ON STENDHAL'S *THE RED AND THE BLACK*

We go, and many of us insistently return, to *The Red and the Black* for a variety of motives, and to enjoy a rich and diverse experience. Many look for the man, Henri Beyle, behind his fictional creatures; few have confessed themselves, yet concealed themselves, more. Those who like to undertake, through literature, a wistful journey into the past read the novel, whose subtitle is "Chronicle of the XIXth Century," as an index of political and social criticism, and as a novel of manners.

The most admirable gift of its author, however, was his talent for psychological analysis: he put on the mask of an ironic sceptic dissecting the human heart, but he was in truth an arch-romantic, fascinated by what was, and still is, for his compatriots—and several others as well—the most important affair in life: love.

—from the introduction by Henri Peyre, Professor of French Literature at Yale University and author of *Contemporary French Novel* and *Life, Literature and Learning in America*

STENDHAL

THE RED AND
THE BLACK

A Story of Provincial France

Translated by
Charles Tergie

with a new introduction by
Henri Peyre

COLLIER BOOKS
NEW YORK, N.Y.

Introduction

"I shall be read in 1930," stated the author of *Le Rouge et le Noir* in 1830, at the age of forty-seven. It is one of the many prophecies, or boasts, of a novelist who was little appreciated by his contemporaries. He might better have said "in 1950," if he had had an American audience in mind. Up to the middle of the present century his two most famous novels, translated by Scott Moncrief in 1925 and 1926, had obtained pathetically small sales. As late as 1943, when paper was rationed to publishers, Modern Library dropped *The Charterhouse of Parma* from its list. But, since World War II, the general reader and the college student have claimed *The Red and the Black* as one of their favorite works of fiction, siding belatedly with other enthusiasts of Stendhal—Tolstoy, Nietzsche, Balzac, Zola, Hippolyte Taine, Paul Bourget, Maurice Barrès, Gide, Proust, Léon Blum, and Simone de Beauvoir. To many Frenchmen today, none of their novelists is so dear as Stendhal, even though others have been more powerful or more polished as technicians. He alone inspires the youth with a passionate admiration. Jean Giono, Roger Vailland, Claude Roy, Jean Dutourd, among the living novelists of France, imitate the manner of Stendhal to an extent that is almost paralyzing to their originality. The finest critics bring out volume after volume on the writer who hated pedantry above all else.

We go, and many of us insistently return, to *The Red and the Black* for a variety of motives and to enjoy a rich and diverse experience. Many look for the man, who was born Henri Beyle, behind his fictional creatures; few have confessed themselves, yet concealed themselves, more. Those who like to undertake a wistful journey into the past, through literature, read the novel as an index of political and social criticism—its subtitle is "Chronicle of the XIXth Century"—and as a novel of manners. The most admirable gift of its author, however, was his talent for psychological analysis: he put on the mask of an ironical sceptic dissecting the human heart; but he was in truth an arch-romantic, fascinated by what was, and still is for his compatriots and several others as well, the most important affair in life—love. Unsuccessful as he often was in his dealings with the other sex, which he probably idealized very much, Stendhal succeeded in giving life and truth to several women in his books. He is extraordinarily shy and chaste in his novels, yet the debauchery of sex and brutality which our age has witnessed in fiction has only enhanced his greater truth. Stendhal's searching analysis has managed to become creative; it never dissolves the mysteriousness of his characters. Finally, those self-conscious novels, technically very subtle, ingeniously constructed, never forsake an elusive quality which, for lack of any other term, must be called "naturalness" and "poetry." But their poetry does not detract, as happens with Flaubert, Hardy, or Proust, from our eager interest in the plot and in the manner in which the characters react to their strange situations. "What's the use of writing a novel at all," said their author, "unless it keeps a lovely marquise awake until two in the morning?"

Like many imaginative writers, Stendhal composed in order to give some reality and solidity to the inner world of his dreams, to avenge himself for some frustrations and rebukes he had suffered in his youth, and to reach a clearer knowledge of himself by projecting his own being into others. His passion for clarity was remarkable (even for a Frenchman) and he did not, like some of his compatriots, mistake logic for clarity or confusion for profundity. He could be all the deeper for being clear.

He was born in Grenoble in 1783, six years before the Revolution broke out. As a child, he felt oppressed by his father, whom he hated; in the novel Julien Sorel feels estranged from his vulgar and calculating father, and he adores his mother. When, as a young man, Stendhal was sent to Paris to study mathematics, he felt very self-conscious, awkward and abnormally shy, a provincial and uncouth lad incapable of talking gallantly and wittily in Parisian salons. He observed men of lesser merit and of scant intellectual power who held high social positions, and he became determined to rebel against a social order in which merit was not recognized, or to climb ruthlessly to a position of influence. Inordinately sensitive and easily hurt, shy in the presence of women, abusing—as Madame de Sévigné put it of her son-in-law—the right which men enjoy to be ugly, he took refuge in solitude and study. He became an officer in Napoleon's armies, showed his calm courage in the retreat from Moscow in 1812, and saw all his hopes and dreams shattered by the fall of the Emperor. He then turned to his first love, literature, writing his best-known books in the 1820's and 1830's.

Eager for success, like many young men after the French Revolution whose motto was "Why not I?", he dutifully studied ideology, the term given, at that time, to an analytical attempt made by Antoine Destutt de Tracy and Pierre Cabanis, among others, to examine the workings of the human mind. The young man from Grenoble thus hoped to learn how to repress his romantic proclivity to enthusiasm and, like Julien Sorel, to control himself and conquer women through careful calculation. "Burning with love, but the head controlling the heart," is one of his favorite phrases. By nature he was tender and passionate, prone to falling rapturously in love. He applied himself to curbing his rash feelings, thus to refine and intensify his own desire, to allow what he called "crystallization" to take place in the person whom he loved and whom his desire, held in check, was gradually to inflame. His little book *De l'Amour* is one of the most perspicacious ever written on that ever elusive subject, falling in love, with its whys and wherefores and, more puzzling still, falling out of love, "le désamour."

Moreover, as Léon Blum and Jean Starobinski, two of the most acute Stendhalians, have noted, Stendhal cherished disguises and assumed dozens of pseudonyms to flee from his own identity. He wished to disassociate himself from his father, from a provincial world of pettiness and thrift, from his dull middle class, even from his own country. He would have liked to have been an Italian, called himself a Milanese because he had been happiest in Milan, and borrowed his pseudonym Stendhal from a small city in Germany.

He desperately feared that his own lack of physical charm (he was corpulent and his features lacked delicacy) would prevent women from loving him. He idolized women and placed them on a pedestal: his heroes love most ardently when they are away from the objects of their love. Imprisoned Fabrice, in *The Charterhouse of Parma,* was able to transfigure his beloved to his heart's content, since she was not there to upset the dream through silly remarks, unchaste behavior, or any gesture or move which would impede the crystallization process. Like medieval knights, Stendhal's young men worship inaccessible women, of high social rank and surrounded with glamour, or actresses who, even if they are accessible, bring to their lover the illusion that he is sharing the bed of Chimène, Phèdre, Juliet, or Desdemona.

In real life, Stendhal enjoyed the favors of Countess Curial from 1823 to 1825, but she then abandoned him. Alberte de Rubempré, whom he loved, fell in love with Stendhal's closest friend instead. But, in 1829, a very young Italian girl of nineteen, Giulia Ranieri, threw herself at him. Stendhal, for once, applied his formulized strategy, and asked her to wait a few months. Still her infatuation persisted. "I deem it a miracle to be loved at forty-seven," jotted down Stendhal.

It was at this time, after a "happy" love affair, compensating him for the "fiascoes" he often spoke about, that he composed *The Red and the Black*.

In that mood of exaltation, he hit upon the story of a murder committed by an upstart who had been loved, then forsaken, by a woman of higher social rank. He used the subject for *The Red and the Black*, lent several features of the young Giulia Ranieri to Mademoiselle de la Mole, utilized other minor incidents of his career, and lent much of himself to Julien Sorel. Stendhal was convinced that most good writing is done fast and his novel was composed quickly and impulsively. It aroused little attention when it appeared, late in 1830, as France was emerging from a revolution, and the literary world was engrossed by the victory of the Romantics. But the aged Goethe praised it in Germany, and slowly the novel rallied admirers and created the new taste by which it ultimately was to be appraised as one of the world's great novels.

"Politics," Stendhal said in regard to *The Red and the Black*, "is a stone tied around the neck of literature and drowns it in less than six months." The political chapters of the novel have managed to eschew dullness and few readers today find them dated. Irony is their saving grace. Stendhal denounces the selfishness and the greed of the Church ("the Black") which attracts the unscrupulous and ambitious young men who, some years earlier, would have donned a uniform ("the Red") and fought under Napoleon. To the Voltairien novelist, most of these young men, except for the lovable and modest Pirard, are hypocrites. He is equally scornful of the higher middle class (Valenod and even M. de Rênal, who apes the aristocrats) and it is in part as the revenge of an underprivileged young man who, like D. H. Lawrence's characters a century later, undertakes to seduce the wife of a member of the small nobility and the daughter of a marquis.

In the regime of the Bourbons (1815–1930) he describes nothing but venality, greed for money, attachment to property (M. de Rênal's symbolic insistence on his wall), fear of the virtues of energy embodied by Altamira, by Napoleon and his marshals such as Ney, and by Julien himself. Mathilde de la Mole's behavior is governed by her admiration for her heroic ancestor, Boniface; to be worthy of him, she will love Julien, humble herself madly for him and alternately humble him. Stendhal brands the decrepitude of his age in the way most novelists who have been social critics (Balzac, Proust, Faulkner) have done regularly after him. The question that is implicitly posed in all his writings is: men have more comfort and leisure and luxury than they have ever had in our century; why are they not happy? His answer is: because they lack passion and generosity and yearning for "grandeur."

The structure of *The Red and the Black* is much less self-conscious and less impeccably elaborate than that of the novelists (Henry James, James Joyce, William Faulkner) who follow Flaubert, the great technician who banished chance and casualness from the art of fiction. Stendhal retains all the charms of an amateur, but also the unpredictability and the spontaneity of a workman who chose to improvise and to allow his reminiscences to surge up as he composed. He started from imaginary elements and grafted on them the reality that he had known. There is no ponderous exposition, no working up to crucial scenes as in a drama, no attempt to be subjective, but, as in Flaubert, to turn the novelist into an all-knowing but invisible god. Some ten years after *The Red and the Black* he confessed to Balzac: "I had never thought much about the craft of writing a novel . . . I did not suspect there were any rules." He added: "I take beings whom I have known and I ask myself: with the same habits, . . . what would they do if they had more brain?" The tone is one of casual nonchalance. Digressions abound (on politics, on love, the duel with the coachman). The author analyzes the thoughts of his characters and proceeds from that analysis to their actions. Without systematically resorting to the type of interior monologue which Joyce and Faulkner have subsequently made famous, Stendhal centers the novel on Julien's hesitations, reflections, and schemes. He imparts life to his hero and at the same time he judges him incessantly. Stendhal intervenes in his narrative, multiplying asides as one would for the stage, probably out of shyness, and in order to forestall the reader's objections and to dissipate his unbelief, and out of a desire to establish an atmosphere of intimacy with his public and to abolish aesthetic distance. He thus reaches a quality of naturalness which only Tolstoy has possessed to such a degree.

Stendhal is a master of psychology. M. de Rênal, the old Marquis de la Mole, his son, the priests, the coarse provincials of Verrières are sketched satirically but vividly, with a sparse choice of significant details which make them true as individuals as well as typical of a group. Even when he hates, Stendhal portrays his characters with the sympathy of a creator who becomes each of those whom he depicts. They all gravitate around Julien. That calculating upstart has purposely been created so as not to appeal to the reader's sympathy. At first sight we view him as a cold, perpetually reasoning, unscrupulous hypocrite at the seminary and in society, and as a heartless seducer of women. Soon, however, we realize how duped we have been by Stendhal's determination to reject sentimentality and facility.

Julien is in truth a shy, tender, easily embarrassed, naïve boy who strains every nerve in order to behave like a real man. "I shall be in your bedroom tonight," he whispers to Mme de Rênal after having subdued his own fright and pressed her hand in the garden scene. Once in her room, however, he does not know how to behave and trembles like a leaf. That worshipper of energy does not yet have the daring which Dostoevski will lend to his Raskolnikov: Julien is constantly ready to lapse back into sentiment, pity, tears, doubts about himself. His hypocrisy and his prudent diffidence of all those who socially outrank him, his touchy pride, are only a veneer. He simulates indifference in order to be loved by Mathilde; he plots elaborately so as to arouse her jealousy. But beneath this he constantly asks himself: "What am I?", watches himself feel, think, act—so unsure is he of himself. He is terrified of being ridiculous. He is determined, as Stendhal was in life, to hunt daily for happiness and to win women of great beauty and high rank. When his ambition is fulfilled and Mathilde de la Mole desperately wants him as her husband, when her father, the Marquis, has ennobled him, he spurns that happiness and the success which usually brings monotony in its train. He forsakes his mistress, shoots Mme de Rênal, whose maternal tenderness he still cherished, and for all practical purposes chooses his own death and brings it about.

To create women who seem to us real, complex, mysterious, and yet natural is the rarest achievement in the whole range of fiction. (Balzac, Dickens, Thackeray, Dostoevski may well have failed that test. Tolstoy superbly succeeded.) It cannot be contended that Stendhal's heroines are true to everyday life, but they fascinate us. Stendhal transfigures them with his fiery imagination. Mme de Rênal at first is an almost conventional wife and mother, devoted, faithful, maternal in her tenderness toward pale, shy Julien, not unusually intelligent, afraid to judge her husband. Love for the young man who tutors her children transforms her. She becomes audacious, reckless, prompt to risk any sacrifices for her love, setting up obstacles of wifely obedience, motherly love, religious piety, only in order to smash them and indulge her passion. In that passion, as always in the chaste writing of Stendhal, the senses have hardly any share. Not one love scene is ever in the least suggestive. Imagination and sentiment are everything.

Mathilde de la Mole ranks among the strangest female characters in fiction. She is, like Corneille's heroines, above the common herd, yet not unreal. She is neither a coquettish baby doll, nor a pursuer of pleasure, but, like many young women, she is both cerebral and passionate. Inordinately proud, living in history and in the nostalgia of her chivalrous and indomitable ancestors, she wages a fierce battle between her self-respect and her desire to love a man stronger and more energetic than she who will humble her pride. She has elements of a Lady Macbeth in her, but also of a tender and submissive Desdemona. To love and to marry such a woman might well terrify an ordinary man, but would offer a challenge to one out of the ordinary.

In the magnificent pages of the second half of his novel where the romantic liaison between Julien and Mathilde is delineated, Stendhal has multiplied insights into that passion which he amorously analyzed. Love and hatred alternate, or rather coexist; there is no unity to the human personality. Man and woman, while using the same word "love" to designate their desire and their feeling, in fact connote very different things by it. To love, and to be loved, but not in the same manner, breeds misunderstandings, differences, and eventually an alienation. Love is a force which multiplies life a hundredfold and alone makes it worth living, yet which also distorts: for each of the lovers transforms himself to become what his partner wants him to be, or thinks he is, and imagination, which enhances desire and gives birth to love, can also wear out and melt the crystallization previously achieved.

Such is that relentlessly analytical novel composed by a Romantic who wished to pass for a pure and dry analyst in the midst of the French Romantic era. In his style, which he had worked on, curing it of a tendency to declamation inherited from Jean-Jacques Rousseau, Stendhal cultivated a brevity which is never the mark of poverty, a cool restraint which intensified the passion burning beneath it, a lucidity which Proust and Camus did envy. He had sedulously analyzed himself with the searching probe of an ideologist and of a mathematician. "When I do not see clearly, my whole universe is annihilated," Stendhal used to declare. There are splendidly evocative sentences, contrasting with the voluntary dryness of the style: "The embraces devoid of warmth of that living corpse," says Stendhal of Mme de Rênal's restrained farewell to Julien; or when Julien conquers Mathilde, "There she is, that haughty woman, at my feet," he exclaims. Later, when her changing moods grieve him deeply, Stendhal concisely notes: "One of the most painful moments of his life was when, every morning, on awaking, he learned his unhappiness anew." More strangely and movingly still, in Chapter 30 of the second part, while Julien watches the proud Mathilde whom he is trying to render jealous of another woman, he looks in silence at his mistress and says to himself: "Ah! could I but cover with kisses those pallid cheeks, and that you would not feel it!"

When *The Red and the Black* was published, Stendhal was well over forty and had a stock of memories behind him: he had published several books, notably of Roman journeys and Italian short stories. With *The Red and the Black*, the classical virtues of restraint, or acute analysis, of naturalness of style and of intellectual lucidity were superbly married to romantic flights of imagination, ardor of sensibility, passionate cult of love and eagerness to surrender to it without renouncing one's lucidity and one's intelligence. "No great novel will ever proceed from a superficial mind," decreed Henry James in his *Art of Fiction* in 1888. Stendhal is perhaps the most searching intellect ever drawn to novel writing.

HENRI PEYRE,
Yale University

BOOK I

La vérité, l'âpre vérité.
—DANTON

To the Happy Few

Chapter 1

A Small Town

Put thousands together
Less bad,
But the cage less gay.
    —HOBBES

THE LITTLE TOWN of Verrières can pass for one of the prettiest in Franche-Comté. Its white houses, with their gable roofs of red tiling, spread over the slope of a hill, where clumps of chestnut trees mark every indentation. The Doube flows some hundred feet below the fortifications which the Spaniards built, now lying in ruins.

Verrières is sheltered on the north by a high mountain, a spur of the Jura range. The irregular peaks of Verra are covered with snow from the earliest frosts in October. A brook falls precipitately from the mountain, and takes its course through Verrières before emptying into the Doube, supplying power to numerous saw-mills. These form the common industry, affording to the greater portion of the inhabitants, who are mostly of the peasant class, a certain degree of affluence. It is not, however, the saw-mills that have enriched this little town. It is the manufacture of print cloth called "Mulhouse;" from that has come the general prosperity which has rebuilt nearly every house in Verrières since the fall of Napoleon.

On entering the town one is deafened by the din of a crashing, formidable-looking machine. Twenty heavy hammers, raised by means of a wheel rotated by the stream, fall with a noise that shakes the pavement. Each one of these hammers makes many thousands of nails a day. To the stroke of these enormous hammers pretty little girls are holding bits of iron which are quickly transformed into nails. This pretentious establishment is among the things that most astonish the traveler who comes for the first time among the mountains lying between France and Switzerland. If the traveller asked to whom this great nail factory belonged that is deafening the people walking in Rue Grande, he would be answered, rather indifferently: "Oh, 'tis the Mayor's." A hundred to one, too, if he stopped for a few moments in this Rue Grande, which rises steeply from the banks of the Doube to the top of the hill, he would see a tall man appear, walking with an air of great importance. At sight of him all hats are hastily raised. His hair is gray, and the suit he wears is gray. With his high forehead and aquiline nose, his face altogether is not without some regularity. He is a Knight in several Orders. One sees, too, at first glance, that there is mingled with the dignity of mayor a sort of solid contentment natural to a man of forty-eight or fifty. But this contented self-complaisance, in which is seen an element of something hard and prosaic, soon grates upon the Parisian traveller. The impression is gathered that the sole genius of the man lies in exacting prompt payment from his debtors, and in demurring payment to the very last to his creditors.

This is the Mayor of Verrières, M. de Rênal. He walks across the street with much deliberation, and enters the town hall, disappearing then from the traveller's eyes. But a hundred steps farther, if the latter continued his walk, he would see a very pretty house and, beyond an iron railing leading from it, a beautiful garden. Beyond it the line of the horizon is made up of the hills of Bourgogne, formed apparently just to please the eye. This view is somewhat of a relief to the traveller depressed by the atmosphere of insatiable greed surrounding him.

He is informed that the house belongs to M. de Rênal. It is from the profits he made in his great nail factory that the Mayor of Verrières has built this beautiful stone residence, just lately finished. The report goes that the Mayor is of an old Spanish family; according to his own declaration, his family had been established in the neighborhood long before the time of Louis XIV.

Ever since 1815 he has blushed at being a manufacturer; that year had made him Mayor of Verrières. The terrace walls, retaining various portions of this magnificent garden, which slopes so beautifully from plane to plane down to the Doube, are the reward of M. de Rênal's knowledge of the iron trade. Of course, one must not expect to find those picturesque gardens in France which surround the manufacturing cities of Germany, like Leipzig, Frankfort, or Nuremberg. In Franche-Comté the more walls one builds, stone on stone, on property, the higher does he rise in the estimation of his neighbors. M. de Rênal's gardens, therefore, are a network of walls, and these are the more admired because the ground over which they stretch was not bought at a bargain. That saw-mill, for instance, which, with the name Sorel in gigantic letters on a roof-board, attracted your attention upon entering Verrières, was six years ago located on the very spot on which the wall of the fourth terrace is being built in M. de Rênal's gardens.

Notwithstanding his pride, his honor the Mayor had been forced to make many a concession to this obstinate, hard-headed peasant Sorel. He had to pay him a pretty penny for having him move his mill away. The public stream by which the mill was turned, M. de Rênal, thanks to strong influence in Paris, was then able to turn off in another direction. That privilege he obtained after the elections in 182–.

He gave Sorel four acres for one a hundred feet lower down along the Doube. And, though the new location was far better for his fir-plank concern, Father Sorel—so he is called since he has become rich—knew how to extract six thousand francs in addition from the impatience and property mania which possessed his neighbor.

True, this transaction was criticized by the good people of the place. Only four years afterwards, one Sunday, while M. de Rênal, adorned with the insignia of office, was returning from church, he saw Sorel from a distance, accompanied by his three sons, smiling blandly at him. That smile came like a stab to him, for it vividly recalled the time when he might have driven a much better bargain.

No one that builds a wall, if he wishes to receive public consideration at Verrières, will adopt the plans the masons bring from Italy when, in the spring of the year, they cross the Jura Mountains on their way to Paris. Such an innovation would bring to the imprudent builder the reputation of "a bad head," and he would forever be lost with the sage and prudent folk who dispense good opinion in Franche-Comté.

In truth, these wise people exercise a most annoying tyranny. For that reason is life in the small towns insupportable for one who has lived in that great republic which we call Paris. The tyranny of public opinion—and such opinion—is as stupid in the small towns in France as in the United States of America.

Chapter 2

A Mayor

> *L'importance! monsieur, n'est-ce rien? Le respect des sots, l'ébahissement des enfants, l'envie des riches, le mépris du sage.*
>
> ——BARNAVE

FORTUNATELY for the administrative reputation of M. de Rênal, a big sustaining wall was needed for the public thoroughfare. The street was up grade to a height of nearly a hundred feet above the banks of the Doube. This made it one of the most picturesque views in France. But the street was flooded every spring by the heavy rains, and then the gulleys made it impassable. This state of affairs brought M. de Rênal to the happy necessity of immortalizing his administration by a wall twenty feet high and between sixty and eighty fathoms long.

The parapet of this wall, on account of which M. de Rênal had to make three trips to Paris—the former Minister of the Interior having declared himself a mortal enemy of this promenade in Verrières—is four feet above the ground, and, as if to defy all ministers, present and future, it is lined with blocks of cut stone.

How often have my eyes gazed down the Doube valley, leaning on those massive bluish-gray blocks of granite, with my thoughts far off in dreams of Paris balls! There on the right bank stretch five or six little vales through which the eye perceives winding, thread-like streams. These, then, falling over cascades, rush into the Doube.

The sun is hot in these mountains; from the torrid heat the dreaming traveller seeks the shade of the magnificent plane trees. These, growing in the filled-in earth behind the large sustaining wall, bear proudly their bluish foliage. Indeed, in spite of the opposition of the municipal council, M. de Rênal had thus widened the promenade by more than six feet; and though he is a Conservative, and I myself a Liberal, I will not withhold from him my meed of praise. I sustain his opinion, and that of M. Valenod, the genial Director of the Verrières poorhouse, that this terrace might compare well with that of Saint-Germain at Laye.

18

I have only one objection to the Cours de la Fidélité—this official name is read in a dozen different places, on slabs of marble, and adds another decoration to M. de Rênal—what I find fault with in the Cours de la Fidélité is the barbarous manner in which the plane trees have been cut; they are trimmed away. But the Mayor's is a despotic will, and twice a year the trees in the public places are ruthlessly amputated. The Liberals in the town insinuate, though indeed exaggeratingly, that the official gardener's hand cuts deeper since the Vicar Maslon has contracted the habit of enriching himself from the profits of sheep-shearing.

This young ecclesiastic had been sent some years before from Besançon to keep an eye on abbé Chélan and other curates in the neighborhood. An old staff-surgeon of the army of Italy, who had retired to Verrières, having been in his lifetime, like the Mayor, first a Jacobin and then a Bonapartist, had the temerity one day to complain of the periodic mutilation of these beautiful trees. "I like the shade," replied M. de Rênal, with a haughtiness befitting the occasion; "I love the shade; I have my own trees trimmed with shade in view, and I cannot conceive how a tree can be good for anything else if it does not bring in any revenue, like the useful walnut tree, for instance."

That is the great word which decides everything in Verrières —"revenue." It represents the habitual thought of three-fourths of its inhabitants. "Yield revenue" is reason enough for deciding everything in this little town which seems so pretty to you. The stranger on arriving might be led by the beauty of the fresh deep valleys surrounding it to imagine that the inhabitants have an eye for the beautiful: they speak only too often of the beauty of the neighborhood. Indeed, it cannot be denied that they prize it highly; but that is because it attracts strangers, and these enrich the proprietors of the inns, and thus, through the mechanism of the custom-house, "revenue" is produced.

One fine autumn day M. de Rênal was walking in Cours de la Fidélité, arm in arm with his wife. While listening to her husband, who was talking in a serious tone, Madame de Rênal followed with an anxious eye the movements of her three little boys. The eldest, who might have been eleven years old, was approaching the parapet with a too evident intention of mounting it. A gentle voice pronounced the name "Adolphe," and the child then gave up his ambitious project. Madame de Rênal seemed to be a woman of thirty, but was still very pretty.

"He will indeed be sorry for it, this fine gentleman from Paris," spoke M. de Rênal, in an injured tone, looking paler than usual. "I am not without some friends at the château." The "fine gentleman from Paris" who seemed so odious to the Mayor of Verrières was none other than M. Appert, who had contrived two days before to visit not only the Verrières prison and poorhouse, but also the hospital, which was managed gratuitously by the Mayor and the leading citizens.

"But," said Madame de Rênal, timidly, "what harm can this Paris gentleman do, since you are administering the affairs of the poor with the most scrupulous honesty?"

"He comes only to cast aspersion, and then he will have articles inserted in the Liberal newspapers."

"You never read them, my dear."

"But people talk about these Jacobin articles. That is what is annoying us and preventing us from doing good. As for me, I will never forgive the curate."

Chapter 3

The Welfare of the Poor

Un curé vertueux et sans intrigue est une Providence pour le village.

—FLEURY

THE CURATE of Verrières, an old man of eighty, whom the keen mountain air had given unbroken health and a constitution of iron, had the privilege of visiting the prison, the hospital, and even the poor-house at any time. It was exactly at six in the morning that M. Appert, coming from Paris with letters of introduction to the curate, had found it convenient to arrive at this queer little town. He had immediately gone to the vicarage.

When the curate Chélan read the letter written by Marquis de la Mole, a peer of France and the owner of the richest estates in the province, he remained pensive.

"I am old and beloved here," he said to himself; and then, half aloud: "they would not dare." Turning suddenly to the visitor from Paris, his eyes, in spite of his great age, gleaming with the holy light that announces the joy of doing a good but dangerous act, he said:

"Come with me, monsieur, and be so good as to express no opinion of what we shall see while the warden is present, and especially not in the presence of the overseers at the poor-house." M. Appert, knowing that he had to deal with a man of courage, followed the venerable curate to the prison, the hospital, and the poor-house, asking many questions, but never permitting himself, in spite of strange replies, to pass a single criticism.

The visit lasted several hours. The curate invited M. Appert to dinner, but the latter pleaded that he had some letters to write. He, in truth, did not wish to compromise his generous companion any further. Towards three o'clock they went to the poor-house again, to finish their inspection, arriving later at the prison. There, by the door, they found the warden, a bowlegged giant six feet tall.

"Ah! monsieur," he said to the curate, "this gentleman is M. Appert I see with you?"

"What of it?" replied the curate.

"Only I've received strict orders yesterday from the prefect, by a gendarme who must have galloped the whole night, not to admit M. Appert to the jail."

"I do inform you, M. Noiroud, that this visitor who is with me is M. Appert. You forget that I have the right to visit the prison at any hour, day or night, accompanied by any one I please."

"Yes, monsieur curate," replied the warden, in a low voice, hanging his head like a dog that is compelled to obey for fear of the stick; "only, monsieur curate, I have a wife and children. If I'm informed on, I'll be discharged; I have nothing to live on but my place."

"I should also be sorry to lose mine," said the good curate, with increasing tremor in his voice.

"What a difference!" replied the warden. "You, monsieur curate, have an income of eight hundred francs laid up for a rainy day."

Such are the facts which, commented upon and exaggerated in twenty different ways, were arousing the most hateful passions in this little town of Verrières. Just at this moment they were serving as the text for the little discussion between M. de Rênal and his wife. The following morning he had gone, accompanied by M. Valenod, the poor-house Director, to the house of the curate, to show him his great displeasure. M. Chélan was not the protégé of any one; he felt the full weight of their words.

"Well, gentlemen, I shall be the third curate who will have been removed from this neighborhood at the age of eighty. I have lived here fifty-six years. I have baptized nearly all the inhabitants of this town, which was nothing more than a village when I came here. I marry young folks every day whose grandfathers were married by me. Verrières is my family; but I thought to myself, when I saw this stranger, 'This man, coming as he does from Paris, may indeed be a Liberal—there are only too many of them there—but what harm can he do to our poor and to our prisoners?' "

As M. de Rênal's rebukes, and particularly M. Valenod's, became severer, the old curate cried out, tremblingly: "Well, gentlemen, have me removed. I will not for that reason leave the neighborhood. You know I inherited a farm forty years ago which brings me in eight hundred francs. I shall live on this income; I have not put by money in my position, sirs; and that is why I am not so frightened when told I shall lose it."

M. de Rênal lived happily with his wife, but he was on the

point of getting very angry after she had repeated timidly, "What harm can this Paris gentleman do to the prisoners?" and he had not found a reply. Suddenly she uttered a cry; the second one of her boys had just mounted the parapet of the terrace and was running on it twenty feet above the vineyard, on the other side. The fear of frightening her child, and thereby causing him to fall, made Madame de Rênal dumb. Soon the child, merry with his prowess, remarked his mother's paleness and, leaping down, ran to her side. He received a scolding.

This little incident changed the subject of the conversation.

"I wish decidedly to take Sorel into the house, the son of the plank-sawyer," said M. de Rênal. "He will take care of the children, who are getting too wild for us. He is a young priest, or as much as that; a good Latin scholar, with whom the children will make progress, for he has a firm character, the curate said. I will give him three hundred francs and board. I have had some doubts about his morals; for he was the Benjamin of that old army surgeon, the member of the Legion of Honor who came to make his home with the Sorels on the pretext that he was their cousin. That man couldn't well be but a secret agent of the Liberals; he would say that our mountain air was good for his asthma, but it has not proved so. He had been in all the campaigns with Bonaparte in Italy, and had even voted No, it is said, as to the Empire. This Liberal taught young Sorel Latin, and has left him a number of books he had brought with him. Really, I should never have thought of bringing the carpenter's son near our children; but the curate, just before the interview which has put us on the outs for good, told me that Sorel has been studying theology for three years, with the intention of entering the seminary; he is not, therefore, a Liberal; and he is a Latinist.

"This arrangement is a good one in more ways than one," continued M. de Rênal, looking diplomatically at his wife; "Valenod is very proud of the two Norman horses he has just bought for his carriage. But he has no tutor for his children."

"He might take this one away from us."

"You approve, then, of my plan?" said M. de Rênal, thanking his wife with a smile for her shrewd remark.

"Oh, my dear, how quickly you make up your mind!"

"That's because I am a man of decision, I am; and that the curate has seen. We should not deceive ourselves; we are surrounded by Liberals here. All these linen merchants are envying me; I am sure of it. Two or three of them are getting rich. Well, I like very much that they should see de Rênal's children promenading under the care of a tutor. That will be imposing. My grandfather often told me that he had a tutor in his youth. It may cost me perhaps a hundred crowns; but it should be included under the necessary expenses of living according to our rank." The sudden resolution brought Madame de Rênal to a new train of thought.

She was a tall woman, of good figure, once the belle, it is said, of all this mountain region. There was something ingenuous and youthful in her bearing; to a Parisian that simple grace, so full of innocence and vivacity, might have suggested something voluptuous. Had she been aware that she had this mode of pleasing, she would have been greatly shocked. Neither coquetry nor affectation had ever entered her heart. M. Valenod, the rich Director of the poor, was known to have paid her marked attention, but without success. This put a shining mark on her virtue; for this M. Valenod, a tall, well-built man, with a ruddy face and fine black whiskers, was one of those coarse, bold, noisy fellows that pass for handsome men in the country.

Madame de Rênal, who was of a retiring, unobtrusive disposition, was particularly annoyed at the restless movements and loud voice of M. Valenod. Her indifference to what was called pleasure at Verrières had given her the reputation of being proud. That did not concern her in the least; on the contrary, she was very much pleased to see that the townspeople were coming less frequently to her house. It cannot be denied, too, that she passed for a foolish creature in the eyes of the women; for, without the least shrewdness in managing her husband, she was continually missing the best opportunities for getting beautiful bonnets from Paris or Besançon. Provided she was let alone to walk in her pretty garden she would be perfectly content.

Hers was an unassuming nature that would not rise even to the point of passing judgment on her husband or of admitting that she was not happy with him. She supposed, without ever expressing it, that the sweetest relations do not exist between man and wife. She, indeed, loved M. de Rênal when he spoke of their plans for the children: he had designated the eldest for the army, the second for the law, and the youngest for the church. M. de Rênal was only less disagreeable, on the whole, than any man of her acquaintance.

This marital judgment was not unfair. Through half a dozen stories he inherited from an uncle, the Mayor of Verrières had acquired a reputation for wit and elegance. Old Captain Rênal served before the Revolution in an infantry regiment of the

Duke of Orleans, and when he came to Paris he was admitted to the drawing-rooms of the prince. He saw there Madame de Montesson, the famous Madame de Genlis, M. Ducret, the architect of the Palais Royal. All these personages appeared only too often in M. de Rênal's anecdotes. But gradually the memory of the things that required delicacy to relate became burdensome to him, and for some time he would repeat his anecdotes relative to the House of Orleans only on state occasions. Moreover, as he possessed much refinement, except when the conversation turned on money affairs, he passed, with good reason, for the most aristocratic personage in Verrières.

Chapter 4

Father and Son

E sarà mia colpa, se così è?
——MACHIAVELLI

"MY WIFE has really a good head," said the Mayor of Verrières next morning when he went down to old Sorel's saw-mill; "the reason I gave her was that it would maintain my superior rank. It never occurred to me that if I don't take this little priest Sorel, who, they say, knows Latin like a book, the Director of the poor-house, that insatiable creature, might have the same idea and take him away from me. With what an air of importance he would then talk of his children's tutor! Will this tutor wear the cassock in my house?"

M. de Rênal was absorbed in this idea, when he observed from a distance a peasant nearly six feet tall busily measuring some logs in the towing-path by the river bank. The peasant did not seem much pleased to see the Mayor approach him; for the logs were obstructing the path and were laid there contrary to law.

Father Sorel—for it was he—was greatly surprised, and even to a greater extent pleased at M. de Rênal's singular proposition with reference to his son Julien. He was no longer listening to him with that crestfallen air with which the cunning of these mountain burghers clothes itself so readily. Having been serfs during the Spanish supremacy, they still retain this characteristic of the Egyptian fellah.

Sorel's answer was at first only a long recital of all the respectful formulas he knew by heart. While reciting these empty phrases—delivered with an awkward smile that accentuated the false and almost knavish expression of his face—the active mind of the old peasant was busily searching for the reason that would lead so important a man to take his scamp of a boy. He himself thought very little of Julien, and yet M. de Rênal was offering him the unexpected sum of three hundred francs a year, besides his board and clothes. The last stipulation, which Sorel had the genius to put in at once, had been finally accepted by M. de Rênal.

That request came home to the Mayor with great force.

"Since Sorel is not overjoyed over my proposition, as he naturally should be, it is clear," he said to himself, "that he has received an offer from another direction; and where could it come from if not from Valenod?" It was in vain that M. de Rênal urged Sorel to close the bargain at once; the old peasant's astuteness offered an effective resistance. He wished, he said, to consult his son; as if, in the country, a rich father would consult a son with nothing in the world, but for pure form!

A saw-mill run by water power consists of a shed built on the bank of a stream. The roof is supported by a framework resting on four large wooden posts. At a height of eight or ten feet, in the middle of the shed, is the saw swaying up and down, while a very simple contrivance pushes the logs before it. A wheel turned by the water produces both these movements—that of the saw sliding up and down, and that by which the logs are slowly brought in front of it.

Approaching his mill, old Sorel, in stentorian tones, called for Julien. No one answered. He could only see his eldest sons, a race of giants, trimming fir logs with their heavy axes. They were intently following the black lines traced over the logs; with each stroke of the axe immense slivers were falling away. They did not hear their father's voice. The latter therefore walked toward the shed. When he entered, he looked in vain for Julien, who should have been at work by the saw. He observed him five or six feet higher up, astride a beam beneath the roof. Instead of tending to the machinery, Julien was reading. Nothing was so exasperating to old Sorel. He could have forgiven Julien his slight figure, which was so ill-adapted to heavy work, and was so different from his elder sons; but this mania for reading he despised—he himself did not know how to read.

He called Julien two or three times, but in vain. The attention he was giving to the book, more than the noise of the machinery, prevented him from hearing anything. The latter, then, in spite of his age, leaped lightly upon the shaft supporting the framework of the saw, and from there to the horizontal beam beneath the roof. A violent blow sent into the river the book Julien was holding; a second one, equally violent, aimed at his head, made him lose his balance. He was about to fall twelve or fifteen feet below, on top of the moving machinery, where he would have been crushed, when his father caught him with his left hand as he slipped.

"Now, you lazy good-for-nothing! So you'll then always be reading your damned books when you should be minding the saw? Read them at night when you go to waste your time at the curate's!"

Julien, though stunned by the blow, and bleeding, went to his post of duty by the saw. There were tears in his eyes, less from physical pain than from the loss of the book he loved.

"Come down, you cur, so I can talk to you."

The noise of the machinery prevented Julien from hearing this order. His father, who had climbed down, went to get a pole, not wishing to take the trouble of climbing into the rafters again; with this he struck him on the shoulder. Hardly had Julien reached the floor, when old Sorel, pushing him rudely before him, chased him towards the house. "Lord knows what he is going to do with me," said the boy to himself. Coming near the river, he looked sadly where his book had fallen; it was "Mémorial de Sainte-Hélène," the book he cherished most of all

His cheeks were purple and he kept his eyes on the ground. He was a lad eighteen or nineteen years of age, small in stature, with irregular but delicate features, and of a constitution apparently weakly. His nose was aquiline; and his large black eyes, which in quiet moments showed thought and vivacity, were ablaze now with the fiercest hatred. His dark brown hair, growing very low on his forehead, gave him a narrow brow, that in moments of anger looked positively wicked. His face would hardly be remarked among the infinite variety of human countenances by any feature particularly striking. His slight, well-proportioned figure gave evidence more of agility than of strength. From his earliest childhood his extremely pensive air and great paleness had given his father the idea that he would not live long, or that he would be a burden on the family. As he was treated slightingly by all in the house, he only had hatred for his father and brothers. He was always beaten in the Sunday games in the public square.

It was a year since his handsome face commenced to attract the attention of some friendly young girls. Having been an object of disdain to nearly every one as a weakly boy, Julien had worshipped that old surgeon-major who dared one day to speak to the Mayor on the subject of the plane trees.

This army surgeon sometimes paid Father Sorel a day's wages for his son, whom he would then teach Latin and history; that is, what he knew of history—the campaign of 1796 in Italy. Before he died he bequeathed to him his Cross of the Legion of Honor, the arrears on his half-pay, and thirty or forty volumes, the most precious of which had just gone into the public stream.

This was the stream the course of which had been changed by the authority of the Mayor.

Immediately upon entering the house Julien felt his shoulders seized by the powerful hands of his father; he trembled, expecting blows.

"Answer me without lying," the old peasant shrieked into his ears in his harsh voice, while turning him round with the hand, as a child might turn a tin soldier. Julien's large black eyes, welling with tears, were opposite the little gray eyes of the old carpenter, who looked as if he wished to penetrate to the very bottom of his soul.

Chapter 5

A Bargain

Cunctando restituit rem.
—ENNIUS

"ANSWER ME without lying, if you can, you cur. Since when do you know Madame de Rênal? When have you spoken to her?"

"I have never spoken to her," replied Julien. "I have never seen this lady except in church."

"But you have looked at her close, you brazen scamp?"

"Never! You know that in church I see only God," answered Julien, with what he thought enough hypocrisy to avoid a return of blows.

"But there is something up," muttered the peasant, shrewdly. Then, after a moment's silence: "But I'll never learn anything from you, you damned hypocrite. Anyhow, I'm going to get rid of you; and my saw will go the better for that. You've won over the curate or somebody else who has got a good situation for you. Go and pack up your things, and I'll take you to M. de Rênal's, where you will teach the children."

"What shall I get for that?"

"Your board and clothes and three hundred francs in wages."

"I don't want to be a servant."

"You idiot, who is talking about being a servant? Do I want my son to be a servant?"

"But with whom am I going to be at the table?"

The question disconcerted old Sorel; he felt, if he kept on talking, he might say something imprudent. He therefore began to storm at Julien, pouring out upon him a veritable torrent of abuse in which the word "gourmandizer" was most conspicuous. Then he went away to consult his other sons.

Julien saw these soon afterwards leaning on their axes. After observing them for some time without being able to read anything from their expression, he moved to the other side of the shed, so as not to be taken by surprise. He wished to think in quiet of the unexpected event that was changing the course of his life. But he could not think calmly; his imagination was busy representing what M. de Rênal's house would be. All that he would rather give up, he thought, than to come down to eating

with servants. "My father would force me to it—rather die!
I have fifteen francs and eight sous saved up, and I'll run away
this very night; two days over the cross-roads, where I need not
be afraid of the guards, and I am at Besançon. Then I'll enlist
as a soldier, and, if necessary, go to Switzerland. But then
good-by to a career and to the priesthood, that leads to everything!"

His horror of eating with servants was not natural to Julien;
he would not have hesitated at anything equally disagreeable
to get on in the world. But this repugnance he drew from
Rousseau's "Confessions," the only book through which he
looked at life. A collection of "Bulletins de la Grande Armée"
and the "Mémorial de Sainte-Hélène" completed his Koran.
Never did he pin his faith to other books. Like the old army
surgeon, he looked upon all other books as a pack of lies gotten
up by stupid fops just to make a noise in the world.

Together with an ardent disposition, Julien united such an
astounding memory as is often allied with idiocy. In order to
win over the old curate Chélan, on whom, he saw clearly, his
career more or less depended, he had committed to memory
the whole of the New Testament in Latin. He also knew M. de
Maistre's "On the Pope," and with as little faith in the one as
in the other.

As though by agreement, Sorel and his sons avoided speaking
to him for the rest of that day. Towards evening Julien went to
take his theology lesson at the curate's; but he did not deem it
prudent to say anything of the strange proposition that had been
made to his father. "Perhaps it is only a trap," he said to himself; "I must pretend I have forgotten it."

Early next day M. de Rênal sent for old Sorel. The latter,
after a delay of an hour or two, finally arrived with a hundred
excuses and salaams. Then, by urging all sorts of objections, he
had the satisfaction of knowing that his son would eat with the
master and mistress of the house, and on company days alone
with the children, in a separate room. Interposing more objections, as he perceived a decided eagerness on the part of the
Mayor, Sorel asked to see his son's sleeping-room. It was a
large, neatly furnished room, in which the children's beds were
already being brought in. That came like a ray of light to the
old peasant; he soon asked, with the utmost assurance, to see
what clothes his son would receive. M. de Rênal went to his
desk and took out a hundred francs.

"With this money your son may go to the tailor Durand and
order a black suit."

"And if I should take him away from you," asked the peasant, who had all at once forgotten his courtly genuflexions, "might he keep this suit?"

"Of course."

"Well, then," said Sorel, drawling out his words, "it remains only to agree about one thing—the money you are going to give him."

"What!" cried M. de Rênal hotly, "we agreed about that yesterday. It is three hundred francs; I think it is a good deal, if not too much."

"That was your offer; I don't deny it," said old Sorel, his words coming slower than ever. Then, by a stroke of genius quite familiar to those who know the peasants of Franche-Comté, he added, looking steadily at M. de Rênal: *"We find something better elsewhere."*

At these words the Mayor's face fell. He soon composed himself, however, and entered on a profound discussion lasting over two hours. Not a word was spoken but was carefully weighed. In the end the astuteness of the peasant won the day —that was an article not essential to the rich man for earning a livelihood. All the points involved in Julien's new mode of life were carefully reviewed; not only was his salary to be four hundred francs, but it was to be paid monthly, in advance.

"Very well, I will give him thirty-five francs," said M. de Rênal.

"To make it a round sum," said the peasant slyly, "a rich and generous man like you, monsieur Mayor, will make it thirty-six francs?"

"Well—yes," said M. de Rênal; "but let us close it."

For once, anger lent a shade of firmness to his tone. The peasant saw that he must not press any further. Then M. de Rênal began to make progress on his side. He would never give the thirty-six francs for the first month to old Sorel, who was eager to get it for his son. It was dawning on M. de Rênal that he would be obliged to tell his wife of his part in the whole transaction.

"Give me back the hundred francs I gave you," he said firmly. "Durand owes me something; I will go with your son to order the black suit."

After this vigorous move, Sorel prudently took recourse to his respectful formalities; these took a good quarter of an hour. Then, seeing that he had positively nothing more to gain, he took his leave. His last reverence was accompanied with the words: "I will send my son to the château"—so the Mayor's house was called by the officials when they wished to please him.

On returning to his house, Sorel looked in vain for his son. Distrustful of what might happen, Julien had stolen out in the middle of the night to put his books and the Cross of the Legion of Honor where they might be safe. He had brought them to his friend, a young wood dealer, by name of Fouqué, who lived on the top of the mountain overlooking Verrières.

When he appeared again, his father began by saying: "The Lord knows, you damned good-for-nothing, if you will ever have the honor to pay me for what I have given you these many years. There, take your rags and go to the Mayor's."

Julien, surprised at not receiving a blow, hurried away. But scarcely was he out of sight of his terrible father when he began walking very slowly. He judged it would not be amiss with his *hypocrisy* if he stopped a while at the church.

That word should not be surprising. Before arriving at the import of it, the young man had covered considerable ground. In his early childhood the long white coats and black tufted helmets of some dragoons of the Sixth who were returning from Italy, and whom Julien saw tying their horses to the grilled window of his father's house, had made him wild for the army. Later he would listen with delight to the accounts of the battles of Lodi, of Arcole, of Rivoli, which the old army surgeon would give. He would notice with what an impassioned look that old man would gaze at his cross.

But when Julien was fourteen a church was building in Verrières that, for a small town, was indeed magnificent. Four marble columns particularly took Julien's fancy. These later became celebrated in the neighborhood for the mortal hatred they engendered between the justice of the peace and the young Besançon vicar who passed for a Congregation spy. The magistrate came near being removed; such, at least, was the common opinion. Did he not dare to differ with the priest who went every fortnight to Besançon, where, it was said, he had interviews with the Bishop?

In the meantime the magistrate—the father of a numerous family—was handing down decisions that were seemingly unjust, and these were all adverse to the readers of the "Constitutionel." It was only a question, it is true, of a few francs; but one of these fines had to be paid by a nail-maker, Julien's godfather. "What a change!" burst out that man in mighty wrath; "and to think that for twenty years this justice has passed for such a good man!"

All at once Julien ceased to speak of Napoleon; he announced his intention of becoming a priest. And he was constantly seen in his father's mill learning by heart the Latin Bible which had been given to him by the curate This good old man, marvelling at his progress, spent whole evenings instructing him in theology. Before him Julien expressed only the most pious sentiments. Who would have thought that his girlish face, so pale and delicate, concealed the firm resolution to brave a thousand deaths rather than fail to make a mark in life?

For Julien a career meant, first of all, to leave Verrières; he detested the place of his birth. Everything he saw there ran counter to his ideal. For from childhood he had had moments of great exaltation. Later he would delightfully conjure up in his mind beautiful Parisian women who would know and admire him some day for his brilliant career. Why should not one of these fall in love with him just as Bonaparte, while still poor, had been loved by the brilliant Madame de Beauharnais? For many years Julien had not passed a single hour without telling himself that Bonaparte, an obscure, moneyless lieutenant, made himself master of the world by his sword. That thought had consoled him in his griefs, which he thought very great, and redoubled every stray joy.

The building of the church and the decisions of the magistrate came to him then as a revelation. One idea formed itself in his mind that made him wild for weeks, finally mastering him with all the force of a new idea in an ardent soul.

"When Bonaparte arose, France was in dread of disaster; military glory was necessary and fashionable. To-day one sees priests at forty with incomes of a hundred thousand francs, or three times as much as the famous division generals under Napoleon received. There must be men to back them. Here is this justice of the peace, such a fine head, and such a good old man until now, dishonoring himself for fear of displeasing a young vicar of thirty. I will become a priest."

Once, when two years had elapsed after beginning his studies, he was betrayed in the very midst of his piety by the sudden darting out of his old flame. It was at M. Chélan's, at a dinner for the priests, to which the good curate had invited him as a marvel of diligence. It came into his head to praise Napoleon furiously, madly. For that he held his right arm bent across his breast—he had dislocated it, he said, while moving a log—and carried it in that position for two whole months. After that self-inflicted pain he pardoned himself. That was the young man of eighteen, so weak in appearance, looking for all the world considerably less than seventeen years of age, who entered the magnificent church of Verrières with a little bundle under his arm. It was empty, gloomy. On the occasion of some feast the transepts had been decorated with some crimson stuff. In the sunlight this shone with dazzling splendor, with a sort of depressingly religious effect. Julien was ill at ease. Being alone in the church, he sat down in a pew that looked the prettiest. It bore the arms of M. de Rênal. On the altar Julien noticed a piece of printed paper, smoothed out as if it was meant to be read. Examining it, he saw:

"*Details of the execution and of the last moments of Louis Jenrel, executed at Besançon on the . . .*" and there the paper had been torn off. On the back there were the first words of a line: "*The First Step . . .*"

"Who could have put that paper there?" thought Julien. "Poor wretch!" he added, with a sigh, "his name ends like mine"; and he crumpled the piece of paper in his hand.

On going out, Julien thought he saw some blood near the font; it was some holy water that had been spilt, to which the reflection from the red curtains in the windows had given the color of blood. Julien was soon ashamed of his weakness.

"Am I going to be a coward?" he said. "To arms!"

That phrase, repeated so frequently in the old surgeon's recitals of his battles, invariably had a heroic effect on Julien. He arose, and walked rapidly towards M. de Rênal's house.

But when he saw it only twenty steps away, he was seized with unconquerable timidity in spite of his fine resolutions. The iron grating was open; it was so imposing: yet he must enter.

Julien was not the only one whose heart was uneasy over his arrival at the house. Madame de Rênal, who was of an extremely timid disposition, was greatly disconcerted over the idea that a stranger would find it his duty to stand between herself and her children. She was accustomed to seeing her children put to bed in her own room. That morning she had shed many tears when she saw the little beds being carried into the tutor's room. It was in vain that she had begged her husband to have Stanislaus-Xavier's—the youngest boy's—little bed carried back into her own room again.

Womanly delicacy was most marked in Madame de Rênal. She had formed in her mind a most disagreeable picture of a frowzy, uncouth creature in rags, who would be snarling at her children just because he knew Latin—a barbarous language for which her boys would be whipped.

Chapter 6

Ennui

Non so più cosa son,
Cosa facio.
—MOZART (*Figaro*)

WITH THE lively grace that was so characteristic of her when she was not in men's society, Madame de Rênal had just passed through the side door opening on the garden, when she observed near the gate the almost childish, pale, tear-stained face of a young peasant boy. He had on a white shirt, and carried under his arm a neat little ratteen jacket.

The boy had such a fine complexion and such beautiful eyes that something like a romantic thought came to Madame de Rênal to suspect in him only a girl in disguise, with a petition to the Mayor. Her heart was full of pity for the poor creature at the gate, who had not, evidently, the courage to raise his hand to the bell. Madame de Rênal, for the moment free from the disagreeable thought about tutors, advanced a few steps towards him. Julien, with his face turned towards the door, did not see her. He trembled all over when he heard close to him, in a gentle voice:

"What is it you want here, my child?"

Julien turned quickly around. His timidity left him under the kindly look Madame de Rênal gave him. Presently, dazed by her beauty, he forgot everything, even what had recently occurred. Madame de Rênal repeated the question.

"I am here to be the instructor, madame," he said to her, ashamed of the tears which he did his best to wipe away.

Madame de Rênal was dumbfounded; they were then near enough to observe each other closely. Julien had never known a person so well dressed, particularly a woman of such radiant beauty, to talk to him. Madame de Rênal observed the great tears on his cheeks; the latter, though pale at first, were now crimson. She laughed outright, and her laugh had all the abandon of a young girl. She was now amused at herself. What, was this the tutor, the dirty, ragged priest she imagined, who would abuse her children? She could not at first wholly grasp the situation.

"Why, monsieur," she gasped, "you know Latin?"

This word "monsieur" astonished Julien so much that he had difficulty about collecting his thoughts.

"Yes, madame," he replied, shyly.

She was so happy that she hardly dared add:

"You will not, then, scold the poor children too much?"

"I scold them?" asked Julien in astonishment; "why?"

"Then you will be good to them, monsieur," she added, after a moment's silence, in a quavering voice, "will you promise me?"

To hear himself called "monsieur" again seriously, and by a lady so beautifully dressed, was above all Julien's expectations; in all the air castles he had built in his youth he had been convinced that no fine lady would deign to notice him until he had on a smart uniform. Madame de Rênal, on her part, was completely taken by surprise by Julien's fine complexion and large black eyes and black curly hair, curling more than usual after the refreshing plunge he had given his head in the public fountain on the way. To her great joy, she was beholding the reserve of a young girl in this dreaded tutor whose severity she had been fearing so much for her poor children. For such a peaceful soul as Madame de Rênal's, the contrast between what she had feared and what she saw marked a great event. Gradually she overcame her surprise, and then she wondered why she should be standing near the door of her house so close to this half-clad young man.

"Come in, monsieur," she said, somewhat embarrassed.

In all her life a pleasant sensation had never before affected Madame de Rênal to such a great extent. Never before had such a pleasing apparition succeeded such disquieting fears. Her pretty children, upon whom she had bestowed such loving care, would not now fall into the hands of a dirty priest and scold. Arrived scarcely in the hall, she turned to look at Julien again, who was timidly following. His astonishment at beholding such a well-appointed house seemed so pretty to Madame de Rênal. She could not believe her eyes: she thought then that he should by all means be dressed in black.

"But is it true, monsieur," she said to him, stopping for an instant in as much dread of being deceived as she was happy in her belief; "is it true you know Latin?" The words wounded Julien's pride and dispelled the charm in which he had been living for some moments.

"Yes, madame," he replied, endeavoring to assume an injured tone, "I know Latin as much as the curate; and sometimes, even, he is kind enough to say that I know more."

Madame de Rênal noticed that Julien had somewhat of a temper. He had stopped two steps behind her. Approaching him, she said:

"You will not, the first few days, whip my boys? Even when they don't know their lessons?"

The gentle, half-pleading tone of the beautiful woman made Julien immediately forget what was due to his reputation as a Latin scholar. Madame de Rênal's face was near his own; he inhaled the perfume of a woman's summer garments—an astonishing thing for a poor peasant. Julien blushed deeply, saying falteringly:

"Have no fear, madame; I will obey you in everything."

It was at this moment, when the fear for her children was wholly removed, that Madame de Rênal was struck by Julien's extreme beauty. Neither the femininity of his features nor his embarrassment seemed absurd to this timid woman. A virile air, which is commonly regarded as essential to masculine beauty, would have disconcerted her.

"How old are you, monsieur?" she asked Julien.

"I shall soon be nineteen."

"My eldest son is eleven," replied Madame de Rênal, wholly reassured; "he will be almost a companion for you. You can talk sense to him. Once his father punished him, and the child was sick for a week; and yet it was only a light tap."

"How different with me!" thought Julien; "it was only yesterday my father beat me. How happy these rich people are!"

Already Madame de Rênal was eager to catch the slightest shade of meaning in the tutor's mind. Mistaking his sad expression for embarrassment, she asked, with the intention of encouraging him:

"What is your name?"

There was a grace in tone and accent of which Julien felt the whole charm, though unable to account for it.

"I am called Julien Sorel, madame. I am so afraid in coming to a strange house the first time in my life; I have need of your indulgence and your pardon for many things the first few days. I have never been at college; I have been too poor. I have never spoken to any men except my cousin, the army surgeon of the Legion of Honor, and the curate, M. Chélan. He will give you a good account of me. My brothers have always beaten me; don't believe them if they say anything bad about me. Please overlook my mistakes, madame; I will never have any but good intentions."

Julien became reassured during his long speech and had been carefully observing Madame de Rênal. Such is the effect of perfect grace, especially when the person it adorns is unaware of it, that Julien, who prided himself on his knowledge of feminine beauty, would have sworn at that moment that she was only twenty. For an instant he had the daring idea of kissing her hand; but he was afraid of his bold desire. Presently, however, he began saying to himself: "It would be cowardly to refrain from doing what can be useful to me, in removing the contempt of this beautiful lady for a poor workman, just taken from the mill." Perhaps Julien was a little encouraged by the phrase "pretty boy," which he had been hearing for six months on Sundays from the mouths of some young girls. While he was debating with himself, Madame de Rênal was addressing him a few words about the way to begin with the children. The violent conflict in which Julien was engaged made him very pale again, and he said in a constrained tone:

"Never, madame, will I strike your children; I swear it before God." And in saying these words he took Madame de Rênal's hand and brought it to his lips. She was first startled by the movement, then dumbfounded. As it was very warm, her arm was bare under her shawl, and Julien's action in bringing the hand to his lips had entirely uncovered it. She took herself severely to task; it seemed to her that she was not showing herself indignant enough.

M. de Rênal, who had heard them talking, then came out of his room. With the same majestic, magisterial tone he used in performing weddings in the town hall, he said to Julien:

"I want to speak to you before the children see you."

He called Julien into a room, detaining also his wife, who wished to leave them together. When the door had been closed, M. de Rênal seated himself with great pomp.

"The curate has told me that you are a good young man. Everybody here will treat you with respect; and, if you give me satisfaction, I will help you to a little start. I desire that you see neither relatives nor friends; their bearing is not suitable for my children. Here are thirty-six francs for the first month; but I want your word of honor that not a centime of this goes to your father." M. de Rênal was angry at the old man, who had shown himself more astute in the transaction.

"Now, *monsieur*—for everybody here has orders from me to call you *monsieur,* and you shall see the advantage of entering properly into a good family—now, monsieur, it is not proper that the children should see you in a jacket. Have the servants seen him?" asked M. de Rênal of his wife.

"No, dear," she replied, absent-mindedly.

"So much the better. Put this on," he said to the surprised young man, handing him a long coat; "we will now go to Durand, the tailor's."

An hour later, when M. de Rênal returned with the tutor all in black, he found his wife seated in the same place. She felt a quieting effect in Julien's presence; in looking him over she forgot to be afraid. Julien was not thinking of her; in spite of his distrust of men and of fate, his soul at that moment was like a child's. It seemed to him as if he had lived years since he stood trembling in the church three hours before. He remarked Madame de Rênal's cool demeanor; he felt she was angry at him for his daring kiss on her hand. But the proud feeling which the contact of different clothes from what he had been accustomed to wearing gave him made him lose his equipoise; and he was so eager to hide his joy that every movement of his became brusque and ludicrous. Madame de Rênal stared at him in astonishment.

"Serious, monsieur," M. de Rênal said to him, "be serious, if you desire the respect of my children and my servants."

"Monsieur," replied Julien, "I am spoiled by these new clothes. As a poor peasant I have worn only jackets. With your leave I will retire to my room for a while."

"What do you think of this new acquisition?" asked M. de Rênal of his wife.

Something like instinct, of which Madame de Rênal was certainly not aware, made her disguise the truth to her husband.

"I am not as charmed with this peasant as you are; your kindness will make him impertinent, and you will be obliged to send him away in less than a month."

"Oh, well, we shall see. It will cost me about a hundred francs, that's about all, and Verrières will then have frequently seen M. de Rênal's children with a tutor. That I should never obtain if I allowed Julien to be dressed in workmen's clothes. In sending him away, I should certainly take back the black suit I have just ordered for him at the tailor's. He would only take with him what I got for him ready-made, which I have already given to him."

The hour Julien spent in his room seemed only a minute to Madame de Rênal. The children, to whom the tutor's arrival had been announced, were overwhelming their mother with all manner of questions. At length Julien appeared. He was a different man. It would have been wrong to say he was serious; he was the very incarnation of gravity. Being introduced to the children, he began to speak to them in a manner that astonished M. de Rênal himself.

"I am here, gentlemen," he said to them in conclusion of his speech, "to teach you Latin. You know what it is to recite a lesson. Here is the Holy Bible," he said, holding out a little black volume; "it is particularly the history of our Lord Jesus Christ; that part is called the New Testament. I shall have you often recite your lesson; let me recite mine." Adolphe, the eldest boy, had taken the book. "Open it anywhere," continued Julien, "and give me only the first word in the line. I will recite from this book, which should regulate every one's conduct, until you stop me."

Adolphe opened the book, read a word, and Julien recited the whole page as if he were speaking French. M. de Rênal looked triumphantly at his wife. The children, seeing their parents' astonishment, opened their eyes wide also. A servant came to the door, but Julien continued to deliver in Latin. The servant stood stock-still for a minute and then fled. Presently the maid and the cook came to the door. Adolphe had then opened the book in eight different places, and Julien was continuing with uninterrupted fluency. "Oh, Lord, the pretty little priest!" cried the pious cook.

M. de Rênal's self-esteem was becoming acutely sensitive; far from thinking of examining the teacher, he was busy himself scraping up a few Latin words. He at last found himself equal to the task of quoting a verse from Horace. Julien knew only Bible Latin. He replied, contracting his brows: "The holy ministry to which I will devote myself forbids me reading such a profane poet."

M. de Rênal now cited a fairly large number of lines which he said were from Horace. He explained to the children who Horace was, but they kept admiringly gazing at Julien without giving their father the least attention.

The servants being at the door, Julien concluded to make the most of the moment. "Let Master Stanislaus-Xavier," he said to the youngest boy, "indicate a passage from the Holy Book." Little Stanislaus, proud of the distinction, stumbled over the first word of a line, and Julien reeled off the whole page. As if nothing should be wanting to M. de Rênal's triumph, there entered, while Julien was reciting, M. Valenod, the owner of the beautiful Norman horses, and M. Charcot de Maugiron, the sub-prefect of the department. This scene earned for Julien the appellation of "monsieur"; the servants themselves did not dare refuse it to him.

In the evening all Verrières came to M. de Rênal's house to see the prodigy. Julien coolly kept every one at a distance. His reputation spread so rapidly in the town that M. de Rênal, fearing lest some one might take him away, proposed to him a few days later to sign a two years' contract.

"No, monsieur," answered Julien, coolly; "if you wished to send me away I should be obliged to go. A contract that is binding on me and not on you is not just. I refuse."

Julien knew so well how to conduct himself that in less than a month after his arrival M. de Rênal himself respected him. As the curate was in disfavor with de Rênal and Valenod, there was no one to tell of Julien's old passion for Napoleon. On that subject he always spoke with holy horror.

Chapter 7

Elective Affinities

Ils ne savent toucher le coeur qu'en le froissant.
—A MODERN

THE CHILDREN adored him, though he himself did not love them. His thoughts were elsewhere. Whatever the little rogues might do, he never became impatient. Cool, just, dispassionate, he was a model of a teacher. He became endeared to all because he in some way relieved the monotony in the house. He himself entertained only hatred for the high society to which he had come; he was at the foot of the table, to be sure—and that perhaps could explain his hatred. At certain dinners, when company was present, he restrained his abhorrence for his surroundings only with great difficulty. One day—it was the day of Saint Louis—M. Valenod held forth at great length, and Julien was on the point of betraying himself. He fled to the garden, saying he wished to see the children. "What tributes to probity!" he thought. "One would think it is the only virtue. Yet what respect, what scraping homage this man receives, who has most likely doubled and trebled his fortune at the expense of the poor! I wager he makes money even out of the foundling funds, those poor little creatures whose misery is more sacred than any one's. Ah, monsters, monsters! And I, too, I am a sort of a foundling, hated by my father, by my brothers, by my whole family."

A few days before, while walking alone in the little wood Belvédère, that overlooked the Cours de la Fidélité, Julien, carrying his little breviary in his hand, had tried in vain to avoid meeting his two brothers, whom he saw approaching along a solitary path. The jealousy of these coarse fellows was so greatly aroused by his fine black coat and generally neat appearance, but more than all by his evident contempt for them, that they had fallen upon him and left him bleeding and insensible. Madame de Rênal, who was walking with M. Valenod and the sub-prefect, happened to come by chance into this little piece of wood. She found Julien lying on the ground; she thought he was dead. Her shock was so great as to make Valenod jealous.

He was alarmed too soon.

Julien thought Madame de Rênal very pretty, but because of

43

this very beauty he hated her. He deemed her the first stumbling-block to his career. He spoke to her as little as possible, in order to forget the feeling by which he had been led the first day to kiss her hand.

Elisa, Madame de Rênal's maid, did not lose any time in falling in love with the young teacher. She spoke frequently of him to her mistress. Miss Elisa's love made an enemy for him of one of the valets. One day he heard that man say to her: "You don't want to talk to me any more since this dirty teacher has come to the house." Julien did not deserve that insult; for he took especial pains with his person, though that was more or less instinctive with the handsome fellow. M. Valenod's hatred for him also increased. He said publicly that such flirting was not proper for a young priest.

Madame de Rênal noticed that Julien was speaking quite often to Elisa; she learned that those conversations were caused by Julien's poverty. Having only a few changes of linen, he was compelled to have it washed frequently outside, and for these little cares Elisa made herself invaluable. This extreme poverty touched Madame de Rênal, who had never suspected it. She had a mind to make him a present or two, but she did not dare. This inner check was her first painful sensation caused by Julien. Up to this time Julien's name and a feeling of pure, ideal joy had been one and the same with her. Tormented by Julien's poverty, Madame de Rênal ventured to speak to her husband about making him a gift of linen.

"What nonsense!" he answered. "Why give presents to a man with whom we are perfectly satisfied and who serves us well? No, if he slighted his work we should stimulate his zeal."

Madame de Rênal was humiliated by his view of it; before Julien's arrival she would not have noticed it. She never observed the spotless cleanliness of the young theologian's poor shift without asking herself, "How can the young man do it?"

And gradually she came to regard him tenderly.

Madame de Rênal was one of those women who might easily be called foolish after only a fortnight's acquaintance. Of the real world she had no knowledge, and her propensity for conversation was slight. With a faint touch of aloofness in her bearing, she paid but little attention to the gross persons in whose sphere chance had cast her life. Her unaffected, lively temperament might have been brought out to an advantage even by the shallowest kind of an education; but being an heiress, she had been reared by the pious Sisters of the Sacred Heart of Jesus, who were animated by a violent hatred of the French, the enemies of the Jesuits. Madame de Rênal had enough good sense soon to forget all that she had learned in the convent as something absurd; but she put nothing in its place, and remained ignorant. The fulsome flatteries which she received as the heiress of a great fortune, as well as her passionate religious devotion, made her live a wholly inner life. With what appeared as unconditional yielding, which husbands in Verrières cited as an example for their wives, and formed the pride of M. de Rênal, the habitual state of her mind was virtually the effect of a proud spirit.

Up to the arrival of Julien she had not paid the least attention to any one but her children. Their little ailments, their little griefs, their little joys had filled up her entire soul, which had adored only God—when she was at the Sacred Heart in Besançon.

Without caring to speak of it to any one, when one of her boys had fever, she felt as if the child were dead. A loud burst of laughter and a shrug of the shoulders, accompanied with a trite maxim about a woman's nonsense, had constantly greeted such confidences, when from sheer need of expression she would impart them to her husband during the first years of their married life. This sort of pleasantry, especially when it concerned her children, was like a dagger in Madame de Rênal's heart. That was what she found in the place of the importunate and honeyed flatteries in the Jesuit convent in her girlhood. Her education was really made up of chagrin. Too proud to speak of her disappointments even to her friend Madame Derville, she imagined all men were like her husband, or M. Valenod, or the sub-prefect Charcot de Maugiron. The coarseness and brutal insensibility to everything that did not concern money or station or the Cross, the blind hatred for every manifestation of reason that opposed their wishes, seemed natural to the sex, like the wearing of boots.

After long years Madame de Rênal had not yet accustomed herself to the mercenary people in the midst of whom she had to live. Hence the success of the little peasant Julien. She found in the sympathy of his noble, proud soul exquisite joy, and this was heightened by the charm of novelty. Madame de Rênal soon overlooked his extreme inexperience—an additional grace in her eyes—and his rude manners, which she succeeded in correcting. She found he was worth listening to even when he spoke of the commonest things, as of a dog that had been run over by a peasant's cart while he was crossing the street. Her husband would only have laughed at the cruel spectacle, but she saw Julien's finely arched eyebrows contract with pain. Little by little, generosity, humaneness, nobility of soul seemed to exist only in the young priest. For him alone she had all the sympathy and admiration which those virtues enkindle in generous hearts.

In Paris, Julien's attitude towards Madame de Rênal would have been much simplified; but in Paris love is the offspring only of novels. The young preceptor and the timid mistress would have been enlightened as to their mutual relation by three or four romances. Those works of fiction would have outlined for them their respective parts and would have given them a model for their imitation; and that model Julien would have been forced to follow, through sheer vanity, sooner or later, though it might have been devoid of pleasure, and even positively irksome.

In a little town in the Aveyron or in the Pyrenees the slightest incident would have been made decisive by the heat of the climate. Under our darker skies a poor young man who is ambitious only because he has a delicate desire for some pleasures money can buy, sees, without borrowing anything from the novels, a sincerely good woman of thirty, every day occupied with her children. Everything is slow, gradual in the province; it is more natural.

Often, thinking of the young teacher's poverty, Madame de Rênal would be moved to tears. Julien surprised her one day while she was crying. "Oh, madame, has anything happened?"

"No, 'mon ami,' " she replied. "Call the children. Let us take a walk together."

She took his arm, and in a way rather singular to Julien. It was the first time she had called him "mon ami." At the conclusion of the walk Julien remarked that she was blushing very deeply. She talked rather hesitatingly.

"You may have been told," she said, without looking at him, "I am the sole heiress of a rich aunt who lives at Besançon. She overwhelms me with presents. My sons are doing nicely—astonishingly—I would ask you to accept a little present as a token of my gratitude. It is only a matter of a few louis—for linen. But—" she added, blushing more deeply, and coming to an abrupt stop.

"What, madame?" said Julien.

"It would be useless," she continued, lowering her head, "to speak to my husband about it."

"I am small, madame, but I am not low," replied Julien, stopping short, his eyes ablaze with anger, and drawing himself up to his full height. "It is because you have not reflected. I should be lower than a valet if I put myself in a position of hiding from M. de Rênal anything concerning my money."

Madame de Rênal was dumbfounded.

"His honor the Mayor," continued Julien, "has given me thirty-six francs five times since I came to the house. I am ready to show my expense book to M. de Rênal, and, as far as that is concerned, even to M. Valenod, who hates me."

Madame de Rênal remained pale and trembling.

And the walk ended without a renewal of the conversation. Love for Madame de Rênal became more and more impossible for the proud Julien. As for her, she respected him, she admired him. On the pretext for removing the humiliation which she had caused him, she permitted herself the tenderest attention. It brought happiness for an entire week to Madame de Rênal. Its effect was in part to appease Julien's anger; but he was far from seeing anything in it that could resemble personal feeling.

"See," he said to himself, "how these rich people act; they humiliate one, and then they think they can remedy everything with a little nonsense."

Madame de Rênal's heart was too frank and too innocent not to speak, in spite of her resolutions, of the offer she had made to Julien, and of the way she had been repulsed. "What!" replied M. de Rênal angrily, "could you tolerate a refusal on the part of a domestic?" And when Madame de Rênal objected to that word, he said: "I speak, madame, like the late Prince de Condé. When he presented his chamberlain to his second wife, 'All these people,' he said to her, 'are our domestics.' I have read you this passage from the 'Mémoires de Besenval,' a work that is indispensable for people of quality. Every one in your house who is not of noble birth and who receives wages is your domestic. I am going to say two words to this Monsieur Julien and give him a hundred francs."

"Oh, my dear," said Madame de Rênal, trembling, "don't do it in the presence of the servants."

"No; they might be jealous, and with reason," replied her husband, as he walked away, thinking of the large sum.

Madame de Rênal sank into a chair, despairing. "He is going to humiliate Julien, and through my fault," she said, hiding her face in her hands. She resolved never again to impart a confidence to him.

When she saw Julien again, she trembled all over. She was

so miserable that she could not utter a single word. In her despair she had taken his hands and pressed them.

"Ah, well, 'mon ami,'" she said at last, "are you satisfied with my husband?"

"Why shouldn't I be?" replied Julien, with a bitter smile; "yes, he has given me a hundred francs."

Madame de Rênal looked at him, puzzled.

"Give me your arm," she said, with a suggestion of courage in her tone which he had not before remarked.

She ventured to walk as far as the book-store in Verrières with him, regardless of the bookseller's reputation as a Liberal. There she bought some books for the children. But the books were those which she knew Julien wanted. While Madame de Rênal was happy in thus making reparation to Julien, he was marvelling over the number of books in the store. He had never dared enter so profane a place; his heart beat violently. Far from trying to divine what was passing in her mind, he was dreaming only of what chance a young theological student would have of getting some of those books. Finally it occurred to him that with a little address it would be possible to persuade M. de Rênal that he needed the history of the celebrated men of the province for subjects of composition for the boys. After a month of study, Julien saw his plans succeed to such an extent that he ventured, in speaking to M. de Rênal, to mention something even that was very painful to the Mayor. That was nothing less than to contribute to a Liberal's income with a newspaper subscription. M. de Rênal fully agreed with him that it would be wise to give his eldest son a glance into the many works which he might hear mentioned in conversation when he entered the military school; but Julien saw his honor the Mayor very obstinate about going any farther. He suspected a secret reason, but he could not guess what it was.

"I was thinking, monsieur," he said to him one day, "that it would be very inconvenient to have a gentleman's name such as Rênal on the stationer's soiled ledger." M. de Rênal's brow cleared. "It would also be a rather awkward thing," continued Julien, in his humblest tone, "for a poor theological student if it were discovered that his name was on the ledger of a stationer who loaned books; the Liberals would accuse me of having asked for the most infamous works. Who knows but they might go to the length of writing after my name the titles of the most abominable books!" But Julien then tacked; he saw the Mayor's face assume an expression of embarrassment and anger. Julien ceased speaking. "I have got my man," he said to himself.

A few days later the eldest boy, asking about a book advertised in the *Quotidienne*, in M. de Rênal's presence, Julien said: "In order to remove an occasion of triumph for the Jacobin party, and at the same time to have the means of answering Master Adolphe, a subscription might be taken from the stationer's through one of the servants."

"That is not a bad idea," said M. de Rênal, visibly very glad.

"Yet it must be specified," said Julien, with a grave, sad tone so becoming to certain people when they are succeeding in their understakings, "it must be specified that the servant shall not take out a novel. Once in the house, these dangerous books would corrupt madame's servants."

"You are forgetting the political pamphlets," said M. de Rênal, haughtily, intending to smother the admiration which the tutor's uncompromising suggestion had won from the children.

Julien's life was thus a series of little intrigues, and the success of these occupied his mind much more than the marked preference for him which he could not but read in Madame de Rênal.

The moral elevation in which he had passed his life was renewed in the house of the Mayor of Verrières. There, as at his father's saw-mill, he cordially despised the men around him, and was despised in turn. Every day he saw in the conversation of the sub-prefect, of Valenod, and others, how little their ideas corresponded with the truth. His own comment was always, "What knaves or what fools!" The humor of it was that with all his pride he understood absolutely nothing at times what was said.

In all his life he had never spoken with sincerity except to the army surgeon; the few ideas that one had concerned only Napoleon's Italian campaign, and surgery. His youthful courage jested over the details of painful operations. He would say, "I shouldn't have flinched."

The first time Madame de Rênal tried to engage him in a conversation outside of the children's education, he began to speak of surgical operations; she blanched, and begged him to stop.

Julien did not know anything else; and so, passing whole days with Madame de Rênal, the most singular silence would ensue when they found themselves alone. In the drawing-room she found that in spite of his humble demeanor he would look with a certain air of intellectual superiority at her visitors. When she was alone with him for an instant, she would see how embarrassed he became. She was uneasy; her womanly instinct told her that this embarrassment was not the effect of any tender sentiment.

According to the peculiar notions he had of polite society—perhaps such as he found in conversation with the army surgeon—Julien would feel humiliated whenever there was a lull in the conversation while he was in a woman's company, as if the silence were his fault. This sensation was a hundred times more painful in a *tête-à-tête*. His imagination, stored with most exaggerated quixotic notions of what a man should say when alone with a woman, offered him only preposterous ideas in his dilemma. His head soared high among the clouds, yet he could not relieve the painful silence. As a consequence, his bearing became more brusque during the long walks he took with Madame de Rênal and the children. He had utter contempt for himself. If by some ill-chance he was compelled to speak, he would express the most ridiculous ideas. To complete his misery he himself was aware of his absurdity, and grossly exaggerated it. But what he did not see was the expression of his eyes: they were so beautiful, and reflected a soul so ardent, that, like good deeds, they gave a charming sense of something they did not possess. Madame de Rênal observed that when he was alone with her, he would never say anything pleasant except when brought out of himself by something unforeseen; he would never think of turning a compliment. As her friends and family did not spoil her with new or brilliant ideas, she enjoyed immensely the sparks which Julien from time to time would emit.

Madame de Rênal, the heiress of her rich, pious aunt, was married at the age of sixteen, but had never in her life experienced anything that in the least resembled love. Her confessor, the good old curate Chélan, once hinted about Valenod's attentions to her, and he conjured up in her mind then, while on the subject of love, such an unholy picture, that the word meant for her only the most unbridled license. She imagined that the love she read of in the few books which chance threw in her way was exceptional and extraordinary. Thanks to such ignorance, Madame de Rênal, rapt up in Julien, was supremely happy; not the least self-reproach entered her heart.

Chapter 8

Minor Events

> *Then there were sighs, the deeper for suppression,*
> *And stolen glances, sweeter for the theft,*
> *And burning blushes, though for no transgression.*
> —DON JUAN, I. 74

THE SWEETNESS OF LIFE which Madame de Rênal owed partly to her disposition, and partly to her present happiness, was not a little diminished when she came to think of her maid Elisa. That girl, who had just come into an inheritance, went to confession to the curate Chélan, and had avowed her intention of marrying Julien. The curate found real joy in the happiness of this friend of his, and he was greatly surprised when Julien announced his resolution that he would not think of mademoiselle Elisa's offer.

"Take care, my son, as to what is passing in your heart," said the curate, contracting his brows; "I congratulate you on your choice of vocation if it is to that alone you owe your contempt for a competence which is more than sufficient. It is fifty-six years since I am curate of Verrières, and yet, to all appearances, I am about to be removed. It is annoying to me, though I have an income of eight hundred livres. I make you acquainted with these facts in order that you might not entertain any illusions about what you may expect when you become a priest. If you think of truckling to men of power, your eternal damnation is assured. You might make a career, but you will have to oppress the wretched and to cater to the sub-prefect and the great man the Mayor, and minister to their passions. Such conduct, which the world calls tact, might not be absolutely incompatible with salvation in the long run; but in our station one must make his choice between making his fortune in this world or in the next; there is no other alternative. Come, now, my son, think over it, and come back in three days with a definite answer. I behold with pain a dark passion at the bottom of your heart, which does not show me the moderation and the perfect abnegation of earthly goods essential to the priesthood. I augur well of you, but let me say," added the good curate, with tears in his eyes, "I tremble for your salvation as a priest."

Julien was ashamed of his emotion; for the first time in his life he saw himself loved, and he wept for joy. He took a walk in the woods lying above Verrières to hide his tears.

"How queer I am!" he said to himself. "I feel that I should give my life a hundred times for the curate Chélan, and he has just made me out a fool. It is he above all that it is important for me to fool, and he has found me out. The secret ardor of which he speaks is my ambition to make a mark. He believes me utterly unworthy to become a priest, and that, too, when the sacrifice of an income of fifty louis was intended to give him a most exalted notion of my piety and inclination. In the future," continued Julien, "I will rely only on those things in my character of which I am sure. Who would have told me that I should find pleasure in shedding tears or that I should love the one who proves to me that I am only a fool?"

Three days later Julian found a pretext which might have fortified him from the very first. This pretext was a calumny, but—what of it? He confessed to the curate, with much hesitation, that something which he could not disclose, because it would damage a third party, forced him suddenly to renounce the proposal—a defamation of Elisa's character. Chélan noticed something altogether too worldly in his manner, something entirely different from what he should have liked to see in a young Levite.

"My son," he said to him again, "try to be a good, estimable, and accomplished bourgeois rather than an uninspired priest."

Julien replied with a great show of earnestness; the young seminarist's words were fervent; but the tone, the ill-concealed gleam in the eye, alarmed the good Chélan. It was an earnest of no mean ability; the words of cunning, prudent hypocrisy came with great fluency. As to tone and gesture he showed that he had lived only with peasants, and great models had not come within the sphere of his vision. He had not the opportunity of hearing orators admirable alike for their delivery as for their eloquence.

Madame de Rênal was surprised to find that the new fortune of her maid was not making that girl any happier. She saw her going continually to the curate, and returning from him with tears in her eyes. At last Elisa herself spoke to her of her marriage proposal.

Madame de Rênal thought she would succumb. A sort of fever robbed her of her sleep; she lived only when she saw either the maid or Julien under her eyes. She could only think of them and of the happiness they would find in their little home.

A small household managed on an income of fifty louis was painted by her with the most ravishing colors. Julien might very easily become an attorney at Bray, the sub-prefecture two leagues from Verrières—and—in that case she would see him sometimes.

Madame de Rênal believed she would go mad. She complained to her husband, and then really fell sick. The same evening her maid came to wait on her. She noticed that the latter had been crying. She hated Elisa at that moment, and was treating her with little kindness. She was quick, however, in making reparation, and then Elisa's tears fell faster. She said that if her mistress would permit she would tell her of her trouble.

"Go ahead," replied Madame de Rênal.

"Oh, madame, he refuses me; some wicked people must have told tales on me, and he believes them."

"Who refuses you?" asked Madame de Rênal, scarcely daring to breathe.

"Who, madame, who, if not this M. Julien?" replied the maid, sobbing. "The curate has not been able to win him over. The curate thinks that he should not refuse a good girl because she is only a maid. After all, M. Julien's father is only a carpenter, and he himself—how did he earn a living before coming here?"

Madame de Rênal was no longer listening; her great joy bereft her almost of her reason. She had it repeated to her several times that Julien had declined in a manner not calculated to show a change of purpose.

"I will make a final effort," she said to her maid; "I will speak myself to M. Julien."

Next day, after breakfast, Madame de Rênal gave herself up to the delight of pleading the cause of her rival, and of seeing Elisa's hand and fortune firmly refused, for a whole hour. From mere monosyllables Julien passed little by little to a long and spirited reply to Madame de Rênal's representations. She could not stem the tide of happiness that inundated her heart after so many days of anguish. She fainted away. When she came to and had been brought to her room, she sent every one out. She was wildly agitated.

"Is it right that I should love Julien?" she asked herself.

This discovery at any other time would have plunged her into remorse and would have made her perfectly wretched; but now it appeared to her only as a singular phenomenon. Worn out by all that she had experienced, she was insensible to all self-reproach.

Madame de Rênal wished to go about her work, but from sheer exhaustion she fell into a profound slumber. When she awoke she was not frightened at herself in the least.

She was too happy to take anything amiss. Naïve, innocent, the good woman had never tortured her soul to question a new happiness or a new grief. Having been absorbed before Julien's arrival in that mass of work which, outside of Paris, falls to the lot of every good housewife, Madame de Rênal used to think of passion as one might think of the lottery—a delusion, a pleasure sought by fools.

The dinner bell rang; Madame de Rênal blushed when she heard Julien's voice as he was bringing in the children. Adroit, since she commenced to love, in explaining her heightened color, she complained of a frightful headache.

"That's how women are," said M. de Rênal, with a loud laugh. "There is always something to fix in those machines."

Although accustomed to that sort of raillery, the tone grated on Madame de Rênal. To divert her attention she looked at Julien. That one, if he had been the ugliest of men, would have pleased her at that moment.

Industrious in his imitation of the ways of the nobility, M. de Rênal had moved in the beginning of spring to Vergy, a village made famous by the tragic adventure of Gabrielle. A few hundred paces from the picturesque ruins of an ancient Gothic church was M. de Rênal's cottage, a four-towered affair, with a little garden around it that was laid out after the manner of the one in the Tuileries, with boxwood hedges, and walks lined with chestnut trees. An adjoining field studded with apple trees served as a promenade. At one end of the orchard stood a dozen magnificent walnut trees; their immense foliage rose to a height of twenty-four feet.

"Each of these damned walnuts," M. de Rênal would say when his wife admired them, "costs me half an acre in farming; nothing can grow in their shade."

The country was new to Madame de Rênal. Her admiration passed even to the ecstatic. The feeling which was now dominating her gave her courage and resolution. The day after their arrival at Vergy, Madame de Rênal hired workmen at her own expense while her husband was away on official business. Julien had given her the idea of a little sanded path around the orchard to the walnut trees that would permit the children to walk in the morning without their feet becoming wet from the dew.

This idea was put into execution in less than twenty-four hours after being conceived. Madame de Rênal gayly passed the whole day with Julien, directing the workmen.

When the Mayor returned from town, he was greatly surprised at finding a walk had been laid out. His arrival also surprised Madame de Rênal; she had utterly forgotten that he existed. For two months after that he spoke in the most aggrieved fashion of the hardihood with which such an important *alteration* had been made without consulting him; but as Madame de Rênal had had it done at her own expense, he was somewhat consoled.

She passed the days running with the children in the orchard chasing butterflies. They had made nets of some light gauze for the capture of these poor *lepidoptera*. That barbarous word Julien had taught her; for she had ordered from Besançon the fine work of Godart, and Julien had told her of the singular habits of these insects. These were pitilessly transfixed on pins and placed on a large card made for that purpose by Julien. It served as a subject of conversation between him and Madame de Rênal. He was no longer exposed to the cruel torture he had suffered from silence. They talked unceasingly and animatedly, always on indifferent topics. This active, busy, gay life was pleasant to all except to mademoiselle Elisa, who found herself overburdened with work. Never during the carnival, she would say, when the ball took place at Verrières, had madame paid so much attention to her toilet. She dressed two and three times a day.

It must be said that Madame de Rênal, who had a beautiful skin, wore no dresses which left her arms or breast too much exposed. She was a beautiful woman, and her style of dressing was exceedingly becoming.

"Never *have you been so young*, madame," said some friends of hers who had come to dine at Vergy.

Singularly enough—something that may receive little credence—Madame de Rênal was painstaking about her dress wholly without any distinct motive. She simply took pleasure in it, and, with no ulterior thought, she passed all the time, when she was not chasing butterflies with her children, making herself gowns. Her single trip to Verrières was occasioned by a desire to buy some new summer dress goods which had just come from Mulhouse. She was accompanied on her return by a young woman, a relative of hers. Since her marriage Madame de Rênal had become very intimate with Madame

Derville, who had formerly been her companion at the Sacred Heart.

Madame Derville laughed considerably at what she called her cousin's foolish ideas. "Really, I should never think of such things," she said. Such unexpected sallies as would have been called bright in Paris, Madame de Rênal was ashamed of as a piece of folly when she was alone with her husband. But Madame Derville's presence gave her courage. At first she would express herself rather timidly; but when the women were alone for a long time, Madame de Rênal would become greatly animated, and a long forenoon would pass like a moment and leave the two friends bright and gay. During this visit, Madame Derville found her cousin less gay than usual, but much happier.

Julien, on his part, was living a child's life. Since their coming to the country he was as happy in the butterfly chase as his pupils. With constraint and plotting removed, with no men around him, and with no fears any more of Madame de Rênal, he gave himself up to the pure pleasure of existence.

When Madame Derville came, he looked upon her as his friend; he hastened to show her the view to be had at the foot of the new walk under the large walnut trees, equal, if not superior, to the most beautiful in Switzerland or by the Italian lakes. By climbing the steep bank rising a few feet farther away, a great precipice could be seen, fringed with oak saplings, stretching clear to the river. It was to the top of these perpendicular rocks where the happy, free Julien, feeling as if he were master of the domain, conducted the two friends, enjoying hugely their admiration of the beautiful scenery.

"It is like Mozart's music to me," Madame Derville said.

His brothers' jealousy and the presence of his despotic father had spoiled for Julien the country in the neighborhood of Verrières. At Vergy he did not find any of these; for the first time in his life he could not see an enemy. When M. de Rênal went to town, and that was often, he could read. Soon, in place of reading at night, he could give himself up to sleep, though still taking care to hide his light under a vase. During the day, between the children's lessons, he would go to these rocks with a book which formed the guide of his life and the object of his affections. He found in it at once happiness, joy, and exaltation.

Certain things which Napoleon said of women, and several discussions on the merits of fiction in his reign, gave him then for the first time ideas which young men of his age would have known long before.

The summer heat came on apace. The evenings were then regularly passed under a large lime tree a few steps from the house. The darkness there was profound. One evening, while Julien was conversing, and enjoying the pleasure of talking well before young women, he touched, in making a gesture, Madame de Rênal's hand resting on the back of one of the painted garden chairs. The hand was quickly withdrawn, but Julien thought that it was his duty to bring it about so that the hand would not be withdrawn when he touched it. The idea of this duty, and of ridicule, or, rather, of a feeling of inferiority if he failed to perform it, took away all his pleasure.

Chapter 9

An Evening in the Country

La Didon de M. Guérin, esquisse charmante!
—STROMBECK

HIS EXPRESSION the next day, when he saw Madame de Rênal again, was strange. He looked upon her as an enemy with whom he was about to struggle. His look, so different from the night before, almost made Madame de Rênal hysterical. She had been kind to him, and he seemed angry. She could not remove her eyes from him.

Madame Derville's presence caused Julien to speak less, and to occupy himself more with what he had in his heart. His sole concern all that day was to fortify himself with the reading of his inspired book. This imparted new strength to his soul. He greatly shortened the children's lessons, and then, when Madame de Rênal's presence came to recall him to his battle for glory, he decided that it was absolutely necessary that she should allow her hand that night to rest in his.

As the sun set and the hour of decisive battle approached, Julien's heart beat most violently. Night came. He observed, with a joy that removed a great weight from his heart, that the night would be very dark. The sky, heavy with great clouds, seemed, together with a very warm wind, to announce a storm. The two cousins came out very late. Everything they did that night appeared most singular to Julien. Yet they liked the weather, which for certain delicate souls seems to increase the pleasure of loving. They soon sat down; Madame de Rênal by the side of Julien, and Madame Derville near her. Preoccupied with what he was about to do, Julien had nothing to say, and the conversation lagged.

"Shall I then tremble and be discouraged before my first duel?" he said to himself. For, distrusting himself and others, he recognized only too well his own state of mind. In his mortal anguish all dangers would have seemed preferable. How often did he not wish that something might happen that would compel Madame de Rênal to leave the garden and return to the house! The inner conflict in which Julien was engaged was too great to leave his voice steady. Soon, too, Madame de Rênal's voice quavered, though Julien did not notice it. The dreadful combat in which his duty and timidity had become involved was too painful to permit him to notice anything outside of himself. The cottage clock had just struck a quarter to ten, and he had not yet accomplished anything. Julien, mortified over his cowardice, said to himself, "When ten o'clock strikes, I will do what I said all this whole day I would do, or I will go to my room and blow my brains out!"

After another period of anxiety, during which the excess of emotion made Julien almost mad, ten o'clock struck. Every stroke of the clock reverberated in his heart, producing an effect as of physical contact.

At last, when the last stroke was still heard, he stretched out his hand and seized Madame de Rênal's. It was quickly withdrawn. Julien, without knowing what he was doing, seized it again. Although moved himself, he was struck by the icy coldness of the hand he took; he pressed it convulsively. Another effort was made to withdraw it, but finally the hand remained in his.

His heart was filled with joy; not that he loved Madame de Rênal, but it was an end to his frightful torture. In order that Madame Derville might not suspect anything, he thought he would begin to speak. His voice now rang out clear and strong. Madame de Rênal, on the other hand, betrayed so much emotion that her friend, who thought she was ill, proposed to return to the house. Julien scented danger. "If Madame de Rênal," he argued, "went back to the house I should be in the same horrible position in which I passed the whole day. I have not held her hand long enough to see any advantage that I have gained." While Madame de Rênal was considering the idea of returning to the drawing-room, Julien was tightly pressing the hand that was now abandoned in his. Madame de Rênal, who had already seated herself again, said faintly:

"I feel, indeed, a little ill; but the open air will do me good."

These words confirmed Julien's happiness, which at that moment was great indeed. He spoke on; he forgot even to dissemble. Indeed, he appeared most agreeable to the two friends who were listening to him. Nevertheless, there was still a want of courage in the eloquence that came to him all at once. He was in mortal dread lest Madame Derville, feeling the rising wind which presaged a storm, might be inclined to return to the house by herself; he would then remain alone with Madame de Rênal. He was possessed of sufficient blind courage for spontaneous action, but he felt that it was now beyond him to say the simplest word to her. However lightly he might bear his self-reproach, he was, after all, to be beaten, and the advantage which he had just acquired would forthwith disappear.

Happily for him, that night his lively, dashing conversation found grace with Madame Derville, who very often found it as insipid as a child's. As for Madame de Rênal, with her hand resting in Julien's, she was not thinking of anything. She seemed only to have a delicious sense of living. The hours passed under that grand lime tree—said to have been planted by Charles the Bold—were for her one long delight. She listened with rapture to the rustling of the wind in the thick foliage and to the scattering drops on the leaves. Julien did not remark a certain circumstance that would have greatly reassured him: Madame de Rênal, who had been obliged to withdraw her hand to help her cousin pick up a vase of flowers that had been overturned by the wind near by, was hardly seated again before she gave him her hand without the least hesitancy, as if the matter had long been agreed upon.

Midnight had long struck, and it became necessary to leave the garden. They separated, and Madame de Rênal, on retiring, had such transports of love that she did not make herself a single reproach. Happiness allowed her even no sleep.

On the other hand, a leaden slumber took possession of Julien, fatigued as he was from the warfare which all that day timidity and pride had waged in his heart.

Next morning he arose at five o'clock, and—what might have been cruel for Madame de Rênal if she had known it—he scarcely gave her a thought. He had done his duty. Filled with happiness over this feeling, he locked himself in his room and gave himself up with renewed pleasure to the reading of his hero's exploits. By the time breakfast was served he had forgotten, in the reading of the records of the Grand Army, all his conquests of the night before. He said to himself lightly, as he went down to the drawing-room, "I must never tell the woman I love her."

Instead of looks expressive of love which he expected to meet, he encountered the frowning face of M. de Rênal. The latter, on his arrival from Verrières two hours before, had not concealed his great displeasure at the fact that Julien had spent the entire morning without attending to the children. No one could be more disagreeable than this overbearing man in an angry mood when he had the means of showing it. Each sharp word her husband uttered sent a pang to Madame de Rênal's heart. As for Julien, he was so deeply plunged in ecstasy, and so greatly occupied with the great things that had passed before his eyes for several hours, that he could hardly concentrate his attention on M. de Rênal's tirade. At last he said, brusquely:

"I was sick."

The tone of this reply would have piqued a much less sensitive man than the Mayor of Verrières. The latter had a mind to reply to Julien by throwing him out of doors; he was restrained only by his rule of never doing anything hastily.

"The young fool," he said to himself, "has in a way established himself in my house. Valenod might take him, or he might marry Elisa, and in either case he would have his laugh on me, after all."

Despite the wisdom of these reflections, M. de Rênal's anger burst out in a torrent of words that finally enraged Julien. Madame de Rênal was on the point of bursting into tears. Hardly was breakfast over when she asked Julien to give her his arm for a walk. She leaned on him then with most marked friendliness. To all that she would say, Julien could only reply in a suppressed voice:

"That is what rich people are!"

M. de Rênal was then walking very close to them, and his presence increased Julien's anger. Then for the first time he felt that Madame de Rênal was leaning on him. The sensation caused him horror. He repulsed her violently, disengaging his arm.

Fortunately M. de Rênal did not notice this new piece of impertinence; it was noticed only by Madame Derville. Her friend burst into tears. At that moment M. de Rênal was throwing stones at a little peasant girl who was walking over a corner of the orchard.

"M. Julien, please restrain yourself; you must know that we all have our moods," said Madame Derville, quickly.

Julien gazed at her coldly, with eyes expressive of the most sovereign disdain. His look surprised Madame Derville, and it would have surprised her still more had she divined its real meaning. She would have seen there something like a vague desire for atrocious vengeance. It is without doubt such moments of humiliation that have made the Robespierres.

"Your Julien is very violent; he frightens me," said Madame Derville to her cousin in a whisper.

"He is right to be angry," the other replied. "After the astonishing progress which the children have made, what difference does it make if he passes a morning without teaching them? Really, men are hard." For the first time in her life

Madame de Rênal had a feeling of resentment against her husband.

Julien was about to give vent to the great hatred he entertained for the rich. Happily, M. de Rênal, having called his gardener, was occupied with him in barring the little path around the orchard with fagots. Julien did not respond in the slightest to the kindly attentions of which he was the object for the remainder of the walk. For hardly had M. de Rênal disappeared when both women, pretending to be tired, asked each an arm. Between these two women, whose cheeks were red with embarrassment caused by the disagreeable incident, the pallor and gloom of Julien's face formed a strange contrast. He despised these women and all their tender sentiments.

"Oh," he said to himself, "not five hundred francs to finish my studies! How I should like to send these people walking!" Absorbed in these gloomy reflections, what little he deigned to hear of the kind words of the two friends irritated him as being devoid of sense, vapid; in a word, feminine.

Just to be speaking and to keep up a lively conversation it occurred to Madame de Rênal to say that her husband had come from Verrières because he had made a bargain with one of the farmers for May straw. (In that neighborhood mattresses are filled with May straw.)

"My husband will not join us," said Madame de Rênal. "With his gardener and his man he is going to be busy filling the mattresses in the house. This morning he put straw in all the beds on the first floor; he is now on the second."

Julien changed color. He gave Madame de Rênal a wild look and took her aside, Madame Derville permitting them to withdraw.

"Save me!" cried Julien. "You alone can do it; for you know that the valet has a mortal hatred for me. I must confess to you I have a portrait, madame; I have hidden it in the mattress."

"You have a portrait?" asked Madame de Rênal, scarcely able to stand.

Her look of dejection was perceived by Julien, who immediately profited by it.

"I have another favor to ask of you, madame: I beg you not to look at that portrait; it is a secret."

"A secret?" repeated Madame de Rênal, faintly.

Though raised among purse-proud people who were sensible only to money interests, love had already made her heart generous. In spite of being cruelly wounded, it was with the simplest devotion that Madame de Rênal asked the necessary questions of Julien in order to acquit herself of the commission.

"So, then," she murmured as she was walking away, "it is a little round box of soft black cardboard?"

"Yes, madame," answered Julien in that hard tone which danger imparts to men.

She went up to the second story, with a pallor as if she were going to her death. To complete her misery she felt as if she were about to faint; but the necessity of rendering that service to Julien gave her strength.

"I must get that box," she said to herself, walking faster.

She heard her husband talking to the valet in Julien's very room. Fortunately they passed into the children's apartment. She raised the mattress and thrust her hand into the straw with such violence as to scratch her fingers. Of this she was not aware, though usually sensitive to such little pains; for almost at the same time she felt the polished surface of the box. She seized it and disappeared.

Hardly was she delivered from the fear of being surprised by her husband than the horror which the box caused her nearly made her ill.

"Julien, then, is in love, and I hold here the portrait of the woman he loves!"

Seated on a chair in the hall leading to that room, Madame de Rênal was a prey to all the horrors of jealousy. Her great lack of experience at that moment was again useful to her; astonishment was tempering her grief. Julien appeared, seized the box without thanking her, without a word, and ran into his room, where, making a light, he proceeded immediately to burn it. He was pale, exhausted. He exaggerated the greatness of the risk he had run.

"Napoleon's picture," he said to himself, shaking his head, "found hidden in the room of a man who professes such a mortal hatred for the usurper; found by M. de Rênal, such an extremist, and so angry! And to cap the imprudence, on the back of the portrait, lines written in my own handwritting, to leave no doubt of the greatness of my admiration; and every one of those transports of admiration is dated! There is one from day before yesterday. My whole reputation is spoiled, ruined, in a moment," Julien said to himself, seeing the box burn, "and my reputation is all I have. I live on nothing else; and yet, what a life! Good Lord!"

An hour later his fatigue and the pity he felt for himself softened him a little. He met Madame de Rênal, and taking her hand, kissed it with more sincerity than he had ever used. She blushed with happiness, though at the same instant she rudely repulsed him. Julien's pride, wounded only so recently, made him at this moment positively foolish. He saw in Madame de Rênal only a rich woman; he dropped her hand with disdain and walked away. He walked to the garden, absorbed in thought, a bitter smile playing on his lips.

"I walk here calmly like a man that is master of his time. I am not attending to the children. I am exposing myself to humiliation from M. de Rênal, and he would be in the right!" He walked quickly to the children's room.

The caresses of the youngest boy, whom he loved very dearly, calmed somewhat his boiling passion. "This one does not despise me yet," thought Julien. But soon he blamed the calming of his anger as a new weakness. "These children pet me as they would a dog they had bought yesterday."

Chapter 10

A Great Heart and a Small Fortune

But passion most dissembles, yet betrays,
Even by its darkness; as the blackest sky
Foretells the heaviest tempest.
—DON JUAN, I. 73

M. DE RÉNAL, after going through all the rooms, returned to the children's apartment, with the servants carrying the mattresses. The sudden entrance of the man was the last straw with Julien. Paler and gloomier than usual, he made a rush towards him. M. de Rênal stopped and looked at his servants.

"Monsieur," said Julien to him, "do you think that your children would have made as much progress with any other tutor? If not," continued Julien, without giving M. de Rênal time to reply, "how dare you tell me I'm neglecting them?"

M. de Rênal, hardly recovered from his fright, concluded, from the strange tone which he saw the little peasant assume, that the latter had a better offer up his sleeve and was going to leave. Julien, with increasing anger as he went on, added:

"I can live without you, sir!"

"I am sorry to see you so angry," replied M. de Rênal, faltering a little. The servants were only ten feet away, arranging the beds.

"I don't care, sir," Julien answered. "Think of the insulting words you addressed to me, and before ladies, too."

M. de Rênal knew only too well what Julien wanted, and his heart was rent with a fearful struggle. Then Julien, fairly beside himself with anger, cried out:

"I know where to go, sir, when I leave you."

On hearing this M. de Rênal saw Julien already installed at the house of M. Valenod.

"Oh, well, monsieur," he said, sighing, in a tone that might have been occasioned by a surgeon during a most painful operation, "well, you shall have what you want. Beginning with day after to-morrow, which is the first of the month, I shall give you fifty francs a month."

Julien was amazed; he almost burst out laughing—all his anger suddenly disappeared.

"I haven't enough contempt for this brute," he said to himself; "that's without doubt the greatest apology such a low nature could make."

The children, who had been witnessing this scene with open mouths, ran into the garden to tell their mother that M. Julien was very angry, but was going to get fifty francs a month.

Julien followed them mechanically, without even looking at M. de Rênal, who was indeed very angry.

"There's a hundred and sixty-eight francs," the Mayor said to himself, "that Valenod has cost me. I will tell him a word or two about his little scheme for maintaining the foundlings."

A minute later Julien went up to M. de Rênal, saying:

"I want to go to confession to M. Chélan. I have the honor to inform you that I will be absent for a few hours."

"Oh, my dear Julien," M. de Rênal said, with the falsest kind of a laugh, "all day if you like; all of to-morrow, my dear friend. Take the gardener's horse if you are going to Verrières."

"There he goes," said M. de Rênal to himself, "to give his reply to Valenod. He has not promised anything; but let the young man's head cool off a little!"

Julien slipped away quickly, and entered the thick wood lying between Vergy and Verrières. He did not wish to come so soon to M. Chélan. Before entering on a new scene of hypocrisy, he thought he would peer into his own heart to know the varied feelings that were moving him.

"I have won a battle," he whispered to himself as soon as he was in the wood, when he thought no one could see him. "Yes, I have won a battle."

That thought made his position roseate, and imparted to his soul a great tranquillity.

"Here I am with an income of fifty francs a month. M. de Rênal must be very much afraid. But of what?"

The thought that he had been able to frighten a man of means and power, who had an hour before thrown him into a violent rage, made Julien's soul serene again. For the moment he was almost impressed by the ravishing beauty of the primeval forest. Enormous blocks of living rock lay here and there along the mountain side. There grew alongside tall beech trees, as high almost as those rocks, whose shade, three feet away from where the heat of the sun was almost intolerable, lent a delicious freshness.

Julien took breath for a moment in the shade of these great rocks and then started to go up higher. By a narrow, unfrequented path, used only by the goat shepherds, he soon found himself upon an immense rock, where he was sure of being all alone. That physical position made him smile; it pictured to him the moral plane he was burning to reach. The pure air of those high mountains imparted serenity to his soul, even joy. The Mayor of Verrières was the representative in his eyes of all the rich and the insolent on the face of the earth; yet Julien felt that the hatred by which he had been moved, had, in spite of its violence, nothing of the personal in it. If he had ceased to see M. de Rênal he would have forgotten him in a week—him, his house, his dogs, his children—all.

"I have forced him, I don't know how, to make the greatest sacrifice. Yes, more than fifty crowns a year! Only a moment before, I escaped the greatest danger. That's two victories in one day; the second one don't amount to much; but I'll find out how it came about. But to-morrow is time enough for that difficulty."

Julien, standing upright on the high rock, looked at the sky, where an August sun was blazing. Grasshoppers were chirping in the field below. He saw at his feet twenty leagues of country. A hawk he had noticed, after leaving the high crags overhead, was describing in silence its widening circles. Julien's eye mechanically followed the bird of prey, struck by its tranquil, mighty movements. He envied its force; he envied its isolation.

It was the destiny of Napoleon. Would it some day be his?

Chapter 11

An Evening

Yet Julia's very coldness still was kind,
And tremulously gentle her small hand
Withdrew itself from his, but left behind
A little pressure, thrilling, and so bland
And slight, so very slight that to the mind
'Twas but a doubt.

—DON JUAN, I. 71

IN COURSE OF TIME he appeared at Verrières. In leaving the vicarage he met by chance M. Valenod, whom he hastened to tell of the increase in his salary.

On his return to Vergy, Julien did not go down to the garden until nightfall. He felt worn out by the great emotions which had agitated him during the day. "What shall I say to them?" he asked himself uneasily, when he thought of the ladies. He was far from seeing that his thoughts were precisely on a level with the little things that ordinarily fill a woman's interest. Julien was often an enigma to Madame Derville, and even to her friend; and he, in his turn, comprehended only half of what they said—such was the force, indeed, the sublimity, of the movements of passion that were overwhelming the soul of this ambitious young man. With that singular creature the weather was almost continually a storm.

Upon coming into the garden that evening, Julien was disposed to occupy himself with ideas about the pretty cousins. They were awaiting him with impatience; he took his usual place beside Madame de Rênal. It was very dark. He took a white hand which he had been noticing near him, resting on the back of a chair. There was a slight hesitation, but in the end it was withdrawn in a manner that betokened a little anger. Julien was content to have it so, and was continuing gayly the conversation, when he heard M. de Rênal approaching.

In Julien's ears still rang the insulting words of the morning.

"Wouldn't it be," he thought, "a good way of making a fool of this fellow, who is stuffed with all that fortune can give, to take possession of his wife's hand in his own presence? Yes, I'll do it, just because he showed me so much contempt."

From that moment his tranquillity of mind, always unnatural to one of his nature, quickly disappeared. He was burning to have Madame de Rênal consent to let him have her hand. He could think of nothing else.

M. de Rênal was discussing politics with considerable heat. Two or three traders had suddenly become richer than himself and were ready to dispute the elections with him. Madame Derville was quietly listening. Julien, irritated by his speech, brought his chair closer to Madame de Rênal's, the darkness hiding all these movements. He ventured to place his hand very close to the pretty arm which the sleeve left bare. He felt dazed; his mind was reeling; he brought his cheek close to the pretty arm; he pressed his lips to it.

Madame de Rênal trembled. Her husband was four feet away; she hastened to give Julien her hand, and at the same time to push him back a little. While M. de Rênal was continuing his invectives against the good-for-nothing people and the rich Jacobins, Julien was covering the hand which had been abandoned to him with passionate kisses, or, at least, with what seemed such to Madame de Rênal. Yet the poor woman had proof during this fatal day that the man she was secretly adoring loved another. All the time that Julien was absent she had been a prey to the greatest torment. She was beginning to think.

"Should I love him," she said to herself; "I, a married woman? Is it right for me to love? But—I have never had that passion for my husband which absorbs me in Julien. After all, he is only a boy who respects me. My infatuation will pass away. What difference does it make to my husband what sentiments I have for this young man? M. de Rênal would be only irritated by the conversations I have with Julien on trifling things. As for him, he is thinking of his business. I deprive him of nothing in giving it to Julien."

No hypocrisy went with the purity of that simple soul misguided by a passion which until then she had never experienced. She was deceived, but she was not aware of it; though her virtuous instincts were taking alarm.

In these struggles she had been engaged when Julien appeared in the garden. She heard him speak and saw him take his seat by her side. Her heart was in rapture, almost, from that delightful sensation which for a fortnight had astonished her even more than it beguiled. It was all so unexpected to her. After a few minutes the thought came: "Is it enough, then, for Julien only to be present to make me forget all his faults?" She was frightened. It was then she withdrew her hand from him.

His passionate kisses, such as she had never before received, made her immediately forget that he might love another woman. Soon he appeared blameless in her eyes. With the cessation of the sharp pang that was born of her suspicion, her present happiness, of which she had never even dreamt, gave her transports of a wild, boundless love. That evening was a delightful one to all but the Mayor of Verrières, who could not forget the trading upstarts. Julien was thinking neither of his sombre ambition nor of his difficult projects. For the first time in his life he was enthralled by the power of beauty. He was lost in a vague, gentle reverie that, to his nature, was so strange, and was softly pressing the hand that captivated him with its fairness. He was half listening to the rustling of the leaves as they were stirred by the night breeze, and to the distant bark of the dogs from the mill on the Doube.

But his emotion was a pleasure, not a passion. On returning to his room, he thought only of one pleasure, that of taking up again his favorite book. At twenty years of age the idea of the world and of the effect to produce in it is above everything else. But he soon laid the book down. From thinking of the victories of Napoleon, he had seen something new in his own. "Yes, I've won a battle," he reflected. "I must profit by it. I must crush the pride of this haughty gentleman while he is in retreat. That's Napoleon through and through. I will ask him for three days' absence to visit my friend Fouqué. If he refuses I leave him at once; but he will not refuse!"

Madame de Rênal could not close her eyes. It appeared to her as if she had not lived until that moment. She was possessed by the thought of her delightful sensation while Julien was covering her hand with burning kisses.

All at once the frightful word "adulteress" came to her. All that the vilest debauchery could suggest of a wicked, sensual love presented itself vividly to her imagination then. Her ideas now were tarnishing the delicate, divine image which she had made of Julien, and of the happiness of loving him. The future was outlined in awful colors. She saw herself fallen.

It was a horrible moment; her heart had wandered to unknown lands. The night before she had tasted of a rare delight; now she saw herself plunged in cruel despair. She had no idea that there were such sufferings; they disturbed her reason. For an instant she had a notion of confessing to her husband that she was in fear of falling in love with Julien. Happily, she remembered a word of warning given to her on the eve of her marriage by her aunt: that there is danger in confiding in a husband, who, after all, is a master. In very grief she wrung her hands. Her heart was swept by opposing painful sensations. As much as she feared that she was not being loved, so much was she tortured by the idea of a horrible crime—as if she were to be exposed the next day in the pillory in the public square of Verrières, with an inscription explaining her adultery to the entire world.

Madame de Rênal had no real experience; even in her clearest moments, and in the full exercise of her reason, she had never perceived an interval between being culpable only in the eyes of God and being overwhelmed by general contempt.

When the horrible idea of adultery, and the disgrace which, in her opinion, attaches to that crime, left her some repose, she began to think of the charm of living innocently with Julien, of living with him with only a *memory* of the passion. Just then the horrible thought came to her that Julien loved another. She saw him again, turning pale, when he had expressed the fear of losing the picture, of being compromised in having it seen. For the first time then she had surprised a line of fear on his countenance, always so tranquil and noble in her eyes. Never before had he been so moved either before herself or the children. This added pang came to her with overpowering force. Probably Madame de Rênal uttered a cry that awakened her maid. She saw the light of a candle, and, with it, Elisa approaching her bed.

"Is it you he loves?" she cried out, frantically.

The maid, distressed by the suffering in which she found her mistress, happily paid no attention to that singular question. Madame de Rênal became aware of her imprudence. "I have fever," she said, "and I believe I'm a little delirious; stay with me."

Fully awakened by the necessity of self-constraint, she saw herself in a less painful light. Reason took possession again of the domain which had been usurped.

To escape from the steady gaze of her waiting-woman she asked her to read the paper to her. And it was under the monotonous tone with which the girl read a long article from the *Quotidienne*, that Madame de Rênal made the virtuous resolution to treat Julien with extreme coolness when she saw him again.

Chapter 12

A Journey

*On trouve à Paris des gens élégants, il peut y
avoir en province des gens à caractère.*
—SIEYÈS

AT FIVE O'CLOCK the next morning, before Madame de Rênal
appeared, Julien had obtained from her husband a leave of
absence of three days. To his own surprise Julien felt a desire
to see her; he thought of her pretty hand. He went down into
the garden; but Madame de Rênal was long in coming. Yet, if
Julien had loved her he would have seen her by her semi-
consciousness.

Behind the half-drawn curtains, with her face against the
window, she was watching him. At last she decided, in spite of
her resolutions, to appear in the garden. Her habitual paleness
gave way to a heightened rosy color. She was apparently agitated, the naïve soul; constraint and anger were changing that
expression of profound serenity which gave such charm to her
angelic face—an expression that seemed so far above all the
vulgar interests of life.

Julien approached her eagerly; he admired those beautiful
arms which a shawl hastily thrown about her exposed to his
view. The fresh morning air seemed to heighten the brilliancy
of her complexion, so sensitive to every impression from her
agitation during the night. That modest and touching beauty,
suggestive of ideas not to be found in the inferior classes, revealed to Julien a faculty in his soul of which he had never
been aware. In rapt admiration of the charms which surprised
his eager gaze, he was not thinking of the friendly reception
he had calculated upon receiving. He was therefore the more
astonished at the icy coldness which she was at pains to show
him, and through which he could discern the intention of keeping him in his place. The smile of pleasure died away on his
lips; he remembered his station in life, especially as it appeared
in the eyes of a rich and noble heiress. In an instant his face
showed only disdain. He felt a certain contempt for himself for
having delayed his departure for an hour just to meet with such
a humiliating reception.

"It is only a fool," he thought, "who gets angry at people. A stone falls because it's heavy. Shall I always remain a child? When have I contracted the good habit of giving my heart to these people just for their money? If I want their respect and my own, I must show them that it's my poverty that is dealing with their money, but my heart is a thousand miles away from their insolence, and in a sphere too far removed to be reached by their marks of disdain or favor!"

While these thoughts were crowding into the young tutor's mind, his face took on a fierce expression of injured pride. Madame de Rênal was troubled by it. The virtuous indifference which she assumed in greeting him quickly gave way to a lively interest in the sudden change she was witnessing. The meaningless words that were exchanged about health and the fine weather all at once ceased. Julien, whose judgment was not clouded by any passion, very soon found the means of intimating to Madame de Rênal how small was his share in the common friendship; he told her nothing of the little trip he intended to make, but, raising his hat, departed.

As she saw him walk away, her heart sinking with the weight of the disdain which she read in his face—the face that was so pleasing the night before—her eldest boy, who came running from the other end of the garden, cried out, as he embraced her:

"We've said good-by; M. Julien is going away for a while."

On hearing this, Madame de Rênal was seized with a mortal chill; she was unhappy because of her virtue, and unhappier still because of her weakness!

This new event began to occupy her whole mind; it bore her far away from the good resolutions she had formed during her terrible night. It was no longer a question of resisting the man; it was to lose him forever!

She must go to breakfast. To complete her misery, M. de Rênal and Madame Derville spoke only of Julien's departure. The Mayor of Verrières had remarked something unusual in the firm tone with which he had asked leave.

"This little peasant has no doubt some offer from somebody in his pocket. But that somebody, even if it is M. Valenod, should be discouraged by the sum of six hundred francs, by which his annual expenditure must now be increased. Yesterday, at Verrières, I should have asked for three days to think it over; and this morning the little gentleman leaves for the mountain so as not to be obliged to give me an answer. To be obliged to bargain with a miserable laborer playing the insolent—yet that's what we have come to!"

"Since my husband," thought Madame de Rênal, "who does not know how much he has wounded Julien, thinks he will leave us, what must I think? Oh, it is all over!"

In order that she might be free with her tears and not answer any questions from Madame Derville, she complained of a severe headache and went to bed.

"That's how women are," remarked M. de Rênal; "there's always something wrong with those complicated machines." And he walked away, jeering.

While Madame de Rênal was a prey to her cruel passion, Julien was gayly pursuing his way amidst the great beauty along the mountain path. He had to cross the great chain lying to the north of Vergy. The path he pursued, rising gradually from the beech woods, wound zig-zag along the mountain side which hems in the valley of the Doube on the north. Soon the traveller, looking at the lower ridges enclosing the course of the Doube southward, could gaze as far as the fertile plains of Bourgogne and Beaujolais. However insensible the young man was to beauty of this kind, he could not help stopping from time to time to gaze upon this vast and imposing spectacle.

Finally he reached the top of the mountain, which he had to pass in order to reach the solitary valley where his friend Fouqué, the wood merchant, lived. Julien was not in a hurry to see him or anyone else. Hidden like a bird of prey in the midst of the bare rocks fringing the high mountain, he could see from a distance anyone that might approach. He discovered a little cave in the steep side of one of these rocks, and making his way towards it, he soon found himself in that retreat. "Here," he said, his eyes sparkling with joy, "here men couldn't do me any harm." He thought he would yield to the pleasure of putting down his thoughts in writing—a thing that was so dangerous for him elsewhere. A square stone served as a desk. His pencil fairly flew. He became oblivious to everything around him. By and by he noticed that the sun was setting behind the mountains on the other side of Beaujolais.

"Why can't I pass the night here?" he said to himself; "I have some bread, and I am free." At the thought of that word his heart became exalted; pretending even with his hypocrisy, not to feel free with his friend Fouqué. With his head resting on both his hands, Julien, in that nook, was happier than he had ever been in his life, as he sat lost in reverie, dreaming of the happiness of liberty. Unconcernedly he saw the twilight gradually disappear. In the darkness his mind wandered to the contemplation of what one day he imagined he would see in Paris

—a woman more beautiful, more gifted than any he had seen in the country, whom he would love with passion. And he, too, would be loved. And if he left her side for a while, it would only be to cover himself with glory and to deserve her love the more.

A young man raised amid the sad realities of life in Paris, even if he had Julien's imagination, would have been awakened at this point in his romance by cold irony; the great deeds would have disappeared, with the hope that had moved him, to give place to the well-known maxim: "Leave your mistress; you run the risk of being deceived two and three times a day." But this young man saw nothing between him and the most heroic deeds but the lack of opportunity.

A dark night took the place of day, and he had yet to cover two leagues before descending into the hamlet where Fouqué lived. Before leaving the grotto, Julien kindled a fire and carefully burnt all he had written.

His friend was greatly astonished when he knocked at his door at one o'clock in the morning. He found Fouqué at his ledger—a very tall, clumsily built young man, large-featured, with a nose beyond all proportion. There was much kindliness hidden behind that forbidding aspect.

"You've quarrelled with your M. de Rênal; that's why you come here so unexpectedly?"

Julien related to him, in his own way, the events of the preceding day.

"Stay with me," said Fouqué to him; "I see that you know M. de Rênal, M. Valenod, the sub-prefect Maugiron, and the curate Chélan; you know their crafty character. You are in a position to know what's what. You know arithmetic better than I do; you will keep the books. I make a good deal in my business. The impossibility of doing everything myself, and the fear of finding a rascal in the man I should choose for a partner, have prevented me every day from improving excellent opportunities. Only a month ago Michaud de Saint-Amand, whom I had not seen for six years, and whom I met by chance at the Pontarlier sale, made, through me, six thousand francs. Why shouldn't you have made those six thousand francs, or if only three thousand? If I had you with me that day I would have put a higher price on that lot of lumber, and it would have soon been left to me. Be my partner."

This offer had some point for Julien; it somewhat neutralized his folly. All through supper, which, like Homeric heroes, the two friends had prepared themselves—Fouqué living alone—

the accounts were shown to Julien, as well as other proof that the lumber business offered many advantages. Fouqué had a high estimation of the lights and character of Julien.

When he found himself at last alone in his little room—a room built of fir logs—he said to himself: "True, I can make a few thousand francs to take up then the profession of soldier or priest with advantage, according to what may then be the fashion in France. The little sum I'll have then will remove all difficulties. Alone in these mountains I would put away a little of the awful ignorance I have of the many things that society people know. But Fouqué says he will not marry; and he tells me repeatedly that solitude makes him unhappy. It's evident that if he takes one for a partner who has no money to put into the business, it is with the hope of making an inseparable companion of him. Shall I deceive my friend?" Julien cried out, vexed. This creature, with whom hypocrisy and the absence of all sympathy were the ordinary means of safety, could not for once bear the idea of a want of delicacy towards his friend.

But all at once Julien felt reassured; he had a reason for refusing. "What, shall I, like a coward, lose seven or eight years? I should then be twenty-eight; but at that age Bonaparte had won already his greatest achievements. After I'll have gained, obscurely enough, a little money in running to the lumber sales and winning the favor of a few unimportant fools, who tells me I'll still have in me the sacred fire with which a name is made?"

The next morning Julien coolly replied to the good Fouqué, who had already looked at the partnership as settled, that his predilection for the holy ministry at the altar prevented him from accepting. Fouqué was amazed. "Think," he urged, "I'm making you a partner, or, if you like it better, I'll give you four thousand francs a year. And you want to go back to your Rênal, who despises you like the mud on his shoe. When you have two hundred louis in your pocket, what will prevent you from entering the seminary? I'll tell you more. I'll take it upon myself to procure for you the best curacy in the country. For," continued Fouqué, lowering his voice, "I deliver firewood to the ____, and to the ____, and to the ____, and I give them the heart of oak, for which they only pay me as for white wood; but money was never invested better."

Nothing could overcome Julien's choice. Fouqué began to think him somewhat of a fool. On the third day, early in the morning, Julien left his friend, to pass the day amid the mountain rocks. He found his little cell again, but he did not experience again his former peace of soul; his friend's offer had taken it away. Like Hercules, he had not to decide between vice and virtue, but between a mediocrity with assured ease and comfort and all the heroic dreams of youth. "I haven't any real firmness," he said to himself; and his doubts caused him the greatest vexation. "I'm not of the stuff of which great men are made, if I'm afraid that eight years spent in earning a living will take away the sublime energy for remarkable achievements."

Chapter 13

Open-Worked Stockings

*Un roman: c'est un miroir qu'on promène le long
d'un chemin.*

—SAINT-REAL

WHEN JULIEN saw the picturesque ruins of the ancient church
of Vergy, it occurred to him that for two days he had not given
a single thought to Madame de Rênal. "The other day, when I
left, that woman recalled to me the infinite distance that separated us; she treated me like a laborer's boy. No doubt she
wanted to let me know that she regretted giving me her hand
the night before. Yet it's very pretty, that hand. What charm
she has, what gentility her face expresses!"

The opportunity of a mercantile career with Fouqué gave
greater facility to Julien's reasoning; he was no longer so irritated either by his own lively sense of his poverty or by the
thought of his lowliness in the eyes of the world. Placed, so to
speak, on a height, he could use his judgment, and command,
in a measure, poverty or ease. He was far from regarding his
position like a philosopher, yet he was clear-sighted enough to
feel somewhat different after that little journey to the mountain.

He was struck by the marked pain with which Madame de
Rênal listened to a brief account of his trip which she had asked.

Fouqué had had some idea of marrying; it was an unfortunate
love affair. Long confidences on this subject had filled out the
entire conversation between the two friends: Fouqué's happiness had been too great; he found out that it was not he alone
that was loved. All this had astonished Julien; it was something
new. His own solitary life, lying mostly in imagination, had removed him from the possibility of understanding it.

During Julien's absence, life for Madame de Rênal was one
long torture. She, in fact, became ill.

"Indeed," said Madame Derville to her, when she saw Julien
arrive, "indisposed as you are, you must not go into the garden
to-night; the damp air will make you worse."

Madame Derville saw with astonishment that her friend, who
was always being scolded by M. de Rênal for the excessive
simplicity of her dress, had taken out the open-worked stock-

ings and the pretty little slippers which had come from Paris. For three days Madame de Rênal's sole diversion had been to have had a summer dress made for her, by Elisa, of some pretty material that was then in fashion. This dress was finished just a few moments before Julien's return. Madame de Rênal immediately put it on. Her friend was no longer in doubt. "She is in love, poor thing," said Madame Derville to herself. She understood then all the singular symptoms of her malady.

She saw her speak to Julien. Paleness gave way to crimson blushes, and anxiety was vividly pictured in those eyes, that remained fixed on the young tutor. Madame de Rênal was expecting every moment that he would declare himself and tell whether he would leave the house or remain. Julien had no idea of saying a word on that subject; he was not thinking of it. After a fearful struggle with herself, Madame de Rênal ventured to ask him in a trembling voice, in which all her passion was revealed:

"Are you going to leave your pupils here, to go elsewhere?"

Julien was struck by Madame de Rênal's anxious tone and expression. "This woman is in love with me," he thought; "but after this fleeting moment of weakness, that wounds her pride, she will assume her haughtiness again when she has no longer to fear my departure." This view of their mutual position came like a flash to Julien. He replied, hesitatingly:

"I should regret very much to leave such amiable, *well-born* children; yet it may be that I will have to. A man has duties to himself."

In pronouncing the words "well born," one of those aristocratic phrases which Julien had recently acquired, he was animated by a feeling of resentment. "In this woman's eyes," he said to himself, "I am not well born."

Madame de Rênal was admiring his spirit, his beauty, while listening to him. She was dismayed at the possibility of a departure which he intimated to her. All her friends from Verrières, who had come to dine with her in Vergy while Julien was absent, had complimented her—if not envied—on the marvellous young man her husband had the good fortune of securing. It was not because they were aware of the progress of the children. The fact that he knew his Bible by heart, and in Latin, too, had elicited admiration enough to last a century.

Julien, because he spoke to no one, did not know that. If Madame de Rênal had had the least address she would have complimented him on the reputation he had acquired; and

Julien, with his self-esteem assured, would have been gentle and kind towards her, especially since he thought her new dress so becoming. Madame de Rênal, pleased, too, with her pretty gown, and with what Julien said of it, wished to walk about in the garden; presently she admitted she was not in a condition to walk. She had taken the traveller's arm, and, far from increasing her strength, the contact of the arm removed it altogether.

It was dark; hardly were they seated, when Julien, using his old privilege, ventured to bring his lips to the arm of his pretty companion and to take her hand. He was thinking of the boldness with which Fouqué had treated his mistresses, and not of Madame de Rênal; the phrase "well born" still weighed on his heart. He felt his hand pressed, but it gave him no pleasure. Far from being proud or grateful for the feeling which Madame de Rênal showed him, and by signs that were only too evident, her beauty, her elegance, her freshness left him almost wholly unmoved. Purity of soul and the absence of wicked passions, no doubt, lengthen the duration of youth. It is the face that first grows old with most women.

Julien was sullen during the entire evening. Until then his anger had extended only to the accident of social position; but from the time that Fouqué had offered him an ignoble means of reaching a condition of ease he was bearing himself a grudge. Absorbed in his thoughts, though from time to time speaking a few words to the women, Julien dropped Madame de Rênal's hand, unconsciously. That action crushed the poor woman's heart; she saw in it a miserable end.

Assured of Julien's affection, she might have perhaps found strength against him; but in dread of losing him forever, her passion brought her even to her taking of Julien's hand, which was carelessly resting on the back of a chair. That action put new life into the ambitious young man; he would have wished it to be observed by all those noble folk who would regard him so patronizingly, sitting at the foot of the table with the children. "This woman can't despise me," he thought; "in that case I should appreciate her beauty. I owe it to myself to become her lover." Such an idea would not have occurred to him before he had heard the simple confidences of his friend.

The determination he had just formed became an agreeable diversion. "I must have," he said to himself, "one of these two women." He saw that it would have been more agreeable to court Madame Derville; not because he liked her better, but because she had always seen him honored for his knowledge, and not as carpenter's apprentice with a ratteen coat folded under his arm as he had appeared to Madame de Rênal. It was precisely as a young workman, blushing to the whites of his eyes, who had stood at the door not daring to ring, that Madame de Rênal thought of him with the greatest charm.

In thus surveying his position, Julien saw that he could not think of making a conquest of Madame Derville, who, indeed, was as charming to him as Madame de Rênal. Forced to revert to the latter, he thought, "What do I know of this woman's character? Only this: before my trip I took her hand, she withdrew it; to-day I withdrew my hand, she takes it and presses it. A fine opportunity for showing her all the contempt which she has shown to me. The Lord only knows how many lovers she has had! Perhaps she only decides in my favor because we can see each other so easily."

Such, alas! is the evil effect of an effete civilization. At the age of twenty a young man, if educated at all, is yet a thousand leagues from unrestraint, without which love often becomes the most irksome of duties.

"I must succeed," Julien's vanity continued, "with this woman, since, if I ever make a name, and it is thrown up to me that I have been an humble tutor, I can claim that it was love that put me into that position."

Julien moved his hand to a greater distance from Madame de Rênal's because she had taken it again and pressed it. When they entered the house, towards midnight, Madame de Rênal asked him in a whisper:

"Are you going to leave us? Will you go?"

Julien replied, with a sigh:

"I must leave, for I love you passionately. It is wicked—and how wicked for a young priest!"

Madame de Rênal leaned on his arm, and with such abandon that her cheek felt the warmth of Julien's.

The nights for these two persons were quite different. Madame de Rênal was exalted by transports of the highest moral pleasure. A coquettish young girl who begins to love early becomes accustomed to amorous troubles; by the time she reaches the age of the real passion, the charm of novelty has worn off. As Madame de Rênal had never read any novels, every form of her happiness was new to her. Not a suggestion of sober truth came to cool her ardor; not even the spectre of the future. She saw herself as happy ten years hence as she was at that moment.

Even the thought of the virtue and constancy she had sworn to M. de Rênal, which had stirred her to such an extent a few days before, presented itself in vain; she dismissed it as importunate. "I will never yield to Julien," she said to herself. "We shall live in the future as we have been living now for a month. He will be a friend."

Chapter 14

The English Scissors

A girl of sixteen had a rosy complexion, and she put on rouge.

—POLIDORI

As FOR JULIEN, Fouqué's offer had taken away all his happiness; he could not make up his mind.

"Oh, perhaps I'm wanting in character; I should have been a bad soldier under Napoleon. At least," he added, "my little intrigue with the mistress of the house will amuse me for a while."

Happily, even in this petty incident, his heart but lamely responded to his cavalier-like tone. He was afraid of Madame de Rênal's dress. That dress, in his eyes, was the vanguard of Paris. His pride would not allow him to leave anything to chance or to the inspiration of the moment. After Fouqué's confidences and the little that he had read about love in his Bible, he went about formulating a detailed campaign. As he was greatly perturbed, without acknowledging it, he wrote out his plan.

The next morning Madame de Rênal was alone with him for a moment in the drawing-room.

"Have not you another name besides Julien?" she asked.

To this flattering question our hero did not know what to reply. Such a circumstance had not entered into his plan. Without this foolish idea of following a plan, his lively ingenuity would have been equal to the occasion, and the surprise would have served only to add to the vivacity of his ideas.

He felt awkward, and he himself exaggerated his awkwardness. Madame de Rênal quickly overlooked this. She saw in it the effect of charming candor. And what was wanting in this man whom she deemed so intelligent was precisely this air of candor.

"Your little tutor inspires me with distrust," Madame Derville would say to her at times. "He has always a preoccupied air about him and always acts with diplomacy. He is a politician."

Julien was deeply humiliated by his embarrassment in not

being able to reply to Madame de Rênal. "A man like myself," he thought, "must make up for lost ground." And taking advantage of the moment they were passing to another room, he thought it was his duty to give Madame de Rênal a kiss. Nothing was more hazardous, nothing more agreeable, both for him and for her, and nothing more imprudent. They just missed being caught. Madame de Rênal thought he was mad. She was thoroughly frightened, besides shocked. The piece of absurdity reminded her of M. Valenod. "What would happen to me," she thought, "if I should be alone with him?" All her virtue returned: love had eclipsed itself.

She arranged it so as to have one of her children always about her.

The day was a tedious one for Julien; he spent it entirely in arranging, awkwardly enough, a plan of capture. He never looked at Madame de Rênal but it meant an interrogation; he was not foolish enough, nevertheless, not to realize that he was not succeeding in making himself attractive, and seductive least of all.

Madame de Rênal could not recover from her astonishment at finding him so awkward and at the same time so bold. "It is the timidity of love in a man of genius," she finally concluded with inexpressible joy. "Can it be possible that he has never been loved by my rival?"

After breakfast Madame de Rênal returned to the drawing-room to receive M. Charcot de Maugiron, the sub-prefect of Bray. She worked at a piece of embroidered tapestry. Madame Derville was by her side. It was under these circumstances, in broad daylight, that our hero found it agreeable to put out his foot and press that of Madame de Rênal, which, with the open-worked stocking and the pretty Parisian boot, was evidently attracting the attention of the gallant sub-prefect.

Madame de Rênal was terrified; she dropped the scissors, the ball of wool, and the needles; and Julien's movement might have been taken for an awkward attempt to catch the scissors he saw falling. Fortunately, the little English scissors broke, and Madame de Rênal did not delay expressing her regret that Julien was not nearer. "You saw them fall before I did, and you might have prevented it instead of succeeding only in your eagerness in kicking me." All that deceived the sub-prefect, but not Madame Derville. "This pretty fellow," she mused, "has very bad manners; the good breeding even of a country town could not pardon such boorishness." Madame de Rênal found a moment to tell Julien:

"Be careful, I command you."

Julien saw his blunder and became moody. He deliberated a long time with himself in order to ascertain whether he should be angry over the words, "I command you." He was foolish enough to reason: "She could say 'I command' when it is a question about the education of the children; but in responding to my love she admits equality. Love is impossible without equality." And his whole mind was occupied with commonplaces about equality. He repeated angrily the verse from Corneille, which Madame Derville had taught him a few days before:

> ". . . L'amour
> Fait les égalités et ne les cherche pas."

Julien, obstinate in his rôle of Don Juan, with never a mistress in his life, was a perfect fool throughout the day. He had but one clear idea: that he was disgusted with himself and with Madame de Rênal; and that the approach of evening, when he would be seated in the dark by her side, was insupportable. He told M. de Rênal that he was going to Verrières to visit the curate; he left after dinner and did not return until late at night.

At Verrières, Julien found Chélan moving; he had just been removed, and the Vicar Maslon was taking his place. Julien lent a hand to the good curate. He had had an idea of writing to Fouqué that his irresistible inclination for the sacred ministry was preventing him from accepting his kind offers; but after seeing such an example of injustice, it came to him that, after all, it might be more advantageous not to take holy orders.

Julien congratulated himself on the fact that he was benefiting by the removal of the curate of Verrières in leaving a door open for a business career if sober prudence won the day over heroism.

Chapter 15

The Cock's Crow

Amour en latin fait amor;
Or donc provient d'amour la mort,
Et, par avant, soulcy qui mord,
Deuil, plours, pieges, forfaitz, remords.
——BLASON D'AMOUR

IF JULIEN had possessed a little of the acuteness which he so gratuitously claimed for himself, he would have congratulated himself next day on the effect of his visit to Verrières. His absence had wiped away all the effect of his stupidity. He was still sullen, however; towards evening an absurd idea came to him, and he communicated it to Madame de Rênal with rare intrepidity. They were hardly seated in the garden when Julien, without waiting even until it grew sufficiently dark, brought his mouth close to Madame de Rênal's ear, saying to her, at the risk of compromising her irremediably:

"Madame, at two o'clock to-night I will enter your room. I have something to tell you."

Julien was fearful his request might be granted. His rôle of seductor was weighing so heavily on him that if he could have followed his real inclination he would have shut himself up in his room for several days and no more seen the women. He was aware that, by his brilliant conduct of the night before, he had spoilt all the fine appearances of the day preceding, and he did not know to what saint to turn.

Madame de Rênal replied with real indignation to Julien's bold proposal. He thought he could detect a little contempt in her curt reply. He was sure that in her answer, though spoken very low, there were the words, "For shame!" On the pretext of saying something to the children, Julien went to their room, and on his return he sat down beside Madame Derville, quite at a distance from Madame de Rênal. He thus removed all possibility of taking her hand. The conversation took a serious turn, and Julien acquitted himself well. In the few intervals of silence, Julien was fiercely cudgelling his brains. "Why," he thought, "can't I hit upon a plan to make Madame de Rênal show me the affection which for three days has led me to believe she belongs to me?"

Julien was painfully disconcerted by the desperate position to which he had brought himself. Yet nothing would have embarrassed him more than success. When they separated at midnight, his pessimism led him to believe that he was despised by Madame Derville, and that probably he was no better off with Madame de Rênal.

Humiliated and in bad humor Julien did not sleep. He was far from renouncing his plan; nor did he for a moment entertain the idea of living like a child with Madame de Rênal, contenting himself with the chance pleasure each day might bring.

He tired out his brains inventing brilliant plans; a minute later he found them all absurd; in a word, he was far fully wretched when the clock struck two. The sound awoke him, as the crowing of the cock awoke Saint Peter. He saw himself entering on a most painful scene. He had not thought of his bold proposition since the moment he had made it—it had been so gracelessly received.

"I have said to her that I would be with her at two o'clock," he said to himself, rising. "I can be as inexperienced and boorish as it is natural for a peasant's son to be—Madame Derville made me understand that clearly enough—but I will not be weak."

Julien had good reason for congratulating himself on his courage; never had he imposed upon himself a more arduous task. When he opened his door, he was trembling so that his knees gave way under him, and he had to lean against the wall.

He did not put on his shoes. He went to the door of M. de Rênal. He could hear the latter's breathing. It made him miserable. There was no longer any pretext for not going to her. But—what would he do there? He had no idea; and if he had, he was so troubled that he felt he could not execute it.

At last, suffering a thousand times more than if he had been walking to his death, he came into the little hall leading to Madame de Rênal's room. He opened the door with a trembling hand, making a fearful noise. There was a light in the room; a night-lamp was burning on the mantel: he did not expect this new misfortune. Upon seeing him enter, Madame de Rênal jumped quickly out of bed. "Wretch!" she cried. There took place some altercation. Julien forgot his vain projects and returned to his natural rôle: not to please such a charming woman seemed to him the greatest of misfortunes.

His only reply to her reproaches was to throw himself at her feet and to embrace her knees. As she continued with cruel invective he burst into tears. A few hours later, when Julien left Madame de Rênal, he might have said, as they say in the novels, that there was nothing more he could desire. It was due, in fact, to the love which he had inspired and to the unforeseen effect of her charms that he obtained a victory which all his tact could not have produced.

But even in his sweetest moments, victim as he was of a whimsical pride, he pretended to play the rôle of a man accustomed to vanquishing women; he made extraordinary efforts to spoil what he deemed agreeable. Instead of giving himself over to the transports which he aroused, or to the remorse which would follow the excitement, the idea of *duty* always remained before his eyes. He feared he would suffer horrible remorse and everlasting ridicule if he departed from the ideal which he had set before himself. In a word, what made Julien a superior character was precisely that which prevented him from enjoying the pleasures that came under his eyes—like a young girl of sixteen, with a charming complexion, putting on rouge to go to a ball.

Mortally afraid of Julien's coming, Madame de Rênal had dwelt in the greatest alarm. Julien's tears and despair visibly moved her. Even when she could no longer refuse him anything, she repulsed him with unfeigned indignation; but all at once she threw herself into his arms. She abandoned all discretion. She believed herself hopelessly damned, and strove to hide herself from the sight of hell by overwhelming Julien with caresses. In a word, nothing was wanting to the happiness of our hero; not even a passionate tenderness which he awakened in the woman, and which he could not appreciate. Julien's departure did not put an end to the transports that moved her, in spite of herself, nor to the remorse which was consuming her.

"My Lord, to be happy, to be loved, is that all it is?" That was Julien's first thought when he returned to his room. He was in that wandering, perplexed state of mind which follows upon obtaining a long-felt desire. The mind accustomed to desiring finds itself then without an object. Like the soldier returning from parade, Julien was busily engaged reviewing the details of the review. "Did I leave anything out I should have done? Did I play my part well?" And what a part! It was the part of a man accustomed to brilliant success with women!

Chapter 16

The Next Day

He turn'd his lips to hers, and with his hand
Call'd back the tangles of her wandering hair.
—DON JUAN, I. 170

HAPPILY for the glory of Julien, Madame de Rênal had been too greatly moved, too greatly taken by surprise, to perceive the foolishness of the man who in a moment had become all the world to her.

As she was urging him to leave, upon the break of day, she said:

"Oh, God, if my husband has heard any noise, I am lost!"

Julien, who found time to form pretty phrases, remarked by way of reply:

"Would you regret anything?"

"Oh, very much indeed, now; but I should not regret having known you."

Julien found it conformable to his dignity to leave in nearly broad daylight and with great imprudence.

The continued attention with which he studied out his slightest movements in carrying out his foolish idea of acting like a man of the world had just this advantage: that, when he saw Madame de Rênal again, at breakfast, his conduct was a masterpiece of prudence.

As for her, she could not look at him without blushing to the very eyes, and yet she had to look at him. She became aware of her embarrassment, and in her effort to hide it made it much worse. Julien raised his eyes to her only once. At first Madame de Rênal admired his prudence. Soon, as she saw that he would not look at her again, she became alarmed: "Doesn't he love me any more?" she thought. "Ah, I am indeed old for him; I am ten years older!"

While passing from the dining-room into the garden, she pressed Julien's hand. In the surprise which this extraordinary mark of love caused him, he gave her a look of passion. She seemed so pretty to him at breakfast, and with lowered eyes he had spent the time in detailing to himself her charms. His look consoled Madame de Rênal; it did not remove all her

89

misgivings, but these misgivings left no room for remorse when she thought of her husband.

At breakfast her husband did not perceive anything unusual; but that was not the case with Madame Derville. The latter thought she saw Madame de Rênal on the point of confessing everything. All through that day her tried, keen friendship did not spare any hints calculated to bring to her friend a realization of the danger she was running.

Madame de Rênal was burning to be alone with Julien; she wished to ask him if he still loved her. In spite of the unchangeable sweetness of temperament, she was several times on the point of telling her friend how much she was in the way.

In the evening, in the garden, Madame Derville managed it so as to be between Madame de Rênal and Julien. Madame de Rênal, who had thought of the delightful sensation of pressing Julien's hand and carrying it to her lips, could not even say a single word to him.

This disappointment increased her uneasiness. She was devoured by remorse. She had scolded Julien so much for his imprudence in coming to her during the night that she was trembling lest he would not come again. She left the garden early and went to her room. But, yielding to her impatience, she went to Julien's door, placing her ear to the keyhole. In spite of the uncertainty and the passion that were consuming her, she could not summon enough courage to enter. Such an action seemed to her to be of the very lowest—it was the text of a provincial proverb.

The servants had not yet retired. Prudence obliged her at last to return to her room. Two hours of waiting were two centuries of torment.

But Julien was too faithful to what he termed his duty to fail in the detailed execution of what he had set before himself.

As one o'clock struck, he slipped quietly from his room, and, after assuring himself that the master of the house was fast asleep, came to Madame de Rênal. This time he was happier in her company, for he thought less often of the part he was to play. He was all eyes and ears. What Madame de Rênal said of her age helped give him assurance.

"Oh, I am ten years older than you; how can you love me?" she kept on repeating aimlessly, because the thought oppressed her.

Julien could not see the misfortune in it; but he saw it was real, and he almost forgot his fear of appearing ridiculous.

His foolish idea that he was an understudy to another lover, because of his obscure birth, also disappeared. In proportion as Julien's transports reassured his timid mistress, she was deriving some happiness and some power of looking critically at her lover. Happily, he did not have this time that borrowed air which had made of the previous meeting a victory, not a pleasure. If she had become aware of an effort on his part to play a rôle, the sad discovery would have forever robbed her of happiness. She would have seen in it only a distressing effect of the disparity between their ages. Although Madame de Rênal had never thought of theories respecting love, the difference of age, next to that of fortune, affords the greatest occasion for pleasantry in the country whenever the subject turns on love.

In a few days Julien, surrendering to the ardor of his age, became madly in love. "Everyone must agree," he thought, "that she has the heart of an angel; and no one can be prettier." He almost gave up the idea of playing a part. In a moment of abandon he confessed to her all that was troubling him. This confidence brought the passion he aroused in her to an ecstasy. "I have no rival, then," Madame de Rênal said to herself with delight. She ventured to question him about the portrait in which he had been so interested; Julien vowed to her it was of a man.

When Madame de Rênal had sufficient composure to reflect, she could not get over her astonishment that such happiness should exist, and that she should never have suspected it. "Ah," she mused, "if I had only known Julien ten years ago, when I was pretty!"

Julien was far removed from such thoughts; his love was still of the ambitious order; it was the joy of possession—he, a poor, despised creature—of so beautiful a woman. His acts of adoration, his transports on seeing her charms, reassured her a little about the disparity of age. If she had possessed a little judgment —which a woman of thirty in the country can claim for a long time—she would have had misgivings over the duration of a love that seemed to live only in fits and starts and over the outbursts of an overweening self-love. When he forgot his ambition, Julien would admire Madame de Rênal with ecstasy, even to her bonnets and gowns. He could not wholly satisfy himself with the pleasure of smelling their perfume. He would open her mirrored closet and remain for hours at a time gazing at the beauty and arrangement of what he saw within. She, leaning on his arm, would look at him while he admired the jewels and laces which were given to her as wedding presents. "I should have married a man like that," thought Madame de Rênal often. "What a lively spirit, what a ravishing life with him!"

As for Julien, he had never found himself before so near the terrible instruments of feminine artillery. "It is impossible," he would say to himself, "that at Paris there could be anything prettier." Then he would find no objection to his good fortune. Frequently the sincere admiration and delight of his mistress would make him forget the foolish theory which had engrossed him and had made him so ridiculous in the first moments of their *liaison*. There were moments when, in spite of his habitual hypocrisy, he would find great delight in confessing to this beautiful woman ignorance of a great many little things. The position of his mistress seemed to raise him above himself.

Madame de Rênal, on her side, would find ideal pleasure in teaching a number of things to this young man of genius, who, everyone predicted, would one day go very far. Could the sub-prefect or M. Valenod hide their admiration?

As for Madame Derville, she was far from expressing the same sentiments, exasperated as she was by what she guessed, and seeing that her prudent advice was becoming odious to a woman who had literally lost her head. She left Vergy without giving a reason—which they did well not to ask. Madame de Rênal shed a few tears, and very soon it seemed to her that her happiness redoubled. She found herself almost the whole day alone with her lover.

Julien gave himself up the more readily to her pleasant society, because, whenever he was alone for any time, Fouqué's fatal proposition would be a source of disquiet to him. During the first days of the new life, there were moments when he, who had never loved, who had never been loved by anyone, found such delight in being sincere that he was on the point of confessing to Madame de Rênal the ambition which until then had been the essence of his existence. He would have wished to consult her about the strange temptation which Fouqué's proposition held out to him. A little event, however, prevented all frankness.

Chapter 17

The First Deputy

O, how this spring of love resembleth
The uncertain glory of an April day;
Which now shows all the beauty of the sun
And by and by a cloud takes all away!
——THE TWO GENTLEMEN OF VERONA

ONE EVENING, at sunset, while sitting beside his mistress in the
orchard, far from intruders, he was lost in dreams. "Will these
happy moments," he thought, "always last?" He was wrestling
with the difficulty of coming to a decision, and deploring the
coming of care which puts a seal on youth forever.

"Ah," he cried out, "Napoleon was indeed the man sent by
God for young Frenchmen! Who will take his place? Without
him, what will the unfortunate do who, richer even than I, have
some *écus* with which to get a good education and not enough to
make a mark? Whatever one may do," he added, with a deep
sigh, "this painful thought will always prevent us from being
happy."

He saw, presently, Madame de Rênal contracting her eyebrows; she looked coldly and disdainfully: such a way of thinking seemed rather to fit a servant. Having been brought up with
the idea that she was very rich, she took it for granted that he
was likewise. She loved him a thousand times more than her
life, and was not giving a thought to money.

Julien was far from divining those ideas. That contraction
of the eyebrows recalled him to earth. He had enough presence
of mind to compose a speech and to make the noble lady sitting
so close to him on the green bank understand that the ideas he
expressed had been heard by him during his journey to his
friend the wood-merchant. It was, to be sure, the reasoning of
the rabble.

"Well, then, don't mix with such people," said Madame de
Rênal, in the same chill manner which had all at once taken the
place of an expression of the utmost tenderness.

The contracting of the brow, or, rather, his own regret, following his imprudence, was the first check to the illusion which
was captivating Julien. He thought to himself: "She is good and

93

sweet; she likes me very much; but she has been raised in the camp of the enemy. They must be particularly afraid of the class of courageous men who, after receiving a good education, have not enough money to enter on a career. What would become of these nobles if we had the privilege of fighting them on equal terms? I, for example, as Mayor of Verrières, with good principles and as straightforward as M. de Rênal is at bottom, how I should get rid of the vicar, of M. Valenod, and of all their knaveries! How justice would triumph in Verrières! It is not their talents that would prove an obstacle to me. They are blundering all the time."

Julien's happiness that day was on the point of becoming lasting. There was only wanting to our hero the courage to be sincere. He needed only, he thought, the daring to give battle, and immediate battle. Madame de Rênal had been astonished at Julien's remark, because men of her rank were saying that a Robespierre's return was possible chiefly on account of the lower classes, who were being too well raised. Madame de Rênal's coolness lasted for some time and seemed well pronounced to Julien. But it was only the fear of having said something disagreeable that followed her repugnance at his ungracious remark. This trouble reflected itself clearly in her features, so pure and so bland when she was happy and care free.

Julien dared no longer give himself over to his dreams. Becoming calmer and less passionate, he reflected that it was imprudent for him to visit Madame de Rênal in her room. It were much better if she came to him; if a servant met her walking through the house she would have a dozen pretexts to serve her.

But this arrangement, too, had its drawbacks. Julien had received some books from Fouqué which he himself, as a student of theology, could never have asked for at a bookseller's. He dared read them only at night. Often he should be glad not to be interrupted by a visit the waiting for which—that very evening before the little orchard scene—left him in no condition to read. And Madame de Rênal would regard the books in a different light. He had ventured to ask her questions about a number of little things of which he was perfectly ignorant, raised as he had been outside the real world. This ignorance he felt hampered his intelligence, notwithstanding the natural genius attributed to him.

This education in love, directed by a woman extremely inexperienced herself, was a piece of good fortune. Julien immediately came to view society in its bareness. His mind was not beclouded by a recital of what it was two thousand years ago, or only sixty years ago, or of the time of Voltaire or of Louis XV. To his great joy a veil was removed from his eyes; he at last understood what was occurring at Verrières.

At first appeared the complicated plots that had been hatching for two years with the prefect of Besançon. These were supported by letters from Paris, written by most illustrious personages. It all dealt with making M. de Moirod, the best partisan in the neighborhood, the first and not the second deputy Mayor of Verrières. This one had for an opponent a rich manufacturer whom it was absolutely necessary to turn to the second deputyship.

Julien then understood the half-spoken words he had overheard when leading men of the neighborhood dined at at M. de Rênal's house. This privileged class was deeply concerned over the choice of the first deputy, while the rest of the town, and the Liberals least of all, did not suspect even the possibility of it. The importance of it was that, as everyone knew, the east side of the main street of Verrières had to be widened by more than nine feet, for that street had become part of the royal route. Now, if M. de Moirod, who owned three houses where the street was to be widened, should succeed in becoming first deputy, and, as a consequence, Mayor of Verrières, in case M. de Rênal became a national deputy, he could close his eyes so that slight, imperceptible repairs could be made to the houses encroaching upon the public highway, and remain there for a hundred years, perhaps. In spite of the great piety and the well-known probity of M. de Moirod, there was a certainty that he would be tractable, as he had many children. Among the houses that were to be moved back, nine belonged to the best families in Verrières.

In Julien's eyes this plot was far more important than the story of the battle of Fontenoy, a name he saw the first time he opened one of the books sent to him by Fouqué. There were many things that astonished Julien from the time, five years back, he had commenced his evening visits to the curate. But discretion and humility of spirit being the first qualification in a theological student, it had always been impossible for him to ask questions.

One day Madame de Rênal was giving an order to her husband's valet, Julien's enemy.

"But, Madame, to-day is the last Wednesday of the month," answered the man, significantly.

"You may go, then," said Madame de Rênal.

"Well," said Julien, "he is going to that hay store that was once a church, but belongs now to the creed—but to do what? There is one of the mysteries which I have never been able to penetrate."

"It is a very useful institution," replied Madame de Rênal, "but a very singular one. Women are not admitted there; all that I know is everyone talks familiarly with everyone else. For example, this servant is going to find M. Valenod there, and that proud man will not take it ill to be addressed in a very familiar tone by Saint Jean and to answer in kind. If you care to know about the details, I will ask M. de Maugiron and M. Valenod. We pay twenty francs for each servant, so that they will not some day cut our throats."

Time was flying. The recollection of his mistress's charms was turning Julien from his stern ambition. The necessity of not speaking to her of anything sober and serious, being so differently placed, added, though he was not aware of it, to the happiness he enjoyed and to the sway which she was acquiring over him.

At times, when the presence of the observing children compelled them to speak with sober reason, it would be with perfect docility that Julien, looking at her with eyes blazing with love, would be listening to her explanations of the world. Frequently, in the midst of an account of some clever trick in connection with a road or some other matter, Madame de Rênal's mind would all at once begin to wander, as in a dream. Julien would then scold her, and she would permit herself the same intimate gestures with him as with her children. There were days when she had the illusion of loving him like her own child. Was she not continually answering his simple questions about a thousand things just like an innocent boy of fifteen? A moment later she would admire him as her superior. His brilliancy would even frighten her; she saw clearly every day the great man of the future in this young priest. She would see him as the Pope; she would see him as the First Minister, like Richelieu. "Shall I live long enough," she would say to Julien, "to see you in your glory? The place is made for a great man—the government, religion, both need one."

Chapter 18

A King in Verrieres

*N'êtes-vous bons qu'à jeter là comme un cadavre
de peuple, sans âme, et dont les veines n'ont plus
de sang?*
—FROM THE BISHOP'S ADDRESS, DELIVERED IN THE
CHAPEL OF SAINT CLEMENT

ON THE third day of September, at ten o'clock at night, a guard
riding full gallop through the main street aroused all Verrières.
He brought the news that His Majesty the King would arrive
on the following Sunday. It was already Tuesday. The prefect
had authorized, or, rather, ordered, the formation of a Guard of
Honor. The greatest display was to be made. A courier was
despatched to Vergy. M. de Rênal arrived the same night and
the entire town was in a flutter.

Who should be the chief of the Guard of Honor? M. de Rênal
saw at once how necessary it was, in the interests of the houses
in question, that it should be M. de Moirod. It would thus en-
title him to the position of first deputy Mayor. He could not
question the devotion of M. de Moirod, it was beyond all comparison; but he had never mounted a horse. He was a man of
thirty-six, extremely timid, and fearful alike of falling and of
being ridiculed.

The Mayor sent for him at five o'clock in the morning.

"You see, sir," he said to him, "that I ask your advice as
if you already occupied the position where all good men would
place you. In this unfortunate town the manufacturers are
prospering, and the Liberal party, full of millionaires, is
aspiring to power, and will make capital out of everything. We
must consult the interests of the King, of the monarchy, and,
above all, of our sacred religion. To whom, do you think, sir,
can the command of the Guard of Honor be entrusted?"

In spite of the great fear M. de Moirod had of a horse, he
ended by accepting the honor like a martyr. "I will endeavor to
acquit myself with credit," he promised the Mayor.

There was scarcely time to put the uniforms in order which
had served seven years before during the progress of a prince
of royal blood.

At seven o'clock Madame de Rênal arrived from Vergy together with Julien and the children. She found her drawing-room full of Liberal women, who, after holding forth on the union of all parties, asked her to persuade her husband to give a place to their consorts in the Guard of Honor. One of them went so far as to say that if her husband were not chosen he would become bankrupt through sheer chagrin. Madame de Rênal soon sent all of them away. She seemed greatly pre-occupied.

Julien was astonished and rather angry that she should make a mystery of what she was thinking. "I should have foreseen," he said to himself, bitterly, "that her love would fade beside the happiness of entertaining a king in her house. All this bustle has dazed her. She will love me anew when the ideas of her caste no longer trouble her head." Curiously enough, she loved him then even more.

The upholsterers commenced their work in the house; she waited a long time in vain for an opportunity of saying a word to him. Later, as he was carrrying a coat on his arm, he met her walking towards him from her room. They were alone. He wanted to speak to her. She fled, refusing to listen to him. "I am a big fool for loving such a woman; ambition is making her crazy, like her husband."

That she was indeed; a great desire that she would not avow to Julien, for fear of offending him, was to see him, though only for a day, without his sombre black frock. With tact that was truly admirable in a woman as frank as she was, she had ob-tained, first from M. de Moirod, and then from the sub-prefect, M. de Maugiron, that Julien would be placed in the Guard of Honor in preference to five or six young men, sons of well-to-do manufacturers, of whom two were of exemplary piety. M. Valenod, who had intended lending his carriage to the prettiest women in the town, and having his fine Norman horses ad-mired, consented to give one of these horses to Julien, the per-son he hated most of all. But all the members of the Guard of Honor owned or borrowed those fine sky-blue coats with silver epaulets of the grade of colonel which had shone so resplend-ently seven years before. Madame de Rênal wanted a new uniform, and she had only four days in which to send to Besançon for the uniform, arms, and hat suitable for a member of the Guard. What was most agreeable was that she deemed it imprudent to have the uniform made in Verrières. She wanted to surprise him and the town.

After the work of forming the Guard of Honor and the

manifestation of public spirit was finished, M. de Rênal busied himself arranging a grand religious ceremony; the King would not think of passing through Verrières without seeing the famous relic of St. Clement, preserved at Bray-le-Haut, a little distance from the town. It was desirable to have a large assembly of clergy, a thing very difficult to arrange; for M. Maslon, the new curate, wished to have M. Chélan far away, at all costs. In vain M. de Rênal represented to him that it would be imprudent. The Marquis de la Mole, whose ancestors had been for such a long time governors of the province, had been designated for the honor of accompanying the King. He had known M. Chélan for thirty years; he would certainly ask about him on arriving at Verrières; and, if he found him slighted, he was just the man to look for him, accompanied by his entire retinue, in that little house where he had withdrawn himself. What an insult!

"I am dishonored here and at Besançon," replied the abbot, "if he appears with my clergy. A Jansenist, great God!"

"Whatever you may say, my dear abbot," answered M. de Rênal, "I will not expose the administration of Verrières to the possibility of receiving an affront from Marquis de la Mole. You do not know him. He is discreet enough at court; but here in the province his pleasantries are of a satirical, mocking order, calculated only to overwhelm people with embarrassment. He is singularly capable, just to amuse himself, of covering us with ridicule in the eyes of the Liberals."

It was not until Saturday night before that Sunday, when three days had been spent in conferences, that abbé Maslon's pride yielded before the fear of the Mayor, whose courage was fast waning. It was decided to write a very soft letter to abbé Chélan, begging him to be present at the ceremony of the relique at Bray-le-Haut if his great age and his infirmities permitted. M. Chélan secured an invitation for Julien, who would accompany him as sub-deacon.

From early morning on Sunday, thousands of peasants, arriving from the neighboring mountains, were filling the streets of Verrières. The weather was beautiful. Towards three o'clock there was a great stir in all that crowd; a great bonfire was seen on a rock two leagues from Verrières. That meant that the King had just entered within the department line. Immediately the bells, together with the discharges of the old Spanish cannon belonging to the town, proclaimed the common joy over the great event. Half the people climbed to the roofs, and all the women were at the balconies. The Guard of Honor commenced its march. All admired the brilliant uniforms, recognizing here a relative, there a friend. There was much fun made of M. de Moirod's timidity; his hand was ready every moment to lay a prudent hold on the pommel. But one feature made everything else seem common; the first cavalier of the ninth division was a small, handsome young fellow, whom at first no one recognized. There was a cry of indignation or blank astonishment; there was a profound sensation. That young man, mounted on one of M. Valenod's fine horses, was recognized as little Sorel, the carpenter's son. There arose a hue and cry against the Mayor, especially among the Liberals. What, because this little apprentice, disguised as a priest, is the tutor of his brats, did he have the audacity to appoint him a member of the Guard in preference to M. So-and-So and M. So-and-So, rich manufacturers? "These gentlemen," said a banker's wife, "must commit an outrage for this impudent little fellow who comes from the gutter!" "He is sly and carries a sword," answered a neighbor; "he would be traitor enough to slash them right and left."

The remarks of the people of quality touched on more dangerous ground. They wondered if that indiscretion originated with the Mayor alone. There was full justice done to the contempt in which he was held.

While Julien was the subject of so much remark he was the happiest of men. Naturally graceful, he bore himself on a horse better than the greater number of young people in that mountain town. He saw in the eyes of the women that he was the object of their attention. His epaulets, being new, were more resplendent than any of the others. His horse caracoled at every step, and he was mad with joy. His happiness knew no longer any bounds when, passing near the old rampart, the discharge of the old piece of cannon made his horse leap out of line. By a mere accident he did not fall; from that moment he thought himself a hero: he was an ordnance officer under Napoleon and was charging a battery.

There was only one person happier. At first she had seen him pass, from one of the windows of the Town Hall; then, entering a carriage and rapidly making a wide circuit, she arrived in time to shudder when she saw his horse bound out of line. Finally, driving at full gallop, she returned through another town gate in the direction where the King would pass. There, in a cloud of martial dust, at a distance of some twenty paces, she was able to follow the Guard of Honor. Ten thousand peasants shouted, "Vive le Roi!" when the Mayor had the honor of addressing his Majesty. An hour later, when all the speech-making had ended, and the King was about to enter the town, the little cannon again began with its quick discharges. But an accident happened—not to the cannoneers, who had served their apprenticeship at Leipzig and Montmorail, but to the future first deputy-Mayor, M. Moirod. His horse had gently deposited him in the only mud-puddle in the road—a real disaster, for he had to be pulled out to permit the passage of the royal equipage.

His Majesty halted at the pretty new church, which, for that day, was decked out with all its purple hangings. Then the King was to dine, and soon after to resume his carriage and perform his devotions before the celebrated relique of St. Clement. Hardly was the King in the church when Julien galloped toward M. de Rênal's house. There he took off, with a sigh, his beautiful new uniform, his sabre and his epaulets, to put on again his shabby little black coat. He remounted his horse, and in a few minutes he was at Bray-le-Haut, on the summit of a pretty hill. "Enthusiasm is multiplying these peasants," Julien thought. There was not room to turn round in Verrières, yet here there were more than ten thousand around the old abbey. Half demolished by the vandalism of the Revolution, it had been magnificently restored during the Restoration, and there were rumors even of miracles. Julien joined abbé Chélan, who, with many scoldings, made him put on cassock and surplice. He arrayed himself promptly and followed M. Chélan, who was going to the young Bishop d'Agde. The latter was a nephew of M. de la Mole, and had been only recently appointed; he was the one commissioned to show the relique to the King. But he could nowhere be found.

The clergy were becoming impatient. They were awaiting their chief in the gloomy Gothic cloister of the old abbey. There were assembled twenty-four curates to represent the ancient Chapter of Bray-le-Haut, which had consisted prior to 1789 of twenty-four canons. After deploring for a space of an hour the Bishop's youth, the curates decided that it was proper that the Dean should go to Monseigneur and inform him that the King was coming, and that it was imperative they should retire to the choir. The great age of M. Chélan had given him the title of Dean; in spite of the little anger he had shown to Julien, he gave the latter a sign to follow. Julien carried himself well in his surplice. By means of some mysterious ecclesiastical process, his beautiful curly hair had become straight; but, by a forgetfulness which increased M. Chélan's anger, the spurs of a Guard of Honor were visible under the long folds of his cassock.

Reaching the Bishop's apartment, they saw there tall footmen bedecked with lace, who scarcely deigned to reply to the old curate that his Grace was not to be seen. They chaffed him when he tried to explain that in his capacity of Dean of the noble Chapter of Bray-le-Haut he had the privilege of being admitted at all times before the officiating Bishop.

Julien's high-strung temper could not brook the insolence of these lackeys. He began by going through the dormitories of the ancient abbey, opening every door he found. A very small one yielded, and he found himself in a little cell, in the very midst of Monseigneur's valets, all dressed in black robes and with a chain round the neck. Seeing his hurried manner, these gentlemen thought he had been sent by the Bishop, and they let him pass. Taking a few steps, he came into an immense Gothic hall, exceedingly gloomy in effect, with its panels of black oak. The arched windows, with the exception of one, had been walled up with brick. The roughness of the masonry was in no wise disguised, and was sadly in contrast with the magnificent woodwork. This hall, so well known to the antiquaries of Burgundy, was built about the year 1470 by Charles the Bold in expiation of some sin. On both sides were stalls in richly carved wood. One could see there the mysteries of the Apocalypse in relief in different colored woods.

This gloomy magnificence, though spoiled by the view of bare bricks and white mortar, touched Julien. He stood in silence. At the other end of the hall, near that single window where the light entered, he saw a revolving mahogany mirror. A young man in a purple robe and lace surplice was standing with his head bared three steps away from the looking-glass. That piece of furniture seemed strange in such a place—it had been brought there, no doubt, from the city. Julien saw the young man looked stern; with his right hand the latter was gravely bestowing benedictions along the side of the mirror. "What can that mean?" he thought. "Is it some preparatory devotion which the young priest is going through? Perhaps it is the Bishop's secretary. He will be insolent like the lackeys. Well, it makes no difference. I'll try."

He advanced, and crossed slowly over the length of the hall, his look fixed towards that single window where the young man was continually bestowing benedictions. This was executed deliberately, and repeated an infinite number of times, without a moment's pause. The nearer he approached, the more clearly he distinguished his severe manner. The richness of the surplice, with its trimmings of lace, made Julien pause a few feet away from the mirror.

"It is my duty to speak," thought Julien; but the beauty of the hall had affected him, and he was chilled in advance by the hard words that might be addressed to him.

The young man saw him in the glass, and suddenly abandoning his severe expression said to him in an exceedingly soft tone: "Well, then, monsieur, is it all arranged now?"

Julien was stupefied. As the young man was turning towards him, Julien saw the pectoral cross on his breast; it was the Bishop d'Agde. "So young," thought Julien; "six or eight years, at most, older than I," and then he was ashamed of his spurs.

"Monsieur," he replied, timidly, "I am sent by the Dean of the Chapter, Monseigneur Chélan."

"Ah! he has been well recommended to me," said the Bishop in a polished tone that increased Julien's enchantment. "But I beg you pardon, monsieur, I mistook you for the one who is to bring me my mitre. It was not packed well in Paris; the silver thread at the top is horribly spoiled. It will produce the worst possible effect," added the young Bishop, sadly; "and yet they are making me wait."

"Monseigneur, I will get your mitre if your Highness will permit."

Julien's fine eyes produced their effect.

"Go, monsieur," replied the Bishop, with charming politeness. "I must have it right away. I am in great distress for keeping the gentlemen of the Chapter waiting."

When Julien reached the middle of the hall, he saw, as he turned towards the Bishop, that the latter resumed the giving of benedictions. "What can that mean?" Julien asked himself; "no doubt it is an ecclesiastical preparation necessary to the ceremony that is to take place." On arriving in the little room where the valets were stationed, he saw the mitre in their hands. These gentlemen, yielding in spite of themselves to Julien's imperious look, handed Monseigneur's mitre to him.

He felt proud carrying it. In crossing the hall he walked slowly; he carried it with great respect. He found the Bishop seated before the mirror; yet from time to time his right hand, though fatigued, was still bestowing benedictions. Julien helped him put on the mitre. The Bishop shook his head.

"Ah, it will stay," he said to Julien, with a pleased look. "Would you be so kind as to step aside a little?"

The Bishop walked quickly to the middle of the hall, returning then to the mirror with measured steps. He assumed again his severe look and gave blessings with great gravity.

Julien was amazed; he had tried to understand, but he did

not dare. The Bishop stopped, and, giving him a look from which all gravity had disappeared, said:

"What do you think of my mitre, monsieur—is it becoming?"

"Very, Monseigneur."

"Is it not too far back? That would look a little light; yet it should not be worn low over the eyes like an officer's shako."

"It looks very proper to me."

"The King is accustomed to a venerable, and, no doubt, a grave clergy. I should not wish, by reason of my age above all, to appear light to him."

And the Bsihop began again to walk and to bestow benedictions.

"It is clear," thought Julien, daring at last to comprehend it, "he is practising giving the benediction."

After a few minutes the Bishop said: "I am ready. Go, monsieur, and inform the Dean and the gentlemen of the Chapter."

Presently M. Chélan, followed by the two oldest curates, entered by a lofty, finely-sculptured doorway which Julien had not observed. This time he was in his proper place—the last of all—and could not see the Bishop except over the shoulders of the ecclesiastics who were crowding about the doorway.

The Bishop slowly crossed the hall; when he arrived at the threshold, the curates formed in line. After a moment of disorder, the procession began with the intonation of a psalm. The Bishop walked between M. Chélan and another very old curate. Julien moved quite close to Monseigneur as one attached to abbé Chélan.

They followed along the corridors of the abbey of Bray-le-Haut; in spite of the sunlight without, these were gloomy and damp. Finally they came to the cloister. Julien was filled with wonder over the beautiful ceremony. The admiration aroused by the Bishop's youth, the sense of exquisite politeness of that prelate mastered his heart. That politeness was something different from M. de Rênal's, even in his best moods. "The closer one comes to the highest rank," Julien said to himself, "the finer manners one finds."

They entered the church by the side door. All at once a frightful noise reverberated through those ancient vaults. Julien thought they would collapse. It was only the cannon that had just arrived, drawn by eight galloping horses, and, scarcely arrived, had been fired by the Leipzig cannoneers. It was discharged five times a minute, as though the Prussians were ranged against it.

But that glorious noise no more had any effect on Julien. He was no longer thinking of Napoleon and military glory. "So young," he mused, "and to be the Bishop of Agde. But where is Agde, and how much does it bring? Two or three hundred thousand francs, perhaps?"

Monseigneur's lackeys appeared with a magnificent dais. The curate Chélan took one of the poles, but it was Julien that supported it. The Bishop mounted. The latter had really succeeded in making himself look older. The admiration of our young hero knew no longer any bounds. "What can one not accomplish with address?" he thought.

The King entered, and Julien had the good fortune to see him very close. The Bishop delivered an unctuous address, and Julien learned from the Bishop's discourse that the King was descended from Charles the Bold.

Later it became part of Julien's duty to verify the sums which that ceremony had cost. M. de la Mole, who had given the bishopric to his nephew, extended to him the courtesy of defraying all the expenses. That single ceremony at Bray-le-Haut cost three thousand eight hundred francs.

After the Bishop's harangue and the King's reply, his Majesty placed himself under the dais, and piously prostrated himself on a cushion near the altar. The choir was in the stalls, which were raised two steps above the floor. It was on the last step that Julien was seated at Chélan's feet, like a train-bearer near his cardinal at the Sistine Chapel at Rome. There was a Te Deum, a waft of incense, numerous discharges from musketry and artillery, and the peasants were overflowing with happiness and piety. Such a day undid the work of a hundred issues of Jacobin journals.

Julien was six feet away from the King, who was praying with genuine devotion. Then he observed for the first time a little man who wore a black coat almost without any embroidery, but with a sky-blue sash across the breast. He was nearer the King than many of the other dignitaries whose coats were richly embroidered with gold—so richly, to use Julien's expression, as to hide the cloth. He learned a few moments later that this was M. de la Mole. That man had a proud, almost insolent, manner.

"This marquis is not as polished as my handsome Bishop," he thought. "Ecclesiastical rank makes a man gentle and wise. But the King came to worship the relique, and I don't see it. Where can Saint Clement be?"

A little priest, his neighbor, informed him that the venerable relique was in the tower of the building, in the "burning chapel."

"What is a 'burning chapel'?" thought Julien.

But he did not ask the question: his attention became fixed again. When a sovereign makes a visit, etiquette requires that the canons do not accompany the Bishop; but, in starting to walk to the "burning chapel," Monseigneur d'Agde had called abbé Chélan, and Julien ventured to follow.

After mounting a long stairway, they came to a very small door, of which the Gothic lintel was magnificently gilded. It looked as if it had been finished only the day before. At the door, on their knees, were twenty-four young girls belonging to the most distinguished families in Verrières. Before the open door the Bishop fell on his knees in the midst of the circle formed by the pretty girls. While he was praying, these could not sufficiently admire his beautiful lace, his gracious manner, his young, sweet face. At sight of this our hero lost what little self-possession he had left. At that moment he enrolled himself forever for the Inquisition and for the holy faith.

All at once a door opened. The little chapel was steeped with light. On the altar were more than a thousand candles, ranged in eight rows, with bouquets of flowers between each row. The sweet scent of purest incense came out in clouds through the sanctuary door.

The newly-gilded chapel door was very small, but high. Julien noticed that there were candles on the altar that were more than fifteen feet tall. The young girls could hardly keep back a cry of admiration. In the little vestibule of this chapel there were only the twenty-four girls, the two curates, and Julien.

Presently the King arrived, followed only by M. de la Mole and his grand chamberlain. The guards themselves remained outside on their knees, at "present arms."

His Majesty rather threw himself, then knelt, before the altar. Leaning against the gilded door, Julien perceived, over the bare arm of a young girl, the charming statue of Saint Clement, under the altar. It was in the uniform of a young Roman soldier. There was an imitation of a deep wound in the neck, from which the blood seemed to flow. The artist had evidently surpassed himself; the dim eyes, still full of grace, were half closed; a small moustache adorned a charming mouth, which, half-shut, still seemed to pray. At sight of this the young girl nearest to Julien began to shed tears; one of these fell on Julien's hand.

After a moment's prayer, a most profound silence followed, broken only by the distant sound of bells from all the villages within a radius of ten leagues. Then the Bishop asked permission of the King to speak. He delivered a touching little discourse couched in the simplest words. The effect was only too evident.

"Do not forget, young Christian girls, that you have seen one of the greatest kings on earth on his knees before a servant of the omnipotent and terrible God; these servants, though persecuted, assassinated on earth, as you see by the still bleeding wound of Saint Clement, yet triumphed to the very sky. Will you not, young girls, remember this day forever? Will you not always despise impiety? Will you always remain faithful to this great, this terrible, and yet good God?"

With these words the Bishop arose majestically.

"You promise me?" he asked, raising an arm as if inspired.

"We promise," answered the young girls, sobbing.

"I accept your promise in the name of the terrible God," replied the Bishop in a thundering voice. And the ceremony was then at an end.

The King himself shed tears. It was not until a long time afterward that Julien was sufficiently self-possessed to ask where the bones of the saint were that had been sent from Rome to Philip the Good, the Duke of Bourgogne. He was informed that they were in the beautiful wax figure.

His Majesty graciously permitted the young girls who had accompanied him to the chapel to wear a red ribbon on which was the legend: "Hatred to Impiety, Adoration Forever."

M. de la Mole ordered ten thousand bottles of wine to be distributed among the peasants. In the evening, at Verrières, the Liberals thought it wise to illuminate a hundred times more than the Royalists. Before leaving, the King visited M. de Moirod.

Chapter 19

To Think Is To Suffer

Le grotesque des événements de tous les jours vous cache le vrai malheur des passions.

—BARNAVE

IN REPLACING the furniture in the room which M. de la Mole had occupied, Julien found a folded sheet of paper. He read at the bottom of it: "To S. E. M., le marquis de la Mole, Peer of France, Chevalier of the Orders of the King, etc., etc."

It was a petition written in the uncouth handwriting of a cook.

"M. le marquis, I have all my life had religious principles. I was at Lyons, exposed to the bombs at the siege of '93 of execrable memory. I partake of the communion; I go every Sunday to Mass in the parochial church. I have never been wanting in my duty at Easter, even in '93 of execrable memory. My cook—before the Revolution I had many people—my cook sets a slender table on Friday. I enjoy a good reputation in Verrières, and I dare say it is deserved. I march under the dais in the processional beside the curate and the Mayor; I carry on great occasions a large candle, bought at my own expense. Of all this there are certificates in Paris, in the office of the Minister of Finance. I ask of you, monsieur le marquis, the lottery office at Verrières, which will, no doubt, in one way or another, be vacant, the present encumbent being sick, besides voting without discretion at the elections.

"DE CHOLIN."

On the margin of this petition was a postscript signed "de Moirod," which commenced with this line:

"I have the honor of testifying to the good character of the petitioner."

"So this imbecile de Cholin shows me how to proceed," thought Julien.

A week after the King's progress through Verrières, there

were lies and misunderstandings and discussions about the
King, the Bishop of Agde, the Marquis de la Mole, the ten
thousand bottles of wine, the pitiful fall of de Moirod, who,
hoping for a Cross, was not to leave his house until a month
after his fall; but most of all about the extreme indecency of
having "bolted" Julien Sorel, a carpenter's son, into the Guard
of Honor. What discussions on the subject were conducted by
the rich linen manufacturers who, morning and evening,
crowded the café to preach equality! That haughty woman,
Madame de Rênal, she was the author of that awful mistake!
The reason? The pretty eyes and the fresh cheeks of the young
priest told the rest.

Soon after returning to Vergy, Stanislaus-Xavier, the youngest of the boys, had fever; immediately Madame de Rênal became a prey to the most frightful remorse. It was the first time
she had reproached herself for her love in such a fashion; she
seemed to see, as by an inner light, the enormous sin into which
she had allowed herself to be drawn. Although of a profoundly
religious character, she had not thought up to that moment of
the magnitude of her crime in the eyes of God.

At the convent of the Sacred Heart she had adored God with
passion; she had also feared Him with equal intensity. The
struggle which was rending her soul was the more frightful because she could not be reasoned with in her great dread. Julien
found that, far from calming her, the least show of common
sense caused her irritation. It all seemed to her to be only the
language of the devil. However, as Julien himself loved little
Stanislaus dearly, he found it more prudent to speak of his
illness; she then seemed more tractable.

The harrowing remorse robbed her of her sleep. She never
broke the fierce silence under which she laid herself; when she
opened her mouth, it was only to cry out her crime before God
and man.

"I beg you," Julien would say to her, when they found themselves alone, "do not speak to anyone; let me be the only one
that knows of your great trouble. If you love me, do not speak;
the words cannot take the fever away from Stanislaus."

But his consoling words produced no effect; he did not know
that Madame de Rênal took it into her head that in order to
appease the anger of a jealous God she must either hate Julien
or lose her boy. It was because she felt she could not hate her
lover that made her so wretched.

"Oh, go away from me," she said one day to Julien; "for
God's sake, leave this house; it is your presence that is killing

my boy. God is punishing me," she added, lowering her voice.
"He is just; I adore His justice; my crime is horrible, and yet
I was living without remorse! It was the first sign that God had
abandoned me; I deserve to be punished as much again!"

Julien was profoundly moved. He saw there neither hypocrisy nor exaggeration. "She believes she is killing her child in
loving me, and yet the unfortunate woman loves me like her
son. Then there is no doubt about it; there *is* remorse that kills.
There is the grandeur of a feeling! But how can I inspire such
a love—poor, so badly raised, so ignorant, so coarse in all my
ways?"

One night the child was very low. Towards two o'clock in
the morning M. de Rênal came to see him. The child, wasted
with fever, was very much flushed; he did not recognize his
father. All at once Madame de Rênal threw herself at her husband's feet; Julien saw that she was going to tell everything, and
all would be lost.

Happily that singular movement was irritating to M. de
Rênal.

"Good night, good night," he said, impatiently retreating.

"No, listen to me," cried his wife on her knees before him,
striving to retain him. "Here is the whole truth. It is I who am
killing my son. I have given him life, and I am taking it away.
Heaven has punished me. In the eyes of God I am guilty of
murder. I must disgrace myself, humiliate myself; perhaps the
sacrifice will be pleasing to the Lord."

If M. de Rênal had had the least insight he would have
learned all.

"What foolish ideas!" cried he, pushing his wife away from
him as she was about to embrace his knees. "It is all nonsense.
Julien, have the doctor called at daybreak," and he left the
room.

Madame de Rênal fell on her knees, half overcome, convulsively repulsing Julien, who came to her assistance. Julien
was lost in wonder.

"So that is an adulteress," he mused; "is it possible that these
shallow fools of priests are right? Have they, who commit so
many sins, the privilege of knowing the real theory of sin?"

For twenty minutes after M. de Rênal had retired, Julien
watched the woman he loved as she lay still and almost unconscious with her head on the litle boy's bed. "There is a
woman of a superior mould brought to the greatest misfortune
because she has known me!" he pondered.

The hours passed rapidly. "What can I do for her? I must

do something; I cannot do anything here. What have I to do with the men and their shallow pates? What can I do for her? Leave her? But I leave her alone, a prey to the most frightful grief. This automaton of a husband is doing her more harm than good. He might say some harsh word to her just because he is so coarse. She may become mad, throw herself out of the window!

"If I leave her and I do not watch over her, she will tell him everything. And who knows? Perhaps, in spite of the fortune which is coming to her, it might cause a scandal. She might tell everything—good God!—to this abbé Maslon, who, taking the child's illness as a pretext, does not budge from the house—not without some design! In her grief and in her fear of God, she forgets what she knows of men, and sees only a priest."

"Go away," said Madame de Rênal to him, opening her eyes all at once.

"I would give my life a thousand times to know what I could do for you," answered Julien. "Never have I loved you so much, my darling; or, rather, from this moment I am beginning to adore you as you really deserve. What will become of me away from you, knowing that you are unhappy on my account? But I don't consider my own suffering. I will leave; yes, I will—my love! But if I leave you? If I cease to watch over you, to place myself between you and your husband, you will tell him everything, you will ruin yourself. Think with what ignominy he will drive you from your house; all Verrières, all Besançon will talk about the scandal. They will add a thousand crimes to you; you will never lift your head from under such disgrace."

"That is what I ask," she cried. "I shall suffer; so much the better."

"But in this abominable scandal you will also ruin him."

"But I will humiliate myself; I will degrade myself; and perhaps by that I will save my boy. This humiliation in the very eyes of the world will perhaps be a public penitence. As far as I can judge, is it not the greatest sacrifice I can make to God? Perhaps He will graciously accept my humiliation and leave me my boy. Show me a more painful sacrifice and I will make it."

"Let me punish myself, too; I also am guilty. Do you want me to go to the Trappists? The austerity of their life will perhaps appease your God. O God, how I wish I could take Stanislaus's sickness on me!"

"Then you love him!" said Madame de Rênal, rising, and

throwing herself into his arms. Then almost at the same time she repulsed him with horror.

"I believe you, I believe you," she continued, throwing herself on her knees again. "My only friend, why are you not the father of Stanislaus? Then it would not be such a horrible sin to love you better than my son."

"Then shall I remain and love you hereafter as a brother? It is the only reasonable expiation; it might perhaps appease the wrath of the Most High."

"And I," she said, rising, and taking Julien's head between both her hands, holding it at a little distance before her eyes, "I, too, shall I love you like a sister? *Can* I love you like a sister?"

Julien burst into tears.

"I will obey you," he said, falling at her feet; "I will obey you, just as you say. That's all that is left for me to do. I am dazed, I am mad. If I leave you, you will tell your husband; you will ruin both yourself and him. Never, after all the ridicule, would he be elected Deputy. If I remain, you will believe me to be the cause of your boy's death, and you will waste away with grief. Do you wish to try the effect of my absence? If so, I will punish myself for our sin by leaving you for a week. I will go somewhere, wherever you wish; to the abbey of Bray-le-Haut, for example. But swear that you will say nothing to your husband during my absence; remember that I cannot return if you speak."

She promised, and he left; but in two days he was called back.

"It is impossible for me to keep my word without you; I will speak to my husband if you are not here constantly to order me to be quiet, if only with a look. Every hour of my terrible life seems a day to me."

But heaven had pity on the poor mother. Gradually little Stanislaus came out of danger. But the scales had been removed—her reason had discovered the extent of her sin—she could no longer regain her equanimity. Her remorse, so natural in such an ingenuous heart, remained. Her life was both heaven and hell; hell when she would not see Julien, heaven when she would be at his feet.

"I will not fool myself," she would say to him when she gave expression to her love, "I am damned, hopelessly damned. You are young and have yielded to me. Heaven may pardon you; but I, I am damned. I know it by a sure sign; I am afraid. Who would not be afraid in sight of hell? But in my heart I don't repent; I should commit the same sin a second time. Only if

Heaven would not punish me in this world through my children!—it would be more than I deserve. But you, at least, my
Julien," she would cry out, "are you happy? Do you think I
love you enough?"

Julien's distrust and pride were not proof against a sacrifice
so great, so indisputable, and so constant: he adored Madame
de Rênal. "She can be of noble birth and I only a laborer's son,
yet she loves me! No, I am not a valet whose duty it is to play
the lover."

This fear being removed, Julien gave himself up to all the
folly of a lover.

"At least," she cried, when she saw his misgivings over her
love, "I will make you happy during the short time that we
shall be together. Come; to-morrow, perhaps, I may no longer
be yours. If Heaven strikes me through my children it is in
vain that I should try to live only to love you and not to see that
it is my sin that is killing them; I could not survive such a
punishment. Even if I should desire it, I could not; I should
become mad. Oh, if I could only take your sin, as you offered
to take Stanislaus's fever!"

This great crisis changed the nature of the feeling uniting
Julien with his mistress. His love was no longer admiration for
her beauty nor the mere pride of possession.

Their happiness was henceforth of a deeper kind. The flame
in their hearts was more intense and they had transports that
bordered on the delirious. Their happiness, though it might
have seemed greater in the eyes of the world, did not possess,
however, the delicious calmness, the serenity, the unalloyed joy
of the first days of their love, when Madame de Rênal's sole fear
was that she was not sufficiently loved in return. Their happiness
sometimes presented itself to them under the aspect of a heinous
crime. In their happiest moments, and apparently in their
calmest, Madame de Rênal would suddenly cry out:

"Oh, great God, I see my doom!" and she would convulsively
press Julien's hand. "What frightful punishment! but I deserve
it." She would embrace him, clinging to him the more tenderly.

Julien would try in vain to calm her agitation. Then she
would take his hand and cover it with kisses, and murmur, with
her head thrown back in gloomy reverie:

"Perdition is too much of grace for me; I have had a few days
on earth with him, but the hell of my children's death—yet at
that price perhaps my sin would be pardoned. Oh, good God, do
not bestow mercy at such a price! These poor children have not

offended Thee! I—I alone am guilty; I love a man who is not my husband."

Julien would then see Madame de Rênal becoming more quiet. She tried, too, to be more self-contained; she did not wish to spoil the life of the one she loved. Between their love, their remorse, and their joy, the days passed with great rapidity. Julien put aside even his habit of reflection.

Mademoiselle Elisa happened one day to go to Verrières on some lawsuit, and there she found M. Valenod much incensed against Julien. She hated the tutor, and frequently talked about him.

"You will not betray me, monsieur, if I tell you something?" she said one day to M. Valenod. "Employers keep things quiet in cases of importance, but poor servants are never forgiven for telling things."

After a lengthy introduction, which M. Valenod's impatient curiosity tried in vain to abridge, he learned something most mortifying to his vanity. That woman, the most distinguished in all the neighborhood, whom for six years he had surrounded with such attention—that proud woman whose disdain had made him blush—had taken for a lover that little workman disguised as a tutor. And in order that nothing should be wanting to the dejection of the Director, Madame de Rênal was adoring her lover.

"And," added the maid, with a sigh, "M. Julien was not giving himself the least concern over his conquest; he has not left off his usual chilliness with Madame."

Elisa was not certain of anything taking place until the family had moved to the country, but she believed that the *liaison* dated far back.

"It is on that account," she added, spitefully, "that he then refused to marry me. And I, stupid, went to talk to Madame de Rênal and to ask her to speak to him for me."

The same evening M. de Rênal received from town a long, anonymous letter which informed him with great detail of all that was passing at his house.

Julien saw him turn pale while reading the letter, and direct some searching looks towards him. All that evening the Mayor seemed preoccupied; it was in vain that Julien paid unusual attention to him in asking about the genealogies of the best families in Bourgogne.

Chapter 20

Anonymous Letters

Do not give dalliance
Too much the rein; the strongest oaths are straw
To the fire i' the blood.

—THE TEMPEST

As THEY WERE leaving the drawing-room, Julien had time to say to her:

"We must not see each other to-night; your husband is suspicious. I could swear that the long letter he was reading was an anonymous one."

Happily Julien locked the door of his room. Madame de Rênal had a foolish idea that what he said was only a pretext for not seeing her. Losing her head completely, she came to his door at the usual time. Julien, who heard the noise in the hall, immediately blew out his lamp. There was an effort to open the door; was it Madame de Rênal or the jealous husband?

Early the next morning the cook, who liked Julien, brought him a book on the cover of which was written in Italian: "Look on page 130."

Julien impatiently looked for page 130, and there he found pinned the following letter, hastily, badly written, and wet with tears. Ordinarily Madame de Rênal took pains in writing; he was touched by this detail and forgot for a moment her great imprudence.

"You did not want to let me in last night; it was one of the times when I believed I had never understood you; your look frightened me; I am afraid of you. Oh, heavens! have you never loved me? In that case would that my husband might find us out and shut me in a prison for the rest of my life somewhere far from my children. Perhaps God wishes it so. I should die soon; but you—you would remain a monster.

"Don't you love me? Are you tired of my follies, of my remorse, cruel, cruel one? Do you want to ruin me? I will give you an easy way of doing it. Go, show this letter in all Verrières; or, better, show it only to M. Valenod. Tell him that I love you; but no, don't utter such a blasphemy. Tell him that I adore you;

115

that life did not begin with me until the day I saw you; that in all the mad moments of my youth I never dreamed of the happiness which I owe to you; that I have sacrificed my life, that I have sacrificed my soul! You know that I would sacrifice even more for you.

"But does he know such sacrifices, that man? Tell him, in order to anger him, that I defy everybody, and that there is only one misery for me in the world, and that is to see a change in the one man who holds me to life. What happiness it would be for me to lose it, to offer it as a sacrifice, and to fear no more for my children's sake! I do not for a moment doubt, dearest, that if that was an anonymous letter it came from that miserable person who, for six long years, has been pursuing me with his coarse voice, with his recital about his horses, with his infatuation, and with the eternal tale about his wealth.

"Was it an anonymous letter? Cruel one, that is what I wished to speak to you about. But, no; you are right. Pressing you in my arms, perhaps for the last time, I should never have been able to talk about it calmly as I do when I am alone; for now our happiness will never be as smooth again. Would you feel badly over it? Only when you would not receive some amusing book from M. Fouqué. The sacrifice will be made to-morrow. Whether it was or was not an anonymous letter, I say that I am going to tell my husband that *I* have received an anonymous letter, and that it is necessary to give you a purse immediately, to find some plausible pretext, and without delay, to send you back to your father.

"Oh! dearest, we are going to be separated for two weeks—for a month, perhaps. Go! I will do you the justice to say you will suffer as much as I will. Yet that is the only way of removing the effect of that letter. It is not the first my husband has received, and with reference to me, too. Oh, how I used to laugh at it! My whole purpose now is to make my husband believe that the letter came from M. Valenod. I have not the least doubt but that he is the author of it. If you leave the house, do not fail to go to Verrières. I will try to have my husband take us there for a fortnight or so, so as to show the fools that there is no estrangement between him and me. Once at Verrières, try to be agreeable to everybody, even with the Liberals; I know all the women will take you up.

"Don't embroil yourself with M. Valenod, and don't assault him as you threatened one day to do. On the contrary, be as nice to him as possible; the main thing is that it should be believed in Verrières that you are going to Valenod's house or elsewhere to be a tutor.

"But that is what my husband will never permit. Should he, however, agree to that, you will at least remain in Verrières, and I shall see you sometimes. My children, who love you so much, will come to see you. My God! I feel that I love my children more since they love you. Oh, where will all this end? But I am wandering. Well, then, you understand what to do. Be agreeable, pleasant, and not overbearing towards those coarse fellows, I beg of you on my knees. They may be the arbiters of our fate. I do not doubt for a moment but that my husband will act only as public opinion shall dictate to him.

"Now, you will get up this anonymous letter. Have patience. Cut out of the book the words that you are about to see, and paste them on the sheet of bluish paper I send you; it is the kind used by M. Valenod. But mind one thing, burn the mutilated pages. If you don't find the words made up, have patience enough to form them letter by letter. To save you trouble I have made the anonymous letter very short. Ah, if you don't love me any more, as I fear, it may seem long enough to you!

" 'MADAME—Your little tricks are well known, and the persons who are interested in hiding them are well informed. From a little of the friendship I have had for you I warn you to cast off the little peasant; if you are wise enough for that, your husband will think that the information he has received was simply a joke, and he might be left under that impression. Know that I know your secret, wretched woman; you must *come to me now.*'

"When you have finished pasting on these words—do you recognize the Director's way of speaking?—leave the house. I will meet you.

"I am going to the village and will return seemingly in great trouble; indeed, I shall be so, anyhow. Oh, God! what I am risking, and all this because you thought you detected an anonymous letter! I will approach with a troubled air, and hand this letter to my husband which an unknown party will have put into my hands. You walk on the road in the woods with the children, and don't come back until dinner time.

"From the top of the rocks you can see the vane of the dovecot. If everything goes well, I will put a white handkerchief there; if not, nothing. Ungrateful, won't your heart find a way of telling me that you love me before you go? Whatever may happen, you may be sure of one thing, I will not survive you a single day after our separation. Ah, wicked mother that I am! Those are meaningless words for me now, dear Julien. I can't grasp them; I can only think of you at this moment; I have written them only so as not to be blamed by you.

"Now that I am about to lose you, what is the good of hiding anything? Yes, I seem cruel to you, but I cannot lie to the man I adore. I have deceived only too much in my life. Go! I forgive you even if you do not love me any more. I have not time to read my letter over. It is a little matter in my eyes to pay with my life for the happy days that I have passed with you; you know what they will cost me."

Chapter 21

Dialogue with a Master

Alas, our frailty is the cause, not we;
For such as we are made of, such we be.
—TWELFTH NIGHT

IT WAS with a childish pleasure that for the space of an hour Julien collected the words. As he was leaving the room he met his pupils and their mother; she took the letter with a simplicity and courage that frightened him by their very calmness.

"Have you pasted on the words?" she whispered to him.

"Is that the woman whom remorse is driving mad?" he thought. "What are her plans now?" He was too proud to ask her, but never before perhaps did she seem so beautiful to him.

"If this does not turn out well," she added, with the same sang-froid, "everything is lost. Hide this little parcel in the mountain somewhere. It may, perhaps, be my only resource some day."

She gave him a little glass box, encased in morocco, filled with money and diamonds.

"Go now," she said.

She embraced the children, the youngest one twice. Julien remained impassive. She left him, walking away rapidly, without giving him another look.

From the time that he had opened the anonymous letter, M. de Rênal's existence was one of torment. He had not been so moved since the duel which he came near having in 1816, and, to do him justice, the prospect of receiving a bullet had made him then far less miserable. He looked at the letter from all points of view.

"Is not that a woman's handwriting?" he said to himself. "In that case, what woman has written it?" He reviewed in his mind all those he knew at Verrières without being able to fasten suspicion on any.

"Has a man dictated the letter? Who can be that man?" Another uncertainty. He was envied, yes, and, no doubt, hated, by the greater portion of those he knew.

"I must consult my wife," he said, from habit, rising from the arm-chair, into which he had sunk.

119

Hardly had he arisen, "Great God!" he said, striking his head, "why, it is she of all that I must distrust! She is my enemy now"; and, from sheer anger, tears came into his eyes. As by a just compensation for that hard-heartedness which is called wisdom in the province, the two men whom he suspected the most just now were his most intimate associates. "Besides these, I have ten other friends, perhaps," and he passed them in review, measuring the degree of consolation each might impart.

"To all, to all," he cried, with rage, "to all of them this horrible event will afford the greatest pleasure."

Luckily he thought himself envied. Besides his superior residence in the town, which the King had just honored forever in passing a night under the roof, he had his château in Vergy. The façade was painted white, and at the windows were pretty green shutters. He was for an instant consoled by the thought of all his magnificence. The fact was that this château was seen from a distance of three or four leagues in sharp contrast with the other country houses, so-called châteaux, which had the humble gray color imparted by the weather.

M. de Rênal could count on the tears and pity of only one of his friends, the parish church warden; but that one was an imbecile, who cried at everything. Yet that man was his only resource.

"What misery can equal mine?" he cried, "what isolation? Is it possible," cried this man, who was truly to be pitied, "is it possible that in my misfortune I have not a single friend of whom to ask advice? I shall lose my reason. Oh, Falcoz! Ducros!" he cried, bitterly.

These were two friends whom he had thrown over in 1814 as they were not of noble birth; he wished to change the basis of equality on which they had associated from childhood.

One, Falcoz, a man of parts and courage, who was a paper merchant at Verrières, had bought a printing establishment in the department capital and had undertaken the publication of a newspaper. The Congregation, however, determined to ruin him, and his journal was suppressed and his copyright taken away. Under those unfortunate circumstances he had ventured to write to M. de Rênal for the first time in ten years. The Mayor of Verrières thought it wise to answer in true Roman fashion:

"If the King's minister did me the honor of consulting me I would tell him: 'Pursue without pity the publishers in the province, and make printing a monopoly like tobacco.' "

Such a letter to an intimate friend was admired in Verrières for a long time, but now M. de Rênal recalled it with horror. "Who would have told me that with my rank, my fortune, and my decorations I should regret that day?" He was in such a rage, now against himself, now against his surroundings, that the night became one unbroken torture. Happily the idea never occurred to him to spy on his wife.

"I am accustomed to Louise," he said to himself, "she knows all my affairs; if I should be at liberty to marry again tomorrow, I could not find one to take her place." Then he pleased himself with the idea that his wife was innocent. That way of thinking left him without the necessity of showing any will power, and put him more at ease. "Oh, well, how many women are not slandered every day? But I," he cried, all at once, walking nervously, "should I suffer as if I were nobody? Am I a fool, that she should mock me with a lover? Why should all Verrières ridicule me? What has not been said about Charmier?" (He was a husband notoriously deceived.) "When his name is mentioned, is there not a smile on everybody's lips? He is a good attorney who surpasses most everybody in a speech; and yet of Charmier they say, 'It is Bernard Charmier'; so they call him by the name of the man who has brought shame upon him!

"Thank God!" said M. de Rênal again, "I have no daughter; and the way I am going to punish the mother will not injure my children's station in life. I can surprise the little peasant with my wife and kill them both together. In that case the tragedy of the affair will perhaps remove the ridicule." The idea made him smile; he pursued it in all its details. "Yes, there is the penal code awaiting me, but, whatever might happen, our Congregation and my friends on the jury would save me."

He examined his hunting knife, which was very sharp; but the idea of blood made him recoil.

"I could crush this perfidious tutor with my fist and chase him out of the house; but what a treat for Verrières and for the entire department! At the suppression of Falcoz's journal, when his editor-in-chief was put in prison, I contributed six hundred francs to have him removed. They say that the little scribbler has dared show himself in Besançon; why, he can blackguard me in such a way as to make it impossible for me to bring him into court. The wretch would insinuate in a thousand ways that he was telling the truth. A man of noble birth, of such rank as I am, is hated by the rabble. I can see myself in those horrible newspapers in Paris. Oh, heavens! what a fall—to see the ancient name of de Rênal steeped in the mud of ridicule! If I ever travelled I should have to change my name; but, abandon the name which is my glory and my strength! Oh, terrible!

"If I don't kill my wife, but turn her out of doors in disgrace, she has her aunt in Besançon, who straightway will give her her entire fortune. My wife will then go to live in Paris with Julien, they will know it in Verrières, and I will still be the dupe."

The unfortunate man saw then, by the pale light of his lamp, that day was breaking; he went out into the garden for a little fresh air. Just then he had almost resolved to keep the matter quiet, for the simple reason that to do otherwise "would be the height of joy" for his friends in Verrières. The little walk in the garden calmed him somewhat.

"No," he said, "I will not deprive myself of my wife; she is too useful to me." He thought with horror of what his house would be without his wife. He had only one other relative, a marquise, who was old, imbecile, and malevolent. One other idea occurred to him, but the execution of it required a display of character which the poor man did not possess.

"If I keep my wife," he said, "I know that I shall find myself some day impatient with her, and I will throw it up to her. She is proud, and we will quarrel; and all that will come before she receives the fortune from her aunt. Then how she will laugh at me! My wife loves the children, and all will then be in her favor; but I—I will live as a fable for Verrières. Why, people will say he did not know enough to get even with his wife. Now, would it not be much better for me to keep my suspicions and not verify them? But then I will tie my hands, and I shall never be able to reproach her with that!"

A moment later M. de Rênal, aroused again by his wounded vanity, commenced to recall laboriously what was cited at billiards in the Casino or in the Cercle Noble in Verrières, when some good talker interrupted the game to amuse himself at the expense of a duped husband. How cruel those pleasantries seemed now!

"Heavens! why can't my wife die? I should then be proof against all ridicule. How I should like to be a widower now! Oh, I could spend six months in Paris in good society!"

After that happy respite that came to him from the idea of being a widower, his imagination returned to the invention of some means of assuring himself of the truth. At midnight, after all had retired, he would scatter some light sawdust before Julien's door; in the morning he would see his footprints. "But that is not worth anything," he cried, impatiently; "that fool of an Elisa would see it, and everybody in the house would know I am jealous."

In another tale that was told at the Casino, a husband had assured himself of his dishonor by affixing a hair with wax as a sort of seal to his wife's door and to that of her gallant. After many hours of uncertainty, that means of enlightening himself on his fate seemed the best, and he was thinking of making use of it, when, turning into a path, he met the woman whom he had wished to see dead. She was returning from the village, where she went to attend Mass. All the time that she thought she would pass in prayer in the church, she was continually representing to herself her husband killing Julien while out hunting, as if by accident, and then later eating out her heart in despair.

"My fate," she said to herself, "depends on what he will think when he listens to me; after this frightful quarter of an hour I shall perhaps find no more occasion to speak of him. He is not a man that is ruled by reason; I might, by the aid of my feeble mind, anticipate him in what he might do or say. It is for him to decide our lot; he has the power; but that fate will depend upon how cleverly I can direct his ideas and how I can prevent him from seeing not even a half. Good God! it requires tact, a cool head. Where shall I find it?"

She recovered her calmness as by enchantment when she came into the garden and saw her husband. His hair and dress told of a sleepless night. She handed him a letter that had been opened, but folded again; he, without opening it, looked at his wife like a madman.

"Here is an abominable thing," she cried, "which a man pretending to know you, and to be under obligations to you, put into my hand as I was passing behind the notary's garden. I demand one thing of you, and that is that you send this M. Julien to his folks without delay."

Madame de Rênal said that quickly in order once for all to get over the horrible idea of having to say it. She was seized with joy upon seeing what an effect it produced upon her husband. From the fixed look he gave her she understood that Julien was right. Instead of worrying over her present trouble, which was real enough, she was thinking: "What genius, what perfect tact, and yet a young man without experience! What height will he not reach? Alas! this will soon only make him forget me." This admiration for the man she adored recalled her to her trouble. She congratulated herself upon her success.

"I have been worthy of Julien," she was saying to herself, with a sweet, secret pleasure.

Without saying a word, for fear of committing himself, M. de Rênal examined the second anonymous letter, composed, as the reader will remember, of the words pasted on the blue paper. "Why, they are making fun of me in all sorts of ways," said M. de Rênal, wearily.

"Fresh insults, and again about my wife!" He was ready to overwhelm her with abuse, but the thought of the fortune from Besançon made him prudent. Consumed, however, by a desire of doing something in his state of passion, he crumpled the second letter in his hand, all the time walking furiously to and fro in order to be at a distance from his wife. In a few minutes he became somewhat calmer.

"We must decide about one thing, and that is to send Julien away," she said, presently. "He is only a laborer's son, after all. You can make it up with him with a little money. Besides, he is clever and will quickly find a place again; at M. Valenod's, for example, or with the sub-prefect, both of whom have children. You will not make him lose anything."

"You talk like the fool that you are," cried M. de Rênal, in a terrible voice. "What common sense can one expect in a woman? You never pay attention to anything reasonable; how can you know anything? Your indifference and laziness are just good enough for chasing butterflies! Worthless creatures, whom we have the misfortune to have in our families!"

"I am going to see to it that Julien asks you for leave of absence for a month to go to the wood merchant, that great friend of his."

"Take care what you are doing," replied M. de Rênal; "what I demand above all is that you do not talk to him. You will get him into a rage, and then you will embroil me with him. You know how touchy this little monsieur is."

"The young man has no tact," Madame de Rênal answered. "He may be clever, you know that; but at bottom he is only a boor. As for me, I have not thought much of him ever since he refused Elisa—there was a sure fortune for him—on the pretext that she visited M. Valenod occasionally."

"Ah," said M. de Rênal, raising his eyebrows, "did Julien tell you that?"

"No, not precisely. He has always spoken to me of an inclination he has for the priesthood; but, believe me, the only inclination these small people have is to get bread. He gave me to understand that he was not ignorant of those secret visits."

"And I—and I—I did not know it," cried M. de Rênal, beside himself with rage, drawing out his words. "I do not know what is going on in my house! So there is something between Elisa and Valenod?"

"Oh, it is an old story, my dear," answered Madame de Rênal, laughing, "and perhaps it is not so bad after all. There was a time when your good friend Valenod would not have been much put out if it were said in Verrières that a little platonic love existed between him and me."

"I had a suspicion of that once," interjected M. de Rênal, clapping his head furiously as he proceeded from one discovery to another. "And you did not tell me anything?"

"Was it necessary to get two friends involved in a difficulty about a little buffoonery on the part of our dear Director? Where is the woman of any standing who has not received his clever, gallant little notes?"

"He has written to you?"

"Oh, yes, a good deal."

"Show me the letters at once, I command you!" said M. de Rênal, leaping towards her.

"I am going to be exceedingly careful with them," she replied, with a calmness that bordered almost on nonchalance; "I will show them to you some day, perhaps, when you are in a better humor."

"At once! Morbleu!" cried M. de Rênal, in mad fury, and yet happier than he had been for twelve hours.

"Will you promise," she replied, "that you will never quarrel with the Director on account of these letters?"

"Quarrel or no quarrel, I am going to take away the foundlings from him; but," he continued, furiously, "I want those letters right away. Where are they?"

"In a drawer in my desk; but I certainly do not intend to give you the key."

"Very well, I can break it," he cried, running towards the room.

In fact he did break with a poker a fine little mahogany secretary which had come from Paris, and which he had frequently wiped off with his coat when he would see a spot on it.

Madame de Rênal had run up the one hundred and twenty steps to the dovecot, to tie a white handkerchief to one of the little iron window bars. She was the happiest woman in the world; with tears in her eyes she looked out towards the mountain woods.

"Undoubtedly," she was saying to herself, "Julien sees this

happy signal from underneath a cluster of those elms." For a long time she listened, irritated by the noise of the grasshoppers and the twittering of the birds. But for that noise, a joyous cry coming from great rocks would have reached her, no doubt. Her eager eye swept over that dense stretch of dark verdure, lying like a level field, which formed the tops of the trees.

"Will he not be clever enough," she asked herself, softly, "to invent some sort of a signal to tell me that his happiness is equal to mine?"

She did not leave the dovecot until she was afraid that her husband might come to look for her. She found him in a boiling rage. He had read over the vapid phrases in M. Valenod's letters—phrases that were never intended to be read with such emotion. Seizing a moment when her husband's furious interjections allowed her to make herself heard, she said:

"I am coming back to my first idea. Julien must leave. Whatever genius he may have for Latin, he is, after all, only a little peasant, often coarse, and always without sense. Every day he pays me some exaggerated compliments, that he has learned by heart from some novel; lamely enough, to be sure, though he thinks he is highly polished."

"He never reads them," cried M. de Rênal, "I am positive of that. Do you suppose that I am master of the house and don't know what is going on here?"

"Well, if he does not read these ridiculous compliments, he invents them; so much the worse. I suppose he must have spoken in that fashion in Verrières, and," continued Madame de Rênal, pretending to make a great discovery, "he must have talked so before Elisa, which is the same as talking to M. Valenod."

"Ah!" cried M. de Rênal, making table and room resound with a tremendous blow of his fist, "the printed anonymous letter and Valenod's letters are written on the same kind of paper."

"At last!" thought Madame de Rênal; but, pretending to be overwhelmed by the discovery, she sank down on a sofa at the other end of the room, seemingly unable to say another word.

The battle was now won; it was all she could do to prevent M. de Rênal from going to speak to the supposed author of the anonymous letter at once.

"Can't you see that to create a scene with M. Valenod, without sufficient proof, is the height of folly? You are envied, monsieur—and whose fault is it? It is owing to your ability, your wise administration, your handsome buildings, the dowry

I brought you, and, more than all, the considerable, though exaggerated, fortune which we expect from my good aunt—all that has made you the first man in Verrières."

"You forget my birth," replied her husband, with a superior smile.

"You are one of the most distinguished men in the province," she continued, impressively. "If the King were at liberty to act as he desired, and could do justice to birth, you would now, no doubt, be a peer. And from such a magnificent position do you want to stoop to be talked about by everybody? To talk to M. Valenod about this anonymous letter is to proclaim to the entire town of Verrières—what do I say? to all Besançon, to the whole province—that this little bourgeois, imprudently admitted into the family life of a de Rênal, has had the means of offending him. If these letters which you have just read should prove that I have responded in any way to M. Valenod's love, you would have the right to kill me—I should deserve it a hundred times—but not to show him anger! Think of it—all your neighbors are waiting only for just such an opportunity to revenge themselves on you! Do you know that in 1816 you had a share in certain arrests, and then that man—"

"I know that you have no regard, no love for me," M. de Rênal spurted out, with all the bitterness which that recollection imparted; "I have not been made a peer."

"I know, my dear," she continued, smiling, "that I will be richer than you; that I have been your companion for twelve years, and that in all these matters I ought to have something to say, especially in this affair of to-day. If you prefer a M. Julien to me," she added, with ill-concealed disdain, "I am ready to spend the winter with my aunt."

That was delivered admirably. There was a firmness in her tone, intrenched with politeness that immediately decided M. de Rênal.

But, following the provincial habit, he continued talking for a long time, and always going over the same ground. His wife patiently let him go on, as there was still a trace of anger in his tone. After two hours, however, he weakened, worn out as he was by a long night of anguish. He outlined his conduct towards M. Valenod, towards Julien, and even towards Elisa.

Once or twice during that scene Madame de Rênal was almost touched by the misfortune of the man who, for twelve years, had been her daily companion; but true passion is egotistical. And, moreover, she was waiting every minute to be informed about the anonymous letter which he had received, and that information had not been forthcoming. Besides, Madame de Rênal was not sure as to what ideas had been suggested to the man on whom her fate depended. In the provinces, it must be known, husbands control public opinion. A complaining husband is only ridiculed—a fact that does not weigh much in France; but if he fails to provide for his wife, the latter is reduced to the level of a scrubwoman at fifteen sous a day, whom some good souls might scruple even about employing. An odalisque in the harem might get to love the Sultan; she has no hope of depriving her all-powerful lord of his authority through finesse, and she knows that while his vengeance is terrible it is not ignoble—a sword thrust, and it is all over. But it is with the blows of public opinion, with the closing of drawing-rooms, that a man kills his wife in the nineteenth century.

The feeling of danger was again wakened in Madame de Rênal when she returned to her room. The disorder in which she found it came as a shock to her. The drawers of all her pretty little cases had been broken open, and even some of the flooring had been raised.

"He was heartless," she said to herself, "to spoil that pretty little desk which he loved so much. If one of the children came into the room with wet shoes he would get fearfully angry. Now, there it is, ruined!"

The scene of violence instantly removed the vestige of regret that had come to her from her too easy victory.

A little before dinner Julien returned with the children. At dessert, when the servants had withdrawn, Madame de Rênal said to him, dryly:

"You have given me to understand that you desire to spend a fortnight at Verrières? M. de Rênal is willing to give you leave; you can go whenever it suits you. The children need not waste their time, though; their compositions will be sent to you every day, and you can correct them."

"Indeed," put in M. de Rênal, sharply, "I give you leave for a week only."

Julien read great trouble in his face.

"He has not yet decided on any plan," he said to her when they were alone for a moment in the drawing-room.

Madame de Rênal related to him hastily all that she had done since morning. "The details to-night," she added, smiling.

"The perversity of womankind!" thought Julien. "What instinct leads them to deceive us?"

"I see that you are both enlightened and blinded by your love," he said to her, coolly; "your conduct to-day is admirable;

but do you think it is prudent for us to see each other to-night? This house is hedged in with enemies. Think of the hatred Elisa has for me."

"That hatred is on a par with the indifference that you are showing now."

"It may be indifference in me to want to save you from a great danger; but suppose M. de Rênal says something to Elisa; she could tell him all in a word! Why couldn't he hide himself in my room, armed to the teeth?"

"What, not even courage!" said Madame de Rênal, with all the pride of a woman of blood.

"I will never stoop to talk of my courage," Julien answered, coldly. "It is base. Let the world judge from facts. But," he added, taking her hand, "you don't know how much I love you, and how great my joy is to be able to take leave of you before this cruel absence."

Chapter 22

Manners and Customs in 1830

Man was gifted with speech to help him conceal his thoughts.

——R. P. MALAGRIDA

HE HAD HARDLY ARRIVED at Verrières, when Julien regretted his injustice towards Madame de Rênal.

"I should have despised her as a weak woman if she had not been equal to that scene with her husband. She acquitted herself like a diplomat, and I sympathize with the vanquished, who is my enemy! There is something of the bourgeois in me; my vanity is wounded because M. de Rênal is a man—the illustrious and vast corporation to which I have the honor of belonging! Oh, I am a fool!"

M. Chélan had refused the lodgings which the more considerate Liberals had offered him after he had been removed from the vicarage. The two rooms he had rented were filled with books.

Julien, wishing to show Verrières what a priest could do, got a dozen fir planks from his father, and carried them himself all the way over Grande Rue. He borrowed some tools from an old friend of his, and soon he had some shelving finished on which M. Chélan's books were arranged in order.

"I thought you had been spoiled by worldly vanity," said the old man to him, with tears in his eyes. "That has made up for your foolishness over that brilliant Guard of Honor uniform, which made you so many enemies."

M. de Rênal had ordered him to go to his house; no one had any idea of what had passed.

On the third day after his arrival, Julien saw no less a personage mounting the stairway than the sub-prefect de Maugiron. It was not until after two hours of insipid chatter and grandiloquent jeremiads on the wickedness of mankind, on the lack of probity in men charged with the administration of public funds, on the dangers besetting poor France, that Julien saw at length the purport of his visit. They were already on the stairway, and the poor, half-disgraced preceptor had respectfully taken the future prefect of a department to the door, when the latter graciously began to talk of Julien's future, and to praise his foresight and genius.

At length M. de Maugiron, after a paternal embrace, proposed to him to leave M. de Rênal's for the house of an official who had children to *educate,* and who, like King Philip, was thanking heaven not so much for having given them to him as for bringing them into the world in the neighborhood of M. Julien. Their teacher would enjoy an income of eight hundred francs, payable not by the month, "which is not genteel," said M. de Maugiron, "but quarterly, and always in advance."

It was now Julien's turn. The latter, after an hour and a half of waiting, had been growing somewhat weary. His reply was perfect and as long as a dissertation. Almost anything could be gathered from it, but nothing definite. It was replete at once with respect for M. de Rênal, with consideration for the Verrières public, and with gratitude for the illustrious sub-prefect. This sub-prefect, astonished at finding more of a Jesuit than himself, endeavored to ascertain something positive. Seemingly enchanted with the opportunity, Julien commenced another reply. Never had an eloquent minister, who wished to seize an opportunity in the Chamber, said less in more words. But hardly had M. de Maugiron departed when Julien burst out in uncontrollable laughter.

In order to profit by his Jesuitical finesse he immediately wrote a nine-page letter to M. de Rênal, giving him an account of all that was said, and asking for advice.

"That fool has not told me the name of the man who is making me the offer; it must be M. Valenod, who sees in my exile the effect of the anonymous letter."

This letter despatched, Julien, as happy as a sportsman would be in coming on a fine autumn day into a field full of game, went out to consult M. Chélan. But, before arriving at the good curate's, his good fortune brought him face to face with M. Valenod, from whom he did not hide the fact that his heart was broken. A poor boy, as he was, might devote himself to the calling which heaven had placed in his heart, but the calling is not all in this wicked world. In order to labor diligently in the Lord's vineyard, and not to be unworthy of his learned colleagues, he must be taught; he must spend two very expensive years at the Besançon seminary. It was indispensable to be economical; it was easier with an income of eight hundred francs, paid quarterly in advance, than with six hundred, which melted away from month to month. On the other hand, did not heaven, in placing him with the de Rênal children, and especially in inspiring in him a real love for them, seem to indicate to him that it would not be proper to leave them for others?

Julien reached such a degree of perfection in that sort of eloquence that he was annoyed, through sheer frequency, by the sound of his own voice. On his return he found M. Valenod's valet in fine livery, who had been looking for him all over town, with an invitation for dinner that day. Julien had never been to that man's house. Only a few days before he was thinking of knocking him down in such a way as to avoid trouble with the police.

Although the dinner was not to take place until one o'clock, Julien found it more respectful to present himself in the Director's library at half-past twelve. He found him there expatiating on his great importance, surrounded by a mass of letters. His long black moustache, his enormous head of hair, surmounted crookedly by a Greek cap, his immense pipe, his embroidered slippers, his heavy gold chains crossed over his breast, everything that went to give him an appearance of an important financier, failed of an impression with Julien. He was only thinking of the caning that he owed him.

He asked the privilege of being presented to Madame Valenod. She was dressing and could not receive. As by a sort of compensation, he had the pleasure of being present while the Director dressed. When they came into the room, Madame Valenod, with tears in her eyes, presented her children to him. She was a leading society woman of Verrières. Her large, masculine face, which was thickly rouged in honor of the occasion, was pathetic with maternal solicitude. Julien was thinking of Madame de Rênal. His present indifference made him susceptible only to those ideas which are occasioned by contrast; and these ideas caused him great emotion when he beheld the furnishings of the Director's house. All was magnificent, new, and costly, as he was told. But to Julien there was something common, coarse, that smelt of stolen money; even to the servants, every one seemed to brace himself against expected contempt.

The collector of taxes, the chief of police, and two or three other public officials presently arrived, accompanied by their wives. These were followed by some rich Liberals. Then dinner was anounced. Julien, ill-disposed for the feast, was thinking of the poor creatures on the other side of the dining-room wall who were waiting for a meal, and whose meat had perhaps been nibbled in order to provide all this coarse luxury.

"Perhaps they are hungry at this moment," he was saying to

himself. His gorge rose; it was impossible for him to eat, even to speak.

It was less than a quarter of an hour later when some notes of a popular song were heard. One of the detained poor was singing.

M. Valenod looked at one of his finely liveried men, and the latter departed. The singing immediately ceased. Just at this moment a valet was handing Rhine wine in a green glass to Julien, and Madame Valenod had observed that the wine cost nine francs a bottle at the vineyard.

Julien held up his green glass, saying to M. Valenod:

"They are not singing that popular song any more."

"Parbleu! no, indeed," answered the Director, triumphantly; "I have made those beggars keep quiet."

That word was too much for Julien; he had acquired the manners, but had not yet the heart suitable to his surroundings, in spite of all his hypocrisy. A great tear rolled down his cheek. He succeeded in hiding it with the green glass, but it was absolutely impossible for him to do justice to the Rhine wine.

"Prevent them from singing!" he was saying to himself. "Oh, Lord! and you permit it!"

Happily no one remarked the tender ring in his tone. The collector of taxes had then intoned a royalist song, and all were singing in chorus. All the time Julien's conscience was saying to him:

"There, now, that is what you will reach. You will not live except under such conditions and in such company. You will perhaps have a position of twenty thousand francs, but while you are gorging yourself, you will have to prevent the poor wretches from singing. You will give dinners with the money that you have stolen from their miserable pittance, and while you are dining, they will be even more miserable. Oh, Napoleon, you were great enough in your time to point to greatness, through the smoke of battle; but to add to such misery in such a cowardly fashion!"

We must admit that Julien's faint-heartedness, as seen in such reflections, might give rise to a poor opinion of him. He might be thought a worthy colleague of those tan-glove conspirators who are laboring to change the destinies of nations without getting a scratch. Julien was violently recalled to his rôle. It was not to dream, that he had been invited to dinner in such good company. A retired linen merchant, a corresponding member of the Academy of Besançon and of that of Uzès, spoke to him across the table, asking him if what was said about his marvellous progress in his study of the New Testament was true.

A profound silence ensued. As if by a miracle, a New Testament appeared in the hand of the savant of the two academies. Julien consenting, a Latin word was read, and then he began to recite. His memory served him well, and he was admired as a prodigy, with genuine after-dinner enthusiasm. Julien looked at the faces of the ladies; several were not bad looking. He particularly remarked the wife of the singer.

"Indeed, I am ashamed to speak Latin so long before these ladies," he said, looking at her. "If M. Rubigneau"—he was the academician—"would be kind enough to read a Latin phrase, I would try to translate it offhand in place of replying with the Latin text." This second test carried him to the pinnacle of glory.

There were present several rich Liberals with a penchant for lucre who had been converted at the last election. In spite of this political finesse, M. de Rênal had never received them at his house. These fine gentlemen, who did not know Julien except by hearsay, and by what they had seen of him when he was on horseback during the King's progress, were his noisiest admirers.

"When will these fools get tired of the biblical talk? They don't understand it," thought he. On the contrary, the style, by its very strangeness, amused them; they secretly made fun of it. At length Julien grew tired.

He arose from the table ceremoniously, just as six o'clock struck, while speaking of a chapter in the new theological work of Ligorio, which he had to learn for the next day to recite before M. Chélan; "for it is my business," he added, suavely, "both to hear lessons and to recite them."

There was a laugh, and he was greatly admired; that was the cleverness in vogue at Verrières. Such is the sway of genius, that when Julien stood up, all the rest arose, regardless of decorum. Madame Valenod kept him for another quarter of an hour; he must, indeed, hear the children recite their Catechism. They made all sorts of blunders, which he alone knew; but he did not care to correct them.

"What ignorance of the first principles of religion!" he said to himself.

He bade good-by and was about to leave, but was detained again. He must hear them recite one of La Fontaine's fables.

"This author is indeed immoral," said Julien to Madame Valenod; "this fable about Jean Chouart ridicules everything that is holy. It is, indeed, criticised severely by the best commentators."

Before leaving, Julien received four or five invitations to dine. "The young man is an honor to the department," cried the dinner company, gayly; they even went so far as to speak of having a fund voted for him from the public treasury, to enable him to continue his studies in Paris.

While that imprudent idea was being expressed in the dining-room, Julien had reached the door. "The canaille!" he muttered three or four times, as he inhaled the fresh air. He considered himself an aristocrat at that moment, he who for so long had been irritated by the condescending smile and overbearing superiority in the polite phrases addressed to him at M. de Rênal's house. He could not but feel the great contrast.

"Even if I should forget," he said to himself, as he was leaving, "that all this money is stolen from the poor; that even a song is not permitted; yet never, never would M. de Rênal think of telling his guests the price of each bottle of wine. And this M. Valenod, in going over his possessions, which he did interminably, does not speak of the house and of his other things if his wife is present, except by saying, 'your house, your land.'"

That lady, displaying all the marks of greed, had enacted an abominable scene while dinner was in progress. A servant had dropped a glass at her feet, and, with its breaking, had "spoilt the set." He had answered her with the greatest insolence.

"What a herd!" thought Julien. "If they gave me half what they steal I should not live with them. One of these fine days I am going to burst out; I cannot hold in any longer the contempt I feel for them."

Yet, in obedience to Madame de Rênal's command, he had to be present at several dinners that were all on the same order. Julien became the vogue; he was even forgiven his uniform of the Guard of Honor. That imprudence, indeed, was the real cause of his success. Soon there was only a question in Verrières as to who would win the battle in getting the young savant, M. de Rênal or the Director.

These two, together with M. Maslon, formed a triumvirate who for many years had ruled the town. The people, as a whole, were jealous of the Mayor, while the Liberals found much cause for complaint on their part. Yet, after all, he belonged to the nobility, and that made him a superior person. But M. Valenod's father had not left an estate of six hundred livres. They recollected the pity they had felt for him when they knew him as a young man wearing a shabby little green coat—and now he had his fine horses, his gold chains, and Parisian clothes.

In his new surroundings Julien had discovered one good man, a geometrician by the name of Gros, who passed for a Jacobin. Julien, vowing that he would never say anything except what seemed false to himself, was obliged to be somewhat careful in the presence of this man.

He received, from time to time, large parcels of themes from Vergy, and was advised in letters to visit his father. To that dire necessity he also submitted. In a word, he was acquiring a fine reputation, when one morning he was surprised by two hands from behind placed over his eyes.

It was Madame de Rênal who had come to town, and who, running up the steps in the greatest haste, having left her children playing with a rabbit, had entered Julien's room.

That was a delightful moment for her, though all too short. Madame de Rênal had just taken breath after her rapid flight up the stairs, when the children entered with the rabbit, which they wished to show to their friend. Julien gave them all a cordial reception, even the rabbit. It seemed as if he were with his own again; he felt that he loved these children, that he enjoyed playing with them. He was struck by the softness of their voices, and by their delicate, gentle little ways. He had to wash his memory clean of all the vulgar habits he had been seeing, and of the disagreeable feelings these had brought him during his exile in Verrières. There was always that terrible contrast between luxury and misery before his eyes. The people with whom he had been dining, beginning with the roast, would make confidences humiliating to themselves and disgusting to their hearer.

"You, indeed, belong to the nobility, and you have a right to be proud," said he to Madame de Rênal, as he told her of the dinners that had been inflicted upon him.

"Why, you are becoming the rage," she replied, laughing at the thought of how much rouge Madame Valenod felt obliged to put on while waiting for Julien. "Ah, I believe she has some designs on you."

The breakfast was delicious. The presence of the children, who, it must be said, were not quite as neat as usual in their appearance, lent additional happiness. The poor children did not know how to show all their joy on seeing Julien again. The servants had not failed to tell them that he had been offered two hundred francs more to educate the little Valenods. When they were not half through breakfast, Stanislaus-Xavier, pale yet from his long illness, suddenly asked his mother how much his dinner set and his cup would bring.

"Why?"

"I want to sell them to give the money to M. Julien, so he would not be bilked if he stayed with us."

Julien embraced him with tears in his eyes. The mother wept, too, as Julien, picking up Stanislaus on his knee, was telling how wrongly the word "bilk" was used. In such a sense, he said, it could be used only in speaking of servants. Seeing the pleasure it gave Madame de Rênal, he went on to illustrate, with clever examples that quite amused the children, what it was to be "bilked."

"I understand," said Stanislaus; "it is just like the crow foolish enough to let go of her cheese, to let it be picked up by the flattering fox."

The delighted Madame de Rênal was covering the child with kisses, leaning now and then a little on Julien, when all at once the door opened and M. de Rênal entered.

His severe, sour look was in sharp contrast with the expression of delight on her face which his presence immediately drove away. Madame de Rênal grew pale, feeling as if she could not utter a word. Julien, however, was equal to the occasion, and boldly began to tell the Mayor about the silver cup which Stanislaus wanted to sell. He was positive, though, it would not meet with a gracious reception. At first M. de Rênal from sheer habit raised his eyebrows at hearing the word "silver." "The mention of that metal," he thought, "means a preface to my purse." But evidently there was something more interesting in this affair than money, and his suspicion was more than ever aroused. The happiness of his family during his absence was not calculated to make things agreeable to a man dominated by harrowing vanity. His wife told him how cleverly Julien had been imparting new ideas to his pupils.

"Yes, yes, I know it; he makes me hated by my own children. Oh, he is a hundred times more agreeable to them than I am, and I am their father! It is of a piece with all disregard of authority in this age! Poor France!"

Madame de Rênal did not stop to consider the hints thrown out in her husband's greeting. She was beginning to see a possibility of spending twelve hours with Julien. As she had a great deal of shopping to do, she said she would take dinner at the cabaret. And whatever her husband might urge to the contrary, she held fast to that resolution. The children were wild over the idea of the "cabaret"—a word by which modern prudery is shocked.

M. de Rênal left his wife in the first notion store they came to, as he had an engagement elsewhere. He returned more morose than in the morning: he had been convinced that the whole town was talking about him and Julien.

In truth, no one gave him the least occasion to suspect anything. M. de Rênal had been asked merely if Julien would remain with him for six hundred francs, or take the eight hundred francs offered by the Director.

Now, the Director, who had met M. de Rênal, had taken his breath away. That was done not without some cleverness. For M. Valenod, coarse, petty, and shameless, was what would be called a buffoon, his prosperous existence since 1815 only accentuating the elegance of his manners. He was an official under the orders of M. de Rênal, but, being much more active and unscrupulous than the latter, had, by dint of much writing and talking, and by utter disregard of all decency and self-respect, succeeded in playing the Mayor against the ecclesiastical authorities. M. Valenod had said to the grocers: "Let me have the two greatest fools among you;" to the lawyers, "Show me the two greatest charlatans in your court;" and to the health officers, "Give me your two greatest quacks." When he had gathered in the scum of each class, he had said to them, "Let us carry on the administration together."

It was the ways of such gentlemen that did not suit M. de Rênal; Valenod's vulgarity, nor even the absurdities of the little abbé Maslon, did not offend him so much. But with all his success, M. Valenod had to intrench himself behind a barricade of insolence to meet the attack of truth people would make. His activity redoubled from the time of M. Appert's visit. He had made three trips to Besançon, and had written many letters with each courier, besides other letters sent by secret messengers who came to his house at midnight. He was wrong, perhaps, in removing the old curate Chélan; for that vindictive action he was looked upon by many of the well-to-do pious people as wicked. It had, besides, put him in the power of the vicar de Frilaire, who was giving him some strange things to do. Such was his position when he yielded to the pleasure of writing an anonymous letter. To increase his embarrassment, his wife had intimated to him that she wished to have Julien at her house. His vanity had completely collapsed.

Under these circumstances, M. Valenod was awaiting the stormy scene with his old confederate, M. de Rênal. The latter was not sparing, to be sure. But the words had no effect; yet the Mayor might write to Besançon, if not to Paris! Some minister's cousin might all at once tumble down on Verrières and take away the Directorship. M. Valenod had thought some time before of allying himself with the Liberals; for that reason several of them had been invited to the dinner together with Julien. He could thus be in a strong position against the Mayor; but the election would come, and it was too evident that the Directorship would be incompatible with an indiscreet vote! This political jugglery, of which Madame de Rênal was aware, was described to Julien while he was escorting her from one store to another in Cours de la Fidélité, promenading as peacefully as at Vergy.

All this time M. Valenod was trying to ward off a sharp encounter with his patron, by showing himself bolder than usual. That day the method succeeded, but it aroused the Mayor's anger even more. Never had vanity arising from the consciousness only of wealth put a man in such a pitiable position as it did M. de Rênal when he entered the cabaret. Never, on the other hand, had his children been so glad and gay. The contrast aroused him anew.

"I am *de trop* in my family, from what I see," he said, as he entered, in a tone intended to be crushing.

By way of reply his wife took him aside, again telling him of the necessity of getting rid of Julien.

The pleasant hours she had passed gave her the ease and firmness necessary to carrying out her plan, the result of two weeks' deliberation.

What troubled the poor Mayor of Verrières more than anything else was the fact that he felt he was everywhere ridiculed for her attachment for this little bourgeois. Then, M. Valenod was as generous as a thief, while he himself had conducted himself rather shabbily in the five or six collections for the Brotherhood of St. Joseph, from the Congregation of the Holy Sacrament, and the rest. When the collectors in Verrières and the neighborhood, adroitly classed on the record as "brother collectors," counted up the contributions, more than once M. de Rênal's name had appeared at the bottom of the list. In vain they said that he was not gaining anything by it.

Chapter 23

The Functionary's Pangs

*Il piacere di alzar la testa tutto l'anno è ben
pagato da certi quarti d'ora che bisogna passar.*
— CASTI

WE SHALL LEAVE the little man to his little cares. Why did this
man take into his house a man of character, while he himself
had the heart of a craven? Did he not know how to select his
people? The distinguishing mark of the nineteenth century is
that when a noble, self-esteemed gentleman meets a man of
courage, he either kills him, or claps him into jail, or humiliates
him otherwise, until the latter sooner or later dies heart-broken.
Here, luckily, it was not a man of character that was suffering.

The great evil in little French towns, as well as in other com-
munities ruled by popular vote, as in New York, is that people
cannot forget that there exist such men in the world as M. de
Rênal. In a town of twenty thousand inhabitants, such men as
he form public opinion, and public opinion is a terrible thing in
countries that have a constitution. Your friend, a noble, generous spirit, living a hundred leagues away, judges you by the
public opinion of your town, formed by the fools or knaves
whom chance has given the means of floating on the surface.
Woe to him that is in any way distinguished!

Soon after dinner they left for Vergy, but in a day Julien
saw the whole family again in Verrières. An hour after their
arrival he discovered that Madame de Rênal was hiding something mysterious from him. She would interrupt her conversation with her husband if he appeared, and would unmistakably
show that she wished him to be at a distance. Julien did not
take it very graciously, and became cold and reserved. Madame
de Rênal, though aware of all this, did not offer to explain.

"Am I going to have a successor?" thought Julien. "Only the
day before yesterday she was so charming to me! But that is
what they say about the way these great ladies conduct themselves—just like the kings: always new attentions to a minister,
who, on returning to his house, finds his letter of dismissal."

Julien observed that, in the conversation which would
abruptly cease at his approach, something was often said about
a large old house belonging to the municipality of Verrières,
that was located opposite the church, in the busiest quarter of
the town.

"What has this house to do with another lover?" Julien wondered. In his uncertainty he was repeating to himself those pretty lines of François Premier, which he had learnt from Madame de Rênal. With how many declarations of love, with how many caresses was not each of these lines accompanied then!

> *"Souvent femme varie*
> *Bien fol est qui s'y fie."*

But M. de Rênal left post-haste for Besançon, the trip having been decided upon in two hours. He had appeared greatly perplexed. On his return he threw a large bundle of papers on the table.

"There is the stupid affair," he said to his wife. An hour later Julien saw a bill poster carrying the large bundle away. He followed him eagerly.

"I am going to find out the secret as soon as he turns the corner."

He stood impatiently behind the bill poster while the latter was pasting on an advertisement. With eager curiosity Julien read the announcement of a public auction of the lease of the large old house that had so often been mentioned in M. de Rênal's conversation with his wife. The auction was announced for the next day at two o'clock in the public hall.

Julien was disappointed; there was such a little interval, he thought. How could the bidders find this out in such a short time? Besides this, the announcement, which had been dated fifteen days before, gave no information. He walked over, therefore, to the house in question. The care-taker, who did not see him approach, was saying mysteriously to a neighbor:

"Bah! bah! It is all in vain. Maslon has promised it to him for three hundred francs, and when the Mayor hedged, he applied to the Bishop through his vicar Frilaire." Julien's arrival seemed to disconcert the two friends, for they ceased speaking all at once.

He came to the auction. There was a crowd in the dimly lighted hall, and all were speaking very familiarly with one another. All eyes were fixed upon the table, where Julien saw a tin plate in which three little candles were burning.

The auctioneer cried out, "Three hundred francs, gentlemen."

"Three hundred francs! Well, that is too bad," said a man in a whisper to his neighbor. "Why, it is worth more than eight hundred; I am going to bid over."

"Oh, there is no sense in that. What will you gain by having

Maslon, Valenod, the Bishop, the vicar, and the entire clique on you?"

"Three hundred and twenty francs," put in the other, crying out.

"You fool!" replied his neighbor; "and here is one of the Mayor's spies," he added, pointing to Julien.

Julien turned quickly around, but the two citizens paid no attention to him. At that moment the last candle went out, and the bailiff slowly announced that the house went to M. de Saint-Giraud, of the Prefecture of _____, for nine years, at three hundred and thirty francs per annum.

When the Mayor left the hall there was a hum of excitement.

"Now, there is thirty francs which de Grogeot's imprudence is worth to the public," cried one.

"Well, M. de Saint-Giraud," replied another, "will be revenged on Grogeot; they will find it out soon enough."

"What a scandal!" said a tall man on the left of Julien. "A house for which I would have given eight hundred francs for my factory; and it would have been a bargain at that."

"Bah!" replied a young Liberal manufacturer. "Does not M. de Saint-Giraud belong to the Congregation? Aren't his sons wealthy? The poor man! The community of Verrières should vote him a pension of five hundred francs, at least."

"And to think that the Mayor could not prevent it," observed a third. "True, he is ultra conservative, but at least he does not steal."

"He does not steal, ha!" interposed another. "Oh, no, somebody else steals; everything goes into one pot, and at the end of the year there is a grand rake-off. But here is little Sorel; let's go."

Julien returned to the house in a bad humor, finding Madame de Rênal in a dejected mood.

"You come from the auction?" she asked him.

"Yes, Madame, where I have had the honor of being taken for the Mayor's spy."

"If he had taken my advice, he would have left the city for a while."

Just then M. de Rênal entered, looking very gloomy. Dinner passed off without a word. Madame de Rênal persuaded Julien to follow the children to Vergy, but the trip was no pleasant one.

Madame de Rênal tried to comfort her husband:

"Oh, you should be used to that, my dear."

In the evening they were seated about the fireplace, and the only distraction from the funereal quiet was the noise made by the burning wood. It was one of those gloomy evenings that intrude themselves sometimes in the liveliest families. Suddenly one of the children cried out joyously:

"The bell rings! the bell rings!"

"Morbleu! if that is M. de Saint-Giraud who is coming to knife me under the pretext of thanking me," cried the Mayor, "I will give him a piece of my mind. Why, it is too much! It is Valenod to whom he is under obligations. I—I—I have simply been taken in. What would these damned Jacobin journals say if they got hold of this little tale and made me another Nonante?"

A tall, handsome man, with large black whiskers, entered, following the servant.

"Monsieur Mayor, I am Signor Geronimo. I have here a letter from Chevalier de Beauvoises, the attaché of the embassy of Naples, written only eight days ago," said Signor Geronimo, looking smilingly at Madame de Rênal. "Signor de Beauvoises, your cousin and my very good friend, Madame, told me that you speak Italian."

The Neapolitan was lively and began making the evening quite gay.

Madame de Rênal insisted on giving him supper. She put the whole house to work, being, above all, desirous of removing from Julien's mind the effect of having been twice taken for a spy that day.

Signor Geronimo was a celebrated singer, a hail-fellow-well-met—a quality, sadly enough, no longer appreciated in France!

After supper he sang a little duet with Madame de Rênal. He related some charming anecdotes, and at one o'clock in the morning the children, when Julien proposed going to bed, made a chorus of objections.

"Another story," pleaded the eldest.

"It is my own, signorino," replied Signor Geronimo. "It was eight years ago; I was a pupil at the Neapolitan Conservatory. Now, mind you, I was your age, but I had not the honor of being the son of the illustrious Mayor of a pretty Verrières." That made M. de Rênal look at his wife with a sigh.

"Signor Zingarelli," continued the young singer, changing his accent in a manner that made the children burst with laughter, "Signor Zingarelli was an awfully severe master. He was not liked at the conservatory, but he wished all to act as if they were enchanted with him. I would leave the conservatory as often as possible, to go to the little San-Carlino Theatre, where I would hear heavenly music; but, mon dieu! how can a man make both ends meet when admission costs eight sous—an enormous sum!" he cried, looking at the children, who were laughing.

"Signor Giovannone, Director of the San-Carlino Theatre, happened once to hear me sing; I was then sixteen years old. 'That boy,' he said, 'is a treasure!'

" 'Do you want me to engage you, my little man?' he suddenly said to me.

" 'And how much will you give me?'

" 'Forty ducats a month.' Gentlemen, that is one hundred and sixty francs. I thought the very heavens were opening.

" 'But how,' I say to Giovannone, 'how can I get the terrible Zingarelli to let me go?'

" *'Lascia fare a me.'* "

"Leave that to me," cried the eldest of the boys.

"Just so, my little monsieur. Signor Giovannone says, 'My dear, first a little contract.'

"Of course I sign it, and he gives me three ducats. I had not seen so much money in my life; then he told me what to do. The next day I went to see the terrible Zingarelli. His old servant let me in.

" 'What do you want, you scamp?' asked Zingarelli.

" 'Maestro,' I replied, 'I am awfully sorry for all that I have done; I will never leave the conservatory again by that grilled door; I am going to apply myself more than ever.'

" 'If I did not fear spoiling the prettiest basso voice that I have ever heard I would put you in the dark room on bread and water for two weeks, you varlet!'

" 'Maestro,' I began again, 'I am going to be the model of the whole school; *credete a me;* but I want to ask a favor. If anyone asks to have me sing somewhere, refuse. Please say that you cannot allow it.'

" 'And who the devil would ask for a bad lot like you? Did I ever let you leave the conservatory? Do you wish to mock me? Get out, get out!' he cried, looking for a soft spot to give me a kick; 'or bread and water, and the dark room!'

"An hour later Signor Giovannone calls on the Director.

" 'I have come to ask you to let me make my fortune,' he says to him. 'Let me have Geronimo; let him sing at my theatre, and this winter I can marry my daughter off.'

" 'What do you want with this scamp?' replied Zingarelli. 'No, you can't have him; and, besides, even if I should consent, he would never leave the conservatory; he just swore to me he would not.'

" 'If it is not of his own accord that he is doing this,' Giovannone replied, drawing the contract out of his pocket, 'why, *carta canta!* here is his signature!'

"Zingarelli, then mad as fury, glues himself to the bell. 'Drive Geronimo out of the conservatory,' he cries, boiling over with rage.

"They drive me out, and I leave, laughing to split my sides. The same evening I sang the air of Moltiplico. Punch, you know, wants to get married, and he counts on his fingers all the things he needs for housekeeping, and he gets mixed up in his calculations."

"Oh, please, monsieur, sing it for us," said Madame de Rênal.

Geronimo sang, and all laughed until the tears came into their eyes. Signor Geronimo did not retire until two o'clock in the morning, leaving the family perfectly charmed with his lively, pleasing manner.

The next day M. and Madame de Rênal gave him letters of introduction which he would find useful.

"And so, everything by finesse," thought Julien. "Here is Signor Geronimo, who is going to London, with an income of sixty thousand francs! Without the acuteness of the San-Carlino Director, his divine voice would not have been known nor admired ten years later. Indeed, I would rather be a Geronimo than a de Rênal; he is not honored so much in society, but he has not the extreme pleasure of being present at auctions like to-day, and lives a gay life."

Julien was astonished at the fact that the weeks he had passed at Verrières in M. de Rênal's house were such a period of happiness for him. He had been disgusted only, or gloomy, at the dinners that were given to him. In that solitary house could he not read, write, think, without being disturbed? He had not been drawn from his lofty thoughts every moment by the cruel necessity of watching the movements of a sordid soul, to match it with cleverness and hypocrisy.

"I could be so happy, and it would all be so easy. I could marry Elisa or become Fouqué's partner. The traveller, after climbing a steep mountain, rests himself at the top, and finds pleasure in repose; but would he be happy if he were compelled always to rest?"

Madame de Rênal's mind was passing through some peculiar phases. In spite of her resolutions, she had told Julien the entire affair about the auction. "He will make me forget every vow I make," she sighed. Yet she would have sacrificed her life without hesitation to save her husband if she saw him in peril. Hers was one of those noble, romantic souls that experience not only remorse, but believe themselves criminal in seeing the possibility of a good act and not doing it. Yet there were days when she could not dispel the image of the great delight she would have if, becoming a widow all at once, she were to marry Julien. He loved her children more than their father did. In spite of his stern justice, he was adored by them. She felt that if she married Julien it would be necessary to leave Vergy, where everything was so endeared to her, and she saw herself living in Paris, continuing the admirable education of her boys. She herself and her children and Julien would be so happy.

Strange effect of a nineteenth century marriage! Marital relations bring it about so that love, if it precedes marriage, surely perishes after it. Yet a philosopher would say that it is because there is nothing to occupy the mind that leads to all the ennui, and that it is really only those dry souls among women that are not disposed to love. Such philosophical reflection would excuse Madame de Rênal, but there was no pardon for her in Verrières. The entire town was busy talking about her love affair. And that autumn life for the little town was therefore less dull than usual.

But autumn passed very quickly, and all had to leave Vergy. The good people of Verrières began to be indignant at the fact that their severe criticisms were making such a slight impression on M. de Rênal. In less than a week some grave persons showed it was their painful duty to hint in well-measured terms, of course, at the gravest suspicions.

M. Valenod had placed Elisa in a noble family where there were five other women. Elisa, fearing that she would not find a place for the winter, had not asked of that family more than two-thirds of what she received at the Mayor's house. She also had the excellent idea of continuing her confession with the old curate Chélan, and of telling him from time to time the details of Julien's love affair.

The day after his arrival, at six o'clock in the morning, abbé Chélan sent for Julien.

"I do not ask of you," he said to him, "I pray you, I beseech you to leave for the seminary at Besançon or for the place with your friend Fouqué, who is always ready to do well by you, within three days. I have seen to everything; it is all arranged; but you must leave, and not come back to Verrières for a year."

Julien did not answer. He was thinking if his dignity should not be offended by the arrangements Chélan made, who, after all, was not his father.

"To-morrow, at this hour, I shall have the honor of seeing you again," he said at length to the curate.

M. Chélan, who wished to finish the matter all at once with the young man, spoke then quite at length. Standing in his most humble attitude, Julien did not open his mouth.

He left soon afterwards to tell Madame de Rênal of his great plight. On her side, her husband had just spoken to her with a good deal of candor. His innate weakness of character, aggravated even more by the fortune coming from Besançon, had decided him to look upon her as perfectly innocent. He had just told her of the queer opinion that was almost publicly expressed in Verrières. The public was wrong; it was all only a sign of envy; but, really, what should he do?

For a moment Madame de Rênal had the illusion that Julien would accept M. Valenod's offer and remain in Verrières. But she was not the simple, timid woman of the year before; her fatal passion, her remorse, had enlightened her. She was indeed grieved to find, while listening to her husband, that a separation of some sort would be absolutely indispensable. "Away from me Julien is again with his ambitions and his projects; it is all natural to a young man who has nothing. And I, I am so rich, and yet my wealth is useless to me now! He will forget me. With his fine disposition he will be loved, and he will love in return. Oh, misery! But why should I complain? Heaven is just. I have not had the strength to remove my guilt, and judgment for the time being is suspended. I could have won over Elisa with money; nothing would have been easier. I did not take the trouble to think for a moment; my thoughts of loving him absorbed all my time; I am lost!"

Julien was struck with one thing in telling her of his proposed departure. There was no selfish objection made, though she tried hard to restrain her tears.

"We must be firm, my dear," she said, cutting off a lock of his hair. "I do not know what I am going to do, but if I die, promise me that you will never forget my children; far or near, try to make good men of them. If there is another revolution, all the nobles will be killed, and their father will emigrate. Look over my little family—give me your hand? There, good-by, my dear. This is the last time we shall be together. With this great sacrifice I hope I shall have the courage to think of my good name again."

Julien was in despair. The simplicity of her farewell was touching.

"No, I will not say good-by to you like that. I will go. Everybody wants me to, and you as well as the rest. But three days after I leave I will be back here at night."

Madame de Rênal's demeanor changed. Julien loved her then, since of his own accord he asid he would be back! Her grief changed straightway to the greatest joy. All became easy to her now. The certainty of seeing him again removed all that was heart-rending to her in these last moments. Madame de Rênal's bearing, like her face, became noble, firm, calm.

M. de Rênal returned soon; he was beside himself with rage. He spoke of the anonymous letter he received two months before.

"I am going to take it over to the Casino to show everybody how infamous this Valenod is, whom I have taken out of the gutter to make him one of the richest men in Verrières! I am going to give him a public insult. I will fight a duel with him. Oh, it is too much!"

"I could then be a widow—good Lord!" thought Madame de Rênal, but almost at the same instant: "If I don't prevent this duel, which I certainly can do, I shall be murdering my husband!"

Never had she managed his vanity with such address. In less than two hours she had made him realize, by using arguments which he could not refute, that such a procedure would be showing more friendliness than ever to M. Valenod. She further urged that it would be advisable to take Elisa back to the house. Madame de Rênal had need of courage to decide taking that girl, who was the cause of all her trouble, into the house again; but the idea came from Julien.

At length, after two or three attempts, M. de Rênal came to the conclusion that Julien should become the tutor of M. Valenod's children in response to public opinion. It was evidently to Julien's interest to accept the Director's offer, but M. de Rênal thought that it would comport more with his own dignity if Julien left Verrières only to enter the Besançon or Dijon Seminary. But what decision should he arrive at? M. de Rênal, seeing an immediate pecuniary sacrifice, was in greater despair than his wife. As for her, she was in the same attitude of mind as a man who, weary of life, had taken a dose of stramonium. It was a matter of indifference to her; she took no interest in it any more. It was just as if Louis XIV should say again that fine mot: *"Quand j'étais roi."*

The next day, early in the morning, M. de Rênal received a most insulting anonymous letter, full of the vilest calumnies. It was the work, no doubt, of some envious subaltern. The letter again led him to the idea of fighting a duel with M. Valenod, fresh courage inciting him to immediate action. Walking out alone, he went to get his pistols, which he proceeded to load.

"Well," he said to himself, "if the régime of Napoleon came again in vogue I should not care in the least. I have some good letters in my drawer that give me sufficient warrant."

Madame de Rênal was frightened by her husband's determined attitude. She told him with bitterness what it would be if she became a widow—an idea which she tried in vain to suppress. She took him aside, and for several hours spoke to him in vain; the anonymous letter still rankling in him. At last she succeeded so far as to decide him to give Valenod only a slap and to give Julien six hundred francs for his expenses at the Seminary. M. de Rênal, cursing a thousand times the day when he took the tutor into his house, did not mention again the anonymous letter.

He consoled himself somewhat with this thought, which he did not express to his wife: he might adroitly work on the romantic ideas of the young man, with the help of the little sum, to induce him to refuse M. Valenod's offer.

Madame de Rênal in vain argued with Julien that, considering the sacrifice he would make in not accepting the position of eight hundred francs a year offered him publicly by the Director, he might honorably accept the gift, but Julien kept on saying:

"I have never had the idea for a moment of accepting that offer; you have accustomed me too much to refined living; the coarseness of those people would kill me."

Cruel necessity, however, with its iron hand, made Julien's will pliant. His pride suggested to him the farce of accepting the Mayor's gift as a loan, and of giving him a five-year note, at interest.

Madame de Rênal still had those few thousand francs hidden in the little hollow in the mountain. She tremblingly offered it to him, knowing only too well that it would be angrily refused.

"Do you want," replied Julien, "to make the thought of our love abominable?"

And so Julien left Verrières. M. de Rênal was now perfectly happy.

At the moment when the money was to be paid over, the sacrifice on the Mayor's part seemed so great to Julien, that the latter absolutely refused. M. de Rênal embraced him, tears streaming from his eyes. Upon Julien's request for a letter of recommendation, he could not express himself enthusiastically enough in exalting Julien's conduct. Our hero had saved up five louis, and thought of asking Fouqué for a like amount. He was very much moved, indeed; but hardly a league from Verrières, where he left so much love behind, he was thinking only of the joy he would have in seeing a capital.

During the three days following, Madame de Rênal lived as in a dream; her life was bearable, for there was still that meeting with Julien to be looked forward to. She counted the hours, the minutes. Finally, on the night of the third day, she heard the signal that had been agreed upon. After overcoming a thousand perils Julien was before her.

She could think only of one thing—that this was her last sight of him. Far from responding to his caresses, she remained almost lifeless. If she forced herself to say that she loved him, it was with an awkward, constrained air. Nothing relieved her from the cruel idea of a final separation.

The incredulous Julien thought for a moment that he had already been forgotten. His words, which were indeed cruel to her, were received only with tears that flowed silently down her cheeks as she gave him convulsive pressures of the hand.

"But, how can I believe you?" replied Julien to the indifferent protestations of his friend. "You would show a hundred times more feeling to Madame Derville, who is only an acquaintance of yours."

Madame de Rênal, petrified, did not know what to answer. "It is impossible to be more unhappy—I hope I shall die—I feel my heart is breaking." Such were the longest answers he could obtain.

When daylight made his departure necessary, Madame de Rênal's tears ceased all at once. She saw him tie the knotted cord to the window without saying a word to him, without giving him a kiss. In vain Julien said to her:

"You have now come to the point that you have so long desired; you can live now without remorse. When your children are the least indisposed, you need no longer think that they are in the grave."

"I am so sorry that you could not kiss Stanislaus," she replied, tremulously.

Julien was profoundly moved in the end by the embraces from this woman who was as cold as death; he could not think of anything else for many leagues. His heart was rent in twain; and, before crossing the mountain, he kept looking back as long as he could see the steeple in Verrières.

Chapter 24

A Capital

Que de bruit, que de gens affairés! que d'idées
pour l'avenir dans une tête de vingt ans! quelle
distraction pour l'amour!

—BARNAVE

EVENTUALLY he saw the white walls beyond the distant mountain; it was the citadel of Besançon.

"What a difference," he said, sighing, "if I could come into this fine city as a sub-lieutenant of one of these regiments of the post."

Besançon is not only one of the prettiest cities in France, but it abounds in brave and intelligent men. Julien, however, was only a little peasant, without any means of approaching distinguished personages. He had received from Fouqué a bourgeois suit, and in that costume he crossed the drawbridge. Having studied the history of the siege of 1674, he wished, before settling himself in the seminary, to see the ramparts of the citadel. Two or three times he came very near being arrested by the sentinels; he was walking in the part prohibited from trespassing by the military authorities, because it produced hay to the value of some twelve or fifteen francs a year. The height of the walls, the depth of the ditches, the formidable looking cannon made a great impression on him. Then walking on the boulevard he passed a café. He stopped, filled with admiration. In vain he read the word "Café" in large characters over the two immense doors; he could not believe his eyes. Making a final effort to overcome his timidity, he entered. The room was thirty or forty feet long, with a ceiling at least twenty feet high. The day was one of enchantment for him. Two games of billiards were going on, the waiters calling out the points. The players were running around the billiard table, pushing away the spectators, tobacco smoke enveloping all in a blue haze. The great stature of the men, their broad shoulders, their heavy walk, their immense long whiskers and their long coats, all attracted Julien's attention. These noble sons of ancient Bisontium never talked, but shouted. They affected, too, a military air, and Julien was lost in admiration. He was thinking of the

151

attractiveness and magnificence of such a great capital as Besançon. He could not summon enough courage to ask for coffee of one of those proud-looking gentlemen who were calling off the points. But the young lady at the cash drawer had remarked the charming face of the young country boy, who, three feet away from the stove, with his little bundle under his arm, was looking at the white plaster bust of the King. This tall, well-formed young woman, dressed suitably for a café, had already asked twice in a very soft voice, so that it could not be heard by anybody but Julien:

"Monsieur? monsieur?"

Julien encountered large, soft, blue eyes, and saw that it was to him they were directed.

He approached the pretty girl's desk as promptly as if he were marching against an enemy. In his quick movement his parcel fell down. What pity this young provincial would inspire in the young collegians in Paris, who, at fifteen years of age, know so well how to enter a café! But these young men, so self-possessed at fifteen, are blasé at eighteen. The shyness that is to be found in the provinces disappears sometimes, too; and then it is exchanged for most ardent desire. In approaching this pretty young girl, who had deigned to speak to him, he would have to tell her the truth, Julien thought. He was becoming bolder in proportion as his timidity decreased.

"Madame, I am here in Besançon for the first time in my life; I should like to have, and I will pay for them, some coffee and rolls."

The girl smiled a little and then blushed. She was afraid for this handsome little fellow when the chaffing attention of the billiard players would be attracted to him; he would then be frightened and never return.

"Come here near me," she said, showing him a marble-topped table almost hidden by the large mahogany desk that projected into the hall.

The young lady leaned over the desk, displaying a superb figure. Julien noticed it, his ideas rapidly undergoing a change. The pretty girl then brought him a cup, some sugar, and a roll. She did not wish to call a waiter for the coffee, knowing that on the waiter's arrival her little tête-à-tête with Julien would be at an end.

Julien thought of this lively, blond beauty, and silently communed with the memories of a former time. The passion of which he had then been the object banished all his timidity now. The pretty girl in an instant read it in Julien's face.

"The smoke makes you cough; come here at eight o'clock to-morrow for breakfast, then I shall be entirely alone."

"What is your name?" asked Julien, with a winning smile.

"Amanda Binet."

"Can I send you in an hour a little package just like this?"

The pretty Amanda reflected a minute. "I am watched. What you ask might compromise me; but I will write my address on a card which you can place on your bundle, and then you can send it to me all right."

"I am called Julien Sorel," said the young man; "I have neither relatives nor friends in Besançon."

"Ah! I see," she replied, gayly. "Are you going to attend the Law School?"

"No," answered Julien; "they have sent me to the seminary."

The greatest disappointment was betrayed in Amanada's face; she called a waiter, having evidently regained her courage. The waiter poured the coffee out for Julien without looking at him.

Amanda was busy for a while at the counter; Julien feeling proud of having talked to her. Some dispute arose at the billiard table, and the cries and shouts of the players echoing through the vast hall were quite astonishing to Julien. Amanda was seemingly lost in reverie.

"If you wish, mademoiselle," he said to her, boldly, "I can say I am your cousin." His confident air pleased Amanda.

"Oh, he can't be a ninny," she thought. She quickly agreed to his proposal without looking at him, for she saw some one approaching the counter.

"I am from Genlis, near Dijon; say that you are also from Genlis, and my mother's cousin."

"I'll not forget," he answered.

"Every Thursday in summer, at five o'clock, the seminarians pass this café."

"If you are thinking of me when I should pass, hold some violets in your hand, will you?"

Amanda looked at him with eyes wide open. Julien was no longer brave, but rash. However, he blushed considerably when he said:

"I feel that I love you passionately."

"Talk lower," she said, looking frightened.

Julien was only recalling the phrases of a little book, "Nouvelle Héloïse," he had found at Vergy. His memory did not fail him. For ten minutes he kept on reciting to the ravished Amanda from "Nouvelle Héloïse." And he was glorying in his courage, when, all at once, the young woman gave him a look that nearly froze him.

One of her admirers had appeared at the door of the café, and was swaggeringly approaching the board, shoulders foremost. He gave Julien a long stare. At once the latter's high-flown imagination was filled with the thought of a duel. He turned pale. Pushing away his cup, he assumed a bold look and gazed back at his rival in defiance. While the latter was familiarly pouring himself out a glass of whiskey, Amanda, with a look, ordered Julien to lower his eyes. He obeyed; and for two minutes he remained immovable in his seat, pale, resolute, thinking only of what was going to happen. He was, indeed, prepared for anything at that moment.

His rival was astonished at Julien's eyes. Swallowing his glass of whiskey at one draught, he exchanged a word with Amanda, stuck both his hands in the pockets of his long overcoat, and walked towards the billiard table in a bullying fashion, all the time looking at Julien sideways. The latter was almost bursting with anger; but he did not know how to issue a challenge. He put down his little bundle, and, with a dandified air, walked towards the billiard table.

In vain prudence told him, "With a duel on your hands immediately on arriving at Besançon your ecclesiastical career is at an end."

"Oh, what is the difference?" he argued then. "It must never be said that I submitted to insult."

Amanda observed his courage, which was in such pleasing contrast with his unobtrusiveness, and in a trice she preferred him to the tall young man in the overcoat. She rose, and apparently seeing only what was passing in the street, walked to where Julien was standing, near the billiard table.

"Be careful how you look at that man; he is my brother-in-law."

"What do I care? He stared at me."

"You want to make me unhappy? Of course, he looked at you. I told him that you were a relative of my mother, and that you had just come from Genlis. He is from Franche-Comté and has never passed Dole, on the way to Bourgogne. So you can say what you like; you need not be afraid of anything."

Julien still hesitated.

She added very quickly, the imagination of a cash girl helping her with an abundance of fiction:

"Of course, he stared at you; but it was just when he asked

me who you were. He is a man that's good natured with everybody; he didn't mean to insult you."

Julien looked at this so-called brother-in-law. He saw him
buy a cue and heard him shout fiercely:

"It's my turn, now!"

He himself passed quickly in front of mademoiselle Amanda,
towards the billiard table. Amanda seized him by the arm.

"You pay me first," she said to him.

"That's so," thought Julien; "she was afraid I would go out
without paying."

Amanda was so flustered that she became red in the face.
She returned the money to him stealthily as soon as she could,
saying to him in a low tone:

"Leave the café at once or I won't love you!—but I *do* love
you—there!"

Julien left, but very reluctantly.

"Is it not my duty," he was saying to himself, "to stare back
at that tall fellow?"

This uncertainty kept him on the boulevard for more than
an hour. He was watching for the man to leave, but, as he did
not appear, Julien went away. He had been in Besançon only
a few hours, and one scruple had already been overcome. The
old surgeon, in spite of his gout, had given him a few lessons
in fencing; that was all Julien could rely on in his present
warlike mood. This fact, however, would not have disconcerted
him if he had known of any other way of provoking a quarrel
except by giving a blow. If it had come to fisticuffs, his rival,
enormous man that he was, would have made short work of
him.

"For a poor devil like me, without money or friends, there's
no great difference between a seminary and a jail; I must put
my clothes in some hotel, where I can again put on my black
suit. If I ever get to leave the seminary for a while, I could then
see mademoiselle Amanda again in these clothes."

It was not bad reasoning; but Julien, though he passed many
hotels, did not dare enter any. At last, as he passed the Hôtel
des Ambassadeurs, his restless eyes encountered those of a
large, florid-complexioned young woman. He came near and
told her his little tale.

"Certainly, my little abbé," said the hostess to him; "yes, I
will keep your clothes for you, and I will even brush them sometimes. Just at this time of the year it is not good to leave clothes
without attending to them." She took a key, conducting him

herself to a room, and asked him to make a memorandum of the contents of his bundle.

"Good Lord! you have a mighty fine face, monsieur abbé Sorel," said the large woman to him, when they came down into the kitchen. "I am going to give you a good dinner, and," she added, in a low voice, "it will cost you only twenty sous instead of fifty, which everybody else pays, for you have to be economical with your little purse."

"I have ten louis," replied Julien, proudly.

"Oh, good Lord!" cried the kind hostess alarmed, "don't talk so loud. There are lots of bad people in Besançon; they will steal it from you in less than a week; but be careful you don't go into any of those cafés; they are a bad lot."

"Is that so?" asked Julien thoughtfully.

"Don't you go to anybody but to me, I will give you your coffee. Sure, you'll always find a friend here and a good dinner, and it will cost you only twenty sous. Sit down; I'm going to wait on you myself."

"I can't eat now," said Julien to her, "I am too nervous; I am going to the seminary after I leave you."

The kind woman did not let him go until she had filled his pockets with good things. Finally Julien walked towards the awful seminary, the hostess standing in the doorway to show him the way.

Chapter 25

The Seminary

Three hundred thirty-six dinners at 83 centimes, three hundred thirty-six suppers at 38 centimes, chocolate to all those entitled to it; how much can be made on the contract?
—THE VALENOD OF BESANÇON

FROM a distance he saw the gilt cross over the door. He walked towards it slowly, feeling as if his knees would give way.

"There is that hell on earth which I shall never leave!"

After some time he summoned enough courage to ring the bell; the sound of the bell reverberated within, as in a sepulchre.

He waited ten minutes before a pale man, in black, came to open the door. Julien looked at him, but was forced to turn his eyes away, the doorkeeper's face was so terrifying. His greenish, flashing eyes roamed like a cat's; his immovable eyelids suggested not a trace of feeling; and over his protruding teeth opened thin, harsh lips. Yet that face did not betray any inherent cruelty, but rather that complete insensibility in which Julien read that whatever he might say would be received with indifference and contempt.

With much difficulty Julien raised his eyes to explain, in a voice which his trembling heart made unsteady, that he wished to speak to M. Pirard, the Director of the seminary. Without saying a word the man made him a sign to follow. They mounted two flights of stairs, guided by a wooden bannister, the rickety steps seeming about to tumble down. A little door, surmounted by one of those large black crosses that are to be seen in cemeteries, was opened, and the doorkeeper ushered him into a low, gloomy chamber, where the sole ornaments on the whitened walls were two large pictures, grimy with age. There Julien was left alone. He felt crushed, panic-stricken; tears would have been a relief to him. A silence as of death reigned throughout the house. In a quarter of an hour, that to him seemed a day, the ill-visaged doorkeeper appeared at a door opposite, and, without deigning to speak, gave him a sign to follow.

He entered a larger room than the first, but very dim. The

157

walls there also were whitewashed, but there was no furniture, save for a little pallet, two straw-bottomed chairs, and a little uncushioned armchair near the door. On the other side of the room, near the little window, where the light streamed through yellowish glass, a stern-looking man in a torn cassock was seated before a table, assorting numerous square cards and writing a few words on them as he laid them away. He did not seem to be aware of Julien's presence. Julien remained immovable in the middle of the room where the doorkeeper had left him. Ten minutes passed; the man in the shabby cassock kept on writing. Julien, from sheer terror, thought he would collapse, though a philosopher might have traced that state of mind only to the influence of unæsthetic surroundings on a soul that loved the beautiful.

The man who was writing finally raised his head. Julien did not at first notice this, but when he did see the face that was turned towards him he was struck with terror. The look was awful. Julien was dimly conscious of a long face covered with red spots, except at the forehead, which seemed to have the pallor of death. Between his red cheeks and white forehead gleamed two little black eyes that were enough to frighten the most courageous. The vast breadth of the forehead was accentuated by the thick hair, black as jet.

"Will you come near or not?" the man said, impatiently.

Julien advanced with less confidence than ever, trembling as he had never done in his life. He stopped three steps away from the little white table where the cards were.

"Nearer," mutterd the man.

Julien advanced, holding out his hand as if seeking support.

"Name?"

"Julien Sorel."

"You are very late," he said, turning again his terrible eyes on him.

Julien could not stand that look; still holding out his hand as if to steady himself, he fell full length on the floor.

The man rang the bell. Julien, though half-dead, then heard steps approaching, and felt himself raised, and seated in the little wooden armchair. The awful man was saying to the attendant:

"He fell apparently from vertigo; there's nothing the matter with him."

When Julien felt strong enough to raise his eyes, he saw that the red-faced man was writing again and the attendant had disappeared.

"I must be brave," said our hero, "and at all costs hide what I feel."

He felt a sharp pain in his heart. "If anything happens to me the Lord knows what they will think of me."

At length the man put down his pen and looked at Julien.

"Are you in a condition to answer?"

"Yes, monsieur," Julien replied, quickly.

"That is well." The black-robed man half arose, looking impatiently for a letter in his table drawer, which opened squeakingly. Having found it, he slowly sat down, looking again at Julien in a manner that bereft the latter of what little life was left in him.

"You are recommended by M. Chélan. He is the best curate of the diocese, the most virtuous man there, and my friend of thirty years' standing."

"Ah! it is M. Pirard to whom I have the honor of speaking," said Julien, faintly.

"Apparently," replied the Director of the seminary, eyeing him severely. There was a new light in those small eyes, which was followed by an involuntary movement of the muscles around the corners of the mouth; it was the physiognomy of a tiger that is tasting in advance the pleasure of devouring its prey.

"Chélan's letter is short," he said, as though talking to himself; *"intelligenti pauca;* in our fleeting time one cannot write too little." He read aloud:

"I recommend to you Julien Sorel of this parish, whom I baptized twenty years ago. He is the son of a rich carpenter who does not give him anything. Julien should prove a remarkable worker in the Lord's vineyard; memory, intelligence, even thought is not wanting. Will the inclination last? Is he sincere?"

"Sincere!" repeated abbé Pirard in an astonished manner, looking at Julien; but the abbé's look was a shade less inhuman. *"Sincere!"* he repeated under his breath, resuming the reading of the letter.

"I ask a stipend for Julien; he will deserve it when he takes his examinations. I have given him a touch of theology from that old and good theology of Bossuet, Arnault, and Fleury. If this young man does not suit you, send him back to me. The Director of the poor, whom you know very well, offers him eight hundred francs a year to be tutor for his children. My conscience is clear, thanks be to God! I am accustoming myself to the terrible blow. *Vale et me ama."*

Abbé Pirard softened his voice a little as he read the signature. He pronounced the name Chélan with a sigh.

"He is at peace with himself," he said. "Indeed, his virtue is deserving of that compensation; may God accord it to me!" He looked up and crossed himself.

After that pious movement Julien had less of that horror which froze his blood on entering the room.

"I have here three hundred and twenty-one aspirants to holy orders," said abbé Pirard at length, in a severe but not menacing tone. "Only seven or eight are recommended to me by such men as abbé Chélan, and so among the three hundred and twenty-one you will be the ninth; but my protection means neither fear nor favor; it means redoubled care and severity in repressing sin. Lock the door."

Julien made an effort to walk, and succeeded in not falling. He noticed that the little window near the door opened on a field; he looked at the trees; the sight made him feel good, as if he saw an old friend.

"Loquerisne linguam latinam?" ("Do you speak Latin?") said abbé Pirard, on his return.

"Ita, pater optime" ("Yes, excellent father"), replied Julien, himself again, though for the space of a half hour no man seemed less excellent to him than this M. Pirard. The conversation continued in Latin. The expression of the abbé's eyes softened somewhat, and Julien was regaining his sang-froid.

"How weak I am," the latter was thinking, "to allow myself to be imposed upon by such saintly appearances! That man may be just as much of a hypocrite as M. Maslon." Julien congratulated himself on having hidden nearly all his money in his boots.

Abbé Pirard eaxmined Julien in theology, and was surprised at his knowledge. His wonder increased when he asked him more particularly with reference to Holy Writ. But when he came to question him about Patristic doctrine, he noticed Julien was totally ignorant, even to the names of St. Jerome, St. Augustine, St. Bonaventure and St. Basil.

"Yes," thought abbé Pirard, "that is the fanatical tendency to Protestantism which I always remarked in Chélan—a too ready acquaintance with Holy Writ."

Julien had just said something, without being questioned on the subject, about the date of Genesis and the entire Pentateuch.

"Ever this interminable reasoning about Holy Writ!" thought abbé Pirard. "Though it is not *private judgment,* is it not the most liberal Protestantism? And, side by side with this imprudent knowledge, nothing about the Fathers to compensate for this tendency!"

But the Director's astonishment knew no bounds when Julien, asked about the authority of the Book, recited to him the entire book of M. de Maistre, in place of maxims about the ancient Gallican Church.

"Singular man, that Chélan!" thought abbé Pirard. "Did he teach him the Book just to show him how to mock at it?"

He tried in vain in his questioning of Julien to find out whether that young man believed seriously in M. de Maistre's doctrine. The young fellow mentioned only what his memory served.

From that moment Julien was perfectly at his ease; he felt that he was again master of himself. After a long examination it seemed to him that M. Pirard's severity was somewhat softened. Indeed, but for his stern principles, which for fifteen years he had adopted in his treatment of the theological students, the Director of the seminary would have embraced Julien for his learning's sake, the answers having been so ready, clear, and precise.

"There is a good, healthy mind," he thought to himself; "but *corpus debile*."

"Do you often fall like that?" he askde Julien in French, pointing with his finger to the floor.

"That was the first time in my life. The doorkeeper's face frightened me," Julien replied, stammering like a child.

Abbé Pirard almost smiled. "That is the effect of the world's vanity. You are accustomed, apparently, to smiling faces, veritable images of lies. Truth is stern, monsieur. Is not our work here on earth stern too? Your conscience must be aroused in order to be on guard against this weakness for the vanities of life."

"If you had not been recommended to me," continued abbé Pirard, resuming the Latin with evident pleasure, "if you had not been recommended to me by such a man as Chélan, I should have spoken to you in the same worldly tone to which, it seems, you have been accustomed. That pension which you ask, I should tell you, then, is the most difficult thing in the world to obtain; but abbé Chélan would indeed be paid but poorly if, after fifty-six years in the apostolic field, he could not command a pension at the seminary."

In conclusion abbé Pirard told Julien not to enter into any secret society or in the Congregation without his consent.

"I promise you on my word of honor," cried Julien, with all the frankness of a sincere man.

The seminary Director smiled then for the first time.

"Such a word is out of place here," he said; "it recalls too much the vain glory of the world where it is made an excuse for sin. You owe me obedience by virtue of the seventeenth paragraph of the Bull of Saint Pius V., *Unam Ecclesiam*. I am your superior ecclesiastic; in this house it is all obedience, my son. How much money have you?"

"There it is," thought Julien; "that is why he called me 'my dear son.' "

"Thirty-five francs, father."

"Make careful note of what you are going to do with this money; you will have to give an account."

The trying interview lasted three hours, then Julien was ordered to ring for the attendant.

"Take Julien Sorel to cell No. 103," said abbé Pirard to the man. To show some distinction, a separate room had been assigned to Julien.

"Take his bag there, too," he added.

Julien looked down and recognized his valise, which had been near him during the whole interview, though he had not noticed it.

As they came to No. 103, a little room eight feet square, on the top floor of the house, Julien noticed that it looked out on the ramparts, where the beautiful valley, separated from the city by the Doube, could plainly be seen.

"What a charming sight!" cried Julien, but he did not know what he was saying. The violent sensations that had rapidly succeeded one another in the little time he had been in Besançon had drained him of all emotion. Seating himself near the window, on the only chair in the cell, he fell into a profound slumber. He did not hear the supper bell nor vespers. It was as if he had been completely out of the world. With the first rays of the sun the next morning, he awoke to find himself lying on the floor.

Chapter 26

The World, or What the Rich Are Missing

> *Je suis seul sur la terre, personne ne daigne*
> *penser à moi. Tous ceux que je vois faire fortune*
> *ont une effronterie et une dureté de coeur que*
> *je ne me sens point. Ils me haïssent à cause de*
> *ma bonté facile. Ah! bientôt je mourrai, soit de*
> *faim, soit du malheur de voir les hommes si durs.*
> —YOUNG*

BRUSHING his coat hastily, he went down stairs. He was indeed late. An assistant proceeded to take him to task, but, instead of excusing himself, Julien only crossed his arms before him, saying, very contritely:

"Peccavi, pater optime." ("I have sinned, excellent father.")

It was a fine beginning. The clever ones among the seminarists saw that they had to deal with a man who was not in the rudiments of the art. Julien, though aware of being the object of general curiosity, showed himself only reserved and silent. Following well-known maxims, he considered his three hundred and twenty-one students enemies; but the most dangerous in his eyes was abbé Pirard.

After a few days Julien, obliged to choose a confessor, had a list presented to him.

"Good Lord! what do they take me for?" he said. "They think that I don't know what *talking means!*" He chose abbé Pirard.

Without a doubt it was a risky proceeding.

A young student, also a native of Verrières, who at the very start declared himself his friend, informed him that if he had chosen M. Castanède, the Vice-Director of the seminary, he would have been more prudent.

"Abbé Castanède is the enemy of Pirard, who is suspected of being a Jansenist," added the little seminarist, leaning towards him.

Everything our hero did at first, like choosing a confessor,

---

* Which Young this is, is not clear; nor is it clear that Stendhal did not simply invent the passage and the ironic author-credit—a type of invention to which he seems wont.

though it appeared clever to him, was evidently very stupid. His vivid imagination led him to regard his intentions as facts, and he already believed himself possessed of consummate hypocrisy. His self-delusion made him almost reproach himself for his too great success in the art.

"Oh, well, it is my only weapon. In another age it would be by daring acts in the face of an enemy that I should have been compelled to *earn my bread*." Julien's self-complacency gave him time to look about him. He saw everywhere the appearance of sterling virtue. Eight or ten seminarists were living in an odor of sanctity and were having visions like St. Thérèse, or like St. François, after receiving his marks in Mt. Vernia in the Apennines. But that was a great secret, and friends were hiding it. These poor, visionary boys were almost continually on the sick list. Another class of boys were combining a robust faith with indefatigable application, working themselves almost sick without accomplishing anything. Two or three were distinguished for real talent, one, especially, by name of Chazel; but Julien held aloof from them all. The rest of the three hundred and twenty-one students were only coarse fellows who were not quite sure that they understood the Latin which they repeated all day long. Almost all were sons of peasants who preferred earning their bread reciting Latin to following the plough.

All this made Julien confident of a brilliant career.

"Everywhere," he would say to himself, "intelligence is in demand when anything is to be done. Under Napoleon I should have been a sergeant; among these future curates I am going to be a grand vicar. All these poor devils," he would add, "grubbing from infancy, have lived, until they came here, on skimmed milk and black bread at home; they had meat five or six times a year. Like the Roman soldiers, who saw in war only a holiday, these boors are delighted with the delicacies of the seminary." Julien never read anything in their dull eyes except the pleasure of a satisfying dinner past or to come.

Such were the young men in the midst of whom he meant to distinguish himself. But what Julien did not know, and what, moreover, everyone took care not to tell him, was the fact that to be first in the different courses in catechism, ecclesiastical history, and in everything else that was taught at the seminary, was in the eyes of all only a resplendent crime. Ever since Voltaire's time, and the establishment of the government under the two Chambers, with its heretical implication of private judgment, by which the people acquired the vicious habit of doubting, the church of France has been regarding books as its real enemies. It is submission that is everything. Progress in studies, even in sacred studies, was therefore suspected—for a good reason. For what would prevent a superior mind from passing to the other side like Sieyès or Gregory? The trembling Church leans on the Pope as its only hope of safety. Only the Pope attempts to destroy the freedom of conscience. The only means at his command is to dazzle the world, sick with this malady, with his magnificent pomp and piety. When Julien half divined the truth, though everything in the seminary seemed to hide it, he became much disheartened. He had been working very hard and was making rapid progress in all his priestly studies. All that, now, he thought absurd, detaching from it all interest. There was nothing for him to do any more.

"I am going to be forgotten by the whole world," he thought. He did not know that M. Pirard had received and had thrown into the fire some letters in which was revealed the greatest passion, in spite of their conventional form. Remorse was in conflict with love.

"So much the better," abbé Pirard thought, "if it is not, after all, a depraved woman whom this young man has loved."

One day abbé Pirard opened a letter that was half effaced by tears; it was a last farewell.

"At last," the letter read, "Heaven has given me the grace to hate, not the author of my guilt, for I will always think of him the dearest thing on earth, but the guilt itself. The sacrifice is made, my dear—not without tears, as you see. The salvation of the beings I have brought into the world, whom you have loved so much, demands it. A just but terrible God will no longer avenge himself on them for their mother's guilt. My dear Julien, don't judge me hastily!"

The last part of the letter was scarcely legible. The address was given as Dijon; but the hope was expressed that Julien would not answer, or at least that he would use only such words as would be proper to a woman who had returned to virtue again.

Julien's melancholy, aggravated by the poor nourishment which the superintendent furnished the seminarians at eighty centimes per dinner, began to tell on his health.

One day Fouqué appeared in his room.

"Well, I have entered at last; I have been to Besançon five times to see you, but always that wooden face! I have stood there at the door waiting for you. Why in the devil don't you ever go out?"

"It is a penance that I have inflicted on myself."

"I see you are quite changed. I am glad to see you, anyhow. Two five-franc pieces just inform me that I was only a fool not to have put them in the right place at first."

The conversation between the two friends was interminable. Julien changed color when Fouqué said:

"By the way, do you know that the mother of your former pupils has taken to religion?" and he spoke in a light manner that went hard with the listener, whose soul was a prey to so many emotions.

"Yes, yes, she is awfully devout. Why, they say she is going to make a pilgrimage. But to the eternal shame of abbé Maslon, who has played spy so long on poor M. Chélan, Madame de Rênal would have nothing to do with him. She goes to confession either to Dijon or to Besançon."

"She comes to Besançon?" asked Julien, his brow flushing.

"Often enough," replied Fouqué.

"Have you a *Constitutionnel* with you?"

"What is that?" Fouqué replied.

"I ask you if you have some numbers of the *Constitutionnel* with you?" Julien retorted, in the most matter-of-fact tone imaginable. "They sell it for thirty centimes here."

"What, even in the seminary, Liberals!" Fouqué cried. "Poor France!" he added, in the soft, hypocritical tone of abbé Maslon.

This visit would have made a deep impression on our hero if that morning the little seminarist from Verrières had not said something to him, pointing to a great discovery. Since coming to the seminary Julien's conduct had been only one long stretch of hypocrisy. Nevertheless, he was disgusted with himself. What was of importance he did sagely enough, but he cared nothing about details; and in the seminary detail was everything. So it happened that already, in the first few days, he had passed among his comrades as an *esprit fort*. But now he was to be betrayed.

For, in their eyes, he had been convicted of an enormous crime; he *thought*, he *judged*, for *himself*, in place of blindly following authority. And, worse than all, abbé Pirard had not been of the least service to him; indeed, the abbé had not once spoken a word to him, except at confession, where he heard more than was told. It would, indeed, have been quite different if abbé Castanède had been chosen. But as soon as Julien became aware of his folly, he was no longer disconcerted. Realizing the full extent of his mistake, he began quickly to remove the distance with which he had kept himself from the students. Then it was that these had their full revenge. His advances were received with disdain, if not with derision. He was made to feel then that since his entrance into the seminary there had not been an hour, particularly during recreation, which did not count either for or against him, with respect to the number of enemies he was making, and that he had not won the friendship even of the sincerer collegians or those less coarse among them. The mistake he had to correct was indeed great, the task difficult. Henceforth Julien was continually on his guard. He was going to remodel his character completely.

The movements of his eyes, for example, gave him a good deal of concern—there was good reason for their being always lowered in such places. "How presumptuous I was in Verrières!" Julien said to himself. "I thought I was living then. I was there only preparing myself for life; here, at last, I am in the world, such as I will find to the very end, surrounded by real enemies. What a terrible task to be forever a hypocrite! It puts Hercules's labors in the shade. The Hercules of our modern times is Sextus V., who for fifteen years deceived, by his modesty, forty cardinals who believed him proud and overbearing in his youth.

"Knowledge is not anything here," he would say grimly. "Progress in dogma, in sacred history, counts for nothing except what show it would make. All that one can say of those things is just calculated to make a fool like me fall into a trap. Pshaw! my real strength consists in my rapid progress in tripping up these humbugs. Do they estimate study at its true worth, or do they judge like myself? How foolish I was! First in the class, which I always am, means only implacable enemies. Chazel, who knows a good deal more, always puts in his compositions something foolish, which brings him down to fiftieth in the class. If he gets the first place it is because of some oversight of his. Ah, a single word from Pirard would have been so much to me!"

From the moment that Julien became undeceived, the long devotional exercises, like *chapelet* five times a week, and the Canticles of the Sacred Heart, so horribly annoying to him at first, were now of the greatest interest to him. Reflecting seriously on himself, and seeking above all not to exaggerate his powers, Julien did not try at first, like the collegians who served as an example to the rest, to do something *significant* every moment; that is, to show a sort of Christian perfection. In the seminary the rule was to eat a boiled egg when progress in a devout life was to be announced.

Julien tried at first to arrive at the stage of *non culpa;* that is, the stage in which the arms, the eyes, and other parts of the body did not indicate anything of the world outside, but only a being absorbed by the idea of the hereafter—the pure, spiritual life.

Julien was continually finding written in chalk on the walls such phrases as this: "What are sixty years of trial compared with an eternity of light, or with an eternity of boiling oil in hell?" Indeed, he did not despise these legends; he understood that it was necessary to have them continually before one's eyes.

"What am I going to do all my life?" he would say to himself. "I am going to sell devout parishioners a place in heaven. How is that place visible, anyhow? By the difference between my exterior and that of a layman?"

After several months of application, Julien still had a habit of *thinking.* His way of looking, and of opening his mouth did not yet announce that implicit faith which is ready to believe and to suffer at the slightest word, so frequently seen in Italian convents and preserved so faithfully in the paintings of Guerchin.

It was with anger that Julien saw himself classed among the self-denying by the coarse peasant boys. On great holidays the students had sauerkraut and sausage. Julien's table companions observed that he was quite indifferent to that delicacy; that was his earliest crime. His comrades saw in it only a little foolish hypocrisy; nothing that he ever did made him more enemies.

"See that bourgeois," they would say, "playing the aristocrat, pretending to despise the best thing we have had for a long time, the proud fool! Damn!"

"Yes, the ignorance of these young peasants is an immense advantage to them," Julien would cry out when he was most discouraged. "When they arrived at the seminary, the professor did not have to rid them of that frightful number of worldly ideas which I brought with me and which they read in my face, whatever I may do."

Julien studied, with an attention that bordered on envy, the coarsest of the peasants who would arrive at the seminary, when their ratteen coat was removed to robe them in black; their education was limited only to an illimitable respect for "hard and flowing cash," as the phrase goes in Franche-Comté, when the heroic and saintly worship of money is to be expressed.

Happiness for these students, as for the heroes in Voltaire's novels, consisted in a good dinner. Julien discovered in most all of them an inherent respect for a man dressed in broadcloth.

"What is there to gain," they would repeat among themselves, "by complaining against a *gros?*"

That was a word used in the Jura valleys for a rich man. How they respected the richest of all, the government, may only be guessed. Not to smile respectfully at hearing the name of the prefect was equivalent, with Franche-Comté peasants, to an imprudence; now imprudence with these poor devils is promptly paid by refusal of bread.

After being almost choked by the disdain he had for them, Julien ended by pitying them. Did it not often happen that the parents of most of his colleagues, on returning to their homes on a winter night, found neither bread nor cabbage nor potatoes?

"What is there astonishing about it," Julien would say, "if in their eyes the happy man is first of all the one who has had a good dinner, and after him the man with a good coat? My fellow students are consistent; they see in the ecclesiastical calling a long continuation of happiness, a good dinner, and a warm suit in the winter."

Julien happened to overhear a young seminarist, who was gifted with an imagination, saying to his companion, "Why couldn't I become Pope like Sextus V., who tended pigs?"

"Oh, they make Popes only of Italians," replied his friend. "But, really, they all draw their lot from among our number for positions of grand vicars or canons and bishops. M——— P———, the Bishop of Châlons, is a carpenter's son, and my father is a carpenter."

One day, during the dogma hour, abbé Pirard called Julien to him. The poor fellow was delighted to step out of the physical and moral atmosphere into which he had been plunged. Julien was again received in the manner that had frightened him so much on his coming to the seminary.

"Explain to me, sir, what is it that is written on this playing card," he said to him, with a look that was calculated to crush him. Julien read:

"Amanda Binet, Café de la Giraffe, before eight o'clock. Say that you are from Genlis—my mother's cousin."

Julien saw his great danger. Abbé Castanède's spies had stolen the card from him.

"The day I came here," he replied, looking at abbé Pirard's brow, the latter's eyes being too much for him, "I was in great perplexity. M. Chélan told me that I should find here a place full of informers and tell-tales, where spying and jealousy among fellow students are encouraged. Heaven has so decreed in order to show real life to young priests and to inspire them with proper disgust for the world and its pomp."

"And so you have fooled me with your fine phrases, haven't you?" replied the abbé furiously. "Little scoundrel!"

"At Verrières," Julien began again, coolly, "my brothers beat me whenever they had occasion to be jealous."

"Indeed, indeed!" cried M. Pirard, beside himself.

Without being in the least disconcerted, Julien continued:

"The day I arrived at Besançon, towards noon I was hungry and I entered a café; my heart was filled with repugnance for so profane a place, yet I thought that breakfast would cost me less there than at an inn. The lady who seemed to be the mistress of the place took an interest in me. 'Besançon is an awfully wicked place,' she told me, 'and I am in dread about you; but if anything happens to you, you can depend on me. Be sure to send for me, but before eight o'clock. If the officers of the seminary refuse to deliver the message, say that you are my cousin, coming from Genlis.' "

"All this is going to be verified," cried abbé Pirard, who, scarcely able to contain himself, was walking to and fro.

"Send him back to his cell."

The abbé followed Julien and then shut the door.

The latter immediately overhauled his grip, at the bottom of which he had hidden the fatal card. But nothing was missing, though there were signs of rummaging. And yet he had had his key about him all the time.

"What luck," Julien was saying to himself, "that I have never taken advantage of the permission to go out given to me so frequently by M. Castanède, and with such incomprehensible kindness! If I had been weak enough to change my clothes and to see the pretty Amanda, I should be lost now." As it was impossible to bring him to commit himself in connection with the clue they had, they had simply resorted to a calumny.

Two hours later the Director summoned him.

"You have not lied," he said to him, looking at him less severely than before; "but to have such an address about you is an imprudence of which you cannot appreciate the full gravity, unfortunate young man! In ten years perhaps you will see what trouble it will bring you."

Chapter 27

First Experience of Life

*Le temps présent, grand Dieu! c'est l'arche du
Seigneur. Malheur à qui y touche!*

—DIDEROT

THE READER will permit a brief account of Julien's life at this
time. Details, indeed, are not wanting, but his experiences at
the seminary might be a little too dark for the soft coloring
given in these pages. It may recall memories to men of the
present day that might mar every pleasure, even that of reading
a tale.

Julien succeeded rather indifferently in his hypocritical efforts. Occasionally he would be so disgusted with himself as to
become completely discouraged: he was not successful even
in base undertakings. The least help from without would have
been an inspiration to him, the difficulties being really not so
very great; but he was alone, like a bark in mid-ocean.

"And even if I should succeed," he would say to himself,
"to spend my whole life in such awful company, amid such
surroundings, it is terrible! With gluttons who think only of
the omelette which they are going to have for dinner; or with
Castanède, for whom no crime is black enough! Yes, there is
power, but at what price, good Lord! The will of man is mighty,
I find that everywhere; but is it powerful enough to overcome
such disgust? The work of great men was easy; whatever danger
they encountered was at least attractive. But who, except myself, knows the rottenness that is surrounding me?"

That was the most trying period in his life. He would have
been mad with delight if he could have enlisted in one of those
fine Besançon regiments. Oh, he might master the Latin, but
of what good would that be for a living? Yet that would be the
end of a career, he thought; the end of everything; as good as
death! That, in the main, tells the story of his miserable days.

"I was so often encouraged because I am so different from
the other young fellows," he would say. "Oh, well, I have lived
long enough to know that difference engenders hate"—a great
truth that came to him during one of his hardest days.

He had worked hard for a week to please one of the students

171

who was giving himself an air of sanctity. He was walking with him in the court, and was almost falling asleep over his companion's nonsense. All at once it began to thunder, and the saintly scholar cried out, repulsing him rudely:

"Here, each one for himself in this world! I don't want to be struck by lightning. Why, the Lord may rend you with a thunderbolt for a heretic like Voltaire!"

Angrily gritting his teeth, Julien cried out to himself, lifting up his eyes:

"Yes, I should deserve being punished by God if you put me to sleep in all this storm. Well, I am going to try and make a conquest of some other fool," he mused.

The hour for abbé Castanède's sacred history lesson came. Abbé Castanède that day taught the young peasants, who had been harassed by hard work and grinding poverty when they were at home, that that creature the government, which to them seemed so terrible, had no real or legitimate power except by virtue of what the vicegerent of God on earth chose to give it.

"Become worthy of the grace of the Pope by the sanctity of your lives, by your obedience; be an instrument in his hands," he said, "and you will arrive at a commanding position, removed from all control; a permanent position to which the government pays one-third and the faithful the rest."

After the lecture M. Castanède stopped for a while in the court.

"It speaks well for a curate when it can be said of him, 'The man is worth so much, the place is worth so much,' " he said to the gathered pupils. "I have known, yes, I have known of mountain parishes where the perquisites were worth more than a metropolitan curacy. There was a great deal of money, too, without counting the capons, the eggs, fresh butter, and a thousand other things. And there the curate is first in everything; not a banquet to which he is not invited."

Hardly had M. Castanède gone to his room, when the students broke up into groups; Julien, not being in any one of them, was left alone like a black sheep. He saw everywhere a coin tossed up in the air: if one of the seminarians could guess head or tail, his companions would immediately conclude that he would have one of the curacies with all the perquisites.

And then came stories. A certain young priest, hardly in his place a year, had given a rabbit to an old curate's servant, and had thereby obtained the privilege of calling on the vicar. A few months later, when the curate died, he was chosen his successor. Another one succeeded in having himself elected to a curacy in a large and wealthy city by dining with an old paralyzed curate and gracefully carving his meat for him. The seminarists, like young men in all professions, exaggerated the effect of these petty means, believing them etxraordinary.

"I must take part in these conversations," Julien said. "When they are not talking about good sausages and good curacies, they entertain themselves with a worldly view of ecclesiastical doctrine, with the dissensions between bishops and prefects, and between mayors and curates."

Julien saw, gradually looming up before him, a second God, more to be feared and more powerful than the other, the Pope. It was whispered, especially when M. Pirard was not near, that if the Pope did not take the trouble to appoint all the prefects and all the mayors in France, it was because he chose to leave it to the King of France when the latter was named the eldest son of the Church.

It was just at this time when Julien believed he sided with the book on the Pope by M. de Maistre. Indeed, he astonished his companions; but that, too, was a misfortune for him. He displeased them when he expressed their own opinions better than they did. Chélan had been as imprudent with Julien as with himself. After imparting to him the habit of thinking correctly and of discarding vain words, he had neglected to tell him that with a man of no influence such a habit is a crime. Julien's fluency of speech was another offence. His comrades only thought of him with horror; they called him Martin Luther, "just because he is so proud of his infernal logic," they would say.

Several young seminarists had the freshness of color that Julien did not possess; but he had white hands that revealed a certain element of refinement. In that institution into which chance had placed him that fact counted for little. The dirty boys with whom he had to live said that it was only an indication of loose manners.

But we fear of tiring the reader with the recital of our hero's miseries; such, for instance, as the habit the strongest fellows contracted of striking him from time to time. He was obliged to arm himself with a piece of iron, and to give evident signs that he was prepared to use it. Signs were, indeed, better in that place than words, where everything passed under the eyes of spies.

Chapter 28

A Procession

Tous les coeurs étaient émus. La présence de Dieu semblait descendue dans ces rues étroites et gothiques, tendues de toutes parts, et bien sablées par les soins des fidèles.

—YOUNG*

JULIEN in vain made himself humble and low. He was not successful—something he had not expected.

"Ah," he would say to himself, "all these professors are very fine, chosen perhaps from a thousand; how is it they don't admire my humility?"

One of them seemed to take him at his word and to make it appear as if he admired it; it was abbé Chas-Bernard, who had charge of the cathedral ceremonies, and who for fifteen years had been watching for a place in the canon. While waiting, he gave instructions in sacred oratory. In his unenlightened period that course was among those in which Julien almost always was first. Abbé Chas took occasion to manifest great friendship for him. After the hour one day, he took his arm and made the rounds of the garden with him.

"Where is he going?" Julien asked himself. Then for hours he heard the abbé speak of the ornaments in the cathedral. There were seventeen chasubles, besides mourning ornaments, and there were also great expectations from the old lady president Rubempré. This lady, who was ninety years of age, had kept for sixty-six years her wedding gown of fine Lyons material brocaded with gold.

"Imagine, young man," abbé Chas would say, stopping short, with eyes wide open, "imagine that that material is stiff with gold. It is generally believed in Besançon that by the lady president's will the cathedral treasury will be increased by more than ten chasubles, not to speak of four or five copes for the great holidays. I will even go farther," added abbé Chas, lowering his voice; "I have reason to think that she will also leave eight magnificent silver flambeaux which, it is said, have been

* See note, page 163.

bought in Italy by the Duke of Bourgogne, one of whose ancestors was the favorite minister of Charles the Bold.

"But what is this man driving at with all this stuff?" Julien thought; "all this adroit preliminary might last a century, and nothing is coming. I must be on my guard; he is sharper than all the rest. With them I can find out the secret well enough in about fifteen days; I see, though, that this man's ambition has been suffering for fifteen years."

One evening, while exercising with fencing, Julien was called to abbé Pirard.

"To-morrow," the abbé said, "will be the feast of Corpus Domini; abbé Chas-Bernard will want you to help him decorate the cathedral. Go and obey." But immediately abbé Pirard called him back, saying in a kindlier tone, "It is left to you now whether you will take advantage of the opportunity, while you are in town, of walking about."

"*In-cedo per ignes,*" said Julien to himself. ("There are enemies hiding.")

Early the next day Julien walked to the cathedral, with eyes on the ground. The sight of the streets and the activity which reigned all around him made him feel good. Everywhere people were standing in front of their houses to watch for the procession. The time that he had spent in the seminary seemed only a moment to him. His mind was now at Vergy and now with the pretty Amanda Binet, whom he might meet, the café being not very far away. He saw Chas-Bernard, from a distance, at the door of his dear cathedral; he was standing there jubilant and joyful. That day would be one of triumph for him.

"I have been expecting you, my dear son," he cried, when Julien was still at a distance. "Oh, you are indeed welcome! The labor for this day will be long and arduous. Let us fortify ourselves first with a little breakfast, then we shall have another at ten o'clock, during high Mass."

"I desire, monsieur," Julien replied, gravely, "not to be alone for an instant. Please observe," he added, pointing to the clock, "that I arrived here at one minute of five."

"Ah, those wicked boys in the seminary have frightened you, have they? You are right to be on your guard against them," said abbé Chas. "But is a road less beautiful because there are thorns by the wayside? Travellers pass on, leaving the prickly thorns to dry away. Now to work, my son, to the work before us!"

Abbé Chas was right in saying that the labor would be arduous. The day before there had been a large funeral in the cathedral, and nothing could be arranged then; in one morning, therefore, it was necessary to cover the three Gothic pillars with a sort of red damask to a height of thirty feet from the top. The Bishop had sent four upholsterers from Paris, but these men could not do all the work, and far from encouraging the Besançon men who assisted them, they merely jeered at them. Julien saw that he would have to mount the ladder himself, his agility serving him well. He took charge of the local upholsterers himself. Abbé Chas was enchanted when he saw him run up the ladder. When all the pillars were covered with the damask, five large bunches of feathers were yet to be placed on the great baldachin over the chief altar. A richly carved crown rested on eight columns of Italian marble, but to reach the centre of the baldachin, on top, it was necessary to walk along an old wooden cornice at a height of forty feet from the floor. The idea of walking on that cornice had almost spoiled the dashing gayety of the Paris upholsterers. They looked down from where they stood, as if measuring the risk they would run. In the end they refused to make the dangerous trip across. Julien took the feathers, and, running up the ladder, placed them in the form of a crown in the centre of the baldachin. As he stepped down the ladder abbé Chas pressed him in his arms.

"*Optime!*" cried the good priest. "Oh, I will surely tell it to Monseigneur."

The ten-o'clock breakfast was a very cheering one. Never had abbé Chas seen his church so pretty.

"My dear pupil," he cried to Julien, "my mother rents the chairs in this venerable basilica, so that I can say I have been nursed in this fine edifice. The Terror of Robespierre ruined us; but when I was eight years old I assisted at the Masses, and they fed me from the daily Mass. No one could fold a chasuble better than I; the lace was never torn. Since the reëstablishment of the Church under Napoleon, I have had the honor of directing everything in this venerable pile. Five times a year my eyes see it bedecked with all these beautiful hangings; but never has it been so resplendent, never has the damask been so beautifully draped around these magnificent pillars."

"At last he is going to tell me his secret," thought Julien; "now that he is talking about himself, he is going to open his heart."

But nothing imprudent was said by that man who was evidently in great exultation. And he had worked so hard!

"Well, it is all right," said Julien, "the good wine was not spared. What an example for me! But this is a feather in his cap!"—a phrase inherited from the army surgeon.

When the *Sanctus* of the Mass rang out, Julien wanted to throw a surplice over his shoulders and follow the Bishop in the procession.

"But the thieves, my dear, but the thieves!" cried abbé Chas, "you are not thinking about that? The procession is going to pass now; you and I will have to watch here. We shall, indeed, be fortunate if we miss only a couple of yards of this fine lace around the pillars; that, too, was a gift from Madame de Rubempré; it is from the famous count, an ancestor of hers; it is of pure gold, my dear," added the abbé, whispering in his ear, apparently very much excited; "nothing gilt about that. I put you in charge of the northern wing; do not leave it, do not go out. I myself will look out in the southern wing and the nave. Look sharp with those who are in the confessional; it is among them that the thieves are found, and they are just waiting for the moment when our backs are turned."

As he finished speaking it struck a quarter to twelve. The sound of the great bell reverberated within, the full, solemn peal moving Julien to his very depths. His imagination carried him far above the earth. The odor of incense, and the rose leaves scattered before the Holy Sacrament by little boys dressed like St. John, combined to bring him to a state of the highest exaltation.

The pealing of the bell should not have given Julien any other idea than that twenty men were working for fifty centimes, aided by fifteen or twenty other devoted men. He should have thought of the cords and of the clapper, and of the danger coming from the bell itself, which had once fallen down. He should have thought, also, of a way of diminishing the pay of the bell-ringers, or of paying them only with some indulgence or other that would leave the Church's purse intact. But in place of such sage reflections, Julien's soul, exalted by the magnificent sound, was wandering in ethereal heights. Never would he make a good priest or a wise administrator! Souls that are thus moved are fit only for artists. Here was seen Julien's defect. Fifty other seminarists, necessarily made attentive to the realities of life by popular hatred and Jacobinism, would have thought only of the wages of the bell-ringers if they had heard the sound from the belfry. They would have examined with the genius of Barême if the degree of emotion it caused was worth the money the ringers received. If Julien had thought of the material interest of the cathedral, his imagination would have gone farther still, perhaps to a saving of forty francs to the vestry, and also another additional expense of twenty-five centimes.

While the procession was making its way through Besançon, stopping now and then before the brilliant stands erected by the authorities, a solemn silence reigned in the church. The light was dim; an agreeable freshness prevailed; it was still fragrant with the perfume of flowers and incense. The silence, the profound solitude, the depth of the nave made Julien's reverie inexpressibly sweet. He had no fear of being troubled by the abbé Chas, who was busy in another part of the church. Though charged to stand guard in the northern wing, his soul was in reality far away from his material surroundings. He was the more free to muse, since in the confessional he could see only a few pious women. His eye really looked without seeing. But his attention was somehow drawn to two richly-dressed women, one kneeling before the confessional, the other seated on a chair. He did not at first notice them particularly, yet, whether it was from a feeling of duty or from the elegant attire of the women, he remarked that there was no priest in the confessional. It was singular, he thought, that these handsome women were not kneeling before the altar if they were devout, or were not in front of some balcony if they were not.

"How becoming that gown is! What grace!" He walked slower, to observe them to better advantage. The one who was in the confessional happened to turn her head slightly on hearing the noise of Julien's footsteps echoing amid all the silence. All at once she gave a cry and fell in a dead faint.

In fainting she fell backwards. As her friend, who was near her, sprang to her assistance, Julien saw, over the shoulders of the fainting woman, a twisted pearl necklace he knew quite well. The woman was Madame de Rênal.

The lady who was trying to raise the fainting woman's head, so as to prevent her from falling at full length, was Madame Derville. Julien, beside himself, sprang forward. Madame de Rênal's fall would perhaps have caused also that of her friend if Julien had not assisted them both. Madame de Rênal's pale face, in which there was not a sign of consciousness, rested on his shoulder. He helped Madame Derville place a chair for the support of her head, he himself remaining on his knees.

Madame Derville, turning around, recognized him.

"Go away, monsieur, go away," she said, with great anger. "Why, it is you above all she must not see; the sight of you will be terrible to her. She was so happy before you came! Your actions are vile! Go, if you have any shame left."

It was all said with such authority that Julien, weakened by his emotion, immediately retreated.

"Oh, she has always hated me," he said to himself, thinking of Madame Derville.

Presently the nasal chanting of the foremost priest in the procession was heard in the church. Abbé Chas-Bernard called to Julien several times, but without making himself heard. At length he took Julien by the arm, as the latter, almost unconscious, was leaning against a pillar. The abbé wished to present him to the Bishop.

"You don't feel well, my son," said the abbé to him, observing his paleness, "and you are hardly in a condition to walk; you have worked too hard." The abbé gave him his arm.

"Come, sit down on this bench here, before the holy water, behind me; I will hide you." They were then opposite the wide entrance. "Now, don't get nervous, we have twenty minutes before Monseigneur comes. When he appears, I will help you rise, for I am strong, even if I am old."

But when the Bishop passed, Julien trembled so that abbé Chas renounced the idea of presenting him.

"Oh, you need not feel it so much, I will find another occasion."

In the evening he brought to the seminary chapel ten pounds of candles, saved, as he said, through Julien's care, by the promptness with which he had extinguished them. The poor boy, nearly extinguished himself, was incapable of a single idea from the time he had seen Madame de Rênal.

Chapter 29

The First Step Forward

*Il a connu son siècle, il a connu son département,
et il est riche.*

—LE PRECURSEUR

JULIEN had not yet emerged from the profound sadness into which he had been plunged in the cathedral, when, one morning, the severe abbé Pirard summoned him.

"I see that abbé Chas-Bernard has written me something good about you. On the whole, I am quite satisfied with your conduct; you are extremely imprudent and heedless without appearing so, yet your heart has so far been good and even generous; the mind is superior. Altogether, I see in you a spark which must not be neglected.

"After fifteen years of labor I am about to leave this institution. My crime consists in having permitted the students private judgment, and in not having protected more strongly the secret society of which you spoke to me in confession. Before leaving I wish to do something for you; I intended doing it two months ago—for you deserve it—if it had not been for that charge concerning the address of Amanda Binet that was found with you. I appoint you Reader in the Old and New Testament."

Julien, full of gratitude, was inclined at first to fall on his knees to offer his thanks to God; but, yielding to a more natural impulse, he approached abbé Pirard, and taking his hand, carried it to his lips.

"What! what is that?" remonstrated the Director, sternly. But Julien's eyes told more than his action.

Abbé Pirard looked at him with astonishment, as a man would naturally do who for fifteen years had lost every trace of emotion. Yet this attention moved the Director; his voice changed.

"Ah, well, my son, I feel attached to you; Heaven knows it is against my own will. I should be just, and have neither hatred nor love for anybody. Your career is a difficult one. I see in you something that is offensive to the rabble. Jealousy and calumny will pursue you. In whatever place Providence will place you, those about you will never look at you but to hate you; and if they pretend to love you, it will be only the more surely to betray you. For that there is only one remedy—trust in God alone, who has given you, in order to punish you for your presumption, this necessity of being despised. Let your conduct be pure; it is the only resource that I see for you. If you hold to the truth without faltering, sooner or later your enemies will be confounded."

It had been so long since Julien had heard a friendly voice that the weakness may be pardoned him—he burst into tears. Abbé Pirard opened his arms; it was a happy moment for both.

Julien was wild with joy. That promotion was the first he had obtained; the advantages were very great. To understand them it must be known that he had been condemned to pass entire months without a moment to himself, and always in immediate contact with young men who were, for the most part, unbearable. Their shouts alone were enough to grate on a delicate organization like his. The noisy merriment of the well-fed and well-clothed peasants was expressed with all the force of iron lungs. Now Julien would dine alone, nearly an hour after the students. He also received a key to the garden, where he could walk about at times when it was deserted.

To his great astonishment, Julien saw that he was being less hated. In fact, he had expected even greater hatred than before. His secret desire that he should not be spoken to, which, nevertheless, was so evident, and which made so many enemies for him, was no longer taken as a mark of hauteur. In the eyes of these coarse fellows who surounded him, it was now only a feeling suitable to his dignity, and so the hatred and scorn visibly diminished, especially among the youngest students, now his pupils, whom he had always treated with much politeness. Indeed, he even came to have partisans; it became rude to call him "Martin Luther."

But why should his friends or his enemies be mentioned? All that is bad enough, and the worse for being true. Yet these are the only teachers of morals the people have, and without these what would become of them? Can a newspaper take the place of a curate?

From the time Julien received his appointment, the Director of the seminary never spoke to him but in the presence of witnesses. There was in this proceeding as much prudence for master as for pupil; but it was above all a *test*. The invariable principle of the severe Jansenist was: if a man has any worth, put an obstacle in the way of all his desires and undertakings;

if he is of the proper stuff, he will know well enough how to overcome all difficulties.

As it was then the hunting season, Fouqué took it into his head to send a deer and a boar to Julien, making it appear as coming from the latter's family. The dead animals were placed in the passage between the kitchen and the refectory, where all the students saw them as they went to dinner. The animals were a great curiosity. The boar, dead as it was, frightened the youngest boys, though they took delight in feeling its tusks. Nothing else was talked of for a week. This gift, which placed Julien's family in a social rank that was to be respected, dealt a mortal blow to envy; he was now placed in unquestionable superiority. Chazel and the most distinguished scholars now made advances, and were almost ready to complain to him for not having informed them of his parents' wealth, and for thus allowing them to be lacking in respect for people of means.

The annual recruiting took place, from which Julien was exempt by virtue of being a theological student. That circumstance moved him profoundly.

"There is another opportunity gone in which, twenty years ago, a heroic career would have opened for me."

As he was walking in the seminary garden he heard some masons who were working on the wall talking among themselves.

"So we must go now; there is the new draft."

"In the time of the *other one*, sure, a mason could get to be an officer, and even a general."

"See what it's now; it is only tramps who are going; veryone who has anything stays at home."

"He who is born miserable stays miserable; that's all."

"Say, is it so, what they say, that the *other one* is dead?" asked a third mason.

"It is the *gros* who say that, that is all. The *other* frightens them."

"Oh, what a difference! How everything went in his time! And to say that he was betrayed by his marshals! Could they be traitors?"

The conversation consoled Julien somewhat. In withdrawing, he said, with a sigh:

"The only king the nation holds in grateful memory!"

During the examination which then took place, Julien acquitted himself brilliantly. He saw that Chazel himself was doing his best. The first day the examiners, who had been nominated by the famous vicar de Frilaire, were somewhat put out to find on their list, either as first or second, this Julien Sorel, who had been designated as the Benjamin of abbé Pirard. There were bets in the seminary that in the general examination Julien would be first, an honor that would carry with it a dinner with the Bishop. But at the conclusion of the session, when the questions turned on the Church Fathers, a cunning examiner, after asking Julien about St. Jerome and his passion for Cicero, began to speak of Horace and Virgil and other profane writers. At the suggestion of his fellow students, Julien had committed to memory a large number of quotations from these authors. Carried away by his success, he forgot where he was, and was reciting and paraphrasing, under the examiner's leading, several odes of Horace. After allowing him thus to enmesh himself for about twenty minutes, the examiner all at once changed countenance and severely rebuked him for having spent his time in profane studies and for harboring useless, if not wicked, ideas.

"I am a fool, monsieur, and you are right," said Julien, modestly, perceiving the stratagem of which he was the victim.

That trick was indeed considered ignoble, even at the seminary; yet that did not prevent abbé de Frilaire, the man who skilfully organized the Congregation in Besançon, and whose despatches to Paris made judges, prefects, and even general officers of the garrison tremble, from putting the number 198 opposite Julien's name. He had the pleasure of thus mortifying his enemy, the Jansenist Pirard.

For ten years his main effort had been directed toward having the latter removed from the seminary. The abbé, following the line of conduct which he had indicated to Julien, was sincere, pious, devoted to his duties; but Heaven in its wrath had given him a bilious temperament, so that he felt deeply every slight, every insult, without being ever able to forget. He would have handed in his resignation long before, but he believed himself useful in the position where Providence had placed him. "I am preventing the progress of Jesuitism and idolatry," he would say.

Before the examination, he had not spoken to Julien for nearly two weeks. On receiving the official notice announcing the result of the examination, he saw 198 placed opposite the name of his pupil, whom he looked upon as the glory of the institution. The only consolation for this stern person now was to concentrate on Julien more attention than usual. It was with joy that he discovered in the latter neither anger, nor a desire for revenge, nor discouragement.

A few weeks afterwards Julien trembled on receiving a letter bearing the postmark of Paris.

"So," he thought, "Madame de Rênal is remembering her promises."

A gentleman signing his name Paul Sorel, saying he was a relative of his, sent him a draft for five hundred francs. It was added that if Julien continued his studies with success in the Latin authors, a like sum would be sent to him every year.

"It is she. Yes, it is her kindness," said Julien, softened. "She wants to console me, but why is there not a word of feeling in it?"

He was deceived about the letter. Madame de Rênal, guided by Madame Derville, had given herself wholly to penitence. Yet, in spite of herself, she often thought of that singular personage who had crossed her path and had changed her entire existence. But she refrained stoutly from writing to him.

If we spoke the language of the seminary, we might recognize a miracle in this gift of five hundred francs, and say that it was M. de Frilaire himself whom Heaven had directed to make a gift to Julien. Twelve years before, abbé de Frilaire had arrived in Besançon with a little slender satchel, which, if the story is true, represented all his worldly goods. Now he was one of the richest men in the Department. In the course of his prosperous career he had bought the half of a piece of property of which the other half had fallen to M. de la Mole. From this grew out a lawsuit between the two men.

In spite of his brilliant position in Paris and his connection with the Court, Marquis de la Mole felt it dangerous to struggle at Besançon with a Grand Vicar who was reputed to make and unmake prefects. In place of petitioning for an indemnity of fifty thousand francs to be put in some way on the budget, and of giving up to abbé de Frilaire this dragging lawsuit about that sum, the Marquis remained stubborn, believing he was in the right—a good reason!

Now, if the question is not out of place, what judge is there who has not a son or a cousin to push forward in the world? In order to enlighten the blindest, it must be said that a week after he received the first judgment, abbé de Frilaire took the Bishop's carriage, and, in his own person, brought the Cross of the Legion of Honor to his attorney. M. de la Mole, somewhat put out of countenance by his opponent's address, and feeling that his attorneys were weakening, asked abbé Chélan for advice, who put him in correspondence with M. Pirard.

The relations between these two had lasted for some years

previous to our history. Abbé Pirard entered with great zest into the affair. After frequent interviews with the Marquis's attorneys, and a diligent study of the case, he came to the conclusion that it possessed merit, and he became openly the solicitor of the Marquis de la Mole, as against the all-powerful Grand Vicar. The latter was outraged at such boldness, and on the part of a little Jansenist at that.

"See! see what nobility is, that pretends to be so powerful!" abbé de Frilaire would say to his friends. "Why, M. de la Mole has not sent a miserable little Cross to his agents at Besançon, and allows them even to be ousted. And yet they write me that this noble peer does not let a week pass without displaying his cordon bleu in the salon of the Lord High Chancellor." In spite of abbé Pirard's activity and M. de la Mole's intimate connection with the Ministers of Justice, and with the most important officials, all that was accomplished after six years of vexation was that the lawsuit had not been lost.

In constant correspondence with abbé Pirard about this affair, into which entered so much passion, the Marquis came eventually to appreciate the abbé's sterling character. Gradually, though there was an immense social distance between the two, their correspondence took a personal, friendly turn. Abbé Pirard informed the Marquis that he was being compelled, through sheer insults, to resign. In the anger which the ignoble trick used against Julien awakened in him, he related the little story to the Marquis. This great lord was not avaricious. Unable to prevail upon abbé Pirard, urge as he might, to accept even a reimbursement for the postal expenses occasioned by the suit, he had sent five hundred francs to the favorite pupil. M. de la Mole himself wrote the letter—a fact that made the abbé reflect.

One day the latter received a little note, requesting him, as it was a pressing matter, to go, without delay, to an inn in a suburb of Besançon. There he found M. de la Mole's steward waiting for him.

"The Marquis has charged me to bring his carriage here. He hopes that after reading this letter you will decide to leave for Paris in four or five days. I will occupy myself, in the meantime, in inspecting the Marquis's lands in Franche-Comté. Then, on the day that you determine, we shall leave together for Paris."

The letter was very brief.

"Leave, my dear monsieur, all this provincial chicanery; come, breathe the calm air of Paris. I send you my carriage, and one who has orders to wait for four days for your decision.

I will wait for you myself at Paris until Tuesday. You need only say yes, on your part, monsieur, to accept one of the best curacies in the neighborhood of Paris. The richest among your future parishioners has never seen you, but he is more devoted to you than you think; it is the Marquis de la Mole."

No doubt the stern abbé Pirard loved the seminary, to which for fifteen years he had given every thought, even if it was peopled with enemies. M. de la Mole's letter was like the arrival of a surgeon charged with performing a painful but necessary operation, though his dismissal was indeed certain. He asked the steward to meet him in three days.

During the first forty-eight hours he was in a fever of uncertainty. At last he wrote M. de la Mole. A letter he wrote to the Bishop was a masterpiece of ecclesiastical style, but somewhat long. He had found it extremely difficult to form unobjectionable and respectful phrases. At the same time, that letter, destined to give a painful hour to M. de Frilaire, sitting opposite his patron, told in detail of his every annoyance, even to the little chicaneries which, though endured without complaint for a period of six years, had at last forced abbé Pirard to leave the diocese. They had stolen the wood from his woodhouse, he said; they had poisoned his dog, besides doing other disreputable things!

When the letter was finished, he had Julien called, though the latter, having retired at eight o'clock like the other students, was already asleep.

"Do you know where the Bishop lives?" he asked him in good Latin. "Take this letter to Monseigneur. I will not hide the fact from you that you are going into a pack of wolves; be all eyes and ears, but not a lie in your replies! Do not forget that the one who is going to ask you questions will find, perhaps, a real joy in knowing that he can injure you. I am indeed happy, my son, in letting you know this before leaving you; for I will not hide from you that the letter you hold is my resignation."

Julien was stupefied; for he loved M. Pirard. Prudence in vain told him: "After the departure of this good man the Sacred Heart party may humiliate me, if not drive me out." He could not give him a thought. But what embarrassed him most was that he wanted to frame a pretty speech, and was not equal to the occasion.

"Well, aren't you going?"

"From what they say, monsieur," replied Julien, timidly, "during your administration you have not laid anything by. I have six hundred francs—" tears compelled him to stop.

"That also will be noted," cried the ex-Director, coolly. "Go to the Bishop; it is late."

It happened that that night abbé de Frilaire did the honors in the Bishop's drawing-room, as Monseigneur himself was dining at the prefecture. It was to M. de Frilaire, whom he did not know, that Julien gave the letter. Julien was astonished to see the man boldly read the letter addressed to the Bishop. The vicar's fine face was expressive of pleasing surprise, yet also of great gravity. While he was reading, Julien, struck by the handsome features, was observing him closely. The face would have been much more dignified if it had not a conscious shrewdness in some features, that bordered almost on deceit. The long nose formed a perfectly straight line with the brow, giving to the profile the lines of a fox. The abbé, who seemed so occupied with M. Pirard's resignation, was attired with an elegance that pleased Julien, who had never seen anything like it in a priest.

Julien did not know until later what was abbé de Frilaire's forte. The latter knew how to amuse his Bishop, an able old man, who was more at home in Paris, and who regarded Besançon as a sort of exile. The Bishop's sight was very poor, and he was very fond of fish; abbé de Frilaire took out the bones whenever fish was served to Monseigneur.

Julien was silently gazing at the abbé, who was reading the resignation for the second time, when all at once the door opened, and a magnificently dressed lackey entered. Julien scarcely had time to turn towards the door when a little old man appeared, wearing the pectoral cross. Julien fell on his knee, and the Bishop, giving him a kindly smile, passed on. The handsome abbé followed the latter, and Julien remained alone in the salon to examine the pious magnificence at his leisure.

The Bishop of Besançon, with ability that remained unimpaired in spite of the Emigration, was seventy-five years of age, and was not at all worried as to the lease of another ten years.

"Who is that seminarian with the fine face whom I think I passed just now? Should they not, according to my rule, be in bed by this time?"

"This one is very much awake, I assure you, Monseigneur, and he brings good news; it is the resignation of the only Jansenist who remains in your diocese. This terrible abbé Pirard has at last understood what we mean."

"Ah, indeed," replied the Bishop, laughing. "I'll wager you cannot replace him by a man as good as he; and to show you how I value this man, I am going to invite him to dinner tomorrow."

The vicar wished to put in a word as to the choice of a successor, but the prelate, little disposed to talk business, replied: "Before taking in another, let's see something about this one. Call that student; truth is in the mouths of children."

Julien was called.

"I am going to be between two inquisitors," he thought. But never did he feel possessed of so much courage.

When he entered, two valets, better attired than Valenod himself, were unrobing Monseigneur. That prelate, before inviting M. Pirard, wished to question Julien about his studies. Happening to question him about dogma, he was greatly astonished. Soon he led up to the humanities, to Virgil, Horace, Cicero. "Those names," thought Julien, "cost me number 198. I have nothing to lose now; I am going to do my best." He succeeded. The prelate, an excellent humanist himself, was delighted.

At the dinner at the prefecture a highly distinguished young lady had recited the poem of the Madeleine. He was in the humor of talking of literature, and so forgot abbé Pirard, and all other affairs, in discussing with the seminarian whether Horace was rich or poor. The prelate recited several odes, but with one his memory was a little treacherous, and Julien forthwith modestly recited the entire ode. What astonished the Bishop more than anything else was that Julien did not leave off his conversational tone; he recited the twenty or thirty Latin lines as if he were speaking of an incident at the seminary. They spoke a long time about Virgil and Cicero, the prelate unable to refrain from passing a pretty compliment on the young student: "No one could have done better."

"Monseigneur," replied Julien, "your seminary can offer you one hundred and ninety-seven young men less unworthy of your high approbation."

"How is that?" asked the prelate, astonished at the number.

"I can prove, by official figures, what I have the honor of saying to Monseigneur. At the annual examination at the seminary, on the subjects that have given me Monseigneur's approval just now, I received the number 198."

"Ah, this is abbé Pirard's Benjamin," replied the Bishop, laughing, and looking at M. de Frilaire. "We should have expected that; it is fair play. Were you not awakened, my son, to be sent here?" he added, addressing Julien.

"Yes, Monseigneur. I have never been out alone from the seminary except once, to help abbé Chas-Bernard decorate the cathedral at the feast of Corpus Domini."

"Optime," said the Bishop. "So it was you who had the courage to place the bunches of feathers on the baldachin. They make me tremble every year; I am always afraid it will cost some man's life. My son, you will go very far; but I do not wish to arrest your career, which will be brilliant, by having you die of hunger," and he ordered some biscuits and Malaga wine to be brought, to which Julien did great honor; but more so abbé de Frilaire, who knew that his Bishop loved to see everyone eat with a good appetite.

The prelate, more and more pleased with the way the evening was passing, touched on ecclesiastical history. He saw that Julien was perfectly ignorant on that subject. The prelate passed to the moral condition of the Roman empire at the time of Constantine. That was the end of the paganism, accompanied then by so much restless doubt, which, in the nineteenth century, brings dismay to so many hearts. Monseigneur noticed that Julien did not even know the name of Tacitus.

"I am, indeed, very glad," said the Bishop, cheerily; "you relieve me of my embarrassment. For ten minutes I have been seeking a way of thanking you for the pleasant evening which you have given me, and, certainly, in a manner which was not expected. I was not looking for a doctor in a pupil at my seminary. Although the gift is not very canonical, I am going to give you a Tacitus." The prelate ordered eight handsomely bound volumes to be brought, and proceeded himself to write on the title page of the first volume a compliment in Latin, for the Bishop prided himself on his Latinity. He ended by saying, in a very serious tone, that contrasted sharply with the rest of the conversation: "Young man, if you are *discreet,* you shall one day have the best curacy in my diocese, and not a hundred leagues from my Episcopal Palace; but you must be discreet."

Julien, burdened with the volumes, left the Bishop as it struck midnight. Monseigneur had not said a word to him about abbé Pirard. Julien was most of all astonished at the Bishop's extreme politeness; he had no idea that such urbanity could be so gracefully united with such dignity. Julien was struck by the contrast he saw when he came to abbé Pirard, who was impatiently awaiting him.

"Quid tibi dixerunt?" he called out, loudly, as he saw him from a distance. ("What have they said to you?")

Julien had great difficulty in putting the Bishop's conversation into Latin.

"Speak French, and repeat Monseigneur's exact words, no more and no less," said the ex-Director of the seminary in his hardest and roughest tones. "What a strange gift on the part of a Bishop to a young seminarist!" he exclaimed, turning the leaves of the superb Tacitus, of which the gilt nearly took his breath away.

Two o'clock struck before he permitted his favorite pupil to withdraw to his own room, after receiving a full account of what had taken place.

"Let me have the first volume of your Tacitus, where the Bishop has written his compliment," he said to him. "This Latin epigram will be a thunderbolt for you in this house after I leave."

"Erit tibi, fili mi, successor meus tanquam leo quærens quem devoret." ("For you, my son, my successor will be like unto a raging lion seeking to devour.")

The next morning Julien perceived something strange in the manner in which his comrades spoke to him. It was more than reserved. "That," he thought, "is the effect of M. Pirard's resignation. It is all over the house that I pass for his favorite; I shall pay for that." There was, on the contrary, complete absence of hatred in the eyes that gazed on him in the corridors. "What can it mean?" he thought. "There must be some trap; I am going to be on my guard." Finally, the little Verrières student said to him with a smile:

"Cornelii Taciti opera omnia." ("The Complete Works of Tacitus.")

At that, everybody, even those who envied him, congratulated Julien, not only on the magnificent gift which he had received from Monseigneur, but also on the two hours' conversation with which he had been honored. Every little detail seemed to be known. From that moment he was no longer envied; everyone bowed and scraped to him.

Abbé Castanède, who the day before had treated him vilely, took him by the arm and invited him to breakfast.

Toward noon, abbé Pirard left his pupils, not without delivering an earnest address.

"Do you desire the honors of the world?" he said to them, "all social advantages, the pleasure of ruling, you who ridicule the laws and are insolent toward all? Or do you desire your eternal salvation? The only thing that you can do is to open your eyes and take your choice between the two roads."

Hardly had he left when the devotees of the Sacred Heart of Jesus trooped into the chapel to intone a Te Deum. No one at the seminary took the ex-Director's address seriously. "He is sour on account of his dismissal," was said on all sides. Not a single seminarian was kindly enough to believe in the voluntary resignation from a place which brought one into close relations with the rich merchants.

Abbé Pirard went to the prettiest suburb of Besançon, where, under the pretext of business, which he did not have, he intended to remain two days.

The Bishop had invited him to dinner, and, to please vicar de Frilaire, tried to spur him on to brilliancy. Dessert had been served, when there arrived from Paris the news that abbé Pirard had been elected to the magnificent curacy of N——, four leagues from the capital. The good prelate congratulated him sincerely on his good fortune. He saw a happy ending to the whole affair, which not only put him in very good humor, but gave him also the highest opinion of the abbé's ability. He gave him a certificate in magnificent Latin, imposing silence on abbé de Frilaire, who was about to remonstrate.

In the evening, Monseigneur displayed his admiration before the Marquise de Rubempré. That was a great piece of news for the upper circles of Besançon; everybody was guessing over the influence that had been used in abbé Pirard's behalf. Abbé Pirard was already seen as Bishop. The shrewdest, believing that M. de la Mole had become Minister, only tolerated that day the imperious airs abbé de Frilaire assumed in society.

The next day abbé Pirard was accompanied by a great crowd in the streets, the merchants even coming to the door of their stores when he went to ask about the Marquis's affairs. For the first time he had been received with politeness. The severe Jansenist, outraged by what he ascertained, consulted long with the attorneys he had chosen for the Marquis de la Mole, and left for Paris.

He had the weakness to tell the two or three friends who accompanied him to the carriage, the coat of arms of which they greatly admired, that, after having managed the affairs of the seminary for fifteen years, he left Besançon with savings amounting only to five hundred and twenty francs. His friends embraced him with tears, saying among themselves, "The good abbé might have spared himself that lie; it was, indeed, too ridiculous." The rabble, blinded by the love of money, could not comprehend that there could be such a man in the world as abbé Pirard, who had been forced for six years to struggle with Marie Alacoque, the Sacred Heart of Jesus, the Jesuits, and the Bishop.

Chapter 30

A Man with Ambition

There is left but one ennoblement, the title of Duke; Marquis is ridiculous, but the word 'Duke' makes people turn their heads.
—THE EDINBURGH REVIEW*

THE MARQUIS DE LA MOLE received abbé Pirard without any of those little formalities that are so polished, and yet can appear so condescending in a great lord. It would have been time lost, and the Marquis was so occupied with his large interests that he could not spare a moment. For six months he had been intriguing at once with the King and with the nation in behalf of a certain Minister, who, as a return, had made him duke. The Marquis had for many years asked in vain of his attorney in Besançon for a clear and precise statement of the lawsuit in Franche-Comté. How could the celebrated attorney explain if he did not understand it himself? But the little note the abbé handed to him explained everything.

"My dear abbé," said the Marquis to him, limiting to five minutes the exchange of personal courtesies, "my dear abbé, in the midst of my so-called prosperity, I have not the time to occupy myself seriously with two or three little affairs that are, however, of some importance—my family and my business. On the whole, I take good care of the fortunes of my house, and I have no reason to complain; I take care also of my pleasures, and that is above everything, at least in my eyes," he added, surprising a look of astonishment on abbé Pirard.

Though a man of a practical turn, the abbé was astounded at hearing an old man talk so frankly about his pleasures.

"Lawyers have died in my service," the Marquis continued; "one of them died day before yesterday of consumption; but for my business in general, would you believe me, monsieur, that for three years I have despaired of finding a man who, while he thinks he is writing for me, deigns to give the least attention to what he is doing? But all this is simply a preface.

"I esteem you, and I can say even, although I see you now for

* The note on page 163 also applies to this unidentifiable quote, given by Stendhal in French.

the first time, I admire you. Would you like to be my secretary at eight thousand francs, or, if you like, at double that amount? I will gain by it, I'll swear, and I will make it part of my business to keep that fine curacy for you until we agree to separate."

The abbé refused, but toward the end of the conversation the embarrassment in which he saw the Marquis placed gave him an idea.

"I left in the seminary a poor young man, who, if I am not mistaken, will have a very hard time of it. If he were not simply a cleric he would by this time be *in pace*. Just now the young man does not know anything except Latin and the Scriptures; but it is not at all improbable that some day he will show a great deal of talent both in preaching and in communal work. I don't know what he will do, but he has the sacred fire, and he will be heard from. I was thinking of recommending him to our Bishop, if there ever came one to us who would concern himself with his diocese."

"Where is this young man from?" asked the Marquis.

"He is said to be the son of a carpenter in our mountains; but I should think that he is rather the natural son of some rich man. I received an anonymous letter with a draft for five hundred francs for him."

"Oh, yes, that is Julien Sorel," said the Marquis.

"How do you know his name?" blushing over the directness of the question.

"That I will not tell you," replied the Marquis.

"Oh, well," said the abbé, "you can try him as a secretary; he is willing to work and is discreet. Anyhow, you can try him."

"Why not?" said the Marquis. "But is he one that would let his pockets be lined by the prefect or the chief of police, or by some other one who is playing spy on me? That would be an objection."

Assured by abbé Pirard, the Marquis took a thousand-franc note, saying, "Send this to Julien Sorel and have him come here."

"One can easily see," said abbé Pirard, "that you live in Paris; you cannot imagine the tyranny that chafes us provincials, especially if we happen to be priests not in good odor with the Jesuits. They will not let Julien Sorel go, and will invent most clever excuses; they will say he is sick, that the letter has been lost, and the like."

"I may take a letter from the Minister to the Bishop," said the Marquis.

"Oh, I was almost forgetting something," said the abbé. "The young man, although of lowly birth, is very proud, and will be of no use whatever if his pride is in the least wounded; you would send him away as a dolt."

"I like that," said the Marquis. "I will make him a companion to my son; will not that be all right?"

Soon afterwards Julien received a letter, written in strange handwriting, coming from Chalons. It contained an order on a Besançon merchant, with the request that he depart for Paris without delay. The letter was signed fictitiously, but, on opening it, Julien trembled; a leaf fell at his feet, the sign agreed upon between him and abbé Pirard.

Less than an hour afterwards Julien was called again to the Bishop, by whom he was received with paternal kindness. While reciting Horace to Monseigneur, the latter congratulated him on the great prospects awaiting him in Paris. He, on his part, with profuse thanks, was waiting for an explanation of it all. Julien could not guess anything; Monseigneur was so kind to him. One of the little priests at a word from the Bishop wrote to the Mayor, who hastened to bring the passport himself; but the traveller's name was left blank.

Before midnight Julien was at Fouqué's house, who was as much astonished as delighted over the future awaiting his friend. "That will wind up with you," said the Liberal elector, "with a place under government, which will oblige you now and then to be scandalized by the newspapers. It is through your shame that I will hear news of you. Remember, though, speaking financially, that to earn a hundred louis in a good concern where one is his own master is better than to receive four thousand francs under the government, even under King Solomon."

Julien saw in this only the narrow spirit of the country bourgeois. He was at last to step on the stage of great affairs. The pleasure of going to Paris, where he imagined there were so many clever, if hypocritical, men, who were quite as polished as the Bishop of Besançon, eclipsed everything in his eyes. He represented himself to his friend, however, as being without the liberty of choice after receiving the letter from abbé Pirard.

At noon the next day there arrived at Verrières the happiest young man alive, intent upon seeing Madame de Rênal. First he went to his friend, the good abbé Chélan, but was received somewhat coolly.

"Do you think you are under any obligations to me?" said M. Chélan, without responding to his salutation. "Come and take breakfast with me while they are getting another horse for you. You will leave Verrières without *seeing anybody*."

"To hear is to obey," replied Julien, with his seminary look, though it was no longer a question of theology or of good Latin.

Jumping on the horse, he rode for about a league, and entered a lonely little wood, where he hid himself. At sunset he mounted his horse again, and reached the house of a peasant who agreed to sell him a ladder and carry it for him to the little wood overlooking the Cours de la Fidélité in Verrières.

"Perhaps I've done wrong," said the peasant, taking leave of him; "but what is the difference? My ladder is sold, and at a profit, and I myself have sown wild oats."

The night was very dark. Towards one o'clock in the morning, Julien, carrying the ladder, entered Vergy. As soon as he could he reached the bed of the stream, about six feet deep, that wound around M. de Rênal's garden between two walls. Julien lightly mounted the ladder.

"What reception will the dogs give me, I wonder?" he thought; but the question immediately presented itself in reality. The dogs began to bark, and came leaping toward him; but he patted them, and they began licking his hands. Climbing from terrace to terrace, over the closed gates, he was quickly under the window of Madame de Rênal's sleeping-room, eight or ten feet above the ground.

There were the shutters with the little heart-shaped opening which Julien knew so well. To his disappointment the opening did not show that there was a light within.

"Good Lord!" he thought, "isn't the room occupied tonight by Madame de Rênal? Where is she sleeping? The family is at Vergy, for the dogs are here; but I may meet M. de Rênal in this room in the dark, or a stranger, and then what a scandal!"

The most prudent thing for him to do was to retire, but such a procedure was out of the question for Julien. "If there is a stranger in the room, I will save myself as best I can, leaving the ladder where it is. But if it is she, what reception is awaiting me? She has begun to repent, and is extremely devout, I have not the least doubt about that; but, anyhow, she has not forgotten everything, since she has written to me." Such reasoning decided him.

With a trembling hand, but yet resolved to see her or die, he threw little pebbles against the shutter. No answer. He rested the ladder against the window and struck the shutter with his hand, softly at first, then louder.

"In this darkness," thought Julien, "I could be shot." This idea reduced the enterprise to a question of mere bravado. "This room is occupied to-night," he thought, "and whatever woman is in the room she is awake now. I have nothing to fear from her; I must try only not to be heard by the people in the other rooms."

He descended, and, resting the ladder against the shutter, mounted again, this time passing his hand through the opening. To his great delight he found the fastening bar. He drew this out, and found that the shutter was not held by anything else, but yielded to his pulling.

"I must open it gradually and let her recognize my voice."

He opened the shutter wide enough to admit his head, and whispered: "It is a friend." He was assured that nothing disturbed the silence of the room, which was wrapped in darkness. It was a bad sign. "Look out for the pistol," he reflected; then, with his finger, he ventured to tap on the window pane. No answer. He gave louder taps. "If I have to break the window I am going to finish this."

As he was giving a loud knock, he thought he saw in the darkness a white form crossing the room. Indeed, there was no doubt he saw a white figure advancing slowly towards him. Then, all at once, he saw a cheek pressed against the glass right opposite his eyes. He drew back trembling, but the night was so dark that even then he was not certain if it was Madame de Rênal. He feared a cry of alarm. The dogs were running around then, and half yelping at the foot of the ladder.

"It is I," he said, louder; "a friend!" The white phantom disappeared.

"Please open. I must speak to you, I am so unhappy," and he knocked at the window as if he would break the glass.

With a little click the window fastener was removed. Then, opening it widely, he lightly leaped into the room. The white form retreated. He took hold of the arms; it was a woman. All his courageous ideas vanished. If it were she, what was she going to say? What was he to do now? When a little cry told him it was Madame de Rênal, he clasped her in his arms. She trembled, having scarcely any force to repulse him.

"Wretch! what are you doing here?" Her tremulous voice could hardly articulate those words. Julien saw that her anger was not assumed.

"I have come to see you after fourteen months of cruel separation."

"Go, leave me instantly. Oh, why has M. Chélan prevented

me from writing to you? I would then have avoided this horror."
She repulsed him rudely. "I have repented of my wickedness.
Heaven has deigned to open my eyes," she said, in a broken
voice. "Go, leave me!"

"After fourteen months of misery I will certainly not leave
you without speaking; I want to know all that you have done.
I have loved you enough to deserve some confidence; I want to
know everything."

Madame de Rênal, in spite of herself, felt in her heart the
imperiousness of his tone. Julien, who was pressing her in his
arms passionately, and was trying to overcome her efforts to
disengage herself, suddenly released her. That movement gave
Madame de Rênal some assurance.

"I want to push away the ladder," he said, "so that we may
not be compromised if a servant, awakened by the noise, should
go around the house."

"On the contrary, go!" she said, indignantly. "What do I
care for anyone! It is Heaven who sees all this, and will punish
me for it. You are deceived by the sentiments which I did have
for you, but which I have no longer. Do you hear, monsieur
Julien?"

He pushed away the ladder softly, so as not to make any
noise.

"Is your husband in town?" he asked her, not out of bravado,
but rather from habit.

"Don't talk to me, or I will call my husband. I am wicked
enough, as it is, not to have driven you out long before this.
Anyhow, I have pity on you," she said, trying to wound his
pride, a point on which she knew he was sensitive.

The refusal on her part to speak familiarly, the manner of
severing a tender relation on which he had counted so much,
made Julien now mad with love.

"What! is it possible that you do not love me any more?"
he said, in his most persuasive tone. She did not reply; she was
weeping bitterly; in truth she had not the strength to speak.

"So, I am completely forgotten by the only person I have
ever loved! Oh, what is life to me!" All his courage had departed when the danger of meeting a man had disappeared. He
was now moved only by love.

She wept a long time in silence. He took her hand, but she
tried to withdraw it; yet after a few nervous movements she
allowed it to remain in his. The darkness was profound, and
they were sitting on the bed. "How different it was fourteen

months ago," thought Julien, his tears falling fast; "and so absence surely destroys all human sentiment!"

"Please tell me what has happened to you," said Julien, a little embarrassed by the silence and by the broken sobs he heard.

"Oh, no doubt," replied Madame de Rênal, in a hard voice, in which there was something severe and reproachful, "my actions since your departure are known everywhere; you were so imprudent! When I was in despair, the worthy M. Chélan visited me. For a long time he tried in vain to obtain a confession from me. One day he had the idea of accompanying me to the church in Dijon where I made my first communion. He was the first to speak." Madame de Rênal was interrupted by her sobs.

"Oh, what shame! I confessed all! The good man was kind enough not to overwhelm me with reproach; he was as much affected as I was. Then every day I wrote you letters which I did not dare send; I put them away carefully, and when I was beside myself with misery, I shut myself in my room and re-read them. Finally, M. Chélan took them away from me. Some of them, more prudent than the rest, he sent to you, but you did not answer."

"I swear I have not received a single letter from you at the seminary."

"Good Lord! Who has intercepted them?"

"Imagine my suspense! Before seeing you in the cathedral I did not know whether you were still alive."

"God has been kind to me in making me understand how much I have sinned against Him, against my children, against my husband," replied Madame de Rênal; "but my husband never loved me with the love I imagined you had for me."

Julien fell into her arms, beside himself with joy; but Madame de Rênal repulsed him again, continuing, firmly:

"My venerable friend, M. Chélan, gave me to understand that in marrying M. de Rênal I had plighted to him all my affections, even those of which I was not aware, and which I had not experienced before our intimacy. Since the sacrifice of those letters, which were so dear to me, my life has been, if not happy, at least quiet. Do not be afraid; you can be a friend of mine, the best of my friends."

But Julien was covering her hands with kisses, and she knew he was still crying.

"Oh, don't cry, you make me unhappy. Now, you tell me what you have done." Julien could not speak.

"I want to know what sort of a life you led in the seminary," she repeated, "since you are going away from there."

Mechanically Julien spoke of the numerous intrigues and jealousies which he encountered at first, then of his tranquil life from the time he was made assistant professor. "It was then," he added, "after a long silence, which doubtless was destined to make me realize, what I see only too well now, that you do not love me any more, and that I am absolutely nothing to you"—Madame de Rênal pressed his hands—"it was then that you sent me the five hundred francs."

"Never," said Madame de Rênal.

"It was a letter postmarked at Paris and signed Paul Sorel, in order to avoid suspicion." They had a little conversation about the possible origin of the letter, and then gradually their manner changed. Without being aware of it both Madame de Rênal and Julien stopped talking formally. Something tender crept into their tone. Though they could not see each other for the darkness, their voices told everything.

Julien passed his arm around her waist, a movement full of danger. She tried to remove his arm, but he, with his usual cleverness, withdrew her attention from it by an interesting little account, and the position of the arm was forgotten. After conjectures about the sender of the letter with the five hundred francs, Julien resumed his recital. He became more self-composed in speaking to her of his past life, which, beside what was taking place at that moment, interested him but slightly. His attention was directed mainly to the manner in which his visit would end.

"Now you must go," she kept saying from time to time, speaking quickly.

"What a shame to show me the door!" he thought; "that will be enough to poison my whole life, and she will never write to me. Lord knows when I will come back here again." From that moment all that was pleasant in Julien's position disappeared.

Seated beside the woman he adored, and pressing her almost in his arms, there in the room where they had formerly been so happy, he saw that she was shedding tears; he felt, by the movement of her breast, that she was choking with sobs. Then, all at once, he became the cool strategist, calculating with as much sang-froid as when, in the seminary, he saw himself the butt of an awkward pleasantry on the part of his stronger comrades.

Julien lengthened his recital, and spoke of his unhappy life since his departure from Vergy.

"So," Madame de Rênal was saying to herself, "after a year's absence, deprived almost entirely of any remembrance of me, while I was forgetting him, he was only thinking of the happy days that he had spent in Vergy!" Her sobs redoubled.

Julien saw the effect of his speech, and understood that he must play his trump card. He began abruptly about the letter which he had just received from Paris.

"I have just taken leave of the Bishop."

"What! aren't you going back to Besançon? Are you going to leave here for good?"

"Yes," replied Julien, resolutely; "yes, I will leave this place where I am forgotten by the one whom I have loved best in all my life, and I will leave it never to see it again. I am going to Paris."

"You are going to Paris?" broke in Madame de Rênal, distractedly, her voice choked by sobs.

Julien had need of this encouragement. He was going to try something that might decide everything against him, and, before that exclamation, he did not know the effect it would produce; now he no longer hesitated. The fear of self-reproach resumed its empire over him, and he added, frigidly, as he rose:

"Yes, madame, I leave you forever; I trust you will be happy. Adieu!"

He made a few steps toward the window and had already opened it. Madame de Rênal sprang toward him and fell into his arms. And so, after three hours' bickering, he obtained all he so ardently desired. If it had come sooner, this return to their tender sentiments, this great love of theirs would have been something divine for Madame de Rênal. But obtained thus, with art, it was only a pleasure. Julien wished, absolutely, in spite of her remonstrances, to light the lamp.

"Do you want," he said to her, "that I should not have the least recollection of having seen you again? Shall the love which is now dwelling in your charming eyes remain lost to me, and shall the whiteness of this pretty hand remain invisible? Think of it! I am leaving you, perhaps for a long time, for a very long time."

Madame de Rênal could not refuse to respond to this idea that brought her again to tears; but dawn was beginning to outline the tree tops on the mountains to the east of Vergy.

Instead of departing, Julien, intoxicated with love, asked Madame de Rênal if he could spend the whole day hidden in her room, and if he could remain until the following night.

"And why not?" she answered. "This backsliding of mine

destroys all my self-respect and effects my everlasting wretchedness, anyhow!" and she pressed him to her breast. "My husband is not the same any more; he is suspicious; he thinks I have led him into this whole affair, and he is angry with me. But if he hears the slightest noise I am lost; he will drive me out like the fallen woman that I am."

"That is M. Chélan's phrase," said Julien. "You would not have spoken so to me before my cruel departure for the seminary. Then you loved me." Julien was rewarded for the sangfroid he put in his tone.

He saw the woman suddenly forgetting the risk she ran with her husband present in the house in thinking of the greater danger of seeing Julien doubt her affection. Daylight grew apace and lighted up the room. Julien again was jubilant with pride when he saw in his arms, and almost at his feet, that beautiful woman, the only one he had ever loved, who, a few hours before, had been held in check by her fear of God and by her idea of duty. Resolutions that had been strengthened by a year's constancy had to yield before his courage.

Soon they heard a noise in the house. Something of which she had not thought before came now to trouble Madame de Rênal.

"That spiteful Elisa is going to come into this room. What are you going to do with this ladder?" she asked him. "Where can we hide it? I am going to carry it to the woodshed!" she cried, all at once, joyfully.

"But you will have to pass the servant's room," replied Julien, astonished.

"I will leave the ladder in the hall, and I will call the servant to go on an errand for me."

"Think of something to say to him in case he notices the ladder in passing it in the hall."

"Yes, my darling," cried Madame de Rênal, covering him with kisses; "you must hide yourself right under the bed. Elisa might come in while I am out."

Julien was astounded at her sudden gayety. "And so," he thought, "the nearness of material danger, far from troubling her, makes her gay, because remorse has left her! What a superior woman! Ah, there is a heart in which it is glorious to reign!"

Madame de Rênal took up the ladder. It was indeed too heavy for her, and Julien came to her assistance. He admired that elegant figure, seemingly so frail, yet strong enough, if necessary, to carry the ladder without aid. She carried it quickly along the corridor on the second floor, where she laid it length-wise against the wall. She called the servant, and, in order to give him time to dress himself, she went to the dove-cot. Five minutes later, when she returned to the hall, the ladder was gone. What had become of it? If Julien had been outside of the house the danger would not have been so great; but at that moment, if her husband saw the ladder, it would be terrible.

Madame de Rênal ran everywhere; finally she discovered the ladder under the roof, where the servant had hidden it. That circumstance was singular, almost alarming.

"What is the difference what happens for the next twenty-four hours? But when Julien is gone, will not all this mean horror and remorse for me?" She had a vague idea of com-mitting suicide at some future time. Yet, after a separation which she had begun to think was eternal, he had come back to her, she saw him again, and what had he not done to show her how much he loved her!

In speaking of the incident to Julien, she said:

"What can I say to my husband if the servant tells him that he found a ladder?" She mused a while. "In twenty-four hours they will find the peasant who sold it to you," and she threw herself into Julien's arms, pressing him convulsively. "Oh, to die like this!" she cried, covering him with kisses; "but that is no reason why you should die of hunger," she added, smiling.

"Come! First I am going to hide you in Madame Derville's room; it is always kept locked."

She went to watch at the end of the hall while Julien ran through.

"Be careful about opening it if anybody knocks," she said, locking the door; "but it will only be the children playing."

"Let them go out into the garden under the window," said Julien, "so I may have the pleasure of seeing them; make them talk."

"Oh, yes, yes," cried Madame de Rênal, withdrawing.

She soon came back with oranges, biscuits, and a bottle of Malaga wine. Bread she had not been able to steal.

"What is your husband doing?" asked Julien.

"He is writing about some business connected with the farmers."

Eight o'clock struck; there was now a good deal of stir in the house. If Madame de Rênal was not seen, they would look for her all over the house; she was, therefore, obliged to leave him soon. She came back, despite all prudence, bringing him a cup of coffee, afraid he would die of hunger. After breakfast she succeeded in leading the children under the window of Madame Derville's room. He found them grown larger and looking a little different. It might have been, perhaps, that his ideas of them had changed. Madame de Rênal talked with them of Julien, the eldest speaking with a great deal of friendship for their former tutor, the youngest scarcely remembering him.

M. de Rênal did not go out that morning; he continually went around the house, busy with the farmers to whom he was selling his potatoes. Until dinner time Madame de Rênal had not a minute to give to her prisoner. When dinner was announced and served, she had the idea of stealing a plate of hot soup. As she noiselessly approached the door, carrying the plate, she found herself face to face with the servant who had hidden the ladder in the morning. He was then advancing quietly in the hall as if to listen; probably Julien was imprudently walking about. The servant retired a little confused.

Madame de Rênal entered Julien's room. When he saw her again, he trembled.

"You are afraid," she said to him. "Well, I—I would brave any danger without flinching; I am afraid of only one thing, that is when I will be alone after you leave," and she ran away.

"Ah," said Julien, admiringly, "remorse is the only danger before which that soul recoils."

In the evening she returned; M. de Rênal had gone to the Casino, his wife telling him she had a severe headache. Sending Elisa out on an errand, she retired to her room, and hastened to open it for Julien. She found that Julien was indeed famished. Madame de Rênal went down to the pantry to look for bread; and then Julien suddenly heard a cry. Madame de Rênal came back and told him that, coming into the pantry without a light, and feeling for the shelf where the bread was kept with her arms stretched out, she had touched a woman's arm. It was Elisa who had uttered the cry Julien heard.

"What was she doing there?"

"Oh, she was stealing sugar, or perhaps she was spying," said Madame de Rênal, with complete indifference. She had found a paté and a loaf.

"What have you there?" asked Julien, pointing to the pockets of her apron.

Madame de Rênal had forgotten that she had filled them with bread at dinner. Julien pressed her in his arms with more passion than ever. Never did she seem to him so beautiful. "Even at

Paris," he was saying to himself, confusedly, "I should not meet a finer character."

She had all the awkwardness of a woman little accustomed to such manœuvres. Yet she possessed the genuine courage of a person fearing only dangers of a higher order and far more terrible.

While Julien was devouring the food and his mistress was joking with him about the simplicity of the repast, the door of the room was suddenly shaken with great violence. It was M. de Rênal.

"Why have you locked yourself in?" he cried.

Julien had only time enough to slip under the sofa.

"What! you are all dressed?" said M. de Rênal, entering; "you are eating, and you have locked the door?"

Ordinarily, such a question, asked with conjugal indifference, would have disconcerted Madame de Rênal; but now she felt that her husband only had to lower his eyes to see Julien, seated as he was in the chair the latter had occupied a moment before, opposite the sofa, and the very danger of the situation gave her self-possession. The headache served as an excuse.

While telling her at length about the game of billiards he had won at the Casino, which had netted him nineteen francs, her husband cried out: "Why!"

She saw on a chair, three feet from them, Julien's hat. With increased self-possession she began to undress, and, passing quickly before her husband, threw her skirt on the chair on which the hat lay. M. de Rênal soon left her.

She begged Julien to commence again to tell her about his life at the seminary. "Yesterday I was not listening to you; I was only thinking, while you spoke, of summoning enough courage to send you away." She was the incarnation of imprudence and they talked very loud. At two o'clock in the morning they were interrupted by a violent blow against the door.

"Open right away, there are thieves in the house. Saint Jean found a ladder in the hall this morning."

"This is the end, now," said Madame de Rênal, throwing herself into Julien's arms; "he is going to kill us both. He knows there are no thieves in the house. I will die in your arms, happier in my death than I have ever been in my life!" She did not reply to her husband, who was getting angrier every moment; she only embraced Julien with greater passion.

"Save Stanislaus's mother!" he said to her, with a look of authority. "I am going to leap out of the window, into the yard, and escape through the garden. The dogs will recognize me.

Make a bundle of my clothes and throw it into the garden as soon as you can; in the meantime let him break in the door. Above all, no confession! I forbid you. It is better that he should be suspicious than certain."

"You will kill yourself jumping," was the only reply; it was her only concern.

She went to the window with him. Then, taking just enough time to hide his clothes, she opened the door to her husband, who was in a boiling rage. Looking all over the room and into the closet without saying a word, he disappeared. Julien's clothes were thrown out to him and he seized them, running quickly towards the other side of the garden on the river bank. As he was running he heard the whistle of a ball and at the same time the report of a gun.

"It is not M. de Rênal," he thought; "his aim is not as good as that."

As the dogs were running silently by his side, a second ball struck the paw of one of them, for the animal began to yelp with pain. Julien leaped over the terrace wall, and, running for fifty paces alongside of it, turned in another direction. He heard voices calling to him to halt, and distinctly saw the servant, his enemy, take aim again.

A farmer on the other side also took aim; but Julien had already reached the river bank, where he proceeded to dress himself.

An hour later he was a league away from Vergy, on the Genoa road. "If they have any suspicions," thought Julien, "they will look for me on the road to Paris."

BOOK II

Elle n'est pas jolie.
Elle n'a point de rouge.

—SAINTE-BEUVE

Chapter 1

The Pleasures of the Country

O rus quando ego te aspiciam!
——HORACE

"MONSIEUR IS, I suppose, expecting the Paris mail?" said the innkeeper to him where he stopped for breakfast.

"To-day's or to-morrow's, it makes no difference," replied Julien.

The mail coach arrived. There were two empty seats.

"Hello, 'tis you, my dear Falcoz," said a traveller who hailed from Geneva to another one climbing into the coach at the same time with Julien.

"I thought you were fixed for good in the neighborhood of Lyons," said Falcoz, "in a delicious little valley by the Rhone."

"Nicely fixed! I've just escaped."

"What! you escaping? You, Saint-Giraud, with that fine face of yours? You've done somehing bad, have you?" Falcoz replied, laughing.

"Pshaw! as you please! I am escaping from the abominable life a fellow leads in the provinces. I love the freshness of the woods and the rustic quiet, as you know. You frequently accused me of being romantic. I've never in my life wanted to hear anything about politics, and it's politics that drove me away."

"But what party do you belong to?"

"To no party; that's what's my ruin. Here's my political platform: I love music, I love painting, and a good book is an event for me. I am going on forty-four years. How long am I to live yet? Fifteen, twenty, thirty years at most. Oh, well! I believe that in thirty years the Ministers will be a little sharper, but as honest as ever! The history of England is my mirror for the future. Always a king trying to increase his power here; an ambitious deputy hungering for glory and a few hundred thousand francs like Mirabeau there; and so our rich provincials will never sleep well. They'll call that being "liberal," and "loving" the people. The hankering for a peerage or for a seat in the Privy Council is enough to spur on everybody. In the ship of state everybody wants to be captain because it pays well.

Isn't there the least bit of a place for a common passenger?"

"Well, well, it's natural for you to joke like that, with your disposition. Have the late elections chased you out of the province?"

"My misfortune dates back earlier. Four years ago I was forty, and I had five hundred thousand francs; now I am four years older, and, probably, I have fifty thousand francs less, which I have lost in the sale of my Monfleury château near the Rhone—a superb location! At Paris I was tired of the perpetual comedy of what you call the civilization of the nineteenth century. I was hungering for good fellowship and simplicity. So I buy myself a little piece of ground in the mountains near the Rhone—nothing prettier on earth! The vicar of the village and the neighborhood squires courted me for a space of six months. I gave them dinners, of course. I have left Paris, I tell them, in order not to talk nor hear anyone talk about politics. You can see it; I haven't subscribed to a single paper. The fewer letters the letter carrier brings me, the better. It was not the vicar's fault. Anyhow, I was asked for a thousand things. I wanted to give every year two or three hundred francs to the poor. But they asked donations for pious associations, for the St. Joseph, for the Virgin, and the rest. I refused, of course. Then they insulted me. I was foolish enough to take it seriously. I can't go out of a morning to enjoy the mountain scenery without finding something to take me out of my reveries and disagreeably recall me to man and his wickedness. At the processions of the Rogation, indeed, of which the song pleased me—I think it's a Greek melody—they didn't bless my fields, because the vicar said they belonged to an infidel. The cow of a pious old peasant woman dies. She says that it's because of the nearness of a pond belonging to me—an infidel, a Paris philosopher—and eight days after, I find my fish with their whites up, poisoned with lime. Treachery surrounds me in all forms. The Justice of the Peace, good man as he is, but fearful for his position always, decides against me. The rustic quiet becomes a snare and a delusion. Once abandoned by the vicar, who is chief of the Congregation in the village, and no longer supported by the retired captain—the chief of the Liberals— all fall away from me, even to the mason whom I have supported for a whole year, and to the wheelwright, who wants to sauce me when he tends to my wagons. Then in order to have some support and to win a few of my lawsuits, I become a Liberal; but, as you say, these devilish elections come, they ask me for my vote."

"For an unknown candidate?"

"Not at all; for a man I know only too well. I decline. Frightful imprudence! From that moment, with the Liberals also on my hands, my position becomes intolerable. I believe that if it had entered the vicar's head to accuse me of murdering my servant, there would have been twenty witnesses from both parties who would have sworn they saw me do it."

"You want to live in the country without indulging your neighbors, without even listening to their scandals? What idiocy!"

"Well, anyhow, it's all over; Monfleury is sold. I lose fifty thousand francs, true; but I am happy! I leave that hell of hypocrisy and chicanery. I am going to seek solitude and rustic quiet at the one place in France where they are still to be found —in a fourth story overlooking the Champs Elysées. And then I will deliberate, if I don't commence my political career there in the Roule quarter, in giving bread to the parish."

"All that wouldn't have happened under Bonaparte," said Falcoz, with anger and regret in his eyes.

"Well and good; but why wasn't he able to remain in his place—your Bonaparte? All that I'm undergoing now is his work!"

At this point Julien became more attentive. He had understood from the first that the Bonapartist Falcoz was the old school friend whom M. de Rênal had thrown over in 1816, and the philosopher Saint-Giraud was a brother of the Chief of Department in the prefecture of ____, who knew how to turn the houses of the Commune to good account.

"And all that your Bonaparte did," continued Saint-Giraud. "A harmless man of forty, inoffensive, too, with a fortune of five hundred thousand francs, can't settle in the provinces and enjoy peace; the priests and the nobility drive him out!"

"Oh, don't speak ill of him," cried Falcoz. "Never had France enjoyed such esteem in the eyes of the nations than during the thirteen years of his rule. Then there was something of glory in everything one did."

"Your emperor—what the devil!—" replied the forty-four-year-old gentleman, "was not great, except on the battlefield and when he restored the finances in 1802. But what does his conduct after that mean? With his chamberlains, his pomp, and his receptions at the Tuileries, he only gave a new edition of monarchical nonsense. It had been removed for a time, and a century or two might have passed without it. Only the nobles and the priests want to go back to the old régime, only they don't have the hand of iron with which to convince the public."

"Why, that's the language of the old pamphleteer!"

"Who is chasing me away from my property?" continued the pamphleteer, angrily. "The priests whom Napoleon recalled with his Concordat, and who are not treated as the state treats physicians, attorneys, astronomers, in whom it sees only citizens, without troubling itself about their means of earning a livelihood. Would there now be your insolent gentlemen if your Bonaparte had not made them barons and counts? No; that's old now. After the priests, it is these petty little country gentlemen who have been most overbearing to me and forced me to become a Liberal."

The conversation seemed to be interminable: it was a subject that was to occupy the attention of France for half a century. As Saint-Giraud kept on repeating that it was impossible to live in the provinces, Julien timidly mentioned the example of M. de Rênal.

"Well, young man, you're just right," cried Falcoz. "He became the hammer so as not to be the anvil, and a terrible hammer at that! But I see him hoodwinked by this Valenod. Do you know that fool? There's one for you! What will your M. de Rênal say when he finds himself removed one fine morning, and Valenod in his place?"

"He will remain alone with his crimes," said Saint-Giraud. "You are acquainted in Verrières, young man? Well, well, Bonaparte—confound him and his monarchical nonsense!—has made possible the de Rênals and the Chélans, who have led the way for the Valenods and the Maslons."

This conversation, with its pessimistic politics, astonished Julien, and drew his attention away, for a moment, from his voluptuous reveries.

He was not much impressed with the first sight of Paris, at a distance. His air-castles of the future were still in contrast with his recollection of the twenty-four hours that he had just spent at Verrières. He swore to himself never to abandon his friend's children, and to leave nothing unturned in order to protect them if the insolence of the priests produced a republic, together with persecution of the nobility. What would have happened on the night of his arrival at Verrières if, at the moment of placing the ladder against the window of Madame de Rênal's bedroom, he had found the room occupied by a stranger or by M. de Rênal? How delightful were the first two hours, when she was so eagerly desirous of seeing him, and when he was pleading his cause before her, seated by her side in the dark! A heart like

Julien's is pursued by such recollections for a lifetime. The rest of the interview was the same as in the first period of their love, fourteen months before.

Julien was aroused from his profound reverie by the stopping of the coach. They had just come on the postal premises, Rue J.-J. Rousseau.

"I want to go to Malmaison," he said to a cabman, who drew near.

"At this hour, monsieur? Why?"

"None of your business."

To Malmaison all real devotion turns. We shall not relate Julien's transports at Malmaison. He wept with emotion. Indeed, in spite of those new, white walls in the park? Yes, for Julien, as for posterity, nothing came between Arcole, St. Helena, and Malmaison.

As it was evening, Julien hesitated before it. He had strange notions of this place of "perdition." A great mistrust prevented him from admiring Paris as it was. He was touched only by the monuments left by his hero.

"Here I am in the centre of intrigue and hypocrisy. Here rule the protectors of the abbé de Frilaire."

On the evening of the third day, curiosity led him to the project of seeing everything before presenting himself to the abbé Pirard. The abbé tartly explained to him the mode of life he was to lead at M. de la Mole's house.

"Now, if in a few months you do not make yourself useful, you will return to the seminary, but in good grace. You will live with the Marquis, who is one of the great lords of France. You will be dressed in black, but as though in mourning, not like an ecclesiastic. I require that three times a week you will pursue your theological studies at the seminary where I will introduce you. Every day, at noon, you will present yourself at the library of the Marquis, who will employ you in writing letters on pending lawsuits and other affairs. The Marquis makes a note on the margin of every letter he receives, as to what sort of an answer it requires. I have represented that in three months you will be able to write replies in a way that he will be able to sign eight or nine out of a dozen that you will present for his signature. At eight o'clock at night you will put his desk in order, and then you will be at liberty."

"It may be," continued abbé Pirard, "that some old lady or some pleasant-voiced gentleman might show you some great advantages, or, more boldly, offer you a purse to show them the letters received by the Marquis."

"Well, monsieur?" cried Julien, reddening.

" 'Tis singular," said the abbé, with a bitter smile, "that, poor as you are, and after a year at the seminary, you still have virtuous indignation. You must have been exceedingly blind. Is that the force of blood?" said the abbé under his breath, as if speaking to himself.

"What is singular," he added, looking at Julien, "is that the Marquis knows you. I don't see how. He is going to give you, to start with, a hundred louis extra. He is a man who is all caprice; that is his failing. He will have some puerilities with you. If he is satisfied with you, your income may reach in a leap to eight thousand francs.

"But mind you," continued the abbé, severely, "he isn't giving you all that money for your pretty eyes; it is a question of usefulness. In your place, indeed, I should talk very little, especially with anyone unknown to you.

"Ah!" said the abbé, "I have some information for you. I was forgetting M. de la Mole's family. There are two children; a daughter, and a son of nineteen, who is elegant, indeed, yet is sort of a fool, who don't know at noon what he will do at two o'clock. But he has character; he is brave, too; he has been in the Spanish campaign. The Marquis hopes—I do not know why—that you may become a friend to the young Count Norbert. I have said that you were a good Latinist; perhaps he counts on your teaching his son a few ready-made phrases from Cicero or Virgil. In your place I shouldn't allow myself to become familiar with this handsome young man, and before yielding altogether to his polished manners, which are somewhat spoilt by cynicism, I should see them more than once.

"I will not hide from you that our young Count may despise you at first, because you are only a little bourgeois. His ancestor was a courtier, and had the honor of having his head cut off in Place de Grêve, on the 26th of April, 1574, for a political intrigue. You are the son of a Verrières carpenter, and, what is more, in his father's employ. Consider well these differences, and study well the family history in Moreri; all the flatterers who dine at the house make delicate allusions to it from time to time.

"Take care how you answer Count Norbert's pleasantries, who is chief of the Hussars and a future peer of France; and give me no cause for regret, in consequence."

"It seems to me," said Julien, blushing considerably, "that it is my duty even not to answer a man that looks down on me."

"You have no idea of that disdain; it will show itself only in exaggerated compliments. If you are to be a fool, you will allow yourself to be taken in by them; but if you are to make a mark, you would seem to be."

"When that doesn't suit me, would I seem ungrateful if I return to my little cell, No. 108?"

"No doubt," replied the abbé, "all the flatterers of the house will calumniate you; but I—I will be myself. *Adsum qui feci.* I will say that the resolution came from me."

Julien was dejected by the abbé's bitter, discouraging tone. It had completely spoilt his last reply. The fact was, the abbé had a conscientious scruple about his affection for Julien, and it was with a sort of religious terror that he went over to the other extreme.

"You will see, also," he added, with the same ill grace as if performing a painful duty, "you will see Madame de la Mole, the Marquise. She is a tall, blonde woman, pious, proud, perfectly polished, and insignificant. She is the daughter of the old Duke de Chaulnes, so well known for his royal prejudices. This great lady is a sort of an abridged, accentuated form of what is really the character of women of her rank. She doesn't hide, indeed, that the fact she has ancestors who went to the Crusades is her only claim to distinction. Money is indeed an after consideration. Does that surprise you? We are not in the provinces any more, my son.

"You will see in the Salon some great lords speaking of our princes in an exceedingly light fashion. As for Madame de la Mole, she respectfully lowers her voice every time she names a prince, and more so when it is a princess. I should not advise you to say in her presence that Philip II. and Henry VIII. were monsters. They were kings, and that gives them inalienable right to the respect of men like you and me, of ignoble birth. However," added M. Pirard, "we are priests; for she will take you for one. Under that title she considers us mere valets that are necessary to her salvation."

"Monsieur," said Julien, "it seems to me that I shall not remain long in Paris."

"Indeed; but notice there's no fortune for men of our class, except by the side of the great dignitaries. With a sort of indefinable something that is in your character—at least as far as I can see—if you do not rise, you will be persecuted; there is no middle ground for you. Don't fool yourself. Men see that it does not give you any pleasure when they talk to you; under our social conditions you are doomed to misery if you do not reach greatness.

"What would become of you at Besançon, without the caprice of the Marquis de la Mole? One day you will understand all that queer action in your behalf, and, if you are not a fool, you will have eternal gratitude for him and his family. How many poor abbés, wiser than you, have lived for years in Paris, with their fifteen sous and with their ten sous for argumentation, at the Sorbonne? Recall what I related to you last winter about the first years of the Cardinal Du Bois. Your pride, perhaps, is greater than his talent?

"I, for example, who am a quiet and mediocre kind of a man, I hope to die in my seminary. I have been foolish enough to become attached to it. Ah, indeed! I was about to be removed when I handed in my resignation. Do you know what I had then? I had a capital of five hundred and twenty francs, no more no less. Not a friend, hardly an acquaintance or two. M. de la Mole, whom I had never seen, drew me out of a difficulty; and he only had to say a word, and I should have received a curacy where the parishioners are people of means and of no extraordinary vices, and the income would have made me ashamed, so out of proportion would it have been to my work! I have never spoken to you so long except to put a little ballast into that head of yours.

"Oh, yes! another word. I have the misfortune of being irascible; it is possible that you and I may cease to speak. If the Marquise's pride or the lame pleasantries of her son should make the house decidedly uncomfortable, I advise you to finish your studies in some seminary at a distance of thirty leagues from Paris, and rather toward the North than toward the South. There is more civilization in the North, and," he added, lowering his voice, "I must tell you that the neighborhood of Paris newspapers makes little tyrants afraid.

"If we continue to find pleasure in seeing each other, and if the Marquise's house is not agreeable to you, I will make you my vicar, and I will give you half of what the curacy brings in. I owe you that, and more, too," he added, interrupting Julien's reply of thanks, "for the singular offer which you made me at Besançon. If, in place of having five hundred and twenty francs, I had not had anything, you would have come to my assistance."

The abbé's voice ceased to be sharp. To his great shame, Julien felt tears in his eyes; he was dying to throw himself into his friend's arms. He could not refrain from saying, with all the courage he could summon:

"I have been hated by my father from the cradle; that was

one of my greatest miseries, but I will not complain any more of chance. I have found a father again in you."

"Now, now," said the abbé, embarrassed; then assuming his old authority as Director of the seminary: "You must not call it chance, my child; always say Providence."

The cab stopped. The coachman raised the bronze knocker on an immense door. It was the Hôtel de la Mole, and in order that the passers-by might not be in doubt, those words could be read on a slab of black marble over the door.

This ostentation displeased Julien. "They are so afraid of the Jacobins; they see a Robespierre and his charrette behind every hedge. Though frequently laughing over it, yet they advertise their house so that the canaille would recognize it and pillage it in case of an uprising." He communicated this thought to abbé Pirard.

"Ah, poor child, you will soon be my vicar. What a frightful idea is that of yours!"

"There is nothing more simple."

The proud bearing of the porter, and especially the clean court, struck him with admiration. The weather was beautiful.

"What magnificent architecture!" he said to his friend.

It was one of those mansions with a low façade in the Faubourg St. Germain that were built at the time of Voltaire. Vogue and architectural beauty were then never so far apart.

Chapter 2

Debut

A memory ridiculous and touching: One's first drawing-room appearance, at eighteen, alone and unsupported! A woman's glance was enough to terrify me. The more I tried to please, the more gauche I became. I formed the falsest ideas of everything; either I gave myself up without grounds, or I cast a man as my enemy because he gave me a dark look. But still, amid the frightful pangs of my shyness, how truly fine a fine day seemed!

—KANT

JULIEN stood stock still in amazement.

"Now collect yourself," said abbé Pirard; "you have just said something dreadful, and now you are only a child. Where is that *nil mirari* of Horace? Remember that the crowd of servants here are going to sneer at you after they see you established here; they will see in you only an equal unjustly placed above them; they will be hail-fellow-well-met, and will offer you good advice, but only to lead you to some egregious folly."

"Let them try," said Julien, defiantly, biting his lip.

The drawing-rooms they passed through on the first floor before arriving at the Marquis's library would have seemed to you, reader, rather depressing than magnificent. Indeed, if they had been offered to you, you would have declined with thanks. Dulness and wearisomeness seemed native there. But Julien was more than ever enchanted.

"How can anyone be unhappy," he thought, "when one lives in such a splendid place?" Presently they arrived at the most cheerless room of all, where it was scarcely light enough to see. There they found a thin little man, with fine, sparkling eyes, in a blond wig. The abbé turned toward Julien and introduced him; it was the Marquis. Julien scarcely recognized him, for he was so polite; he was no longer that haughty lord whom he had seen at the abbey Bray-le-Haut. It seemed to Julien that his wig was too thick, and that observation relieved him somewhat of his shyness. The descendant of the friend of Henry III. gave the impression, at first, of lacking in dignity; he was so thin and restless. Julien, however, noticed that the Marquis was politer even than the Bishop of Besançon. The interview did not last three minutes.

As they walked out the abbé said to Julien:

"You looked at the Marquis as if you were looking at a picture. I am not so polished among these people; you know more about such things than I do, but it seemed to me your steady gaze was not the politest thing in the world."

They went back to the cab. Down the boulevard they stopped, and the abbé led Julien to a great apartment. Julien saw no furniture; all he could see was a magnificent clock, with figures that, according to his ideas, were quite indecent. Just then a gentleman, very elegantly attired, smilingly approached, and Julien half saluted him. The gentleman then smiled again, familiarly laying his hand on Julien's shoulder. The latter, in his surprise and anger, trembled and fell back. Abbé Pirard, in spite of his gravity, was shaking with laughter. The gentleman was only a tailor.

"I give you your liberty for two days," said the abbé to him as they were leaving; "it is not until then that you will be presented to Madame de la Mole. If it were anyone else but I, you would be kept like a young girl during the first moments of your stay in this modern Babylon. Just go ahead at once if you have any inclination to be wild, and I will be quit of my weakness for you. Day after to-morrow this tailor will bring you two suits. Don't forget to give a five-franc piece to the boy who helps try them on. By all means don't let your voice be known to these Parisians. Just say a word and they will know how to lampoon you; that is their forte. Come to me at noon, day after to-morrow; go now where you like. Oh, I was forgetting. Order yourself some boots, some shirts, and a hat at the addresses which I give you here."

Julien looked at the handwriting.

"Yes, it is the handwriting of the Marquis," said the abbé; "he is a very active man who sees everything, who likes to act better than to command. He is going to take you with him just to spare himself that sort of annoyance. You think you will be able to do everything that active man will indicate with only a hint? Well, that is what the future will show. Be careful!"

Julien entered the shops indicated by the addresses without saying a word. He noticed with what respect he was received, the shoemaker even writing his name on his book as M. Julien de Sorel.

At Père la Chaise, a very obliging gentleman, who was an out and out Liberal, offered to show him the tomb of Maréchal Ney, which discreet politics left without the honor of an epitaph. But on leaving this Liberal, who pressed him to his breast with tears in his eyes, Julien missed his watch.

Rich with such experiences, he presented himself at noon the next day to abbé Pirard, who gazed on him for a long time in silence.

"You may turn out to be a perfect fool," said the abbé to him, severely.

Julien looked well enough, but somewhat crestfallen. He was handsome, though; but the abbé was too provincial himself yet to see that Julien had that stoop of the shoulders which in the provinces is considered both elegant and imposing. When the Marquis saw Julien, he looked at him with different eyes.

"Would you have any objection if M. Sorel took dancing lessons?"

The abbé was petrified.

"No, not at all," he answered; "Julien is no priest."

The Marquis ran up the little bare staircase two steps at a time: he was going himself to install our hero in a pretty apartment which looked out on the garden. He asked him how many shirts he had bought.

"Two," replied Julien, intimidated slightly to see a great lord come down to such details.

"Very well," replied the Marquis, in a serious, imperative tone that somewhat sobered Julien, "very well; go and get twenty-two more. Here is your first quarter's salary."

As he left the room, the Marquis called an old man:

"Arsène," he said to him, "you will wait on M. Sorel."

A few minutes later Julien found himself alone in a magnificent library. It was a delicious moment. In order not to be surprised, he hid himself in a little dark corner, whence he gazed rapturously at the finely bound volumes.

"Why, I can read all that," he was saying to himself. "How can I ever find it disagreeable here? M. de Rênal would be put in the shade by the hundredth part of what the Marquis has done for me; but here are the copies I have to make."

After that was done Julien ventured to approach the books. He was wild with joy when he took out a volume of Voltaire. Opening the door to see if anyone came, he gave himself up to the pleasure of turning over each of the eighty volumes. They were magnificently bound, the chef-d'œuvre of the best bookbinder in London. That was all that was needed to bring Julien's admiration to ecstasy.

An hour later the Marquis entered, and, looking at the copies, noted with astonishment that Julien had written *cela* with two "l's."

"So all that the abbé has told me about his knowledge is a little fairy tale!" The Marquis was quite disconcerted, yet he said, gently:

"You are not sure of your spelling, are you?"

"That is so," said Julien, without thinking in the least of the injustice he was doing himself. He was softened by the kindness of the Marquis, and was thinking, by contrast, of the acrid tone of M. de Rênal.

"It will be time lost, this experiment with the little priest from Franche-Comté," thought the Marquis, "for I needed a man who is sure."

"*Cela* is written with only one 'l,' " said the Marquis to him. "When you have finished copying, look in the dictionary for the spelling of the words of which you are not sure."

At six o'clock, when the Marquis called him, he looked with evident pain at Julien's feet.

"I must blame myself," he said; "I did not tell you that at half-past five o'clock you must dress."

Julien looked nonplussed.

"I mean that you must put on stockings; but Arsène will remind you of it. To-day I will make excuses for you."

As he said this, M. de la Mole led Julien into the drawing-room, which was resplendent with gilt. On such occasions M. de Rênal would not have failed to walk fast in order to pass first through the door; that little vanity of his old patron made Julien walk on the heels of the Marquis, causing the latter a good deal of pain from his gout.

"Oh, he is such a stick when he walks!" the latter muttered to himself. He presented him to a tall, imposing-looking woman, his wife. Julien found her overbearing, somewhat like Madame de Maugiron, the wife of the sub-prefect of the arrondissement of Verrières, when she would be at a St. Charles dinner.

A little dazzled by the extreme magnificence of the drawing-room, Julien did not understand anything M. de la Mole said. The Marquise, however, scarcely deigned to notice him. There were several men present, among whom he recognized, with indescribable pleasure, the young Bishop of Agde, who was gracious enough to speak to him before the ceremony at Bray-le-Haut. That young prelate, somewhat disconcerted by the appealing glances of Julien, did not care to recognize the provincial.

The gentlemen seemed to be exceedingly quiet. In Paris loud talk is banned, and anything like lively conversation out of place. A pale, tall, handsome young man, with moustaches and with a remarkably small head, came in at half-past six.

"You always make us wait," said the Marquise. At this he kissed her hand.

Julien learned that he was Count de la Mole. He found him charming from the very first.

"Is it possible," he said to himself, "that this is the man whose little sarcasms will drive me out of the house?" But as he was examining Count Norbert, Julien remarked that he was in boots and spurs. "And I," he sighed, "I am in slippers, apparently like an inferior."

The company seated themselves at the table. Julien heard the Marquise utter some words in a reproving tone, just as a well-formed, blonde young woman seated herself opposite to him. She did not appear attractive to him; but, as he looked at her closer, he thought he had never seen such beautiful eyes; but they seemed cold. Then, too, there was an expression of imperious ennui on her face.

"Madame de Rênal had beautiful eyes," he thought, "and fashionable people were always complimenting her; they had nothing in common with these." Julien did not have enough experience to know that what was scintillating so brightly in Mademoiselle Mathilde's eyes was exactly what he had in his mind. When Madame de Rênal's eyes grew bright, it was through the fire of passion or from virtuous indignation at the recital of some wicked deed. Toward the end of dinner Julien found a word to express Mademoiselle de la Mole's style of beauty. "She is sparkling," he thought. Except the eyes, she cruelly resembled her mother, who displeased him more and more, and at whom he no longer looked. On the other hand, Count Norbert seemed admirable from every point of view. Julien was so carried away by him that he no longer had any idea of jealousy or hatred because he happened to be richer or nobler than himself. Julien saw that the Marquis was becoming somewhat bored. At the end of the second course, the latter said to his son:

"Norbert, I bespeak your friendship for M. Julien Sorel, who is going to be my chief assistant, and of whom I intend to make a man, if that is possible. He is my secretary," said the Marquis to his neighbor, "and he writes *cela* with two 'l's.' "

Everybody looked at Julien, who inclined his head, but more markedly toward Norbert. His face, however, left a good impression. The Marquis happened to speak of the kind of education which Julien had received, for one of the company had attacked him on Horace.

"It was precisely in speaking of Horace that I succeeded so well with the Bishop of Besançon," said Julien to himself; "apparently these people know only that author." From that moment he was himself again. It was easier for him now, for he had decided that Mademoiselle de la Mole was not a woman to his liking. Since leaving the seminary he had put men aside without allowing himself to be in the least disconcerted by them. He would have regained his complete self-composure if the dining-room had not been so magnificent.

There were two mirrors, each eight feet high, in which he could see the person addressing him, and these frightened him to some extent. His sentences were not too long for a provincial, and his fine eyes, in which timidity appeared and reappeared with his answers, enhanced the beauty of his expression. He was declared to be attractive.

That sort of an examination gave a piquant turn to the monotonous dinner. The Marquis made a sign to the speaker to push Julien hard. "Is it really possible that there is something in him?" he thought.

Julien replied cleverly, and lost enough of his timidity to show, not that he had genius—an impossible thing in Paris— but that he was possessed of new ideas, even if they were not elegantly expressed and were not always apropos. One could see that he had mastered the Latin.

Julien's adversary was an Academician of Inscriptions, with whom Latin was not precisely a specialty. He found Julien to be a very good humanist. Having no dread himself of blushing, he tried his best to embarrass Julien. In the heat of the combat the young man even forgot the magnificent furniture of the dining-room and began to express ideas on the Latin poets which his opponent had never heard. The latter really admired the young secretary's knowledge.

Luckily there crept into the discussion the question as to whether Horace was rich or poor, an agreeable, pleasure-loving, reckless man, turning out verse to amuse himself, like Chapelle, the friend of Molière and la Fontaine, or a poor devil of a poet laureate, following the court and writing odes on the King's birthday like Southey, the defamer of Lord Byron. Then there was discussed the condition of society under Augustus and George IV., the two epochs when aristocracy was at its zenith; but at Rome it was snatched by Mecenas, who was only a knight, and in England the power of George IV. had been reduced merely to that of the Doge of Venice.

This discussion seemed to draw the Marquis out of the bored state into which he had passed at the beginning of dinner. Julien did not understand all those modern names like Southey, Lord Byron, George IV., which he just heard for the first time; but it escaped no one that whenever the question turned on the history of Rome or on a knowledge that could be derived from the works of Horace or Martial or Tacitus, his superiority was unquestionable. Julien artlessly expressed certain ideas he had learned from the Bishop of Besançon in the various discussions he had had with that prelate. They were found not bad.

After the discussion on the poets, the Marquise, who had made it a rule in life to admire what amused her husband, deigned to cast her eyes on Julien.

"The young abbé's awkwardness, perhaps, is the guise of a well-informed man," said the Marquise to the Academician in Julien's hearing. Conventional phrases sufficed for the mistress of the house. She adopted that phrase in speaking of Julien, and was congratulating herself on inviting the Academician to dinner. "He has amused M. de la Mole," she thought.

Chapter 3

First Steps

*That immense valley, filled with glittering lights
and thousands of people, dazzles my sight. Not
one of them knows me, all are superior to me.
My head reels.*

—*Poemi dell' avvocato* REINA

EARLY NEXT DAY Julien was copying the letters in the library,
when Mademoiselle Mathilde entered by a little secret door that
was hidden by the books. While Julien was admiring that contrivance, Mademoiselle Mathilde appeared very much astonished, if not positively displeased, at meeting him there. Julien
saw that standing there in her curl papers she appeared severe,
almost masculine. Mademoiselle de la Mole was in the habit of
stealing books from her father's library, and Julien's presence
made her usual appropriation impossible that morning. This
made her so angry that she went to look for the second volume
of Voltaire's "Princess of Babylon," a worthy finish to the
eminently monarchical and religious education at the Sacred
Heart! This poor girl, at the age of nineteen, had already the
great need of something stimulating in order to be interested in
a novel.

Toward three o'clock Count Norbert appeared in the library,
with a newspaper in his hand, to prepare for a speech he had to
make that evening. He was very glad to meet Julien, though he
had entirely forgotten his existence; his manner toward him
was perfect. He proposed a horseback ride.

"My father will give us leave to go out until dinner time,"
he said. Julien appreciated the word *us*, and found it charming.

"Why, Monsieur le Comte," said Julien, "if it were a question
of hewing down an eighty-foot tree and of removing the bark
and making planks out of it, I should come out all right; but to
go horseback riding—I have never done that more than half a
dozen times in my life."

"Well, let this be the seventh time."

In reality Julien was recalling the entrance of the King at
Verrières, and thought himself rather an adept equestrian.

Coming back from the Bois de Boulogne, when they were in

225

the middle of the Rue du Bac, he fell in the mud as he tried to avoid a cab. It was well he had two suits of clothes.

At dinner the Marquis, wishing to talk to him, asked him something about the horseback ride. Norbert very generously hastened to reply.

"The Count is very kind to me," said Julien; "I thank him very much, and I know the value of it. He was good enough to give me the gentlest and prettiest horse imaginable; but he could not tie me on, and for lack of that precaution I fell down in the middle of that fine, long street near the bridge."

Mademoiselle Mathilde tried in vain to smother a laugh, and then indiscreetly asked for details. Julien spoke with a good deal of artlessness, unaware of the grace with which he was speaking.

"I augur well for that little priest," said the Marquis to the Academician, "a simple provincial in such a strait! That is what I have never seen and never expected to see; and to think he even tells of his mishap before ladies!"

Julien put his hearers in a good humor over his misfortune, and at the close of dinner, when the general conversation took another turn, Mademoiselle Mathilde asked her brother for the details of the accident. As she continued these questions, and as Julien encountered her eyes now and then, he ventured to reply directly, although he was not addressed, and all three ended by laughing as if they were three young persons in a country town.

The next day Julien heard two lectures on theology, and then retured to copy a score of letters. He found near him, in the library, a handsomely dressed young man, but whose general appearance betokened pettiness and envy.

The Marquis entered. "What are you doing here, Monsieur Tanbeau?" he asked the newcomer, sternly.

"I believed—" replied the young man, smiling slightly.

"No, monsieur, you did not believe; it is some scheme, but it is an unfortunate one."

Young Tanbeau arose, furious, and disappeared. He was a nephew of the Academician, Madame de la Mole's friend, and was devoting himself to letters. The Academician brought it about that the Marquis should employ him as a secretary. Tanbeau, who was working in another room, knowing with what favor Julien had been received, wished to share it, and therefore had come into the library that morning.

At four o'clock Julien ventured, after some hesitation, to present himself before Comte Norbert; the latter was about to go out horseback riding again, and, though somewhat embarrassed, was perfectly polite.

"I believe," he said to Julien, "that you will do all right after a while, and after a few weeks I shall be delighted to go out riding with you."

"I desire to thank you for the kindness you have shown me. Believe me, monsieur," added Julien, very seriously, "I am sensible of my obligation to you. If your horse was not hurt by my awkwardness yesterday, and is not used now, I should like to ride him to-day."

"My dear Sorel, you are running a risk. Suppose I make objections that will recall your prudence? The fact is it is four o'clock, and we have not much time to lose."

When he jumped on the horse, he asked the young Count what one ought do to keep from falling.

"Lots of things," replied Norbert, laughing aloud. "For example, lean backward."

Julien put the horse into a gallop; they were then at Place Louis XVI.

"Ah, you are a bold young fellow," said Norbert. "There are too many carriages in charge of reckless drivers, and once on the ground the tillburys will run over you. They are not going to risk spoiling the horse's mouth by stopping short."

Twenty times Norbert saw Julien on the point of falling, but at last the ride ended without an accident. When they returned the young Count said to his sister:

"I present you to a dare-devil."

At dinner, speaking to his father across the table, he rendered ample justice to Julien's daring. What he said was the greatest praise he could give to a horseback rider.

The young Count had that morning heard the grooms speaking of Julien's fall as they were attending to the horses, and ridiculing him outrageously. In spite of this kindness Julien soon felt how perfectly isolated he was in the midst of the family. All their ways seemed strange to him, and his awkwardness was a source of constant delight to the servants.

Abbé Pirard had left for his curacy. "If Julien is a feeble plant," he thought, "he will perish; but if he is a man of courage, he will come out all right by himself."

Chapter 4

The Hotel de la Mole

Que fait-il ici? s'y plairait-il? penserait-il y plaire?
— RONSARD

IF EVERYTHING seemed strange to Julien in the noble drawing-room of the Hôtel de la Mole, the pale young man, in his turn, appearing always in black, seemed very singular to the persons who deigned to notice him. Madame de la Mole proposed to her husband to have him sent away on business on days when certain personages were to dine.

"I wish to push my experiment to the very end," replied the Marquis. "Abbé Pirard thinks we are wrong in breaking the pride of those around us. 'We lean only on what offers resistance,' etcetera. This one will be remarked only because his face is unfamiliar; for the rest, he is a deaf-mute."

"If I want to recognize the people here," said Julien to himself, "I must write down the name and a word or two about the great people whom I shall meet here."

In the first line he put down the names of five or six friends of the family, who were assiduous in their attentions to him, believing him to be a protégé of the Marquis.

These were poor, spiritless hangers on, to be found in all aristocratic drawing-rooms. In justice to them it must be said that they were not meek to all alike. Every one of them might have allowed himself to be bullied by the Marquis, but would have resented a slighting word from Madame de la Mole.

There was too much pride, too much tediousness in the life of the master and mistress of the house; they were too long accustomed to outraging other people's feelings for their diversion to expect true friendship. Yet, except on rainy days or when their ennui was insufferable, which was, indeed, very rare, they were found to be perfectly polite.

If the five or six men who tried to be patronizing to Julien had deserted the mansion, the Marquise would have been alone, and, in the eyes of women of her rank, lack of company is not to be borne. It is too significant of a fall from grace.

The Marquis was perfect to his wife in this respect, taking care to have the drawing-room always well filled. He did not invite peers alone, for his new colleagues were not polished enough to be always admitted among his friends, nor amusing enough to be received as subalterns. Julien found this out later. The diplomacy that entered into the amusement of the bourgeois was not to be found in such a house as that of the Marquis, except in extreme cases.

Such is the imperious sway of the desire for amusement in this wearisome century, that even on company days everybody fled as soon as the Marquis left the drawing-room. They could not amuse themselves about God, the priests, the King, men of rank, or artists favored by the Court. Nothing could be said about Béranger, the Opposition journals, Voltaire, or Rousseau; in fine, everything that would imply freedom of speech was banned.

Neither an income of one hundred thousand écus nor a cordon bleu could be proof against such a drawing-room law. The least shadow of levity seemed gross, in spite of the high tone and perfect politeness. Everybody, nevertheless, wished to be agreeable, and, therefore, was more or less of a bore.

The young people who came to pay their respects, fearing to speak of anything that would cause the least remark, or that would betray forbidden reading, usually kept quiet after a few passing remarks on Racine and on the weather.

Julien observed that the conversation was ordinarily kept alive by two Viscounts and five Barons whom M. de la Mole had known in the Emigration. These gentlemen enjoyed an income of from six to eight thousand livres. Four of them held out for the *Quotidienne,* but the others stoutly clung to the *Gazette de France.* Each man then had some anecdote to relate; one was about the Château, in which the word admirable was not spared. Julien remarked that the speaker had five Crosses, the rest having only three at most.

There were usually in the hall ten servants in livery, who served ices or tea every quarter of an hour, and at midnight a sort of supper with champagne. For that reason Julien stayed through a whole evening at times; but he could not understand how one could listen seriously to the commonplaces in the finely gilt drawing-room. Sometimes he would look at the speakers to see if they themselves were not mocking at what they were saying. "Why, my M. de Maistre, whom I know by heart, had said that a hundred times better," he would say to himself, "and even he is tiresome." Julien was not alone in perceiving the mental asphyxia. Some consoled themselves with ices, others with the pleasure of saying, for the rest of the evening, "I have just left the Hôtel de la Mole, where I learned that Russia—"

Julien learned from one of his patronizing friends that Madame de la Mole had rewarded the poor Baron Le Bourguignon, a sub-prefect during the Restoration, only six months before, with a prefecture for his marked attention of twenty years.

That great event redoubled the zeal of these gentlemen. If they were sensitive before, they were no more so after that. Rarely was there seen a direct lack of consideration, but Julien overheard now and then at the table two or three little dialogues between the Marquis and his wife that were indeed cruel for those who sat beside them. These noble personages, indeed, did not hide their disdain for anyone who had no seat in the *chariot of the King*. Julien remarked that the word "Crusade" was the only one that imparted anything serious or respectful to their expression. The respect that they usually showed had in it something of complaisance.

In the midst of all this magnificence, Julien was interested only in M. de la Mole. He heard him say one day that Le Bourguignon's promotion was not ungratifying to him, since it was an attention to the Marquise. Julien learned more about it through abbé Pirard.

One morning, as the abbé was working with Julien in the Marquis's library over the eternal lawsuit with de Frilaire, the latter said to him suddenly:

"Monsieur, is it one of my duties, or is it a great kindness, that I should dine with the Marquise every day?"

"Why, it is a signal honor," replied the abbé, scandalized. "M. N., the Academician, who for fifteen years has paid such marked attention to her, has never been able to obtain that for his nephew, M. Tanbeau."

"For me it is the most disagreeable thing in connection with my position here. I was bored less at the seminary; I see universal yawning, even to Mademoiselle de la Mole, who should by this time be accustomed to the amenities of visitors; I am always afraid of falling asleep. Please secure permission for me to dine at forty sous in some insignificant restaurant."

The abbé, who was by this time a veritable parvenu, was very sensitive to the honor of dining with the great lord. While he was endeavoring to explain himself to Julien, a slight noise made them turn around. Julien saw Mademoiselle de la Mole, who had come to look for a book. She flushed. She had heard all; but she really then began to think something of Julien.

"He was not born on his knees," she thought, "like this old abbé. Lord! how ugly that man is!"

At dinner Julien did not dare look at Mademoiselle de la Mole, who, however, was gracious enough to speak to him. That evening a great deal of company was expected, and she asked him to remain. Young Parisian girls do not like gentlemen of a certain age who are not tidy about their dress. Julien did not need much sagacity to perceive that M. Le Bourguignon's colleagues, who had remained in the drawing-room, had the honor of being the object of Mademoiselle de la Mole's sarcasm. Whether it was affectation on her part or not, she was outrageous to these people.

Mademoiselle de la Mole was the centre of a little group that formed almost every night behind the Marquise's armchair. There were Marquis de Croisenois, Count de Caylus, Viscount de Luz, and two or three other young officials, friends of Norbert and his sister. These young gentlemen were seated on a large sofa. At the end of the sofa, opposite the brilliant Mathilde, Julien was sitting on a little low, straw-bottomed chair. That modest position was envied him by all; but Norbert had his father's young secretary remain there, speaking to him from time to time in the course of the evening.

Mademoiselle de la Mole had asked him during the day as to the height of the mountain on which the citadel of Besançon was placed, but Julien could not tell whether the mountain was higher or lower than Montmartre. He frequently laughed outright at what was said in that little group, but he was incapable of putting in a word. It was like a strange language which he understood, but could not speak.

Mathilde's friends were in constant warfare with the people who kept on arriving in the drawing-room. The friends of the house came first under their fire, being better known than the rest. Julien was very attentive, everything having its interest for him.

"Oh, here is M. Descoulis," said Mathilde, "he is not wearing a wig any more. Why, does he want to get the prefecture by his genius? Look how he displays that brow which he says is replete with lofty thoughts!"

"He is a man that knows everybody," said M. de Croisenois; "he frequently visits my uncle the Cardinal. He is capable of nursing a lie with anyone of his friends for years, and he has two or three hundred friends. He knows how to bolster up friendship, he does; that is his forte. He has grovelled before the door of one of his friends at seven o'clock on a winter morning. Yes, he gets angry from time to time, which leads him to write seven or eight letters. Then he becomes appeased, and writes seven or eight letters over the charms of friendship. But it is in frank and candid expansion of soul that this man shines best of all. This manœuvre appears best when he has any favor to ask. One of my uncle's vicars is inimitable when he gives an account of the life of M. Descoulis since the Restoration. I will bring him here some day."

"Bah! I don't believe in anything of the kind; it is only provincial jealousy among these small people," said Count de Caylus.

"M. Descoulis will make a name in history," continued the Marquis; "he has made the Restoration with abbé de Pradt and MM. de Talleyrand and Tozzo di Borgo."

"That man has gone through millions," said Norbert, "and I cannot conceive how he is going to reward my father's little epigrams, which are often abominable enough. 'How many friends have you betrayed, my dear Descoulis?' he asked him the other day, from one end of the table to the other."

"But what if he has betrayed anyone?" asked Mademoiselle de la Mole. "Who is not a traitor?"

"Hello!" cried Count de Caylus to Norbert, "I see M. Sainclair is here, that famous Liberal. What the deuce does he want here? Why, I must go and talk to him; they say he is brilliant."

"But how will your mother receive him?" asked M. de Croisenois; "he has such extravagant, free, independent ideas."

"See," said Mademoiselle de la Mole, "there is that independent man who is bowing to the very ground before M. Descoulis, as he takes his hand! I thought he was going to carry it to his lips."

"Descoulis knows how to use power better than we give him credit for," replied M. de Croisenois.

"Sainclair comes here to get into the Academy. See, Croisenois, how he salutes Baron L. Why, he would be less obsequious if he fell on his knees," said M. de Luz.

"My dear Sorel," said Norbert, "you may be brilliant—but you come from the mountains; never, never, greet anyone the way this great peer did, if he were a god himself."

"Oh, there is brilliancy par excellence! Baron Baton!" said Mademoiselle de la Mole, laughingly, imitating the voice of the footman who had just announced him.

"I think even you are making fun of him. What a name!" said M. de Caylus.

" 'Oh, what's in a name?' he said one day," replied Mademoiselle de la Mole. "Imagine the Duke de Bouillon being announced for the first time in a drawing-room! It is only a matter of being used to it, in my opinion."

Julien withdrew from the sofa, not appreciative enough of the delicate raillery to laugh over it. He was taking it seriously. He saw in the remarks of the young people only a general contempt, of which he disapproved. His provincial or English prudery made him see in it all only spite. Of course, he was mistaken.

"Count Norbert," he said to himself, "whom I have seen spoiling three sheets of paper writing a few lines to his colonel, would be very happy if, in his whole life, he wrote a page like M. Sainclair."

Being unknown, Julien glided among the people unperceived, and successively approached several groups. He followed Baron Baton with his eyes from a distance, desirous of hearing him speak. That brilliant man seemed nervous, and Julien saw that he was not at his ease until he had found three or four piquant phrases. It seemed to Julien that that sort of genius required room for expansion; the Baron was not content with words, but needed at least four phrases of six lines each to shine.

"That man is delivering a dissertation, he is not talking," said some one behind Julien. He turned round and blushed with pleasure to hear the man called Count Chalvet. That man had figured in the "Mémorial de Sainte-Hélène," and in the little bits of history dictated by Napoleon.

Count Chalvet was astute in his remarks, clear, just, vivid, and deep. If he said anything, it appeared clear at once. What he said was facts, and it was a pleasure to listen to him. In politics, however, he was very cynical.

"Oh, I am an Independent," he was saying to a gentleman wearing three badges, whom he was evidently mocking. "Why should I be of the same opinion to-day that I was six weeks ago? Why, my opinion would be my tyrant."

A quartette of grave young gentlemen who surrounded him made long faces, evidently displeased at the light tone. The Count saw that he was going too far. Happily he perceived the good M. Balland, a very Tartuffe of goodness. The Count began to converse with him. It was understood then that the poor Balland was going to be sacrificed.

For the sake of his morals and morality in general M. Balland, after a few very difficult steps in high society, had married, though horribly ugly, a very rich woman, who soon died; then another very rich woman, whom no one ever saw in society. He enjoyed in all humility his income of sixty thousand livres, and had even some flatterers in his train.

Count Chalvet spoke of all that to him without the least pity. There was a crowd of about thirty persons around them, with a smile on everyone, even on the grave young gentlemen, the hope of the century.

"Why does he visit M. de la Mole if he is evidently the butt?" thought Julien. Approaching abbé Pirard, he asked that question of him. M. Balland had glided away.

"Good!" said Norbert. "He is one of the spies around my father; there remains only that limping Napier."

"Is that a riddle?" thought Julien. "But, then, why does the Marquis receive M. Balland?"

The stern abbé changed countenance as he heard the lackeys announce some one again.

"Why, this is like the Basile hole; I see here only men with a damaged character." The abbé did not know the tenor of fashionable society. Indeed, among his Jansenist friends, he was known to have very strong opinions about the men who cleverly find entrance to drawing-rooms through diplomacy or wealth to serve any and every party. For a while he replied to Julien's questions out of the abundance of his grieved heart. Then he suddenly stopped, unhappy over the idea that he was always speaking ill of the world. He thought it was wicked. A bilious man, a Jansenist, and yet a believer in Christian charity, his life in the world was a continual struggle.

"What a face that abbé Pirard has!" said Mademoiselle de la Mole, as Julien approached the sofa again. Julien did not like that, but she was certainly right. M. Pirard was without doubt the most virtuous man in the drawing-room, but his beet-like face, contorted by the stings of his conscience, made him hideous.

"After this, what is there in faces?" thought Julien. "It is when abbé Pirard's scruples are awakened by some little peccadillo that he looks most atrocious; while in this face of a Napier, who is known as a spy to everybody, one reads only happiness and tranquillity." Abbé Pirard had made some great concessions to his party, for he had taken a servant and was well dressed.

Julien then remarked something unusual in the drawing-room; for everyone had his eyes turned to the door. There was a hush all round. The footman announced the famous Baron de Tolly, to whom the elections had directed general attention. Approaching nearer, Julien saw him very distinctly. The

Baron had presided over an election district and had had the luminous idea of throwing out several square bits of paper bearing the vote of one of the several parties; and, in order to compensate himself for the loss, he had replaced them by other bits of paper bearing the vote of one who was more agreeable to him. That little manœuvre was seen by several electors, who straightway proceeded to pay the Baron de Tolly some compliments. The gentleman was still pale from that little affair. Some evil-minded persons even spoke of the galleys. He was received coolly by M. de la Mole, and he slipped out as soon as he could.

"If he leaves so soon, he is going to M. Comte" (a celebrated prestidigitateur), said Count Chalvet; and everybody laughed.

In a group of quiet persons, intriguers, but men of intelligence, who one after another had been ushered into the drawing-room, the little Tanbeau was endeavoring to win his spurs. If he had not yet the cleverness of speech of the people around him, he made up for it, as one could see, by his great energy.

"Why shouldn't that man be sentenced to ten years imprisonment?" he was saying to the group as Julien approached. "It is at the bottom of a dungeon that such reptiles should be placed. They should die out of the sight of men. If not, their venom will prove more noxious than ever. What is the good of fining him a thousand écus? He is poor; well and good; so much the better. But his party will pay for him; he should have been fined five hundred francs and sentenced to ten years solitary confinement."

"Good Lord! who is that monster you are talking about?" thought Julien, who was admiring the young man's vehement tone and energetic gestures. The little, thin, drawn face of the Academician's nephew was positively hideous at that moment. Julien soon ascertained that he spoke of the greatest poet of the age.

"Oh, monster!" muttered Julien, half aloud, generous tears suffusing his eyes. "You little scoundrel!" he thought, "I will see you about that later. There, now, these are the tail-enders of the party of which the Marquis is the head. And the illustrious man he is berating, how many Crosses, how many sinecures, would he not have received if he had sold himself not even to such a disreputable ministry as de Nervale's, but only to some of those honest men who followed him?"

Abbé Pirard made a sign to Julien just as M. de la Mole had whispered something to him. But when Julien, who was listening respectfully to the effusions of a Bishop, was at liberty again, he approached his friend, who was now beset by that abominable little Tanbeau. That little wretch was heaping coals on him as the cause of Julien's success.

"When will death deliver us of that old putrefaction?" It was in such terms, in picturesque biblical style, that the little literary gentleman spoke in that moment of the venerable Lord Holland. He had at his fingers' ends the biography of all prominent men, and he began to review those who might rise to influence under the new King of England.

Abbé Pirard passed into an adjoining room, with Julien following.

"The Marquis does not like scribblers, I warn you. That is his sole antipathy. You can learn Latin and Greek if you like, and the history of Egypt and Persia, and he will honor you as a savant. But don't go to writing a page in French, especially on matters above your station in life. He will call you a scribbler and will take you for a fool. Why, living in the mansion of a great lord, don't you know that famous phrase of the Duc de Castries about d'Alembert and Rousseau? 'How can he reason about anything when he has not an income of a thousand écus?' "

"Everything is known here," thought Julien, "just as at the seminary." He had written eight or ten glowing pages, a sort of eulogy on the old army surgeon, who, he felt, had made a man of him. "And that little drawer has always been locked," said Julien to himself. He quickly ran up to his room and burned the manuscript, returning immediately to the drawing-room. The brilliant nonentities had now left; only the gentlemen with the decorations remained.

Around the table, that had been brought in all set, were seven or eight noble, devout women between thirty and thirty-five years of age. The brilliant wife of the Maréchal de Fervaques walked in, excusing herself for the lateness of the hour, it being after midnight. She took her place beside the Marquise. Julien experienced a great emotion, for she had the eyes and the general appearance of Madame de Rênal.

The group around Mademoiselle de la Mole had not yet diminished. She was busy with her friends, passing compliments on the unhappy Count de Thaler. He was the only son of the wealthy Jew who loaned money to kings when at war with their subjects. The Jew had just died, leaving his son an income of a hundred thousand écus a month and a name that was only too well known. Such a fortune demanded either simplicity of character or moral strength. Unfortunately the Count was a man possessed of not a single virtue that was attributed to him by his flatterers.

M. de Caylus was saying that he could not bring himself to the decision even to ask in marriage Mademoiselle de la Mole, to whom the Marquis de Croisenois, a Duke with only an income of ten thousand livres, was paying a great deal of attention.

"Oh, don't accuse him of having a will," said Norbert, pityingly. That hit off the weakness of Count de Thaler precisely. In that respect he was worthy of being a King. For, taking advice from everybody, he had not the courage to follow any definite plan.

"His face shows that," said Mademoiselle de la Mole.

It presented a singular mixture of indecision and disappointment, with some suggestion of self-importance appearing from time to time. That was usually accompanied with that decisive tone which the richest man in France ought to have, especially when he is handsome and not quite thirty-six.

"He is timidly insolent," M. de Croisenois said.

Count de Caylus, Norbert, and two of the other moustached young men would chaff him as much as they liked, without any suspicion on his part, and send him home promptly at one o'clock.

"Are those Arabian horses that are waiting for you at the door just now?" Norbert asked him.

"Oh, no, it is a less expensive team I have," replied M. de Thaler. "The off horse cost me five thousand francs and the other one is worth only one hundred louis; but I want you to know that I don't use them except at night. Their gait is exactly alike; they are well matched."

Norbert's remark gave the Count the idea that it was quite proper for a man like him to have a passion for horses. He left, and the other gentlemen departed soon after, greatly amused over him.

"And so," thought Julien, as he heard them laughingly go down the stairs, "this gives me an idea of the other extreme of my position. I have not an income of twenty louis a year and I find myself side by side with a man who has twenty louis an hour, and he is made sport of." Such a view cured him of his envy.

Chapter 5

Sensitivity and a Pious Lady

> *Une idée un peu vive a l'air d'une grossièreté,*
> *tant on y est accoutumé aux mots sans relief.*
> *Malheur à qui invente en parlant!*
>
> ——FAUBLAS

AFTER several months' trial, the day came when Julien received from the steward of the house the third quarter of his salary. M. de la Mole had also given him charge of the administration of his estates in Brittany and Normandy, where Julien made frequent visits. He was charged especially with the correspondence relative to the famous suit with abbé de Frilaire. M. Pirard had given him the necessary instructions.

From the short notes which the Marquis pencilled on the margin of the letters he received, Julien could write replies that were almost always signed.

At the theological school his professors complained of his lack of application, but they regarded him none the less as one of their most promising students. Julien had then gone to work with great ardor, and the bloom had departed from his cheeks. But his paleness was viewed sympathetically by the young seminarists. He found these less troublesome and less enslaved to the franc than those at Besançon. They thought he had consumption.

The Marquis had given him a horse. Fearing that he might be met riding, Julien hastened to tell them that the exercise was prescribed by a physician.

Abbé Pirard had brought him into some Jansenist circles, where his astonishment knew no bounds. The idea of religion was inextricably bound up in his mind with hypocrisy and greed. He admired those pious, stern men who were not thinking of revenue. Several Jansenists had shown him friendship and given him some kindly advice. A new world seemed to open before him. He made the acquaintance of that Count Altamira, a Liberal, six feet tall, who in his own country had been condemned to death. That strange contrast, religious zeal and love of liberty, struck him with great force.

A little coolness had come between Julien and the young

Count. Norbert had found that he answered too readily the little ironies of several of his friends. Julien, having made a few awkward passes, had resolved also never to speak to Mademoiselle Mathilde. He was treated uniformly with a great deal of kindness in the house, but he felt that he had been put back to some extent. His good provincial sense explained this to him with the proverb, "Everything is beautiful that is new."

Perhaps he was clearer in his vision than at first, or perhaps the first enchantment of Parisian politeness had passed away. When he would cease work, he would be prey to dreadful ennui. It was the effect of that admirable politeness which is so nicely graduated to every station in life. The most obtuse sensibility would see in it something artificial.

No doubt one might object to the provinces as being possessed of too little polish; but at least one has some heart there. Never was Julien's pride injured in the Hôtel de la Mole; but often, after a day's work, he was ready to burst into tears. In the provinces a restaurant waiter takes some interest in you if an accident befalls you as you enter the café, even if his commiseration over your mishap is only an excuse for repeating his tantalizing regrets. At Paris the great aim of all is to hide that they are laughing at you; but you are always nothing to them.

We pass over in silence a mass of little adventures which might have covered Julien with ridicule had he not been in some way above ridicule. A foolish sensitiveness made him commit a thousand *gaucheries*. All his pleasures took the form of precaution. He practised pistol shooting every day and was one of the best pupils of the most famous fencing master. When he had a little time, in place of reading, as before, he would run to the stable and ask for the most vicious horse, though in his rides with the riding master he almost invariably fell off.

The Marquis found him in every way suitable, because of his quickness, his silence, and his intelligence. Gradually he intrusted all his difficult affairs to him. At times, when his lofty ambition would permit, the Marquis would transact his business with a great deal of sagacity, prudently investing his fortune in houses and lands. But he was subject to caprice, and would throw away a hundred louis and grumble about a hundred francs, being as desirous, like other rich men, of the amusement his business would afford him as of profits. The Marquis had really need of a man to bring some order into his affairs.

Madame de la Mole, although usually very dignified, found occasion now and then to speak lightly of Julien. *The unex-*

pected coming from a sensitive person is the horror of great ladies; for it is the antipodes of convention.

Two or three times the Marquis took his part:

"If he is ridiculous in your salon, he triumphs in the library."

Julien, on his part, found out the Marquise's weakness. She deigned to interest herself in a Baron Joumate, an inane sort of a man, who passed his life at the Château uttering commonplaces. He was tall, thin, and ugly. Madame de la Mole would have been delighted, perhaps for the first time in her life, if she could have made a match between him and her daughter.

Chapter 6

Inflection

Leur haute mission est de juger avec calme les petits événements de la vie journalière des peuples. Leur sagesse doit prévenir les grandes colères pour les petites causes, ou pour des événements que la voix de la renommée transfigure en les portant au loin.

—GRATIUS

FOR A BEGINNER, who out of pride would not ask any questions, Julien did not commit too many follies. One day he was suddenly pushed into a café in Rue St. Honoré by a tall man in a red overcoat, who, having his attention attracted by his dark clothes, looked at Julien just as before at Besançon mademoiselle Amanda's lover had done.

Julien had too often reproached himself for having allowed that first insult to take this stare lightly. Upon demanding an explanation, the man in the overcoat insulted him outright. It all took place in the café, in the presence of a great crowd, even passers-by stopping at the door. By a sort of provincial precaution, Julien always carried pistols about him. He began to finger these nervously, but he had enough self-control to say only to his adversary:

"Monsieur, your address? I despise you!"

The constant iteration of these words made an impression on the crowd.

"That man must surely give him his address."

The man in the overcoat, hearing that decision repeated so often, threw into Julien's face five or six cards. Fortunately none of them struck his face, for he had promised himself not to use his pistols except on the defensive. The man then went away, not without turning around several times, shaking his fist at him insultingly.

Julien arose, bathed in perspiration. "So then, I am in the power of every man," he thought, "if I am to be moved so lightly at every turn. How can I kill that humiliating sensitiveness?" he muttered, with rage. "But where can I find a second?"

He did not have a friend. True, he formed several acquaint-

241

ances, but all eventually, at the end of six weeks, kept at a distance from him.

"I am unsociable," he thought, "and now I am cruelly punished for it."

Then he thought of looking up an old lieutenant of the 96th, called Lieven, a poor devil with whom he had frequently fenced. With him Julien was sincere.

"I should like very much to be your second," said Lieven, "but on one condition: if you don't wound your man you shall fight with me on the spot."

"Agreed!" cried Julien, enchanted, and they went to the address of M. C. de Beauvoises, as indicated on the card, in Faubourg St. Germain.

It was seven o'clock in the morning. Not until he presented himself did Julien think that this might be the young relative of Madame de Rênal who was formerly with the Embassy in Rome or in Naples, and who had given a letter of introduction to the singer Geronimo.

Julien had given to the tall footman one of the cards that had been thrown at him and one of his own. After he and his second had been kept waiting three-quarters of an hour, they were shown into an elegantly furnished room, where they found a tall young man dressed like a fashion plate. His features had the perfection and inanity of Greek beauty; his head, carried remarkably erect, was covered with beautiful blond hair, carefully dressed.

"It was to have himself fixed up that way," thought the lieutenant of the 96th, "that this damned fool made us wait." His robe, his morning pantaloons, everything, even to his embroidered slippers, was marvellously correct. His face, noble though expressionless, announced something conventional and clever—the ideal diplomat à la Metternich. Napoleon did not have a relish for such cleverness in the officers about him.

Julien, to whom the lieutenant of the 96th explained that to be kept waiting so long after the cards had been tossed in his face was even a greater insult, entered rather brusquely. He intended at first to be insolent, but he was checked by the demand for good breeding. Julien was so astonished at M. de Beauvoises's politeness and tone, in which dwelt a reserve of authority, and more than all, at the admirable elegance all around, that in the twinkling of an eye he gave up the idea of being insulted. His man surely was not the man of the day before!

His astonishment was so great at finding such a distinguished gentleman in place of that coarse fellow whom he was seeking that he could not find a single word. He presented one of the cards that had been thrown at him.

"That is my name," said the young diplomat, on whom Julien's black coat at seven o'clock in the morning did not make a great impression, "but I do not understand how the honor—"

The pronunciation of the last few words imparted to Julien a little of his former anger. "I have come for our little affair, monsieur," Julien explained.

M. Charles de Beauvoises, after thinking a little, seemingly satisfied with the cut of Julien's coat, said to himself: "He is from Staub, that is clear. That vest is in good taste and the boots are also good; but, on the other hand, that black coat so early in the morning! That is good to escape a bullet with."

After the explanation he resumed his perfect politeness, assuming almost a tone of equality with Julien. The affair being a delicate one, the conversation lasted some time, but toward the end Julien could not refuse the evidence. That elegant young man before him offered not the slightest resemblance to that ruffian who had insulted him the night before.

Julien was very much disgusted when he left. He had observed Chevalier de Beauvoises's self-complacency; it was thus he called himself, when Julien called him simply "monsieur." He admired that gravity which was more or less in reserve, but was never wholly abandoned. He was astonished at his peculiar way of moving his tongue in pronouncing certain words. Yet, with all that, there was no longer any reason for seeking a quarrel.

The young diplomat, indeed, very graciously offered to fight the duel, but the ex-lieutenant of the 96th, having sat through a whole hour, his legs straight out before him, his hands on his hips, with elbows back, decided that his friend M. Sorel would not seek a German quarrel with a man because the latter's cards had been stolen.

Julien walked out in a bad humor. Chevalier de Beauvoises's carriage was in the court before the step. By chance Julien happened to raise his eyes, recognizing his man of the night before in the coachman. To see him and to pull him off his seat by his long coat and to pound him with his fist was all done in a trice. Two footmen ran to their comrade's assistance and gave Julien a number of blows. The latter then drew out his pistol and fired, the servants taking to their heels. All that was the affair of a moment.

Chevalier de Beauvoises, who walked down the step with the utmost self-possession, asked in a lordly tone:

"What is this? What is this?"

He was evidently very curious about it, but his diplomatic importance did not permit him to show any more interest. When he found out what the affair was about, his gravity disputed in his face with a little humor—something that should never appear in a diplomatic countenance.

The lieutenant of the 96th understood that M. de Beauvoises wished to fight, but he had the diplomacy to reserve to his friend the privilege of initiative.

"Indeed," he cried, "that is ground enough for a duel!"

"I think so too," replied the diplomat. "I am going to chase out this rascal," he said to his footman. "Let another man get up on the box."

The carriage door was opened, the Chevalier doing the honors to Julien and his second. Then they looked around for a second for M. de Beauvoises, who indicated a secluded spot. The conversation was friendly enough; there was nothing singular in the scene except the diplomat in his gown.

"These gentlemen," thought Julien, "though very noble, are not as tired of life as those who dine at M. de la Mole's; and I see why," he added, an instant later, "why they permit themselves so many indecencies at times." The conversation had turned on dancers who had been well received by the public in a ballet given the night before. The gentlemen had alluded to some piquant anecdotes of which Julien and his second, the lieutenant of the 96th, were absolutely ignorant.

Julien was not foolish enough to pretend to know them, and readily confessed his ignorance.

That candor pleased the Chevalier's friend, who related more stories with greater detail.

One thing astonished Julien as the carriage stopped for a moment at an altar constructed in the middle of the street for the procession of Corpus Christi. The gentlemen had permitted themselves many questionable pleasantries. The curate, according to them, was the son of an archbishop. Never at the house of the Marquis de la Mole, who wished to become a Duke, had any one dared say such a thing.

The duel was quickly over. Julien received a wound in the arm, which was staunched with handkerchiefs. They fortified him with brandy, and Chevalier de Beauvoises begged Julien to permit him to take him home in the same carriage that had brought them to the scene of the duel.

When Julien indicated the de la Mole mansion, there was an exchange of glances between the young diplomat and his friend. Julien had his second there, but he found the conversation of the other gentlemen infinitely more amusing than that of the good lieutenant of the 96th.

"My Lord! a duel! is that all it is?" thought Julien. "Oh, how glad I am that I found that coachman again! What would it have been for me if I had not resented that insult in the café!"

The amusing conversation was not interrupted. Julien understood then that diplomatic affectation is not without its uses.

"Ennui, then, is not inherent," he said to himself, "in conversations between men of quality. These gentlemen amuse themselves about the Corpus Christi procession, venturing, even, to tell with the utmost detail some risqué anecdotes! They need only reason in political affairs, and that lack is more than compensated by the grace of their manner and the perfect impassiveness of their expression."

Julien felt very strongly drawn to them. "How glad I should be to see them often!"

They had hardly gotten away when Beauvoises went to seek information. It was not very encouraging; he was very curious to know about his man. Would it be proper to make him a visit? The little information he received was not calculated to make him feel very proud.

"Oh, that is horrible!" he said to his second; "it is impossible that I can ever acknowledge that I fought a duel with only M. de la Mole's secretary, and that because my coachman stole my visiting cards! That much is sure, there is something of the ridiculous in the whole affair."

The same evening de Beauvoises and his friend were telling everybody that this young Sorel, otherwise a very proper young man, was the natural son of an intimate friend of Marquis de la Mole. That passed without difficulty. Once the rumor was started, the young diplomat and his friend deigned to call on Julien during the two weeks he remained in his room.

Julien confessed to them that he had only once in his life been to the opera.

"That is frightful," he was told. "Why, it is the only place to which people go. The first time you go out it must be to see *Count Ory.*"

At the opera, de Beauvoises presented him to the famous singer Geronimo, who was enjoying great success. Julien almost courted the Chevalier; the mixture of self-respect, of mysterious importance, and of fatuity had a charm for him.

True, the Chevalier stammered a little, because he often had the honor of seeing a great lord who had that impediment in his speech. Never, however, had Julien seen united in one person the folly that amuses and the perfection of manner that a poor provincial should do his best to imitate. He was, therefore, frequently seen at the opera with Chevalier Beauvoises. That companionship was making a name for him.

"Oh, indeed!" said M. de la Mole to him one day; "so, then, you are the natural son of a rich gentleman of Franche-Comté, my intimate friend?"

The Marquis interrupted Julien as the latter was about to protest that he had not assisted in any manner in spreading that rumor: "M. de Beauvoises did not want it known that he fought a duel with a carpenter's son."

"I know it, I know it," said M. de la Mole to him. "It is left for me now to make the story true or false; but I wish to ask a favor of you which will take only half an hour of your time. At the opera, at half-past eleven, you must be in the vestibule when the great people are leaving. I see in you yet some provincial mannerisms of the country. You must get rid of them. Besides, it is not a bad idea to have you know, if only by sight, the important personages to whom I may send you on business one day. Go to the box office in order to make yourself known; you have received cards."

Chapter 7

An Attack of Gout

And I got the promotion not on my own merits
but because my master had the gout.

—BERTOLOTTI

THE READER is perhaps surprised over that free and easy tone. We have forgotten to say that for about a week the Marquis had been confined to his home by gout. Mathilde and her mother were at Hyères with the Marquise's mother. Count Norbert saw his father only for a moment. They were friendly to each other, but they had nothing to say. M. de la Mole, reduced only to Julien, was astonished to find so many good ideas in him, and often had him read the paper to him.

The young secretary after a while was able to pick out the most interesting passages. There was a new newspaper which the Marquis abhorred, swearing he would never read it; yet every day he spoke of it. Julien laughed. The Marquis, disgusted with contemporary history, had him read from Livy, the sight translations of the Latin text affording him a great deal of pleasure.

One day the Marquis said to him in that excessively polite tone which made Julien so impatient:

"Permit me, my dear Sorel, to make you a present of a blue coat. When you find it convenient to take it and to come to me, you will be in my eyes that young man, the brother of Count Chaulnes; that is to say, the son of my friend the old Duke."

Julien did not understand what he meant. The same evening, however, he came to see him in a blue coat. The Marquis treated him like an equal, and Julien saw the difference in the polite tone. He would have sworn before that caprice of the Marquis that it was impossible to be treated with greater consideration. "What admirable tact!" Julien thought.

When he rose to leave, the Marquis excused himself for not being able to accompany him to the door on account of his gout.

That singular event greatly engrossed Julien's mind. "Is he having sport with me?" he asked himself.

He went to consult M. Pirard, who, less polished than the

247

Marquis, replied to him only with a laugh and passed to another subject.

The next day Julien presented himself to the Marquis in his black coat, with his portfolio and letters for signature. He was received in the old way; but in the evening, in his blue coat, it was the same as the night before.

"Since you do not get tired of the visits that you are kind enough to make to a poor sick man," said the Marquis to him, "you must tell him about the little incidents of your life; but candidly, and without thought of anything but to state it clearly and interestingly. For one must amuse one's self," continued the Marquis; "that is the only thing real in life. True, it is something to return safe from a war, or to receive a present of a million; but if I had Rivarol beside my chair he would relieve me of an hour of suffering and weariness every day! I knew him very well at Hamburg during the Emigration." And the Marquis related some stories about Rivarol and the Hamburgers, who join four words to make one.

M. de la Mole, reduced solely to the society of the little abbé, wished to arouse the latter by piquing Julien's pride in an appeal to his sense of honor. Since the truth was asked, Julien resolved to tell all, but to keep in reserve only two things—his frantic admiration for a name which always put the Marquis in a bad humor, and his perfect agnosticism, which was not proper for a future curate. His little affair with Chevalier de Beauvoises appeared in course of time.

The Marquis laughed until the tears came into his eyes at the scene in the Rue St. Honoré with the coachman who had insulted him. It was a frank, free hour in the relations between patron and protégé. M. de la Mole interested himself in this singular character. At first he had smoothed over Julien's awkwardness in order to enjoy it, but he soon found it more interesting to correct it. "All the other provincials who arrived in Paris admire everything; he holds everything in contempt. They have too much affectation; he not enough. Only fools can take him for a fool."

The attack of gout did not leave him during the cold season, which lasted several months.

"A man attaches himself to his little foible," the Marquis said to himself. "Why should I be ashamed of attaching myself to this little abbé? He is original; I will treat him like a son. Oh, well, where is the foolishness? This little caprice, if it lasts, will cost me, perhaps, a little five hundred louis in my will."

Once the Marquis knew the fine character of his protégé, he put some new affair in his hands every day.

Julien remarked with horror that the great lord would give contradictory decisions on the same subject, that might lead to difficulties. Julien no longer worked with him, but carried about a little book in which he wrote down his instructions, and the Marquis then went accordingly. Julien had also taken an assistant, who transcribed the instructions as to the disposition of several matters on a separate book. This book also contained copies of every letter that was written.

That idea at first seemed to be the very height of folly and tiresomeness; but in two months the Marquis saw the advantage of it. Julien proposed to hire a clerk who came from a banker to keep an account of every item of income and expenditure in connection with the letters with which Julien dealt.

These measures gave the Marquis such a clear idea of his affairs that he had the pleasure of undertaking two or three new speculations without the aid of an agent who always stole from him.

"Take three thousand francs for yourself," said he one day to his assistant.

"Monsieur, my conduct might be criticised."

"What difference is it to you?" replied the Marquis, piqued.

"Be good enough, then, to take a check and write with your own hand on this account book. This check will give me three thousand francs." It was abbé Pirard who gave him the idea of the entire book-keeping system.

The Marquis, with the annoyed face of a Marquis de Moncade, made that memorandum while listening to the report of M. Poisson, his steward.

In the evening, when Julien appeared in his blue coat, there was nothing said about the affair. The Marquis's kindness flattered our hero's pride to such an extent that, in spite of himself, he had a feeling of attachment for the amiable old man; but not in the sense in which it is understood in Paris. He was, after all, not insensible; and no one, since the death of the army surgeon, had spoken to him with so much kindness.

He remarked with astonishment that the Marquis had a consideration for him that he had not seen even in the old soldier.

He understood then that the army surgeon was prouder of his Cross than the Marquis was of his cordon bleu. The Marquis's father was a great lord. One day, at the conclusion of a morning meeting, Julien, dressed in his black coat, was quite entertaining to the Marquis. The latter detained him for two hours, and insisted upon giving him some bank notes his agent had just brought from the Bourse.

"I hope, Monsieur le Marquis, I am not lacking in respect for you if I ask for the privilege of a word?"

"Go on, my young man."

"It is to ask the Marquis to be gracious enough to allow me to refuse the gift. It is not the man in the black coat that is addressed now; it might spoil the charm which you are good enough to recognize in the man in blue."

He saluted him with great respect and left without raising his eyes.

This trait amused the Marquis. That night he spoke of it to abbé Pirard.

"I want to assure you of one thing, my dear abbé: I know of Julien's origin, and I command you not to keep back any information on that matter. His procedure this morning was nobility itself, and I myself will ennoble him."

After some time the Marquis could walk out.

"Go to London for two months," he said to Julien. "The special courier and others will bring you the letters which I receive, together with my notes; you will write the answers and send them back, putting each answer with the letter. I have calculated that the delay will be only a matter of five days."

On going to Calais, Julien was astonished at the trifling character of the business for which he was sent away.

We shall not describe the sentiment of hate and horror with which he touched English soil. With his boundless passion for Bonaparte, he saw in each officer a Sir Hudson Lowe; in each great lord a Lord Bathurst, ordering the indignities of St. Helena, for which he received the reward of ten years in the Ministry.

At London he was conscious most of all of his infatuation. He had entered into a friendship with some young Russian nobles.

"You are predestined, my dear Sorel," they said to him; "you have naturally what we try so hard to cultivate, that cool, calculating air by which you manage to be a thousand leagues away from your surroundings."

"You don't understand your age," said Prince Korasoff to him; "always do the opposite of what is expected of you. On my honor, it's the only religion now. Don't be either foolish or affected; for then people will expect of you foolishness and affectation, and that will be the end of you."

Julien covered himself with glory one day in the drawing-room of the Duke Fitz-Folke, who had invited him to dinner together with Prince Korasoff. They waited an hour for him. The manner in which Julien conducted himself in the midst of the twenty persons who awaited him is yet spoken of by the young secretaries of the London Embassy. His expression on his entrance was inimitable. He desired to see, despite the persuasions of the *dandies,* his friends, the celebrated Philip Vane, the only philosopher whom England had produced since Locke. This philosopher had just finished his seventh year in prison.

"The aristocracy do not take him very lightly," thought Julien. "Vane is unhonored, vilified."

Julien found him very cheerful in spite of the rage of the aristocracy.

"There," Julien said to himself, as he walked out of the jail, "he is the only man I have seen in England."

"The most useful idea with tyrants is that of God," Vane had said to him. We shall suppress the rest of the philosophy as cynical.

On his return M. de la Mole asked him: "What amusing idea do you bring me from England?" Julien did not answer. "What idea do you bring with you, amusing or not?" asked the Marquis, again.

"First," said Julien, "the wisest Englishman is a perfect fool for one hour of the day; he is possessed with the mania for suicide, which is the god of that country. Second, genius loses twenty-five per cent in value on arriving in England. Third, nothing in the world is as beautiful, admirable, softening, as English scenery."

"Now, it is my turn," said the Marquis. "First, why did you say at the Russian Ambassador's ball that there are in France thirty thousand young men twenty-five years of age who ardently desire war? Do you think that that is agreeable to Kings?"

"A man does not know what to say when speaking to those diplomats," said Julien; "they have a way of commencing serious discussions. If one holds to what is written in the newspapers, he is taken for a fool; if one permits himself something true and trite, they are astonished. One does not know what to say in reply. And next morning you are informed by the First Secretary of the Embassy that you have said something awkward."

"Not bad," said the Marquis, laughing. "Well, I bet, Monsieur Wiseacre, that you don't know what you have done in England."

"Pardon me," replied Julien; "I have been to dinner once a week at the house of the English Ambassador, who is the most charming of men."

"You have gone to seek that Cross I have here," replied the Marquis. "I don't want you to take off your black coat—though I am accustomed to your entertaining conversation when you are dressed in blue—until further notice. Now, listen; when I see that Cross, you shall be the younger son of my old friend Duke de Chaulnes, who, no doubt, has seen diplomatic service for six months. Now notice," added the Marquis, seriously, with an abrupt gesture; "notice that I do not want you to leave your present position. It is always as embarrassing for the protector as for the protégé. If my lawsuits bother you too much, or if you are no longer agreeable to me, I will provide a curacy for you like that of our friend abbé Pirard, that is all," added the Marquis, dryly.

That Cross was a satisfaction to Julien's pride. He spoke longer than usual in reply. He did not take the remarks amiss, though they were capable of various interpretations, a shade of hardness being quite evident.

The Cross brought him one singular visit. It was that of Baron Valenod, who came to Paris to thank the Minister for his baronetcy and to have an audience. He was about to be named Mayor of Verrières in place of M. de Rênal. Julien was very much amused when Valenod gave him to understand that it was discovered that M. de Rênal was a Jacobin.

The fact of the matter was that in the election for which preparations were being made, the new Baron was a candidate of the Ministry, and at the College of the department, which was indeed very extreme in sentiment, it was M. de Rênal who had been carried by the Liberals.

In vain Julien tried to find out something about Madame de Rênal. The Baron seemed to remember their ancient rivalry and remained uncommunicative. He ended by asking Julien for his father's vote in the elections which were about to take place. Julien promised to write.

"I will beg you, Monsieur le Chevalier, to present me to the Marquis de la Mole."

"In fact, I should," thought Julien; "but such a fool! In truth," he answered, "I am too small a man at the Hôtel de la Mole to take it upon myself to present anyone."

Julien told everything to the Marquis in the evening. He

related to him Valenod's pretensions, also his record during the year 1814.

"Not only," replied M. de la Mole in a serious tone, "shall you present this new Baron to me, but I am going to invite him to dinner for day after to-morrow. He will be one of our new prefects."

"In that case," Julien answered, coolly, "I ask for my father the position of Director of the Poor."

"All right, it is granted," said the Marquis, resuming his good humor. "I was expecting some moralizing; but you are coming out."

M. de Valenod told Julien that the holder of the lottery office in Verrières had just died. Julien took it upon himself to have the place given to M. Cholin, that old imbecile whose petition he had picked up in the room occupied by M. de la Mole. The Marquis laughed good naturedly over the petition which Julien recited as he was presenting a letter for his signature asking the Minister of Finance for that place.

Hardly had Cholin been named when Julien learned that the place was asked by a petition from the department for M. Gros, the celebrated geometrician. That good man had an income of only fourteen hundred francs a year, and had loaned every year six hundred francs to the last incumbent to help him support his family.

Julien regretted what he had done. "Well, what is the difference?" he said to himself; "some injustice must be done if I am to succeed. And yet I must hide it all under fine phrases. Poor Gros! It is he who merited a Cross, and it is I who have it! Yes, I must act as for the government that gave it to me."

Chapter 8

Which Decoration Brings Distinction?

> *"Your water does not refresh me,"* said the
> thirsty genie. *"Yet it's the coolest well in all the
> Diar Bekir."*
>
> ——PELLICO

ONE DAY Julien came back from the fine estate at Villequier on
the Seine, in which M. de la Mole took a good deal of interest.
Of all his possessions that alone had belonged to the celebrated
Boniface de la Mole. He found at the house the Marquise and
her daughter, who had arrived previously from Hyères.

Julien was fashionably dressed now and knew the art of
Parisian life. He was wholly indifferent toward Mademoiselle
de la Mole. He seemed to have forgotten altogether the time
when she asked him so gayly about the details of his fall.

Mademoiselle de la Mole thought he had grown tall and was
looking pale. Neither his figure nor his general appearance had
anything of the provincial. There was not a trace of it in his
conversation. Still there was something too serious, too positive
about him. In spite of these qualities, arising mostly from his
pride, she saw nothing of the subaltern in him; only he looked
at too many things too seriously. One could see that he was a
man who would stand by his word.

"He lacks vivacity, though he is not dull," said Mademoiselle
de la Mole to her father, teasing him about the Cross which he
had given to Julien. "My brother has been asking you for it for
eighteen months, and he is a la Mole."

"Yes, but Julien has something of the unexpected about him;
that is what never happens to the la Mole of whom you are
speaking."

Duke de Retz was then announced.

Mathilde was seized with a frightful yawning, remembering
the antique gilt and the old visitors of the house. She represented to herself a most tedious picture of the life to be resumed
in Paris, and yet at Hyères they had wished they were back.

"And I am only nineteen years old—a blissful age, according
to all these gilded fools!"

She looked at eight or ten new volumes of poetry that had

254

accumulated while they were in Provence. She had the misfortune of being more clever than MM. de Croisenois, de Caylus, de Luz, and her other friends. She knew beforehand all that they would say about the beautiful scenery of Provence, about poetry and the rest.

Her beautiful eyes, in which dwelt so much ennui, and, what is worse, so much despair of finding real pleasure, rested on Julien. "Anyhow," she thought, "he is not exactly like the others."

"M. Sorel," she said, with that lively, curt, almost masculine voice which young women of high society use, "M. Sorel, are you going this evening to M. de Retz's ball?"

"Mademoiselle, I have not had the honor of an introduction to the Duke."

One might have thought that the words and the title were scorching the proud provincial's lips.

"He asked my brother to bring you; and if you should be there I should like to have you give me some details about the estate at Villequier. We may go there in the spring. I should like very much to know if the château is habitable, and if the neighborhood there is as pretty as people say. There are so many things said that are not true."

Julien did not reply.

"Come to the ball with my brother," she added, dryly.

Julien bowed respectfully.

"So even at a ball I must give an account to the members of the family. Am I not paid like a clerk?" he added, with increased ill humor. "The Lord knows if what I am going to tell the daughter will not thwart the projects of the father, brother, and mother. It is a veritable prince's court; one must be a perfect nobody, and yet give no one occasion to complain. How this tall girl displeases me!" he thought, looking at Mademoiselle Mathilde as she walked away in answer to a sign from her mother, who wished to present her to some friends. "She is not stylish, her gown hangs from her shoulders, she is paler even than before the trip. Her hair is of that blond which is almost colorless; light seems to pass through it. But how proudly she greets anyone. What haughtiness in her brow, in that look! What queenly airs!"

Mademoiselle de la Mole had called her brother just as he was leaving the drawing-room.

Count Norbert, approaching Julien, said:

"My dear Sorel, do you want to go at midnight to M. de Retz's ball? He has expressly asked me to bring you."

"I know how to appreciate the kindness," replied Julien, bowing low. His ill humor prevented him from saying anything more in reply to the polite, brotherly tone in which Norbert had addressed him. He was thinking only of the way he should accept the invitation, in which he thought there was something patronizing.

In the evening, at the ball, he was struck by the magnificence of the Hôtel de Retz. The entrance was covered with an immense canopy of pink canvas covered with gilt spangles; it was beautiful. Underneath the awning the court was transformed into an orange grove and a rose garden in bloom. It took infinite labor to sink the vases deep enough so that the rose bushes and the orange trees might appear standing straight out of the earth. The carriage drive was sanded. The whole thing seemed extraordinary to our provincial; he had never had an idea of such magnificence.

In a trice his imagination, now greatly stimulated, bore away all his ill humor. In the carriage, on the way to the ball, Norbert, too, was delighted, as everything was in the dark; but hardly had they entered the court than the rôles changed. Norbert could see only a few details which, in the midst of all this magnificence, seemed to have been overlooked. He knew exactly the cost of each rose, and, when he came to add it up, Julien noticed that his friend was almost jealous and growing glum. As for him, he was carried away. He was full of admiration when he entered the first drawing-room, where dancing was going on.

All surged toward the second door, but there was such a crush that it was almost impossible to advance. The decoration of the second drawing-room represented the Alhambra of Grenada.

"She is the queen of the ball, you must admit," said a young man with moustaches, whose shoulder was pressed against Julien's breast.

"Mademoiselle Fourmont, who all winter has been the most beautiful woman," replied his neighbor, "sees now that she must take second place. Watch her singular manner!"

"Really she has shaken out every sail to please. See! See that gracious smile when she thinks she is alone in the quadrille. Indeed, that is fine! Mademoiselle de la Mole seems to be mistress of it all and is now making her triumph. She knows it, too! There, see that! She is afraid of being too agreeable to the one she is talking to now."

"Good, that is a good way to make them run after her."

Julien made vain efforts to see the seductive woman. Seven or eight tall men were in the way.

"There is a good deal of coquetry in that splendid carriage of hers," replied the young man with the moustaches.

"And those fine blue eyes that are lowered so slowly that one might think they were just on the point of betraying themselves," replied his neighbor. "Mon dieu! there is nothing more beautiful!"

"See how the pretty Fourmont looks common beside her!" said a third. "For all the world she seems to say, 'See what I could be if you were a man worthy of me.'"

"Who can be worthy of the superb Mathilde?" said the first. "He must be a prince, a hero in war, and only twenty years of age!"

"The natural son of the Emperor of Russia, for whom, in case a marriage like that takes place, a little sovereignty would be created. Or, perhaps, only that Count de Thaler with his insignificant provincial manners."

The door was not crowded then, and Julien could enter.

"Since she is thought so remarkable by these fops, she is worth studying," he thought. "I want to see what is the attraction for these people."

As he was scrutinizing her very closely, Mathilde looked at him. "Duty has called me," said Julien to himself; but all his soberness was only in his expression. Curiosity led him to advance eagerly, and he was also hastened by Mathilde's dress, which was cut very low from the shoulders; in a manner, indeed, that flattered his own pride very little. "There is something youthful in her beauty," he thought. Five or six young men were between them, among whom Julien recognized those who had spoken together at the door.

"You, monsieur, who have been here all winter," she said to him, "do you not think that this is the prettiest ball of the season?"

He did not reply.

"This Coulon quadrille is quite perfect, and these ladies dance it beautifully."

The young men turned around to see who was the fortunate man whose reply was so eagerly sought.

"I don't think I am a good judge, mademoiselle. I spend my time writing; it is the first ball of such magnificence I have ever attended."

The young men with moustaches were scandalized.

"You are very good, Monsieur Sorel," one replied, with very

marked interest. "You see all these balls, these fêtes, like a philosopher—like Jean Jacques Rousseau—these follies astonish you, but do not charm."

That was sufficient for Julien: it removed all illusions. His mouth took on an expression of disdain, perhaps a little too exaggerated.

"Jean Jacques Rousseau," he replied, "is in my eyes only a fool when he tries to judge society. He does not understand it, and he has the ideas of a footman who has fallen heir to a fortune."

"Yes, but he has given the *contrat social!*" replied Mathilde, with veneration.

"While preaching about the republic and the overturning of royal dignity, this parvenu becomes mad with joy if a Duke turns aside in his after-dinner walk to accompany one of his friends."

"So the Duke de Luxembourg, at Montmorenci, accompanies a certain M. Coindet on the outskirts of Paris," resumed Mademoiselle de la Mole, with the abandon of a first enjoyment of pedantry. She was almost as happy over her knowledge as the Academician who discovered the existence of King Feretrius. But Julien's eye remained penetrating and severe. Mathilde had a moment of enthusiasm, and his pretence of indifference was plainly disagreeable to her. She was the more astonished at this since it was always she who usually made that impression on others.

At that moment the Marquis de Croisenois advanced eagerly toward Mademoiselle de la Mole. He came within three feet of her without being able to get nearer for the crowd. He looked at her, smiling at the obstacle that was in his way. The young Marquise de Rouvray, Mathilde's cousin, was near him, leaning on the arm of her husband, to whom she had been married only a fortnight. The Marquis de Rouvray, very young himself, had all the love which a man usually shows when he contracts a marriage of convenience as arranged by the notaries and finds also his wife perfectly beautiful. M. de Rouvray at the death of his aged uncle was to succeed him as Duke.

While the Marquis de Croisenois was smiling at Mathilde through the crowd, she herself raised her beautiful eyes to him and those around him.

"Can there be anything more stupid," she was saying to herself, "than that group? This Croisenois, who wants to marry me, is kind, polished, and has perfect manners, like M. de Rouvray. Except for the weary moments they make one spend, these gentlemen would indeed be amiable in every respect. He, too, has followed me throughout the ball with an air of complacency.

"A year after marriage my carriage, my horses, my gowns, my château at a little distance from Paris—all that would be as nice as possible. It would be all that is necessary to make a young upstart like Countess de Roiville die of jealousy; but after that——?"

Mathilde was tired of it all.

Marquis de Croisenois then approached and talked to her, but she was scarcely listening. For her the sound of his voice was confused with the babble of the ball. Her eye mechanically followed Julien, who had withdrawn to a respectful distance, still proud and disdainful.

Far from the crowd she saw in a corner Count Altamira, who, in his country, had been sentenced to death. Under Louis XIV., one of his relatives had married a Prince de Conti; that fact protected him somewhat from the Congregation.

"I see only the death sentence that distinguishes that man," thought Mathilde; "that is the only thing he has not bought. Ah! that is an epigram—a pity it is not anything to be proud of!" Mathilde was too well-bred to mingle epigrams with her conversation, but she had just enough vanity to make her conceit not too pronounced. A look of satisfaction took the place of tedium in her eyes.

Marquis de Croisenois, who kept on talking, thought he was becoming interesting and talked with greater animation.

"Who is wicked enough to object to my phrase?" Mathilde asked herself. "I could reply to a critic that the title of Baron or Viscount can be bought; a Cross is given. My brother has just received something; what did he do? It was a promotion; that is easily obtained. Ten years in garrison, or a relative who happens to be Minister of War, and one can be chief of a squadron. As to a great fortune—that is still the most difficult thing to obtain, and, therefore, is most meritorious. How funny it is the exact opposite of what we read in books! Well, as for fortune, there is marriage."

M. Rotchschild was announced.

"Really, my epigram has some truth in it, after all. The death sentence is still the only thing left which people do not care anything at all about."

"Do you know Count Altamira?" she asked M. de Croisenois. She seemed to be coming back from a great distance, and the question was so little in accord with what the poor Marquis had been saying that his amiability all but left him. "He seems to be an intelligent man and quite famous."

"Mathilde is odd," he thought. "That is an inconvenience; but she would give such a fine social position to her husband. I really do not know how this Marquis de la Mole conducts his affairs, but he is closely in touch with the best men in all the parties. He is a man that is not likely to go down. Besides, Mathilde's eccentricities might pass for genius. With noble birth and fortune, genius is not an absurdity, but a distinction. And sometimes, when she has a mind to, that mixture of brilliancy and depth makes her perfect."

"How difficult it is to do two things at once!" he said, indifferently, in answer to Mathilde. "Who does not know this poor Altamira?" Then he told her the history of the ridiculous, absurd conspiracy.

"Extremely absurd! Bring him here," she said to the Marquis, who seemed very much put out.

Count Altamira, with his haughty, almost impertinent look, was one of the most ardent admirers of Mademoiselle de la Mole. In his eyes she was one of the most beautiful women in Paris.

"How beautiful she would look on a throne!" he said to M. de Croisenois, and he went on in that strain uninterrupted.

There are many who would maintain that nothing in the nineteenth century is worse than a conspiracy. It is the same as being a Jacobin; and what is worse than a thwarted Jacobin?

Mathilde looked somewhat mockingly at Altamira, not seeming very much interested.

"A conspirator at a ball! That is a fine contrast!" With his black moustaches, she thought she saw in him a veritable lion in repose. But she soon found that his genius lay only in one direction, in the practical end. Except that he desired a liberal government in his own country, the young Count did not find anything worthy of his attention.

He left Mathilde with pleasure, although she was the most beautiful woman at the ball. But he had caught a glance of a Peruvian general. Discouraged by the attitude of Europe, as assumed by M. de Metternich, poor Altamira was forced to think that when the South American States had become strong and powerful they might give to Europe the liberty which Mirabeau had given to them.

A crowd of moustached young men were now again surrounding Mathilde. She saw very well that Altamira was not enthralled by her charms, and was, therefore, somewhat piqued at his departure. She saw his black eyes sparkle as he was talking to the Peruvian general.

While Mademoiselle de la Mole was looking at the young Frenchmen who surrounded her with that profound, serious air which her rivals despaired of imitating, she was thinking: "Which one of these would allow himself to be sentenced to death even if he had every opportunity?"

That singular look flattered those who were dull, but disconcerted the rest. The latter feared the utterance of some biting epigram.

"A noble birth gives a hundred qualities the absence of which would to me be an affliction. I see that in Julien," thought Mathilde. "But noble birth has none of the qualities of the soul which can lead to such heroism as is implied in a death sentence."

Just then someone close to her said: "This Count Altamira is the second son of Prince San Nazaro-Pimental. It was a Pimental tried to save Conradin who was decapitated in 1268; one of the oldest families of Naples."

"There, now," said Mathilde, "that proves my maxim admirably. Noble birth removes the force of character that could lead to any such heroism. But I must make up my mind not to reason this evening, since I am a woman like the rest. Well, I suppose I have to dance."

She yielded to the insistent invitation of M. de Croisenois, who for an hour had been asking her for a gallop. In order to be diverted from the serious reflections her philosophy had given her, Mathilde tried to be unusually gracious, and M. de Croisenois was charmed.

But Mathilde found no diversion either in the dance or in the desire to please one of the handsomest men at court. No woman could have had greater success; indeed, she was the queen of the ball. She was not blind to that fact, but she seemed quite indifferent.

"What a vain life I should spend with such a man as de Croisenois," she said to herself, as he escorted her to her seat an hour later. "What is the pleasure to me," she said, sadly, "if after an absence of six months I see him at a ball which is the talk of all the Parisian women? And yet I am surrounded here with attentions in a class of a society than which none can imagine better. The only bourgeois here are a few peers and one or two like Julien, perhaps. However," she added, with increasing sadness, "what advantages has not chance given me? An illustrious ancestry, fortune, youth, everything except happiness. The most doubtful of all my advantages are those of which they spoke this evening. Mind, I think, is one of them; for I made them all afraid, evidently. If they started on a serious subject, at the end of five minutes they would be all out of breath as if they had made a great discovery; and I had been telling them about that very thing for nearly an hour. A pity I have this advantage for which Madame de Staël would have sacrificed everything; and yet—it is a fact—I am dying of ennui! Why should I try to find life a little less wearisome by changing my name for that of Marquise de Croisenois?

"But," she added, almost crying, "is he not a perfect gentleman? He is the chef-d'œuvre of the breeding of our age. One cannot look at him without finding that he can say something agreeable, something bright to you; he is so gallant; but this Sorel is singular. I have as much as told him that I wished to speak to him, and he has not deigned to appear again."

Chapter 9

The Ball

> *Elegance of dress, luster of candlelight, perfumes; so many pretty arms and beautiful shoulders; bouquets, the exalting strains of Rossini, the paintings of Ciceri! I am quite beside myself!*
>
> —TRAVELS OF UZERI

"YOU LOOK CROSS," said the Marquise de la Mole to Mathilde; "yet let me tell you, that is not proper at a ball."

"I have only a bad headache," she replied; "it is so warm here."

Just at this moment old Baron de Tolly, as if to corroborate Mademoiselle de la Mole's statement, fainted and fell, and had to be carried away. Some one said something about apoplexy, which put somewhat of a damper on the evening. Mathilde did not concern herself about that, for she had made up her mind never to look at old men or at anyone else known to speak on sad subjects. She danced in order to avoid a conversation about apoplexy. But nothing of the kind had taken place, for the next day the Baron came out all right.

"But M. Sorel is not coming toward me," she said to herself, after she had danced a while. She looked for him everywhere, finding him finally at the other end of the room. He seemed, strangely enough, to have left off that air of reserve, that sneering English look that was so natural to him.

"He is conversing with Count Altamira, my man who was sentenced to death," Mathilde said to herself. "His eye has a severe look; he seems to be a prince in disguise; he looks prouder than ever."

Julien then came where she was standing, still talking with Altamira. She looked at the latter steadily as if to ascertain those high qualities which lead a man to such sacrifice.

As he passed near her he was saying to Count Altamira:

"Yes, Danton was a man."

"Oh, my! would he be a Danton?" Mathilde said to herself. "But his face is so noble and Danton was so horribly ugly, a butcher, I believe!"

263

Julien was then very close to her, and she did not hesitate to call him. For a young girl, she was rather proud of asking the extraordinary question, "Was not Danton a butcher?"

"Oh, yes, in the eyes of certain people," Julien replied, with an expression of ill-disguised disdain, his eyes still flashing from the animated conversation he had had with Altamira. "But, unfortunately for well-born people, he was an attorney at Mery-sur-Seine; that is to say, Mademoiselle," he added, mischievously, "he began just like some peers I see here now. 'Tis true that Danton was quite at a disadvantage in the eyes of beauty, he was so very ugly."

The last few words were spoken rapidly, in a strange, awkward manner. Julien waited an instant, slightly leaning over, seemingly humble in his pride. He seemed to say, "I am paid to answer you, and I have given you 'value received.' " He did not deign to raise his eyes to Mathilde. On her part, with her beautiful eyes wide open and fixed on him, she seemed to be in the beseeching attitude of a slave. Then, as the silence continued, he looked at her as a footman looks at his master for an order. Although his eyes met Mathilde's, which were still strangely fixed on him, he moved away with marked effort.

"He who is so handsome," Mathilde finally said to herself, coming out of a reverie, "to eulogize ugliness in such a fashion! Never does he speak of himself; he is not like Caylus or de Croisenois. This Sorel looks something like my father when he appears as Napoleon at a ball." She had forgotten all about Danton by this time.

"Well, really, I am weary to-night."

She seized her brother's arm, and, in spite of his objections, compelled him to walk around the ballroom. The idea occurred to her to follow up the conversation of Altamira with Julien.

There was an enormous crowd. She caught up to them just as two steps ahead of her Altamira was going to take an ice. Half turned round, he was still speaking to Julien. He saw an embroidered arm, that also took refreshment, at his side; the embroidery seeming to arouse his curiosity. Then, turning round to see the person to whom the arm belonged, his noble eyes instantly took on an expression of disdain.

"You see that man?" he whispered to Julien, "that is the Prince d'Araceli, the Ambassador from X—. This morning he asked for my extradition of the French Minister of Foreign Affairs, M. de Nerval. Look, there is he down there playing whist. M. de Nerval would not hesitate to give me up, for we gave you some two or three conspirators in 1816. Well, if I am given back to my King, I shall be hanged in just about twenty-four hours, and it will be one of those pretty gentlemen with the moustaches who will use his fist on me besides."

"The wretches!" cried Julien, half aloud.

Mathilde was not losing a syllable of their conversation; her ennui seemed to have disappeared.

"Not exactly wretches," replied Count Altamira. "I spoke to you about the King in order to give you a good idea of the thing. Now look at the Prince d'Araceli; every five minutes he looks at his Golden Fleece. He cannot get enough pleasure of seeing it on his breast. That man at bottom is only an anachronism. For a hundred years that Fleece has been a signal honor, but that long passed away before him. To-day, with all these members of the nobility, one must be a d'Araceli to be enchanted with it all. He would have destroyed a whole town to obtain it."

"Is it at that price that he obtained it?" asked Julien, anxiously.

"No, not precisely," answered Altamira, coldly. "Perhaps he threw into the river some thirty or so rich farmers who were supposed to be Liberals."

"What a monster!" said Julien.

Mademoiselle de la Mole leaned over so far as to have her pretty hair touch his shoulder.

"Now you are very young," replied Altamira. "I was telling you that I have a sister married in Provence. She is still pretty; good, sweet-tempered, she is an excellent woman about a house, faithful to all her duties, pious, but not to an extreme."

"What is he coming to?" thought Mademoiselle de la Mole.

"And she is happy," continued Altamira; "she was the same in 1815. Then I hid myself at her house on the estate near Antibes. Oh, well, as soon as she learned of the execution of Maréchal Ney she took to dancing."

"Is it possible?" asked Julien, dumbfounded.

"That is the spirit of the party," replied Altamira. "There is no more real passion in the nineteenth century; it is for that reason that people get so weary of life in France. The greatest cruelties are committed without cruelty."

"So much the worse," said Julien; "at least when one commits crimes he should do it with a certain amount of pleasure. The good of it is only in that, and it cannot be justified except by such a reason."

Mademoiselle de la Mole, forgetting herself entirely, had come almost between Altamira and Julien. Her brother, whose arm she had taken, accustomed to obeying her, was looking elsewhere in the ballroom; and in order to keep himself in countenance was looking as if he had been stopped by the crowd.

"You are right," Altamira was saying; "everything is done without a thought, even crimes. I can show you in this ballroom ten men, perhaps, who may be condemned to death as assassins; they are not thinking of it, nor is the world. Many people are moved almost to tears if their dog breaks a leg. At Père la Chaise, where flowers are strewn over the graves, as you pleasantly remarked at Paris, we learn that they unite in themselves all the virtues of a valiant knight, and they speak of the heroic actions of their ancestors who lived under Henry IV. If, in spite of Prince d'Araceli's kindness, I am not hanged, and I ever get to enjoy my fortune in Paris, I will invite you to a dinner with eight or ten assassins who are honored and who have no remorse. You and I will be almost the only ones of pure blood at that dinner; but I, I will be hated and despised as a sanguinary monster and Jacobin, and you will be sneered at for being a man of the people who has intruded himself into good company."

"True enough," said Mademoiselle de la Mole. Altamira looked at her astonished; Julien, on the other hand, not deigning even to look.

"Now notice that the revolution at the head of which I am placed," continued Count Altamira, "has not succeeded, simply because I did not want to have three heads cut off, and distribute among our partisans the seven or eight millions in our treasury, to which I have the key. My King, who is dying now to hang me, and who, before the Revolution, would speak to me so familiarly, would have given me the Grand Cordon of his order if I had let those three heads fall and if I had distributed the money in our treasury. I should have obtained at least a partial success, and my money would have bought a constitution— So goes the world! It is a game of chess!"

"So, then," replied Julien, his eyes aflame, "so you did not know the game; now—"

"I should have let those heads fall—is that what you mean to say? And I should have been a Girondist, as you spoke to me the other day? Now, I shall tell you why," continued Altamira, gloomily. "When you have killed a man in a duel, that is not as horrible as having him butchered by an executioner."

"My Lord!" replied Julien, "the end justifies the means. If I, in place of being a mere atom, had a little power, I would let three men hang to save four." His eyes had that disdainful look which announces an utter contempt of men. His look met Mademoiselle de la Mole's; but far from changing to anything more gracious, seemed to grow more intensely contemptuous. She felt repulsed, but it was no longer in her power to forget Julien. She withdrew, taking her brother with her.

"I think I will get some punch and dance a little," she said to herself. "I am going to pick out what is best here, and produce an impression at all cost. Well, here is that famous fop, Count de Fervaques." She accepted the latter's invitation for a dance.

"I must find out which of these two is most impertinent, but to enjoy the sport I must make him talk."

She danced the rest of the quadrille mechanically. Her escort did not wish to lose any of Mathilde's brilliant repartee. M. de Fervaque was somewhat confused, and being at a loss for elegant words, simply looked. Mathilde was decidedly cruel to him and made of him a positive enemy. She danced till morning, utterly exhausting herself. In the carriage, however, what little strength she had left she spent in regrets and worriment. She had been despised by Julien, and she could not despise him in return!

Julien was filled with happiness. Enchanted by the music, the flowers, the beautiful women, and the elegance everywhere, and, more than all, by his own imagination, which was wandering in distinctions for himself and liberty for all, he was saying what a beautiful ball it was; how nothing, nothing had been wanting.

"Yes, thought was wanting," replied Altamira, his face betraying that contempt the more piquant for being hidden under politeness.

"But you have thought, Monsieur le Comte. Haven't you still the thought of the conspiracy?"

"I am here because of my name; but thought is hated in your drawing-rooms. One must not rise above a line from vaudeville; then he will be appreciated. But the man who thinks, if he has any energy, and if there is anything new in what he says, why, he is called a cynic. Was not that the name which one of your judges gave to Courières? You put him in prison just like Beranger. Whoever amounts to anything with you the Congregation throws into prison, and the good company applauds. That is because your effete civilization cannot rise above conventionality; you never rise above military bravado; you will have your Murats, but never Washingtons. I see in France only vanity. If a man speaks vivaciously or expresses an unusual idea, the host thinks himself scandalized."

At these words the Count's carriage stopped before the Hôtel de la Mole. Julien was in love with the conspirator. Altamira had paid him this compliment, evidently coming from profound conviction: "You have not that French lightness, and you understand the principle of practical ends." It just happened that the evening before Julien had seen *Marino Faliero*, a tragedy by Casimir Delavigne.

"Has not Israel Bertruccio more character than all the rest of the Venetian nobles?" our recalcitrant plebeian was saying to himself, "and yet those people lived in the year 700, a century before Charlemagne. Why, all those who were at the ball tonight can date back their nobility only to the thirteenth century, and that only lamely. So, then, of all those Venetian nobles, with all their high birth, it is Israel Bertruccio one thinks of, after all. A revolution annihilated all titles coming from social caprice. Immediately a man reaches high rank if he knows only how to look at death. Genius itself weakens——

"What would Danton be to-day in an age of Valenods and de Rênals? Not even a substitute for a King's governor! What am I saying? Why, he would have sold himself to the Congregation; he would have been Minister; for, after all, this great Danton stole. Mirabeau also sold himself. Napoleon stole millions in Italy, otherwise he would have had to stop short through sheer poverty like Pichegrue. Only La Fayette never stole. Must a man steal? must a man sell himself?" thought Julien. Face to face with that question, he spent the rest of the night reading the history of the Revolution.

The next day, writing the letters in the library, he only thought of the conversation with Count Altamira.

"In fact," he said to himself, after a long reverie, "if these Spanish Liberals had compromised the people with their crimes, they would not have been swept away with such ease. They were such proud, foolish fellows, like myself!" he cried, all at once, bounding out of his chair.

"What difficulty is there in judging those poor devils who once in their life have dared to act? I am just like a man who, leaving the table, cries out, 'To-morrow I shall not dine, but that will not prevent me at all from being light and gay as I am to-day.' Who knows what one will find half way when he sets himself to do something great?" Those lofty thoughts were disturbed by the sudden entrance of Mademoiselle de la Mole. He was so greatly moved by his admiration for the great qualities of Danton, of Mirabeau, and of Carnot, who never knew defeat, that his eye rested on Mademoiselle de la Mole without seeing her. When, finally, he became aware of her presence, his face fell. Mademoiselle de la Mole noticed it with bitterness. She asked him for a volume of Vely's history of France which was on the top shelf, compelling Julien to look for the larger of the two ladders in the library. He mounted the ladder, looked for the volume, and handed it to her mechanically.

In replacing the ladder, he struck one of the glass doors with his elbow. The noise of breaking glass as it fell on the floor at last aroused him, and he forthwith began making apologies to Mademoiselle de la Mole. He was then extremely polite, that was all.

Mathilde saw that she had disturbed him and that he would have preferred to occupy himself with his own thoughts. She looked at him for a long time, and finally withdrew, and Julien saw her quietly walk away. He enjoyed the contrast between the simplicity of her dress now and her elegance of the night before; the difference in her expression was also striking. That young girl, who had looked so proud at Duke de Retz's ball, seemed at that moment to look almost pleadingly. "Really," Julien thought, "that black gown makes her figure beautiful, and she has the carriage of a queen; but why is she in mourning? If I ask anyone for the reason why she is in mourning it will be considered rude." Gradually Julien's enthusiasm disappeared.

"I must read over all the letters I have written this morning; Lord knows how many mistakes I have made."

As he was reading over the first letter, he heard the swish of a gown near him. Turning quickly around he saw Mademoiselle de la Mole just two steps from the table, laughing. This second interruption made Julien angry. As for Mathilde, feeling deeply that she was nothing to the young man, she was laughing only to hide her embarrassment. She succeeded.

"Evidently you are thinking of something very interesting, M. Sorel? Is it not something in connection with a curious anecdote about a conspiracy which has brought Count Altamira to Paris? Tell me what it is about. Oh, I won't tell, I swear." She was astonished at the word herself when she heard it pronounced. What! she was thinking of asking a favor of an inferior?

With increasing embarrassment she said lightly: "What has inspired you, who are ordinarily so cold, in this Michael Angelo prophet?"

That indiscreet question wounded Julien. He was furious.

"Did Danton do well to steal?" he asked her, fiercely. "Should the rebels of Piedmont in Spain have betrayed the people by their crimes? Should they have given men without brains all the places in the army and all the Crosses? And these people who wear the Crosses, did they not dread the return of the King? Was it necessary to pillage the treasury of Turin? In a word, mademoiselle," he said, approaching her impetuously, "must the man who wants to remove ignorance and crime from the world be regarded as a monster and an impostor?"

Mathilde, frightened, unable to withstand his gaze, fell back. She looked at him for a minute, and then, ashamed of her fear, walked slowly out of the library.

Chapter 10

Queen Marguerite

*Love! In what madness do you not contrive to
make us find pleasure?*

—LETTERS OF A PORTUGUESE NUN

JULIEN re-read the letters. When the dinner bell rang, he said
to himself:

"How ridiculous I must have looked to that Parisian doll!
How foolish it was of me to tell her what I really think! But
perhaps my stupidity was not so great after all; the truth on
this occasion was worthy of me. But why should she ask me
about my private opinions? That is indiscreet on her part, she
is so unconventional. My opinion of Danton is not part of my
contract with her father."

When he entered the dining-room, Julien noticed that Mademoiselle de la Mole was in mourning. He noticed it the more
because no one else in the family was dressed in black. During
dinner all that enthusiasm which had possessed him throughout
the day vanished. Happily the Academician who knew Latin
was also at dinner.

"There is a man," said Julien to himself, "who would not
think me impertinent if I presume to question him about Mademoiselle de la Mole's mourning costume."

Mathilde was then looking at him rather singularly. "This
coquetry of women here," he thought, "is exactly as Madame
de Rênal painted it. I was not polite enough to her this morning
when I did not yield to her fancy for talking. Oh, later her
haughty disdain will have revenge! Well, I dare her to do her
worst. Ah! how different she is from the one I lost! What natural
charm! what naïveté! I knew her thoughts before she expressed
them; I saw them rise in her mind. I never found any opposition
in her heart, except that fear of the death of her children. That
was a natural affection, though, and she was lovely to me even
when she suffered. Oh, I was a fool! The ideas I had of Paris
prevented me from appreciating that sublime, that magnificent
woman. What a difference now in what I find here! Dry and
disdainful vanity, selfishness, nothing else!

"Let me get hold of that Academician," said Julien, when

dinner was over. He approached the latter as he was passing into the garden, and shared his anger at the success of "Hernani."

"Ah, if we were still in the time of *lettres de cachet*," he said, "then they would not have dared!" cried the Academician, with a Talma gesture.

Picking a flower, Julien quoted some lines from Virgil's "Georgics," remarking that nothing was equal to the verses of abbé Delille. In a word, he flattered the Academician in every way. Then assuming a most indifferent air, he said:

"I suppose that Mademoiselle de la Mole has inherited a fortune from the uncle for whom she is wearing mourning?"

"What! you are in the house," replied the Academician, stopping short, "and you don't know her hobby? Really, it is strange that her mother should permit anything like that. But, confidentially, it is not precisely through force of character that anyone shines in this house; but Mademoiselle de la Mole has enough for them all, and leads them by the nose. To-day is the 30th of April," and the Academician drew himself up, giving Julien a significant look.

Julien in return smiled as knowingly as he could.

"What connection can there be between leading the house by the nose, wearing mourning, and the 30th of April?" he was asking himself. "I must be more of a fool than I think."

"I must admit——" he said to the Academician.

"Let's walk around the garden," broke in the Academician, enchanted at the prospect of a long and learned conversation. "Yes; is it possible that you do not know what happened on the 30th of April, 1574?"

"And where?" asked Julien, astonished.

"In Place de Grève."

To Julien this was not much information. Curiosity and the expectation of something tragic, both in accord with his character, gave his eyes that brilliancy which a narrator loves so well to see in a listener.

The Academician, pleased at finding a ready ear, related at length how on April 30, 1574, the handsomest young man of his day, Boniface de la Mole, and the Piedmontese, Annibal de Coconasso, had been executed in Place de Grève. La Mole was adored by Queen Marguerite of Navarre.

"Notice," added the Academician, "that Mademoiselle de la Mole's name is Mathilde-Marguerite. La Mole was, in his day, the favorite of Duke d'Alençon, and the most intimate friend of the King of Navarre, afterward Henry IV., the husband of his mistress. On Mardi Gras of the same year, 1574, the court was at Saint-Germain with poor King Charles IX., who was then dying. La Mole wished to release his friends whom Queen Catherine de' Medicis was holding as prisoners near the court. He had two hundred horsemen under the walls of Saint-Germain. But Duke d'Alençon became afraid, and la Mole was handed over to the executioner. But what affects Mademoiselle Mathilde more than anything else is, as she has told me, that seven or eight years ago, when she was twelve years of age—for she has a head, I tell you! a fine head!" and the Academician looked up to the sky—"what touched her more than anything else in this tragedy is that Queen Marguerite of Navarre, who had hidden herself in a house near Place de Grève, asked the executioner for her lover's head. And the same night, at midnight, she took the head into her carriage and drove to a little chapel at the foot of the hill of Montmartre."

"Is it possible?" Julien asked, visibly affected.

"Mademoiselle de la Mole despises her brother because, as you see, he takes no stock in that old story, and does not wear mourning on the 30th of April. It is since that famous execution that all male members of the family have that name in order to recall the la Mole's intimate friendship for Coconasso. This Coconasso, like the Italian that he was, is known also as Annibal, and," added the Academician in a whisper, "this Coconasso was, if we are to believe Charles IX., one of the most cruel assassins of August 24, 1572. But how is it possible, my dear Sorel, that you do not know these things, you who are in the house?"

"So that is why twice at dinner Mademoiselle de la Mole called her brother Annibal," Julien thought.

"It is strange that the Marquise should allow such nonsense. But the husband of that fine girl would find it charming."

The last remark was followed by some satirical allusions. The spiteful pleasure in the Academician's eye repelled Julien.

"Here we are, like two valets, busy talking about our masters," he thought. "But nothing should surprise me in this Academician." One day Julien had surprised him on his knees before the Marquise de la Mole: he was begging her for a receivership under the tobacco tax for his nephew in the provinces.

In the evening Mademoiselle de la Mole's maid, who was paying attention to Julien just as Elisa had formerly done, informed him that her mistress's mourning costume was not put on for effect, but was one of her peculiarities, rooted in her character. She really loved that la Mole who was beloved by the greatest queen of her age and who died in an attempt to free his friends. And what friends—a first prince of the blood and Henry IV!

Accustomed to the naïveté which Madame de Rênal evinced at all times, Julien saw only affectation in the Parisian women; and when he was in the least disconcerted, he could not say a word to them. Mademoiselle de la Mole, however, seemed to be the exception. He no longer took her expression and carriage as signs of indifference and hauteur. He held long conversations with her, too, when, after dinner, they would walk together in the garden, before the open windows of the drawing-room. She told him one day that she was reading d'Aubigné's and Brantôme's histories.

"Peculiar reading," Julien thought, "for a girl, and the Marquise does not permit her even to read Walter Scott's novels."

One day she told him, her eyes shining with pleasure as a proof of her sincere admiration—a trait properly belonging to a woman of the reign of Henry III.—that she had just read in the "Mémoires" of l'Etoile: "Having found her husband unfaithful, she had thrust a dagger into him."

Julien's vanity was flattered. A person to whom everyone paid so much court, and who, according to the Academician, ruled the whole house, was speaking to him in a manner that almost resembled intimacy!

"Oh, but I am fooling myself," thought Julien. "It is not from familiarity, it is only from the necessity of talking. I pass for a savant. I will now have to read Brantôme and d'Aubigné and l'Etoile; I could then talk about some of the anecdotes of which Mademoiselle de la Mole was speaking to me. I must give up the rôle of a passive confidant."

Little by little his conversations with the young girl, who was always so dignified and yet so much at ease, became more interesting. He gradually forgot his sombre rôle of an ever discontented plebeian. He saw she was well informed, even intelligent. Her opinions in the garden were quite different from those she expressed in the drawing-room. Sometimes she evinced an enthusiasm and a frankness which were in sharp contrast with her usual proud, cool bearing.

"The wars of the League were the heroic days of France," she said to him one day, her eyes sparkling with enthusiasm and intelligence. "Then everyone was struggling to obtain something different in order to make his party triumph, and not simply to gain a Cross as in the time of your Emperor. You must agree that then there was less egotism and less pettiness. How I love that century!"

"Your Boniface de la Mole was the hero of it," he interposed.

"At any rate he was loved as much as one could well be. What woman living now would not have a horror of touching the decapitated head of her lover?"

Just then Madame de la Mole called her daughter.

Hypocrisy to be useful should be hidden; and Julien, as was seen, had spoken to Mademoiselle de la Mole half in confidence of his admiration for Napoleon.

"There is the great advantage they have over us," said Julien, now alone in the garden. "The history of their ancestors raises them above vulgar ideas, and they do not have to think of a livelihood. It is terrible," he added, with bitterness; "I have no right to think of those great things. My life is only a series of hypocrisies because I have not a thousand francs."

"What are you thinking of, monsieur?" asked Mathilde, who came back hurriedly.

Through pride he frankly told her of what he was thinking, blushing considerably as he went on. He endeavored to express by his proud speech that he was asking for nothing. And never had he seemed so handsome to Mathilde. She saw in his face a degree of feeling and candor which she had never before observed.

Less than a month after that Julien was walking pensively in the garden, without a trace of that hard, resigned expression which a consciousness of one's inferiority imparts. He had just conducted to the door of the drawing-room Mademoiselle de la Mole, who pretended to have hurt her foot while running with her brother.

"She leaned on my arm in such a peculiar way," Julien said to himself. "Am I only a fool, or is it really so, that she thinks something of me? She listens to me in such a gentle way, even when I tell her of all that I suffer from my pride, she who is so proud with everybody. Wouldn't it be a surprise if she were seen with such an expression in the drawing-room? But, really, her manner is so sweet, and she does not show it to anybody else."

Julien tried not to exaggerate that marked friendship. He looked upon her as a friend, but one who is also armed. Every day when they met, before resuming the intimate tone of the night before, they would almost ask themselves, "Shall we be friends to-day or enemies?" Julien felt that if he allowed himself to be offended in the least by this haughty girl he would lose all. "If I am to get angry, is it not easier that it should take place right now in defending my rights than later, when I would be compelled to stand on my rights against possible contempt?"

Several times when Mathilde was in a bad humor she attempted to act toward him as a great lady. She did it warily, but Julien was on his guard.

One day he interrupted her rather rudely with: "Has Mademoiselle de la Mole any orders for her father's secretary? He must take those orders and execute them with due respect." That was all he said. He was not paid to communicate his ideas, he thought.

This sort of life removed the ennui he found in that magnificent salon where everybody was afraid, and where it was not permissible to speak lightly on any subject.

"It would be so gratifying to me if she loved me. Whether she loves me or not," thought Julien, "I have for a confidante an intelligent girl before whom everybody in the house trembles, and more than all this Marquis de Croisenois. This young man is so polished, so kind, so brave, uniting in himself all those advantages of birth and fortune of which only one would put me at my ease! He is madly in love with her; he ought to marry her. What letters has not M. de la Mole made me write to the two notaries? And I who am only an inferior with a pen in hand, two hours later, here in the garden, I triumph over these pleasant gentlemen! Really her manner is so direct. Perhaps she hates a future husband in him.

"And what friendliness she shows toward me! Well, I am only a fool! Or is she really courting me? The more cool and respectful I show myself to her, the more eagerly she looks for me. Oh, that might be only a fancy or an affectation, but I see her eyes light up so when I come upon her suddenly. Can the Parisian women feign so far? Well, what is the difference? She looks like it, and let us enjoy the appearance. Mon dieu! how beautiful she is! How her eyes charm me when I see them close, looking at me, as they often do! How different this spring is from last year, when I lived discontented, in self-contempt, in the midst of three hundred dirty hypocrites! I was almost as bad as they were."

In his moody days Julien would think, "Ah, this young girl is only amusing herself with me; she is in compact with her brother to mystify me; but she seems to despise her brother's lack of energy so much! He is brave, and that is about all; she tells me he dare not have a thought to which the world might take exception. I am always the one who is obliged to speak up for him. A young girl of nineteen! At that age can one be true all day long to one's hypocritical plan? On the other hand, when Mademoiselle de la Mole fixes her blue eyes on me with that singular expression of hers, Count Norbert always withdraws; that is what is suspicious. Should he not become indignant over the fact that his sister is attractive to a *domestic* of the house, as I have heard Duke de Chaulnes speak of me?"

At that recollection his anger took complete possession of him.

"Is it from the love of the old French in the crazy Duke? Oh, well, she is pretty," continued Julien, with a fierce look. "I shall have her, and I shall have her soon; and let the man look out who is going to cross my path."

That idea engrossed Julien; he could not think of anything else. Days passed like hours. Every moment, though he tried to occupy his mind with something serious, the same thought would always recur to him. He would rise with a start every quarter of an hour, his heart palpitating, his head throbbing, crying out, "Does she love me?"

Chapter 11

A Girl's Dominion

J'admire sa beauté, mais je crains son esprit.
—MÉRIMÉE

IF JULIEN had carefully observed Mathilde's manner in the drawing-room, instead of exaggerating her beauty, or flying into a rage over the haughtiness of the family she was forgetting on his account, he would have known what it was in her that ruled everyone in the house.

When anyone offended Mademoiselle de la Mole, she could revenge herself with a remark so well turned and apparently so innocent that the wound it inflicted would be aggravated the more one thought of it. When the matter concerned her pride, she could be positively cruel. Indifferent to the aims of her family, she always seemed cold in their eyes.

After all, aristocratic drawing-rooms are nice only to speak of when one leaves; but that is all. After the first few days the chill politeness becomes an obsession; that Julien found out after his first disillusion.

"Politeness," he said to himself, "then, is only the mask of a bad temper in the vulgar."

Mathilde was often bored, and would have been bored, perhaps, anywhere, and at any time. A biting epigram was a real diversion, a real pleasure. It was, perhaps, in order to have victims that were a little more amusing than her distinguished parents, the Academician, and five or six others who paid her very marked attention, that she held out hope to the Marquis de Croisenois, to Count de Caylus, and to three other young men of high distinction. These became for her only new subjects for epigram.

It must be admitted that she had exchanged letters with these young men. The young woman was not conventional, that was all. A lack of prudence could not be charged to the pupils of the noble Convent of Sacré Cœur.

One day Marquis de Croisenois returned to Mathilde a most compromising letter she had written him the day before. He thought that his suit would be advanced by this mark of great prudence. But it was imprudence that Mathilde loved in her correspondence. Her pleasure then consisted in playing with his fate, not addressing a word to him for six weeks. The letters of the young men amused her; she found them all alike; all expressed the deepest passion, the greatest melancholy.

"They are all perfect to a man, ready to leave for Palestine," she would say to her cousin. "Can you imagine anything more insipid? Such are the letters I have received all my life. These letters change every twenty years, according to the kind of life that is in vogue. They would not be so flat in the time of the Empire. Then society young men would have said or would have done something which was really great. Duke de N., my uncle, was at Wagram."

"What greatness is required to give a sword thrust?" asked Mademoiselle de Sainte-Hérédité, Mathilde's cousin, "and when they do that they speak of it so often!"

"Oh, well, I like to hear about it. To be in a real battle, in a battle with Napoleon, where ten thousand soldiers are killed, that is a sign of courage! To expose oneself to danger elevates the soul and raises it from that bored state into which my poor admirers are plunged. And it is contagious, this ennui. Has any one of them an idea of doing something extraordinary? They are eager for my hand, a fine ambition! I am rich, and my father would promote his son-in-law. Ah, how I should love to find one who is the least bit interesting!"

The vivacious, clear, picturesque manner of looking at the world made her language somewhat intemperate. Frequently she would see a cloud pass over the eyes of her polite friends. They almost admitted among themselves that her unconventional tone had some ring in it that did not chime with womanly delicacy. On her part she was quite unjust to the handsome gallants that crowded the Bois de Boulogne. The future had no terrors for her—what more could she desire? Fortune, noble birth, intelligence, beauty, as people admitted and as she herself believed, she had all!

Such were the thoughts of the most envied heiress in Faubourg Saint-Germain when she was pleased to promenade with Julien. She was astonished at his pride, and admired still more his bourgeois sense.

"He will be a Bishop yet, like abbé Maury," she thought. The unfeigned indifference, however, with which he listened to her weighed upon her.

She related to her cousin every detail of her conversation and found that she never succeeded in describing fully his face. All at once she was seized with an idea.

"I am happy! I love him!" she said to herself one day, in a transport of joy. "Yes, I love him! At my age, where can a young, handsome, intelligent girl find anything pleasing except in loving? It is all in vain; I shall never love de Croisenois, de Caylus, or the rest. They are perfect—too perfect, perhaps—they weary me!"

There flitted through her head the passionate scenes from "Manon Lescaut," "Nouvelle Héloïse," and "Lettres d'une Religieuse Portugaise." Of course it must be an extraordinary passion; a light love was unworthy of a girl of her age and her birth! She never applied the name of love except to that heroic sentiment which prevailed in France in the time of Henry III. and of Bassompièrre. Such a love does not yield basely to obstacles, but accomplishes marvels.

"Oh, how unfortunate it is for me there is not such a court as that of Catherine de' Medicis or of Louis XIII.! I feel that I should be equal to all that is noble and grand. What should I not do with a man of heart like Louis XIII. sighing at my feet! I would lead him in Vendée, as Baron de Tolly often says, and there he would reconquer his realm, and no more a constitution, and Julien would aid me! Now, what is lacking in him? Name and fortune. He will make himself a name and he will acquire a fortune. Now, there is nothing lacking in de Croisenois, but all his life he will remain only a Duke, half ultra, half Liberal, a hesitating sort of a creature, removed from both extremes, and therefore second-rate everywhere!

"What noble action is there which does not look risky at the time it is undertaken? It is when it is accomplished that it seems possible to ordinary creatures. Yes, it is love with all its miracles that is about to reign in my heart. I feel the flame in me! Heaven will grant me that favor! It is not in vain that all these advantages have accumulated on one creature; my happiness will be worthy of me. Every day will be different from the day before. I feel already that grandeur and that inspiring courage from loving a man even when he is placed so far beneath me. Now see, but will he deserve me? At the very first weakness he goes; I will let him alone. A girl of my birth, and with the romantic character that everyone gives me, cannot tie herself to a fool.

"Wouldn't that be the rôle I should play if I loved the Marquis de Croisenois? I should have a new edition of the happiness of my cousin, which I utterly despise. I know in advance what the poor Marquis is going to tell me and all that I am going to say in reply. What sort of love is that which makes a person yawn, even though there is devotion? I should have a clause in the marriage contract, just as it was with my cousin, about which the parents will come to some agreement, if they do not fall out at the last moment over some new conditions introduced by the notary."

Chapter 12

Another Danton?

Le besoin d'anxiété, tel était le caractère de la belle Marguerite de Valois, ma tante, que bientôt épousa le roi de Navarre, que nous voyons de présent régner en France sous le nom de Henry IV. Le besoin de jouer formait tout le secret du caractère de cette princesse aimable; de là ses brouilles et ses raccommodements avec ses frères dès l'âge de seize ans. Or, que peut jouer une jeune fille? Ce qu'elle a de plus précieux: sa réputation, la considération de toute sa vie.

—MÉMOIRES DU DUC D'ANGOULÉME,
fils naturel de Charles IX.

"BETWEEN Julien and myself there would be no contract, no notary; all that will be heroic, all that will be natural. As regards nobility, which he lacks, it will be the love of Marguerite of Valois for the young de la Mole, the most distinguished man of his time. Is it my fault if the young men are so enslaved to convention that they become pale at the least suggestion of something out of the ordinary? A little trip to Greece or Africa is for them the height of rashness, and even then they do not go except in flocks! When they find themselves alone, they are afraid, not of a Bedouin lance but—of ridicule!

"My Julien, on the contrary, loves to do everything alone. Never in that exceptional character is there the least idea of seeking help from others; he despises others; it is for that reason that I do not despise him.

"If with his poverty Julien were a nobleman, my love would be only common foolishness, a flat mésalliance. I should have nothing to do with him; there would not be anything in it of that which characterizes a great passion—the immense difficulties to be overcome, the dark uncertainty of events."

Mademoiselle de la Mole dwelt so completely in these charming reflections that she praised Julien before Marquis de Croisenois and her brother next day with an eloquence that amazed them.

"Look out for that young man who is all energy!" cried her

brother. "If we have another revolution, he will be just the one to lead us to the guillotine!"

She then began to tease her brother and Marquis de Croisenois about the fear they had of a man of action.

"It is nothing at bottom but the fear of finding something unexpected; of stopping short in the presence of the unforeseen. It is always, gentlemen, that dread of ridicule, a monster that, unfortunately, has been dead since 1816."

"There is no longer any ridicule," said M. de la Mole, "in a country where there are two parties." His daughter understood that.

"So, gentlemen," she said to Julien's enemies, "you will be afraid all your life; and it will be said of you: 'It was not a wolf, it was only the shadow!' "

Mathilde left them directly, ruffled by her brother's remark. The next day, however, she saw in it the greatest praise.

"In this age in which all energy is dead, his courage makes them afraid. I will tell him what my brother said. I want to see what answer he will make; but I will wait until his eyes shine, then he won't lie to me. Ah, he would be a Danton!" she added, after a long reverie.

"Yes, should a revolution occur again, what would de Croisenois and my brother do? Well, it is written in advance; sublime resignation! Ah, they are like lambs led to the slaughter! Their only fear when they die would be of not being in good form. Julien would risk his head fighting a Jacobin who would come to arrest him even though he should see no means of escape." The last thought made her pensive again, but she put aside her painful ideas.

The remarks of MM. de Caylus, de Croisenois, de Luz, and her brother recurred again to her mind. These gentlemen were always speaking lightly of Julien, as the humble and hypocritical priest. "But," she thought, her eyes bright with joy, "the bitterness and frequency of their sarcasm show that he is the most distinguished man we have had here this winter. What do I care for their sarcasm and their ridicule? He is great, and that is where the shoe pinches with these gentlemen who are so self-indulgent. Yes, he is poor and has studied to become a priest. They are Chiefs of Squadron and have never had occasion to study; it is easier.

"In spite of all the disadvantages of his eternal black coat and his priestly look, the poor boy, though compelled to earn a livelihood, has a character that makes them tremble. That is plain. And that priestly look disappears as soon as we are alone together; and when these gentlemen say anything brilliant, don't they look first at Julien? I have noticed that quite often. And yet they know that he never talks unless he is addressed first. It is only to me he talks; he believes I have a lofty soul. He replies to their remarks in a way only to seem polite. But with me he talks for hours at a time. He is not sure of his ideas until I find some objection to them. Well, my father, who is a superior man and who will advance the fortune of our house, has great respect for Julien. Everybody hates him, but no one really looks down on him except my mother's devoted friends."

Count de Caylus had, or feigned to have, a great fondness for horses. He passed his days in his stable and often took breakfast there. That great passion, joined to his habit of never laughing, gave him prestige among his friends. He was the lion of his set.

When they met again the next day behind Madame de la Mole's easy chair, M. de Caylus, finding Julien was not present, attacked, with the support of de Croisenois and Norbert, Mathilde's good opinion of Julien, and almost as soon as he saw Mademoiselle de la Mole enter. She understood the attack and was charmed by it.

"There they are," she thought to herself, "all of them leagued against a man of genius who has not an income of ten louis and who never answers them except when he is addressed. They are afraid of him in his black coat; what would it be if he wore chevrons?" She was never more brilliant.

From the first signs of the attack she overwhelmed de Caylus and his allies with the utmost sarcasm. When the first artillery fire of the brilliant officers was silenced, she said:

"Suppose, to-morrow, some squire from the Franche-Comté mountains should find that Julien is his natural son and give him his name and some ten thousand francs. In six weeks he would have a moustache like you gentlemen; in six months he would be an officer of hussars like you gentlemen; and then his strength of character would no longer be amusing. I see, monsieur, you who are going to be a Duke, that you are reduced to this bad reasoning of old: the superiority of the nobility of the court to the nobility of the country. But what will there be left if I drive you further, if I am malicious enough to give Julien a Parisian Duke for a father, who was a prisoner of war at Besançon in Napoleon's time, and who, from conscientious scruples, declares him his son on his deathbed?"

All these hints at illegitimate birth were found in bad form by MM. de Caylus and de Croisenois. That was all they saw in

Mathilde's arguments. Though Norbert was prejudiced, his sister's words were so convincing that he became somewhat grave in his reply, wholly belying his smiling face.

"Why, are you sick, my dear?" Mathilde asked him, with a touch of seriousness in her tone. "You must be sick, indeed, to answer my trifles with your morals. Morals! you! Do you want a place with a prefect?"

Mathilde soon forgot Count de Caylus's irritation, Norbert's bad humor, and M. de Croisenois's silent despair. She stoutly maintained the idea which had taken possession of her.

"Julien is sincere enough with me," she said to herself. "At his age, penniless, and as unhappy as he can be from his astonishing ambition, he must need a friend—a woman. Perhaps I am that friend; but I do not see any love in him. With the boldness of his character he would have spoken to me of it." This uncertainty, together with her musings, which occupied every moment of Mathilde's time, and in which every time Julien spoke to her she inserted new arguments, drove away all that ennui to which she had been a prey. As a daughter of that great man who might become a Minister and sell his woods to the clergy, Mademoiselle de la Mole had been the object of the most fulsome flatteries at the Convent of the Sacré Cœur. That injury was never undone. She had been told that, considering her advantages of birth and fortune, she should be happier than anyone else. In that is the source of the weariness and disappointment of princes and of their follies. Mathilde had not escaped the harmful influence of that education. With all her intelligence she was not proof against the flatteries of the convent.

From the time that she was sure that she loved Julien there was a new interest for her in life. Every day she congratulated herself upon what she had done in encouraging her passion. "It may be dangerous," she thought; "so much the better, a thousand times better! Without a great passion I should be languishing at the happiest period of my life, which is always said to be from sixteen to twenty. I have already lost my best years. I am obliged, in lieu of pleasure, to listen to the gossip of my mother's friends, who at Coblenz in 1792 were not, I suppose, as strict as their words indicate to-day."

It was while Mathilde was agitated with uncertainty that Julien did not understand the steady gaze which she would fix upon him. He felt also an increased coolness in Count Norbert, and new haughtiness, new pride in MM. de Caylus, de Luz, and de Croisenois. This he noticed several times in the course of an evening when he shone more brilliantly than his station in life warranted.

"Yes, it is impossible that I am mistaken," Julien said to himself. "Mademoiselle de la Mole looks at me in a queer way; but when her beautiful blue eyes are fixed steadily on me with the greatest abandon, I read in them something of sang-froid and recklessness. Is it possible that it is from love? How different from the look of Madame de Rênal!"

One evening Julien, after following M. de la Mole into his room, returned to the garden. As he was quietly approaching the group around Mathilde, he caught a few words that were spoken very loud. She was teasing her brother. Julien heard his name pronounced twice distinctly. When they saw him, a profound silence immediately ensued, Mademoiselle de la Mole and her brother being too much occupied with the previous conversation to start on another subject. MM. de Caylus, de Croisenois, de Luz, and a friend of theirs greeted Julien icily and left.

Chapter 13

A Conspiracy

Disconnected remarks and chance meetings become most cogent proofs in the eyes of a man of imagination if he has some fire in his heart.
——SCHILLER

THE NEXT DAY Julien again surprised a conversation about himself between Norbert and his sister. Becoming again quiet on his arrival, his suspicions knew no longer any bounds. "Have these people conspired to make a fool of me?" he thought. "I must admit that is much more natural, more probable than a pretended passion on the part of Mademoiselle de la Mole for a poor devil of a secretary. In the first place, have such people passions? To hoax is their forte. They are jealous of my little superiority in speech; and jealousy is a weakness of theirs. It is all clear now, Mademoiselle de la Mole wished to persuade me that she is distinguishing me just to make a spectacle of me to her admirer."

This cruel suspicion changed Julien's entire position. It engendered a love in his heart that he could not eradicate. It was founded only on Mathilde's beauty, or, rather, on her queenly airs and admirable costumes. In that respect Julien was only a parvenu. A beautiful woman in high life is what most astonishes an intelligent provincial. It was not Mathilde's character that gave Julien cause for reverie. He had enough sense to know that he did not understand her; all that he saw might be only affectation. For example, Mathilde would not for all the world miss Mass on Sunday; she always accompanied her mother. And if in the drawing-room some one forgot himself and indulged in a distant allusion to the true or supposed interests of the throne or altar, Mathilde would immediately become reserved and cold. Her look, which was usually so vivacious, would become haughtily impassive, like that of an old family portrait. Yet Julien was sure that she always had in her room one of Voltaire's philosophical works. He himself would often steal some of the volumes of the handsome edition. By slightly pushing the neighboring volume forward, he would conceal the absence of the one he would take away. But soon he discovered that another person was reading Voltaire. He had recourse to a seminary trick, by placing bits of hair on the volumes which he supposed would interest Mademoiselle de la Mole. They would disappear for weeks at a time.

M. de la Mole, who was angry with his bookseller for sending him spurious Memoirs, had ordered Julien to buy for him some piquant works; but in order that the venom might not spread in the house, the secretary had orders to place the books in a little bookcase in the Marquis's own room. Yet he was very certain that, although these new books were hostile both to the interest of the throne and the Church, it was not long before they disappeared. It was certainly not Norbert who read them. Julien, exaggerating all this, believed Mademoiselle de la Mole to have the duplicity of Machiavelli. That witch of a woman seemed charming to him. Indeed, with his hypocrisy, it was the only charm he could appreciate. But he was carried away more by his imagination than by his love. It was in dreaming over the elegance of Mademoiselle de la Mole's figure, her excellent taste in dress, her white hands, her beautiful arms, and her flowing movements that he found himself in the depths of love. Then, to put the climax to this dream, he believed her a veritable Catherine de' Medicis. Nothing was too deep nor too wicked for the character which he conjured up. It was the ideal of a Maslon, a de Frilaire, a Castanède, admired by him in his youth; it was, in a word, his ideal of Paris. Could there be anything more pleasant than to believe in the depth or the wickedness of a Parisian character?

"It is impossible that this trio are mocking me," thought Julien. He would not be understood, indeed, if that gloomy, cold look in response to Mathilde was not observed; for a bitter irony repulsed the assurances of friendship which Mademoiselle de la Mole ventured to give him once or twice.

Moved by the sudden check, the young girl, though naturally cold, became more impassioned than ever. But there was a good deal of pride in Mathilde's character, and the feeling that placed her entire happiness on another person was extremely bitter.

Music as sung by Frenchmen tired Mathilde to death; and yet Julien, who made it his duty to be present when the opera was over, noticed that she allowed herself to be taken there quite frequently. He thought he saw a loss of self-possession in her actions. Frequently she would reply to her friends in a most outrageous fashion. It seemed to him that she treated the Marquis de Croisenois with the utmost disdain.

"That young man must be madly in love with money not to

let the girl go, rich as she is," thought Julien. And as for himself, feeling outraged in his manly dignity, he had nothing but increased coolness for her. His remarks to her at times were indeed far from polite.

However resolved he was not to be fooled by Mathilde's marked interest, Julien, whose eyes were beginning to open, became somewhat embarrassed.

"Yes, you polished men and women of society are triumphing over my ignorance," he said to himself. "I must leave and put an end to all this business."

The Marquis had just intrusted to him the administration of some lands and houses in lower Languedoc. It was necessary for him to go there, he said, and M. de la Mole reluctantly consented. Except as to his ambition, Julien had become a wholly different man.

"At bottom they have not fooled me yet," Julien said to himself preparatory to his departure. "Whether Mademoiselle de la Mole's persiflage to those gentlemen is real or not, by which she endeavors to give me confidence, I am only amused. If this is not a conspiracy, then Mademoiselle de la Mole's action toward me is inexplicable; but it is more pronounced toward Marquis de Croisenois than myself—— Yes, indeed, her lack of feeling for him is real. And I—I have had the pleasure of cutting out that young man who is as noble and rich as I am poor and plebeian. That is my greatest triumph; that will amuse me on the coach, riding over Languedoc."

He had not spoken of his departure, but Mathilde knew that he was going to leave Paris the next day and for a long time. Excusing herself on the plea of a severe headache, which she said the closeness of the room made worse, she went into the garden, followed by Norbert, Marquis de Croisenois, de Caylus, de Luz, and other young men. These her biting sarcasm soon put to flight. She looked at Julien in a strange manner.

"That look is perhaps a little comedy, but that rapid breathing and all that anxiety I see! Bah!" he cried to himself, "what do I know about it? Here I see only the most finished woman in Paris. That labored breathing which has almost affected me, she must have learned from Leontine Fay whom she loves so much." They were then alone and were at a loss of what to say.

"No, Julien has no feeling for me," Mathilde was saying to herself, visibly unhappy. As he was taking leave of her she pressed his arm, saying in an altered voice, that was scarcely recognizable: "You will receive a letter from me to-night."

Julien was taken by surprise. "My father," she continued,

"has a just esteem for the services which you render him. You must not leave to-morrow; you must find a pretext," and she ran off.

Her figure was so charming, she had such a beautiful foot, and she ran with such grace that Julien was enchanted. But could anyone guess what his second thought was after he saw her disappear? He was offended by the imperative tone in which she said "You must." Louis XV likewise, when he was about to die, objected strongly to the word "must" that was lamely used by his chief physician; and Louis XV was not an upstart!

An hour later a servant brought Julien a letter. It was a simple declaration of love.

"There is not too much affectation in that style," Julien said to himself, trying, by a literary criticism, to hide the joy which contracted his face and produced a smile in spite of himself.

"There," he cried all at once, "her passion is too great to be held in restraint. I, a poor peasant, I have a declaration of love from a great lady. As for myself, it is not bad," he added, restraining his joy as much as possible, "if I were able to maintain my dignity. I have never said that I loved her." Then he began to study the characters; Mademoiselle de la Mole had a pretty English style of writing. He had to do something physical to divert his mind from the joy that was inundating his heart.

"Your departure obliges me to speak. I cannot bear the thought that I shall not see you again——"

One thought came to Julien which interrupted his examination of Mathilde's letter and redoubled his joy. "I have come out ahead of Marquis de Croisenois!" he cried. "He is always so serious with her! And his moustache and brilliant uniform! He always has something pretty to say at the right time and in the right place!"

Julien experienced a moment of delight. He walked up and down the garden, perfectly wild with joy. Later he went to the library and presented himself to Marquis de la Mole, who fortunately had not gone out. He proved to him, as he showed him certain papers that had come from Normandy, that affairs there obliged him to postpone his departure for Languedoc.

"I am very glad that you are not going to leave," said the Marquis to him when they finished talking business; "I am so glad to have you here." Julien left. That remark came as a sting to him.

"And I—I am going to seduce his daughter, and prevent the marriage with Marquis de Croisenois, who would make her a brilliant future! If he does not become a Duke, his daughter at least will have the *tabouret*."

Julien had the idea now of leaving for Languedoc in spite of Mathilde's letter and the explanation he had given to the Marquis; but that gleam of virtue soon became extinguished. "How good of me!" he said to himself; "I, a plebeian, to have pity on a noble family! I, whom Duke de Chaulnes calls a servant! How does the Marquis double his fortune? By selling an estate when he learns at the Château that the next day there will be a coup d'état. And I, placed at the bottom of the ladder by a cruel Providence, I, to whom noble birth has not been given, and not an income of a thousand francs,—no, not even bread! yes, to tell the truth, not even bread!—shall I refuse a pleasure that is thrown at me? A limpid stream which comes to quench my thirst in that wasting desert of mediocrity which I traverse with such pain? No, indeed! 'Each one for himself and the devil take the hindmost' in this life!"

He recalled the looks of disdain which Madame de la Mole, and especially her friends, had given him.

The pleasure of triumphing over the Marquis de Croisenois ended in putting his virtuous instincts to utter rout. "How I should like to see him in a rage! With what assurance I should now give him a sword thrust!" he cried out, assuming guard. "Before this I was a nobody, basely abusing the little courage I had; but with this letter I am his equal! Yes," he said to himself, with infinite pleasure, drawing out his words, "the Marquis and I have been weighed in the scales, and the poor carpenter from the Jura has been found the heavier.

"Well, here is my reply: 'Don't imagine, Mademoiselle de la Mole, that I am forgetting my station in life. I wish to give you to understand that it is for that carpenter's son that you are betraying a descendant of the famous Guy de Croisenois who followed St. Louis in the crusade.' "

Julien could not contain his joy. He was obliged to go down into the garden, feeling that his room, into which he had locked himself, was all too narrow for him. "Here I am, a poor peasant from the Jura," he repeated to himself from time to time. "I am doomed to wear this sombre black coat all my life. Oh, twenty years earlier I should have worn a uniform like them! Then a man like me would either be dead or would be a general at thirty-six."

The letter which he pressed in his hand gave him the figure and attitude of a hero. "Now, it is true, in this black coat at forty there may be an income of a hundred thousand francs and a cordon bleu like Bishop de Beauvais."

"Oh, well," laughing like Mephisto in the play, "I am cleverer than they are; I know how to select my uniform for this age"; and he felt his ambition redouble with his attachment for his ecclesiastical coat. "How many cardinals of lowlier birth than mine have not come to the height of power? My fellow country-man Granville, for instance!"

Gradually Julien became calmer. Prudence returned. He said to himself, like his master Tartuffe, whose part he knew by heart:

> *"Je ne me firai point à des propos si doux*
> *Qu'un peu de ses faveurs après quoi je soupire*
> *Ne vienne m'assurer tout ce qu'ils m'ont pu dire."*

"Tartuffe was also betrayed by a woman. But my reply may be shown. For this I have this safeguard," he added, slowly but fiercely. "I will begin with the most compromising phrases in Mathilde's letter. Yes, but four servants of M. de Croisenois can fall upon me and take away the original! Oh, no, I am well armed, and I am known for shooting servants. Well, but one of them may be bold and pounce upon me? He might have been promised a hundred napoleons for it. I will either kill him or wound him; and that is all that is wanted. I am thrown into prison, in due course of law I appear in the police court, and I am sent away with all justice and equity on the part of the judges to keep MM. Fontan and Magalon company at Poissy. There I shall be thrown pell-mell with some four hundred criminals, and I will be pitied by them, too, I suppose," he cried, rising impetuously. "Have they pity for the Third Estate when they are with them?" That was the last vestige of gratitude for M. de la Mole, the thought of whom was torturing him at this moment.

"Softly, gentlemen! I see this little Machiavellistic trick! Abbé Maslon and Castanède at the seminary could not have done it better. You take away that letter, and I will be the second edition of Colonel Caron at Colmar. But, gentlemen, I am going to send the letter away, well concealed in a package, to M. abbé Pirard. He is a good man, a Jansenist, and is not likely to be seduced by gold. Yes, but he may open the letter? I am going to send it to Fouqué!" Julien's face and his entire look expressed something atrocious. There was revealed in it crime in its most naked form. It was the look of an unfortunate man at war with society.

"To arms!" cried Julien, and with a bound he cleared the steps in front of the house. He entered a copyist's office on the street, whom he frightened by his abrupt entrance. "Here, copy this," he said, showing him Mademoiselle de la Mole's letter. While the copyist was writing, he himself wrote to Fouqué, begging him to keep for him a valuable package. "But," he said, interrupting his writing, "at the post-office they may open my letter—no——" He went and bought a big Bible at a Protestant bookstore, in the cover of which he concealed Mathilde's letter. He had it all wrapped up, and the package was sent by mail, addressed to one of Fouqué's workmen, who was unknown in Paris. That done, he returned joyfully, leisurely, to the Hôtel de la Mole.

"Now, mademoiselle!" he cried, locking himself in his room and taking off his coat. He wrote:

"It is Mademoiselle de la Mole who sent through the hands of Arsène, her father's valet, a too charming letter to a poor carpenter from the Jura, evidently for the purpose of playing on his credulity." And he repeated the most telling phrases of the letter he had received. His own letter would have done honor to the diplomatic prudence of the Chevalier de Beauvoises. It was then only ten o'clock. Julien, intoxicated by his happiness and by his sense of power, so unknown to a poor devil of a carpenter like him, went to the Italian opera. He heard Geronimo sing. Never had music had such an effect on him; he felt like a god.

Chapter 14

Thoughts of a Young Girl

*Que de perplexités! Que de nuits passées sans
sommeil! Grand Dieu! Vais-je me rendre méprisable? Il me méprisera lui-même. Mais il part, il
s'éloigne.*

—ALFRED DE MUSSET

IT WAS NOT without a struggle that Mathilde had written. As
soon as she had felt an inclination for Julien it conquered that
pride which from her earliest childhood had held her heart in
thrall. That proud, indifferent soul was for the first time carried
away by passion. Yet, if her pride was conquered it was still
faithful to its wonted course. After a struggle of two months
with her new sensation she had resumed her usual moral attitude.

But Mathilde began to see a gleam of happiness. And that
faint spark which has such power over courageous, intelligent
souls had to struggle for a long time with her dignity and self-importance.

One day she came to her mother at seven o'clock in the morning to beg her to let her go away to Villequier. The Marquise,
not even deigning to look, told her to go back to bed. It was the
last effort she made in the direction of common prudence and
traditional ideas.

The fear of doing wrong and of violating the ideas held by
de Caylus, de Luz, and de Croisenois had little influence with
her. These, she felt, did not understand her. She would have
consulted them if there had been a question of buying a carriage or an estate.

Her real dread was that Julien might be displeased with her.
"But perhaps he has only the appearance of a superior man."
She abhorred lack of character; that was her only objection to
the handsome young men who paid her such attention. The
more gayly they chatted about the world and the rest, believing
her to be interested, the more they lost prestige in her eyes.
They were brave and that was all. "And in what way brave?"
she asked herself. "In a duel; but a duel is only a form. Everything is known in advance, even as to what one must say in

falling. Lying on the grass, with his hand over his heart, he must generously pardon his adversary and say something brilliant about a beautiful woman, often an imaginary one, who is going to a ball, even on the day when you are dying, in order not to arouse suspicion. Oh, yes, they brave danger at the head of a squadron that is gleaming with steel. But solitary, singular, unexpected danger—no, indeed!"

"Bah!" Mathilde said to herself, "it was at the court of Henry III. that men were found as great in character as by birth. If Julien had been at Jarnac or at Moncontour I should not have the least hesitancy! In those days of action and force Frenchmen were not mere figureheads! On the day of battle there was less anxiety than at any other time. Their life was not wrapt up like an Egyptian mummy under a cover which is the same to all and always the same. Yes, there was no less courage required in going alone at eleven o'clock at night from the Hôtel de Soissons, dressed like Catherine de' Medicis than to-day to go to Algiers. A man's life was a series of dangers. To-day civilization has removed danger. No more spontaneity and initiative! If it is shown in ideas it becomes matter for epigram; if it is shown in action there is not enough cowardice to mock at it. But whatever folly fear makes us commit is quickly overlooked. A degenerate and wearisome age, indeed! What would Boniface de la Mole have said if, rising from his grave with his head severed, he had seen, in 1793, seventeen of his descendants allow themselves to be taken like lambs and guillotined two days afterwards? Death was certain, but it would have been in bad taste to defend oneself and to kill one or two Jacobins! In the heroic days of France, in the days of Boniface de la Mole, Julien would have been Chief of a Squadron and my brother the conventional young priest, with wisdom in his eyes and reason in his mouth!"

A few months before, Mathilde, despairing of finding a character different from the rest, had found some pleasure in writing to one or two society young men. That unconventional performance, which was considered so imprudent in a young girl, could have dishonored her in the eyes of Marquis de Croisenois and of Duke de Chaulnes, his father, and of the entire Chaulnes household, if, on seeing the marriage project falling through, they would have wished to know why. Then Mathilde could not sleep, though her letters were only replies. But in this one she ventured to write that she was in love, and she wrote *first.* "Oh, how horrible! And to a man placed on the lowest rung of the social ladder!" That circumstance, if discovered, would have brought her lifelong dishonor. Which one of the ladies who visited her mother would have dared take her part? What would be said to soften the blow of contempt coming from all drawing-rooms? To speak was bad enough, but to write! "There are things that should never be written," cried Napoleon, when he learned of the capitulation of Baylen; and it was Julien who had taught her that!

But that was not all. Mathilde's anguish came from another source. Forgetting the terrible effect on society, and the ineffaceable stain and contempt she would bring upon herself in thus outraging her caste, Mathilde had written to a person of an altogether different nature from that of de Croisenois and his compeers. The depths, the unknown quantity in Julien's character frightened her even in his ordinary relations with her; and she bade him to become her lover, perhaps her master! "What would not be his pretensions if once he had complete control over me? Oh, well, I will say just as Medea: 'In the midst of all perils there remains *myself*!' "

Julien had no veneration for noble blood, she knew. If that is the case, perhaps he would have no love for her. In the midst of all this doubt and terror her feminine pride returned.

"There should be nothing ordinary in the lot of a girl like myself," cried Mathilde, impatiently. Her pride, inculcated in her from her cradle, struggled with her daring. It was just at this juncture when Julien's proposed departure brought the matter to a crisis.

Late in the evening Julien was malicious enough to have his trunk taken down by the porter. He called the valet to take it down. "This little matter may not be noticed," he said to himself; "but if it succeeds, she will think I am gone." And he fell asleep over his little joke, while Mathilde could not close her eyes.

Early the next day Julien left the house unperceived, returning before eight o'clock. Hardly was he in the library when Mathilde appeared at the door. As he handed her his reply, he thought it was his duty to speak to her. It was, indeed, a very convenient moment, but Mademoiselle de la Mole evidently did not wish to listen, and disappeared. Julien, on the other hand, was well pleased; he really did not know what to say to her.

"If all this is not a game put up by Count Norbert, it is clear that it is my cold look that has kindled the love which that proud girl takes pains to show me. I should be more than an ordinary fool if I should allow myself to have a feeling for this tall blond doll." His reasoning left him colder and more calculating than ever.

"In the battle that is being arranged now her noble birth will be the breastworks in this military position between her and me; it is there that all the manœuvring must take place. Indeed, I have done wrong in remaining in Paris; this postponement of my departure exposes me somewhat if all this is only a game. What harm was there in leaving? I could have laughed at her if they are laughing at me now. If there is anything in her feeling, I could have increased it a hundredfold." Mademoiselle de la Mole's letter had given Julien such an access of vanity that, laughing at what was happening, he had really forgotten about his proposed departure. It was the fatality of his character to be so extremely sensitive to his own weaknesses. He was put out by this and was giving almost no thought to his former victory.

When it was nine o'clock Mademoiselle de la Mole again appeared on the threshold of the library. She threw him a letter and ran away.

"Why, it seems this is going to be a regular letter romance!" he cried, picking it up. "The enemy has a masked battery. I—I will be on my guard with coolness and virtue."

He was asked for a decisive answer in a manner that augmented his joy. He took pleasure in hinting broadly for two long pages at the persons who desired to amuse themselves at his expense, and it was only by way of remark at the end of the letter that he decided to leave anyhow the next morning. The letter finished, he said, "The garden is a good place to put it," and he went there. He looked at the window of Mademoiselle de la Mole's room. It was on the first floor, near her mother's suite, but there was a high entresol. The first floor was so high that, as he was walking under the linden trees with the letter in his hand, Julien could not be seen from Mademoiselle de la Mole's window, the arch formed by the trees intercepting the view. "But, my!" said Julien to himself, "this is imprudent if the whole thing has been gotten up to make a fool of me. To be seen carrying a letter would be to play into the hands of the enemy."

Norbert's room was just over his sister's, and if Julien left the walk under the trees, the Count and his friends could follow his every movement. As Mademoiselle de la Mole appeared at her window, he half showed her the letter. She nodded her head. Julien quickly returned to his room, and by chance met the beautiful Mathilde on the stairway, who seized the letter, with eyes blazing with passion.

"What passion there would be in the eyes of poor Madame de Rênal," said Julien to himself, "when, after six months of intimacy, she would receive a letter from me! But even in her I believe I have never seen such passionate eyes." He did not allow himself to continue the comparison. "But, what a difference!" he added. "In her elegant morning gown, in her charming carriage, Mademoiselle de la Mole, thirty feet away, would be taken by any man to belong to her high rank. That is what I call intrinsic worth."

Madame de Rênal did not have a Marquis de Croisenois to sacrifice to him. He only had for a rival that vulgar subprefect Charcot, who called himself Maugiron because there were no more Maugirons.

At five o'clock Julien received a third letter, thrown at him from the library door. Immediately, as before, Mademoiselle de la Mole had fled.

"What a mania for writing, when talking is so much more convenient! The enemy wants letters from me, and many of them, that is clear." He was not in a hurry to open it. "Some more elegant phrases," he thought. But he paled as he read the eight short lines:

"I must talk to you; I must talk to you this evening. At one o'clock in the morning come to the garden. Take that garden ladder near the well and place it against my window, and come to me. It is moonlight now, but that makes no difference."

Chapter 15

Is It a Conspiracy?

Ah! How cruel is the interval between the conception of a grand project and its execution! What vain terrors! What doubts! Life itself is at stake. And something much more is at stake: honor!

—SCHILLER

"THIS IS getting serious," thought Julien, "and a little clearer, too. Why, this fine young woman can talk to me in the library with the greatest ease. The Marquis, in his fear that I might show him some accounts, never goes there. Why, M. de la Mole and Count Norbert, the only persons who ever go there, have been away nearly the whole day! We could easily find out when they return to the house. And Mathilde, for whose hand a sovereign prince is not too noble, wants me to act so abominably imprudent! Well, it is clear that they want to ruin me, or, to say the least, to have sport with me. First they wanted to cause my downfall through my letters; but I had made them too prudent. Now they want something clearer than day. These fine gentlemen think I am a fool. The devil! In bright moonlight to mount a ladder to the first floor, twenty-five feet high! It will take enough time to let everybody see me, even from the neighboring houses! Wouldn't I look fine on the ladder!"

Julien returned to his room and commenced packing his trunk, whistling. He was resolved to leave without even making any reply. But that sage resolution did not bring him peace.

"But, suppose," he said all at once, after locking his trunk, "Mathilde is in earnest? Then in her eyes I become a consummate coward. I cannot boast of my birth, therefore I need great qualities which form *my* capital and are to be shown in just such actions."

For a quarter of an hour he reflected. "Why should I refuse to do it?" he concluded, finally. "She will think I am a coward. I not only lose the most brilliant society woman, as they all said at Duke de Retz's ball, but also the extreme pleasure of seeing the Marquis de Croisenois sacrificed,—a Duke's son, who himself some day will be a Duke—a charming young man who has all the advantages that I lack—fortune and birth! Regret will follow me all my life, but not so much on her account, there are so many mistresses—— 'But there is only one honor,' said old Don Diegue. And here I quickly recoil before the first peril; for the duel with M. de Beauvoises was only a farce. It is all different now. I may be shot point blank by a servant, but that is the least danger; I may be disgraced. It is getting serious, my boy," he added, with the gayety and accent of a Gascon; "it is a question of honor! Never will a poor devil, placed by chance at the very bottom of the social scale, have another such occasion. Oh, I may acquire a fortune, but to be inferior always——" He reflected a long time, walking rapidly to and fro, and stopping short from time to time, as thought after thought came.

A magnificent marble bust of Cardinal Richelieu had been placed in his room, and that now attracted his gaze. The bust seemed to look at him rebukingly, as if reproaching him for the lack of daring which should be natural to the French character. "In your time, oh great man! should I have hesitated? So much the worse," he cried out at last, "if the whole thing is a trap. It is worse, more compromising for a young girl! Everybody knows that I am not a man to keep quiet. They will have to kill me then. It was all right in 1574, in the time of Boniface de la Mole, but no one would dare do it to-day; people are not the same. Mademoiselle de la Mole is so envied, four hundred drawing-rooms would resound with her disgrace, and with such pleasure!

"The servants are always talking among themselves about her marked preference for me; I know it, I have heard them say it. On the other hand, there are her letters, they can prove that I have them on my person. They can take them away from me after they surprise me in her room; I should then have to deal with two, three, or four men—how can I tell? But where will they get these men? Where can they find these hirelings in Paris? The law, they are afraid of the law, even de Caylus, de Croisenois, and de Luz!

"The singular situation and the ridiculous figure I should cut when held by them might tempt them. Look out for Abelard's fate, M. le Secrétaire! Oh, well, they will carry away marks from me. As for the letters, I can put them in a safe place."

Julien made a copy of the last two letters he had received and hid them in a volume of that handsome edition of Voltaire in the library, taking the originals to the post-office. When he returned, he thought with terror and surprise: "Into what folly am I throwing myself?" For a full quarter of an hour he thought of his course of action for the night.

"But if I refuse, I shall despise myself in consequence all my life; it will be a matter of regret for me, and for me such a regret is the greatest pain. Did not I show it in my affair with Amanda's lover?

"How can I be the rival of a man bearing one of the greatest names of France, and I myself an inferior? Really it is only cowardice at the bottom of my not going there. That decides me now," Julien cried out, leaping up. "Besides, she is so pretty. If this is only a betrayal of me, how foolish she has been on that account! If it is all a hoax, gentlemen, I will make the joke a very serious one, and I will do it this way. But if they tie my arms as soon as I enter the room? If they place some ingenious trap? It is all like a duel," he said to himself, laughing, " 'parade everywhere,' as my fencing master used to say. But, good Lord! to finish it all one of the two must forget to play. Besides, here is the reply I can make." He drew out his pistols from his pocket, pulling the trigger back, ready to fire.

There were some hours yet before anything could be done, so Julien wrote to Fouqué. He said: "My friend, do not open the enclosed letter except in case of accident. If you hear that anything strange has happened to me, then erase the proper names from the manuscripts which I send you and make eight copies of them, which please send to the newspapers in Marseilles, Bordeaux, Lyons, and Brussels. Ten days later have the manuscripts printed and send the first copy to Marquis de la Mole; fifteen days later scatter the others at night in the streets of Verrières."

All this being arranged as in a tale, Julien enjoining Fouqué from opening it except in case of accident, provided, nevertheless, against a possible compromise of Mademoiselle de la Mole. Julien finished arranging the package when dinner was announced.

He felt his heart beat violently. His imagination, busy yet with what he had written, represented everything tragical to him. He saw himself seized by the servants, tied hand and foot, and lowered into a hole, gagged. Then a servant stood guard over him. He saw, too, that if the honor of the family demanded that there should be a tragic end to the affair he might be finished with a poison, which would leave no trace behind. It could then be said that he had died naturally, and he would be carried back into his room dead.

Moved by his dramatic imagination, he looked at the liveried servants when he entered the dining-room, and closely studied their faces. "Which of these have been selected for the affair of to-night?" he asked himself. "The traditions of Henry III.'s court are so continually kept up in this family that they would be rasher than other persons of their rank if they believed these to have been outraged." Observing Mademoiselle de la Mole's face to see if he could read there any family projects, he saw she was pale. He was carried back by her expression to the Middle Ages. She had never assumed such a magnificent air; she was indeed beautiful and imposing. He was really then becoming in love. *"Pallida morte futura"* ("Pale from approaching death"), he was saying to himself.

After dinner he remained a long time in the garden, but Mademoiselle de la Mole did not appear. To talk to her now would have removed a great weight from his heart.

It must be admitted he was afraid. When he had decided to act, he abandoned himself to that feeling without shame. "Provided I have the necessary courage at the moment of action," he said to himself, "what difference does it make if I feel so now?"

He went to reconnoitre the place and to examine the rungs of the ladder. "That is an object," he said to himself, smiling, "that is destined to serve me here as well as in Verrières. What a difference, though! Then," he added, sighing, "I was not obliged to be on my guard against anyone when I was exposing myself for her! And what a difference, too, there is in the danger! I might have been killed in the garden by M. de Rênal, but there would not have been the least dishonor for me; my death could have been easily explained. Here what tales will there not be told in the house of de Chaulnes and the rest! I shall serve as a fable. For two or three years, perhaps," he resumed, smiling, "I shall be talked about." But that idea made him serious.

"And what can even justify me? Supposing Fouqué does print the pamphlet, that will be only an additional infamy. Yes, I have been admitted into a house, and, in return for the hospitality I have received and the kindness that has been shown me, I print a pamphlet on what has taken place there; I attack a woman's honor. Ah, let me rather be fooled a thousand times!" It was, indeed, a wretched night for him.

Chapter 16

One O'clock in the Morning

> *Ce jardin était fort grand, dessiné depuis peu d'années avec un goût parfait. Mais les arbres avaient figuré dans le fameux Pré-aux-Clercs, si célèbre du temps de Henri III, ils avaient plus d'un siècle. On y trouvait quelque chose de champêtre.*
>
> —MASSINGER

HE WAS about to countermand the order to Fouqué when eleven o'clock struck. He noisily drew the bolt of his door as if he had been locked in his room against his will. Softly he made the rounds of the house to see what was going on, especially on the fourth floor, where the servants slept. But there was nothing out of the ordinary. One of the maids had company, and the servants were gayly partaking of punch.

"Those who are laughing so," thought Julien, "surely cannot be a party to to-night's affair; they would be more serious." Then he placed himself in an obscure corner of the garden. "If the plan is to hide some of the servants, they would have to come along the garden walls if they are charged to spy on me. If M. de Croisenois is concerned in this matter, he ought to find some less compromising means for the young woman he wishes to marry, by surprising me before I enter her room." He made a careful examination of the premises. "It is a matter that concerns my honor," he thought, "and if I fall into some stupidity, I shall never excuse myself by saying I did not think of it."

The night was exasperatingly clear. Toward eleven o'clock the moon rose, and at half-past twelve it shone resplendent on the front of the house.

"She is mad!" Julien said to himself. When one o'clock struck there was still light in the room occupied by Norbert. Julien had never been so afraid in his life; he only saw the danger of the enterprise, unaided as he was by any enthusiasm.

Taking the ladder, after reflecting for a few minutes longer, he placed it against Mathilde's window. He mounted it softly, pistol in hand, astonished at not being attacked. As he approached the window, it was noiselessly opened.

"Oh, here you are, monsieur," said Mathilde to him with emotion. "I have been following your movements for an hour."

Julien was greatly embarrassed; he did not know what was expected of him. He felt no love whatever. In his embarrassment he thought he might venture to do something; he made a pass as if to embrace Mathilde.

"Go away!" she said, repulsing him.

Quite pleased at the rebuff, he threw a hasty glance around him. The moon was so bright that there were dark shadows cast in Mademoiselle de la Mole's room. "There might be men hidden there, for all I know," he thought.

"What have you in your coat pocket?" Mathilde asked him, pleased at finding a subject for conversation. She was indeed suffering agonies. All the reserve and timidity natural to a well-born girl came back to her most cruelly.

"I have all sorts of arms and my pistols," replied Julien, now well pleased at finding something to talk about.

"You must lower the ladder," said Mathilde.

"It is large and might break the windows down below."

"There is no need of breaking the windows," replied Mathilde, trying to resume her ordinary tone. "It seems to me you could lower the ladder with a cord, which you can tie to the top rung. I always have cords here."

"And that is a woman in love," thought Julien; "and she has even dared to tell me that she loves me! All this coolness and prudence in her precautions tell me plainly enough that I do not triumph over de Croisenois, as I foolishly thought.

"But how I follow her in every way! Oh, well, what is the difference? Do I love her? I only triumph over the Marquis in this: that he will be exasperated to know that he has been replaced, and angrier still when he finds it is myself. With what pride he looked at me last night at the café Tortoni, pretending not to know me! And how spitefully he saluted me when at last he could not help himself!"

Julien, tying the cord to the top of the ladder, commenced to lower it gently, leaning far out over the balcony so that the windows below might not be touched.

"A fine opportunity to kill me if anybody is hidden in Mathilde's room!" he thought. But only a profound silence ensued. The ladder touched the ground and Julien succeeded in laying it along the wall, in a bed of exotic flowers.

"What will my mother say," asked Mathilde, "when she sees all her beautiful plants in disorder? You must throw the cord away," she added, with the utmost sang-froid. "If it is seen leading to the balcony it will be a circumstance difficult to explain."

"And how shall I leave?" asked Julien, suavely, affecting the Creole tone of one of the maids in the house, a native of San Domingo.

"You? Why, you are going to leave by the door," replied Mathilde, ravished at the thought. "Ah, that man is worthy of my love!" Julien let the cord drop into the garden.

Mathilde happened to press his arm; he thought he was seized by an enemy. Turning quickly around, he drew out a dagger. She thought then that someone was opening a window. They remained motionless, not daring to breathe, the moon shining full in to the room. The noise ceased, and they became calm again. Then their embarrassment returned. Julien satisfied himself that the door was locked and all the bolts in place. He was thinking of looking under the bed, but he did not dare; two or three servants might have been hidden there. Finally, feeling that he would have occasion to reproach himself for lack of prudence, he ventured to look.

Mathilde experienced now all the anguish from the side of imprudence. The situation caused her horror.

"What have you done with my letters?" she asked, abruptly.

"What a fine thing to disconcert the gentlemen if they are listening!" thought Julien.

"They are hidden in a large Protestant Bible, which the diligence is carrying far away from here," he replied. He spoke very distinctly, in order to be heard by anyone who might have been hidden in the two mahogany wardrobes which he had not dared examine. "The other two have been sent by post and are going in the same direction as the first."

"Why have you taken all these precautions?" asked Mathilde, frightened.

"Why should I lie?" thought Julien. Then he told her all his suspicions.

"That explains the coolness of your letters," cried Mathilde, not at all tenderly.

Julien did not notice the tone, but the familiarity it implied nearly turned his head. His suspicions vanished, and he ventured to press in his arms the beautiful girl for whom he had so much respect. This time he was only half repulsed. He had recourse to his memory, as he had formerly done at Besançon with Amanda Binet, reciting some of the most beautiful passages from "Nouvelle Héloïse."

"You are a man of courage," she replied, without too much

attention to his phrases. "I wanted to test your valor, I admit. Your first suspicions and your resolution show you to be more intrepid than I gave you credit for."

As Mathilde tried to speak familiarly with him, she was evidently more conscious of this new mode of speech than of what she was saying. As it lacked tenderness Julien found no pleasure in it, but was rather astonished at the absence of anything like charm in it all. He commenced to reason about it. He saw himself esteemed by this proud girl who never gave unqualified praise. And reasoning thus he gained some satisfaction for his vanity.

It was not that passion which he had formerly experienced with Madame de Rênal. There was no tenderness in his heart. He simply felt happy because his ambition had been satisfied; and Julien, above all, was ambitious.

He spoke again of those of whom he was suspicious and of the precautions he had taken. While speaking, he was thinking of the means he should adopt to profit by his victory.

Mathilde, still in the greatest embarrassment and almost overwhelmed by what she had done, seemed delighted to find some subject for conversation. They spoke of seeing each other again. Julien again enjoyed the effect produced on her heart by the bravery of which he now gave further evidence. They spoke of those around them who might poke their noses into their affair, and particularly of little Tanbeau, who was surely a spy. Neither he nor Mathilde, however, was without resource.

"What can be easier than to meet in the library to arrange all that? I can come without suspicion into any part of the house," added Julien, "and even into Madame de la Mole's room." That room it was absolutely necessary to cross to reach the girl's; but if Mathilde should find it better that he should come by way of the ladder, he was ready to expose himself to that little danger.

While listening to him, Mathilde experienced her first shock by the air of triumph he assumed. "He is my master now," she was saying to herself, a prey to remorse. Her reason brought terror to her heart as a reward for the awful folly she had committed. She would have killed both him and herself then if she had had the power. When her will silenced remorse to some extent, her maidenly modesty made her miserable. She had never thought of the horror of the situation.

"Anyhow, I must talk to him," she said to herself; "at least that is the rule; one must speak to a lover." She then tried to do what she felt was her duty. With a tenderness in word rather than in voice she related to him all she had experienced during the last few days. She had decided, she said, that if he dared climb up to her window as she had ordered him to do, she would belong to him entirely. But never was anything said in a calmer tone.

There was a singular absence of warmth between them. For all the world it looked as if unwilling love was dragged in by force. What a moral lesson for a young imprudent girl! Was it worth the trouble of jeopardizing her whole future for such a moment?

After a hesitancy that seemed to be the reflex of positive hatred, Mathilde became his mistress, her womanly reserve yielding to her fixed resolution. But all her transports of love remained mechanical. Passion is, after all, only a model which is imitated rather than realized. Mademoiselle de la Mole was only thinking that she owed a duty to herself and to her lover. "The poor boy," she thought, "was very brave, and I should make him happy, or it is I who lack character." But she would have staked her soul if she could have removed the cruel necessity in which she found herself. Yet she was mistress of herself withal. Not a regret, not a single self-reproach marred that singular rather than happy night for Julien.

How different from his last twenty-four hours at Verrières! "These fine Parisian ways have spoiled everything, even love!" he was saying to himself, with a keen sense of injustice. He gave himself up to these reflections after he had been hidden in a large wardrobe on first hearing a noise in the next room, occupied by Madame de la Mole.

Mathilde followed her mother to Mass.

The servants left the room for a while, and Julien lightly glided out before they came back to finish their work. He mounted his horse and went to the outskirts of the most solitary woods around Paris. He was more astonished than happy. What happiness he did feel was like that of a young sub-lieutenant who, as a reward of daring, has just been named colonel by his general. He felt himself lifted to a great height. All that was above him the day before was now on a level with him, if not beneath him. Gradually, as he rode farther, Julien's happiness increased in proportion.

If Mathilde had nothing tender in her heart it was because, strangely enough, she had simply fulfilled a duty. There was no spontaneity in her throughout the night, except from the side of the misery and shame she found in place of that happiness of which she had read in novels.

"But am I sure about that?" she asked herself; "don't I love him?"

Chapter 17

An Old Sword

I now mean to be serious—it is time,
Since laughter now-a-days is deem'd too serious,
A jest at vice by virtue's called a crime.

—DON JUAN

SHE DID NOT come down to dinner. In the evening she was in the drawing-room for a while, but did not look at Julien. That seemed strange to him, but he thought, "I don't know their way of doing; she will give me some good reason for that." Yet moved by curiosity, he studied Mathilde's features. He could not disguise the fact that she looked cold, almost angry. Apparently she was not the same woman who the night before had feigned the transports of love. Were they too violent to be true?

The next day, and the day after, there was the same coldness on her part. She would not look at him; she did not seem to be conscious of his existence. Julien, a prey to uncertainty, was now far away from that triumph in which he had exulted the first day.

"Is it, perhaps," he was asking himself, "a return to virtue? But that idea belongs too much to the bourgeois to suit the proud Mathilde. Ordinarily in her life she does not give a thought to religion; she only cares for it as a useful means for the interests of her caste. But through sheer delicacy could she not reproach herself for what she had done?" Julien felt that he was her first lover; yet he thought, "I must admit that there was nothing free or spontaneous in all that. Never before have I seen her so proud as then! Did she despise me? It is quite likely that she is reproaching herself now. Is it because I am not born well?"

While Julien, with the prejudices that came back to him from his recollection of Verrières, was following the chimera of a tender mistress who would not think of her own existence when she was making her lover happy, Mathilde's vanity made her furious toward him. Since she had not been bored for nearly two months, she had no more fear on that account; and Julien,

309

without being in the least aware of it, had lost his greatest advantage.

"I have made myself a master," Mademoiselle de la Mole said to herself, a prey to the greatest chagrin. "Yes, he is now filled with pride. But if I drive him to extremes he will revenge himself by telling everyone of the nature of our relations!" Mathilde had never had a lover, yet in such a situation, where the most phlegmatic acquire tenderness, she was moved only by the bitterest reflections.

"He has a despotic empire over me since he reigns by terror, and can punish me atrociously if I displease him in the least!" That idea alone sufficed to make Mathilde perfectly wretched. Courage was the first characteristic of her nature. For the rest it was a game of toss-up.

On the third day, as Mademoiselle de la Mole persisted in avoiding him, Julien, evidently against her wishes, followed her into the billiard-room when dinner was over.

"Well, monsieur, you think you have acquired inalienable rights over me," she said to him, with ill-concealed anger. "In spite of my wishes, which I have shown plainly enough, you want to talk to me. Do you know that no one has ever dared to do anything like that?"

The conversation between the two was indeed a queer sort. Without the least suspicion on their part, neither one having much stability, one was animated only by the greatest hatred for the other. They soon came to the conclusion that they would forever part.

"I swear that I will keep it secret," said Julien; "and I will add that I will never speak to you. Then your good name cannot suffer." He left her with a bow.

He could easily accomplish what he thought was his duty, for he was far from believing himself in love with Mademoiselle de la Mole. Three days after he had been shut up in the wardrobe he had not a particle of feeling for her. But all was changed when he saw himself separated from her. His memory cruelly retraced every little circumstance of the eventful night, though that night had left him only cold. The same night of their quarrel Julien became perfectly delirious, for he was obliged to avow to himself that he was really in love with Mademoiselle de la Mole. That discovery was accompanied with a great inner struggle. All his ideas seemed to have overgone a complete change.

Two days afterwards, in place of being disrespectful to M. de Croisenois, he almost embraced him, with tears in his eyes.

His misfortune, however, did not deprive him of all sense, and he decided to leave for Languedoc. He packed his trunk and went to make arrangements for a coach. He thought he would collapse when, on arriving at the office, he learned that there was only a place for the next day in the Toulouse coach. Ordering it to be kept for him, he went back to the house to tell the Marquis of his proposed departure. M. de la Mole had gone out. More dead than alive Julien went to the library to wait for him. He dreaded meeting Mademoiselle de la Mole there.

She was there, and she looked daggers at him as he entered. Taken by surprise, overwhelmed as he was by his misery, Julien was weak enough to say to her in a most piteous tone: "You don't love me any more?"

"I have a horror of giving myself up to the first comer," said Mathilde, tears of anger starting in her eyes.

"To the first comer!" cried Julien, springing toward an old Crusader's sword that hung in the library as a curiosity. His despair, which was indeed very great when he spoke to Mademoiselle de la Mole, was increased a hundred-fold at beholding her tears. He would have been the happiest man in the world to have killed her at that moment. As he drew the sword out of the scabbard, Mathilde, taken out of her gloom by a new sensation, advanced boldly toward him, her tears ceasing to flow. The thought of Marquis de la Mole, his benefactor, presented itself vividly to Julien.

"I kill his daughter," he was saying to himself, "what horror!" He made a movement to throw the sword away. "Of course," he thought, "she will only laugh when she sees the melodramatic movement." That thought calmed him completely. He observed the blade curiously, as if he were looking for a nick there. Then, putting it into the scabbard with the greatest unconcern, he replaced it on the bronze hook. The whole scene lasted only a minute; but Mademoiselle de la Mole remained in utter astonishment.

"I was on the point of being killed by my lover!" she said to herself, thinking of the great days of Charles IX. and Henry III. She stood silent before Julien, without a trace of anger in her eyes. She was indeed charming at that moment. Certainly no woman ever looked less like a doll than she did—the thought which gave Julien the greatest repugnance to the Parisian women.

"I am going to show some weakness for him," thought Mathilde, "and that will be just enough to show him that he is my master, and precisely when I was going to speak to him so firmly!" She hastened away.

"Mon dieu! how beautiful she is!" exclaimed Julien, as he saw her turn away. "And she is the one who threw herself into my arms with such abandon a week ago! Ah, that will never come back! It is my own fault. When she was so charming to me, I should not have been so sensitive. Yes, I have a coarse and miserable nature."

The Marquis then appeared, and Julien hastened to tell him of his departure.

"Where?" asked the Marquis de la Mole.

"To Languedoc."

"No, if you please, there is something better in store for you if you leave for the north to-night. No; not if, in military fashion, I keep you a prisoner here. You will oblige me if you are absent only two or three hours; I may have occasion to need you at any moment."

Julien bowed, and retired without saying a word, leaving the Marquis greatly astonished. He was not in a condition to say anything more. He went to his room and locked the door. There he could exaggerate to his heart's content the bitterness of his lot.

"I cannot even go away! Lord knows how many days the Marquis is going to keep me in Paris. Good God! what will become of me? And not a friend whom I can consult. Abbé Pirard would not let me finish my first word, and Altamira would advise me to join myself to some conspirator. Oh, I am a fool! I know it. I am a fool! Who will give me advice? What will become of me?"

Chapter 18

Painful Moments

*And she admits it to me! She goes into the most
minute of details! Her lovely eyes, fixed on mine,
depict the love that she feels for another!*

—SCHILLER

MADEMOISELLE DE LA MOLE was charmed by the idea that she
had been on the point of being killed. She even went so far as
to say to herself: "He is worthy of being my lord and master if
he has had the courage to think of killing me. How many of
the handsome society young men could reach such a moment
of passion? Oh, he was so handsome when he got up on the
chair to put the sword back! After all, I was not such a fool to
fall in love with him." At that moment, if any honorable means
had presented itself for renewing their intimacy, she would have
hailed it with delight.

Julien, after locking himself in his room, became a prey to
the most violent despair. In his folly he thought of throwing
himself at her feet. If, in place of hiding himself in his room,
he had gone into the garden or in another part of the house,
he would have had occasion to change his despair for the greatest joy.

The address with which he had enacted the sword scene
created a favorable moment for him. The generous thought
lasted throughout the day. Mathilde was drawing a charming
picture of the brief moments she had loved him, and was regretting they were past.

"Indeed," she said to herself, "my passion in the eyes of the
poor boy lasted only from one o'clock in the morning, when I
saw him come up the ladder with pistols in his hand and in
the side pockets of his coat, until eight o'clock. It was a quarter of an hour later, at Sainte-Valère, that I began to think he
might try to frighten me into obedience."

After dinner Mademoiselle de la Mole did not flee from
Julien, but, accosting him, requested that he would follow her
into the garden. He obeyed.

Mathilde, yielding to the love she again felt for him, found
inexpressible delight in walking by his side. Curiously she

313

looked at his hands, which, in the morning, had seized a sword to kill her. After such a procedure there was no longer any question of referring to their previous conversation.

Gradually Mathilde began to speak to him confidentially about herself, finding great pleasure in such conversations. She even told him of the stray feeling of love she had for M. de Croisenois and M. de Caylus.

"What! for M. de Caylus also?" cried Julien. All the bitter jealousy of an abandoned lover broke out in that word.

But Mathilde, though aware of this, was not in the least disconcerted. She continued to torture Julien, detailing to him her former sentiments in the most intimate tone imaginable. He felt she was describing what really had taken place. He was unhappy to find that while she was speaking she was really finding out his own feelings. Jealousy could not go any farther. The suspicion that a rival exists is cruel enough; but to find that the love is described in the utmost detail by the woman one adores is without doubt the greatest misery imaginable. How Julien's pride was punished for believing himself preferred to de Croisenois and de Caylus! With great bitterness he exaggerated to himself every little advantage they had over him. He utterly despised himself. Yet Mathilde seemed adorable to him. Language could not describe his great admiration. As he was walking with her he looked at her hands, her arms, marvelling over her queenly carriage. He was tempted to fall at her feet, exhausted by his love and misery, and cry, "Pity!"

"And this beautiful woman, superior to all that I have ever seen, who once loved me, now loves M. de Caylus!" Julien could not doubt Mademoiselle de la Mole's sincerity; the tone of veracity was so marked in all she said. That nothing should be wanting to his misery, there were moments when, in order to think of the feelings she once had for M. de Caylus, Mathilde spoke of him as if she really loved him. Certainly there was love in that accent; Julien saw it clearly.

He had a greater weight in his heart than he could bear. How could the poor boy, wretched as he was, guess that it was only to be talking to him that Mademoiselle de la Mole took so much pains to tell him of her former inclination for M. de Caylus and M. de Luz? It was impossible to express Julien's anguish. He had to listen to the detailed accounts of her love for others in the same walk under the trees where, a few days before, he was waiting for one o'clock to strike to go to her room. His suffering was unbearable.

For a week his despair continued. Mathilde sometimes

seemed to seek him, and at other times barely avoided speaking to him; and the subject of conversation, to which she returned with a sort of cruel pleasure, was always a recital of the feelings she had for the others. She told him of the letters she had written, quoting even the very words she used. Towards the end she seemed to him to look upon him with a cruel malignity, his despair seeming to give her a measure of happiness.

Julien, indeed, had no experience and had never read any novels. If he had been less awkward and had just a little self-possession toward that young girl whom he loved so dearly, he would have said, even while she was making those strange confessions to him: "Well, I admit I am not as good as those gentlemen, yet I love you!" And she might have been happy to hear that. It would have depended entirely upon the manner in which it was said. Anyhow, he would have come out advantageously from a situation which was becoming monotonous even to Mathilde herself.

But Julien broke out with, "Then you don't love me any more, and I adore you!" when he was in despair. That was the worst step he could have taken. It destroyed in a second all the pleasure Mademoiselle de la Mole found in speaking to him about her feelings. She had just begun to be surprised that he was not getting angry over her talks about her love. She even imagined, just before he made that foolish remark, that perhaps he did not love her after all.

"His pride has no doubt extinguished his love for me," she was saying to herself; "he is not a man to see others, like de Caylus, de Luz, and de Croisenois, preferred to him with impunity. No, I shall never see him at my feet."

A few days before, laboring under his despair, Julien had praised those gentlemen to the very skies. That did not escape Mademoiselle de la Mole, to whom it came as a surprise. The passionate Julien, in praising a rival whom he saw loved, found an assuagement of his own grief. But his frank, stupid remark changed all in a second. Mathilde, assured now of being adored by him, despised him utterly. She was walking with him when he made that declaration, but she immediately left him, and her last look was of the utmost contempt. When she returned to the drawing-room she did not look at him once during the entire evening.

The next day the same contempt held sway in her heart. There was no longer any question about treating him, as she had done for a week, as a most intimate friend. The very sight of him seemed offensive to her. Mathilde's feelings had almost a tinge of disgust. She could not express all the contempt she felt on beholding him.

Julien, of course, had no idea of what was passing in Mathilde's heart during that entire week; but he certainly became aware of his fall. He had the good sense, however, to meet her as rarely as possible, and then without looking at her. Yet it was not without great pain that he deprived himself of her presence. He thought his wretchedness would never end.

"A man's endurance could go no farther," he said to himself. He passed his time at the little window in the tower of the house. With the blind closed he could see Mademoiselle de la Mole when she walked in the garden. What were his feelings when after dinner he would see her walking with M. de Caylus and M. de Luz, or some of the others for whom she had told him she formerly had so much love! Julien had never thought that misery could be so poignant. He was on the point of crying out from sheer wretchedness. His soul, usually so firm, had lost its bearings, and he could think of nothing but Mademoiselle de la Mole. He was incapable of the simplest sort of a letter.

"You have become simple," said the Marquis to him one day.

Julien, trembling at the thought that he was being found out, spoke of being ill, and actually persuaded himself that he was sick. Fortunately for him the Marquis joked with him at dinner about the trip he was going to make. Mathilde thought that he might be away for a long time. For many days Julien had avoided her, and all the brilliant young men who had every advantage which this pale, gloomy young man lacked could not draw her out of her reverie.

"An ordinary girl," she was saying to herself, "would have looked for the young man she preferred amid all these gentlemen who attract so much attention in the drawing-room, but an extraordinary character does not go in the rut traced by common persons. To be the companion of such a man as Julien, who lacks nothing but a fortune, which I have, I should continually attract attention; I should not pass unnoticed in life. Far, far from recoiling from any definite change, like my cousin, who, out of fear for others, would not dare even to scold her coachman who drove in the wrong direction, I should be sure of playing a great rôle. The man I have chosen has character and unlimited ambition. What does he lack? Friends, money. I will give him both." She thought, nevertheless, of Julien as an inferior whom she might love whenever she chose.

Chapter 19

The Comic Opera

> *O how this spring of love resembleth*
> *The uncertain glory of an April day;*
> *Which now shows all the beauty of the sun,*
> *And by and by a cloud takes all away!*
> —SHAKESPEARE

BUSY evolving the future and the rôle she hoped to play, Mathilde soon came to regret the dry metaphysical discussions she had frequently had with Julien. But while wearying of her lofty thoughts, she even regretted, too, sometimes, the pleasure she had found by his side. That was not without remorse. Indeed, self-reproach almost overwhelmed her at times. "Well, one may be weak," she said to herself; "it was worthy of a girl like me to forget myself with such a strong man. No, one can see that it was not the fine moustache or his graceful pose on horseback that carried me away; but it was his profound discussions over the future of France, his ideas of the connection between the events which happened here and the Revolution of 1688 in England. I have been led astray," she would say, recoiling before her remorse. "I am a weak woman; but, at any rate, I have not been led away like a fool by external appearances. If there is going to be a revolution, why, why could not Julien Sorel act the part of Roland and I that of Madame Roland? I love that to-day better than Madame de Staël, as immoral conduct would be an obstacle in our age. Certainly no one will reproach me for another weakness; I should die of shame."

Mathilde's reveries were not as lofty as her thoughts occasionally would lead one to suppose. She would observe Julien and find a grace in his every act. "Without doubt," she would say to herself, "I have wilfully taken away every right which that young man possesses. That despair and passion which the poor boy revealed in his declaration of love a week ago prove it. I must admit that I was wrong in getting angry at a word which, after all, showed such admiration and passion for me. Am I not his mistress? That indeed was natural. And really he was so lovely! Julien loved me even after those eternal conversations

317

I had with him about my love for those young men of whom he is so jealous. Ah! if he only knew how little they affect me, how flat they look by his side!"

With these reflections Mathilde was thoughtlessly drawing profiles one day in her album. One profile astonished her, almost taking her breath away, it was so like Julien's! "It is the voice of Heaven! There is one of love's miracles!" she cried, delightedly. "Without thinking of it I have drawn his picture!" Flying to her room, she locked the door and set herself seriously to work to draw Julien's picture. She did not succeed, however; the profile she drew by chance resembled him most of all. Mathilde was enchanted at seeing in it evident proof of her great passion. She did not put away her album until much later, when the Marquise called her to go to the opera. She had but one idea, to look everywhere for Julien and have him bring them home. But he did not appear, and the ladies had the usual callers in their box. In the first act of the opera Mathilde was dreaming only of the man she loved so ardently; but in the second act a phrase sung with a melancholy worthy of Cimarosa made a great impression on her heart. The heroine was singing:

"I must punish myself for my adoration; I love too much."

From the moment she heard that phrase all that had occupied Mathilde's mind before immediately vanished. Though she was addressed, she did not answer. Her mother even scolded her, but she hardly turned round. Her ecstasy reached the exultation and passion Julien had felt for some days. The air with which that phrase was sung seemed to be so applicable to her position that it occupied her every moment she was not thinking of Julien. Thanks to her love for music, she was that evening as Madame de Rênal was when she thought of love. The intellectual love is more brilliant, without doubt, than the real love; but it can claim only a few moments of enthusiasm. It is too conscious of itself, too self-complaisant; far from leading thought astray, it is built up entirely of thought.

When they returned home, Mathilde pleaded fever whenever Madame de la Mole wished her to do anything. She passed part of the evening repeating that little air on the piano; she sang the words which charmed her:

"I must punish myself; I love too much!"

The result was, she succeeded in triumphing over her love. During the next day she took occasion, in order to assure herself of her triumph over her passion, to displease Julien as much as possible. Yet never for an instant did anything he did escape her. Julien was too unhappy and too much moved to guess at the complicated feelings possessing her, just as before he was unable to understand the great favor she showed him. Never was his despair so great. His actions were so little governed by reason that had a melancholy philosopher come to him, and said, "Think only of profiting by what comes to hand; this love that comes from the head, that one sees in Paris, may not last two days," he would not have understood it. But, however exalted he was, Julien had a sense of honor. His first duty was discretion; that he knew. To tell of his grief to the first comer would have been a happiness comparable to an unfortunate one who, traversing a burning desert, feels a drop of water coming from the sky. But he knew his peril; he was afraid he would burst into tears at an indiscreet question that might be put, and so he kept himself locked in his room.

He saw Mathilde walking one day for a long time in the garden; when at last she left, he came down. He picked a rose. As the night was dark, he could give himself up at will to his melancholy without the fear of being observed; it was evidently for his benefit that Mademoiselle de la Mole loved one of those young officers with whom she had just spoken so gayly. She had loved him, too; but she had found out his little worth.

"Indeed, I have very little of it," thought Julien to himself, convinced; "I am really only an ordinary sort of creature, wearisome to others and unbearable to myself." He was disgusted with all the good qualities he had loved with so much enthusiasm. He judged life with an imagination turned on itself—a weakness of superior men.

Several times the thought of suicide presented itself to him. The idea was attractive; it came to him like a delicious sense of repose, like a glass of cold water offered to the wretched traveller overcome by heat and thirst. "But my suicide would only add to the contempt she has for me," he cried out. "What would she think of me?" In such despair the only resource for a man was courage. Julien had not enough spirit to say, "I must dare;" but as he looked at Mathilde's window he saw, through the blinds, that she had just extinguished the light. He looked with his mind's eye into the charming room he had seen only once, his imagination painting all in vivid colors. Then one o'clock struck. To hear the sound of the clock and to say to himself, "I am going to mount the ladder," came like a flash. It was like a stroke of genius; and good reasons came crowding into his mind. "I shall be happy," he said to himself. He ran to get the ladder, but the gardener had passed a chain around it. By means of the barrel of one of his pistols, which he broke, Julien, with almost superhuman strength, broke one of the links. He took up the ladder and placed it against Mathilde's window.

"She will be in a rage, and she will overwhelm me with hatred and contempt; but what do I care? I will give her a kiss, one last kiss, and then I will go to my own room and kill myself. My lips will then have touched her cheek before dying."

He ran up the ladder and knocked on the shutter. Mathilde heard him. She wished to open the shutter, but the ladder was in the way. Julien leaned against an iron bar which held the shutter in place, and, at the risk of falling, gave the ladder a violent push and moved it aside. As Mathilde opened the shutter, he threw himself into the room more dead than alive.

"It is you?" she cried, throwing herself into his arms.

Julien's happiness, like Mathilde's, was indescribable. She denounced herself to him. "Punish me for my cruel pride," she said to him, pressing him in her arms in a way that nearly choked him. "You are my master and I am your slave. I must ask pardon on my knees for rebelling against you." She left his arms to fall at his feet.

"Yes, you are my master," she said, intoxicated with happiness and love. "Rule over me forever; punish your slave whenever she revolts." Then, tearing herself away from him, she lighted a candle, and Julien could hardly prevent her from cutting off nearly half of her hair. "I want to remind myself," she said, "that I am your slave. If ever this pride of mine leads me astray, show me this hair and say, 'It is no longer a question of love or emotion with your heart; but you have sworn to obey. Obey, then, on your honor!'"

But it is more prudent to leave out the description of such blind folly.

Julien's prudence, however, was on a par with his happiness. "I must go down by the ladder," he said to Mathilde, when he saw the light of early morning on the chimneys to the east, beyond the garden. "The sacrifice I make is worthy of you; I am depriving myself of hours of the greatest happiness a human soul can taste. But it is a sacrifice I owe to your good name. If you knew what was in my heart, you would know what this means to me. Will you always be to me as you are now? But your word of honor is enough. You must know that since our first meeting the suspicion has not always been that there were thieves in the house. M. de la Mole has put a watchman in the garden; M. de Croisenois is fairly surrounded with spies. Why, it is known that every night he——"

Mathilde laughed outright at that idea, awakening her mother and a maid. Suddenly her name was called out through the door. She became pale as Julien looked at her; but she merely scolded the maid without even answering her mother.

"But suppose they should think of opening their window; they will see the ladder," said Julien to her. Pressing her again in his arms, he threw himself on the ladder and slid down. In a trice he was on the ground, and three seconds later the ladder was under the trees and Mathilde's fair name was saved.

When Julien had slightly recovered his equipoise, he found himself covered with blood and almost naked; he had hurt himself in his frantic descent down the ladder. His happiness brought back all the energy of his character. If twenty men had fallen upon him he would have attacked them all with pleasure. Fortunately his military prowess was not put to a test. He put the ladder in its usual place and passed the chain around it as before. He did not even forget to cover the holes the ladder had made in the bed of exotic flowers under Mathilde's window. As he was moving his hand over the soft earth in the dark, to assure himself that it was all covered, he felt something drop on his hand. It was one of Mathilde's tresses: she had cut it off and thrown it down to him. She was still at the window.

"This is what your slave offers you," she said to him aloud; "it is a sign of eternal love! I renounce the use of my reason; you are now my master!" Julien, overcome, was on the point of taking the ladder again and going back to her room, but his good judgment prevailed.

It was no easy thing for him to gain entrance into the house. He succeeded, however, in forcing a cellar door. When he came into the house, he was obliged to break into his own room. In the excitement with which he left Mathilde's room he had forgotten the key, which was in his coat pocket. "How in the world," he thought, "will she hide the place where she has cut off her hair?" Finally fatigue overcame even his happiness, and he fell into a profound slumber just as the sun was rising.

He was hardly awake when the breakfast bell rang. He came down into the dining-room, followed soon by Mathilde. Julien's pride had a great satisfaction when he saw love shining brilliantly in the eyes of that beautiful woman who was the object of so much attention. But his prudence took alarm. Under pretext of having little time for dressing, Mathilde had arranged her hair in a way that Julien could see at first glance what a sacrifice she had made for him.

"If such beauty could be spoiled by anything," he thought, "Mathilde would nearly have succeeded!" A whole side of her beautiful hair was cut within half an inch of her head. At breakfast Mathilde's manner corresponded with her previous imprudence. One might have thought that she was taking great pains to let everybody know of her great passion for Julien. Fortunately, that day, M. de la Mole and the Marquise were busy talking about the approaching bestowal of the cordon bleu, in which M. de Chaulnes was not to be included.

Toward the end of the meal it entered Mathilde's head, as she was speaking to Julien, to call him "my master." He blushed almost to the whites of his eyes. Whether by chance, or by design on the part of Madame de la Mole, Mathilde was not left alone for a moment all that day. In the evening, as they were leaving the dining-room, she just had time to say to Julien, "Can't you think of some pretext for me? Mamma has just decided that one of her maids shall sleep in my room."

That day was a glorious one for Julien. He was the happiest man on earth. At seven o'clock the next morning he came down into the library, hoping that Mademoiselle de la Mole would be there. He had written her a long letter; but he did not see her until two hours later, at breakfast. Her hair was dressed with the greatest care; with marvellous art a coiffeur had hidden the part where the tress was cut off. Once or twice she looked at Julien, but calmly and collectively; there seemed to be no longer any suggestion of calling him "my master." Julien's astonishment nearly took his breath away. Indeed, Mathilde had bitterly repented of nearly everything she had done. Thinking of it all calmly, she had come to the decision that he was, after all, a common creature; tarred too well with the same brush as the rest to deserve the extraordinary favors she had bestowed upon him. In fact, love was far away from her that day; she was weary of it.

As for Julien, he was just like a young boy. Uncertainty, astonishment, despair seized him in turn during the meal, that seemed to him an eternity. When he could decently rise from the table, he ran rather than walked to the stable, where he himself saddled his horse and galloped off like mad. He feared to disgrace himself by a sign of weakness. "I must kill my love physically," he was saying to himself, as he galloped in the

Meudon woods. "What have I done that I should deserve such a downfall? I must not do anything, I must not say anything to-day; I must be dead physically, as I am morally." Julien no longer lived; he was steeped in the greatest apathy.

Chapter 20

The Japanese Vase

At first his heart does not grasp the full extent of his misery: He is more vexed than moved. But as his reason returns he gradually senses the depth of his misfortune. All the pleasures of life become nothing for him, he can sense only the sharp points of despair that bite into him. But what good is it to speak of physical pain? What pain felt only by the body is comparable to this?
—JEAN-PAUL

WHEN the dinner bell rang, Julien scarcely had time to dress himself. In the drawing-room he saw that Mathilde was doing her best to keep her brother and M. de Croisenois from going to the soirée at Surenne, at the house of Madame de Fervaques. She could not have been more charming to them. After dinner M. de Luz, M. de Caylus, and several of their friends arrived. One might have thought that Mademoiselle de la Mole had made a cult of friendship and etiquette.

Although the night was charming, she insisted upon remaining in the room. She desired that they should not leave the chair where Madame de la Mole was seated, the blue sofa remaining the rendezvous of the group as in winter. Mathilde had an instinctive aversion to the garden; or, at least, it seemed unattractive to her. In truth it was bound up with her thoughts of Julien.

Despair dulls the brightest mind, and our hero was foolish enough to occupy the little stool which had formerly been the witness of his brilliant triumphs. Now no one said a word to him. Not only was his presence ignored, but worse: a few of Mademoiselle de la Mole's friends who were seated near her, at one end of the sofa, seemed deliberately to turn their backs on him. At least, so he thought.

"That is a direct insult," he said to himself. He affected to study the people who were trying to show him their disdain. M. de Luz's uncle had been ordered to appear before the King, and the handsome officer prefaced his remark by saying that his uncle left at seven o'clock for Saint Cloud, and that he would spend the night there. This information was introduced very adroitly, but it invariably appeared in his conversation with every one.

As he was critically observing M. de Croisenois, he noticed, he thought, some connection between that agreeable young man and his own misery. "I am foolish," thought Julien. "His character is strikingly like the Emperor Alexander, if I can believe what Prince Korasoff told me." During his first year in Paris, Julien, who had just left the seminary, was dazzled by the grace and brilliancy which he observed in the young men. He could not but admit that their real character was just now becoming outlined before his eyes.

"I am playing an unworthy rôle here," he said to himself all at once. He was thinking of leaving the little straw-bottomed chair so as not to appear too awkward, and was cudgelling his brains for some pretext. He appealed in vain to his memory, though it was usually very resourceful. The poor young man arose, with the greatest awkwardness imaginable, and left the drawing-room, his misery evident in every movement. For three-quarters of an hour he had played the part of an inferior, and the fact had not been hidden that he had not even been noticed.

The critical observation he had just made of his rivals prevented him somewhat from regarding his despair too tragically. In order to maintain his pride he recalled what had passed the night before. "Whatever advantage they have over me," he thought, as he walked in the garden, "Mathilde has never been to any of them what she has been to me twice already." But his wisdom did not go any farther; he did not understand the character of that singular woman chance had made the mistress of his life.

The following day he tried hard to kill both himself and his horse with fatigue. In the evening he did not even approach the blue sofa where Mathilde had taken her place as before. He noticed that Count Norbert did not even deign to look at him when he met him in the house. "Something very strange must have occurred," he thought, "he is naturally so polite!" Sleep for Julien would have been the greatest happiness; but, in spite of his physical fatigue, the charming memories of what had passed crowded his imagination. He was not clever enough to see, during his gallops in the woods around Paris, that he left his fate to chance in thinking only of himself without taking Mathilde's character into account. It seemed to him that only one thing remained to lighten his despair: to speak to Mathilde. But what could he say?

He was thinking of this early one morning, when all at once she appeared in the library.

"I know, monsieur, that you want to speak to me."

"Mon dieu! who told you that?"

"I know it; what is the difference to you? If you are wanting in honor, you can ruin me, or at least you can try to do it; but that danger, which I do not think is a real one, will certainly not prevent me from being sincere. I do not love you any more, monsieur; my imagination deceived me."

Under this terrible blow, Julien, fairly beside himself with grief and misery, tried to argue with her. Nothing, indeed, could have been more absurd. To justify oneself under a woman's displeasure! But reason no longer controlled his life, and only blind instinct was driving him to his fate. It seemed to him that as long as he spoke he could modify it. Mathilde was not listening to him; the sound of his voice irritated her. She had not imagined that he would have the audacity to interrupt her. Remorse, nursed by virtue and pride, made her life bitter that morning. She was almost beside herself at the thought that she had surrendered without discretion to a little abbé, the son of a peasant.

"It was almost," she would say to herself, when her misery was greatest, "as if I could reproach myself for a weakness for a servant." With such high-strung natures there is only a step from self-reproach to violent anger, and Mademoiselle de la Mole began to pour out upon him a veritable torrent of contempt. She displayed a dauntless spirit in torturing his pride.

For the first time in his life Julien, the object of a violent hatred, found himself submitting to a superior spirit. Far from thinking of a defence, he began to despise himself. In listening to the cruel words that were nicely calculated to destroy the least good opinion he might have had of himself, it seemed to him that Mathilde was right and that she was only telling the truth. As for herself, she found the greatest pleasure in punishing him, as well as the passion which she had felt for him a few days before. There was no need of inventing the cruel things she addressed to him; she only repeated what her pride had urged against her love for a week past. Each word increased Julien's despair. He wanted to leave the room, but Mademoiselle de la Mole authoritatively held him by the arm.

"Please, please notice," he said to her, "that you are talking very loud; you will be heard in the next room."

"What do I care?" replied Mademoiselle de la Mole. "Who

will dare tell me that they have listened? I am going to kill your pride for good, if you ever had any designs on me."

When Julien was at last able to leave the library, he was so dumbfounded that his very despair diminished.

"Oh, well, she does not love me any more," he repeated to himself aloud, as if to assure himself of his position. "She only loved me for eight or ten days, and I—I loved her all my life! Is it possible that she has no love for me—after only a few days?"

Mathilde was proud of what she had done. At last she had been able to break off completely! Her triumph over such a strong passion made her perfectly happy. "Now this little gentleman will know once for all that he cannot rule over me!"

She was so happy that she really had not a particle of love for him.

After such a humiliating scene, love would have been impossible for a less passionate person than Julien. Without a moment's hesitation Mademoiselle de la Mole had spoken to him with a directness that appealed to him even when he became self-possessed. The conclusion Julien drew after the first moment was that Mathilde was inordinately proud. He firmly believed that all was over now between them. Yet next morning at breakfast he felt awkward and timid before her. That was a weakness that could not have been attributed to him before. In small as well as in great matters he generally knew what to do and what to say. That day after breakfast, as Madame de la Mole asked him for a proscribed little pamphlet which the curate had secretly brought to the house that morning, Julien, in handing it over the table, turned over an old blue Japanese vase. Madame de la Mole arose, and gave a cry as she saw the pieces.

"An old Japanese vase," she said, "given to me by my great aunt, Abbess de Chelles! It was a present from the Dutch to the Duke, Regent of Orleans, who gave it to his daughter." Mathilde followed her mother's movements, delighted at seeing that blue vase broken which had always been an eyesore to her. Julien was silent and appeared greatly troubled. He saw Mademoiselle de la Mole near him.

"Yes, this vase is broken forever," he said to her, "just like the feeling that I once had in my heart. I pray you to excuse the awkwardness of which this is the result," and he withdrew.

"One might think," said Madame de la Mole, as he walked out, "that M. Sorel is proud of what he has done."

Mathilde was greatly struck by his remark. "That is so,"

she said to herself. "My mother is right; that is the feeling that animates him now"; and then the joy which came from the scene of the day before vanished. "Oh, well, it is all over now; there remains to me only a great moral lesson; my error is horribly humiliating; but I have gained enough wisdom to last me all my life."

"Was not that the truth?" thought Julien. "Why does this love which I once had for her torment me yet? Far from becoming extinguished as I hoped, it is becoming even greater. She is foolish—well and good," he said to himself; "but is she less adorable for all that? Can I ever change? Can any one be more beautiful than she is? All that the highest civilization could impart in the way of life, is it not all seen in Mademoiselle de la Mole?"

This recollection of his past happiness took immediate possession of Julien and forthwith destroyed what little reason he had. Reason struggles in vain against recollections of that sort; its own severe measures only increase their charm. The day after the breaking of the old Japanese vase Julien felt himself the most wretched of men.

Chapter 21

The Secret Note

*Car tout ce que je raconte, je l'ai vu; et si j'ai pu
me tromper en la voyant, bien certainement je
ne vous trompe point en vous le disant.*
—FROM A LETTER TO THE AUTHOR

JULIEN was summoned one day by the Marquis. The latter
seemed rejuvenated, his eye seemed so brilliant.

"Tell me something about your memory," he said to Julien;
"I hear it is prodigious. Can you learn four pages by heart and
recite them in London and without changing a word?"

The Marquis was reading the *Quotidienne,* seeking in vain
to hide a serious air which Julien, even when it turned on the
question of the Frilaire lawsuit, had never before remarked in
him. Julien was sufficiently well versed in tact to seem to be
taken in by the Marquis's lightness of tone.

"To-day's *Quotidienne* is not very interesting, but if the
Marquis will permit, to-morrow morning I shall have the honor
of reciting it word for word."

"What! even the advertisements?"

"Yes, monsieur, without missing a word."

"You promise me to do that?" asked the Marquis with some
gravity.

"Yes, monsieur; only the fear of failure can trouble my
memory."

"But I forgot to ask you—no, I do not ask you to swear not
to repeat a syllable of what you are going to hear. I know you
too well to impute anything of that kind to you; I will answer
for you. I am going to take you to a room where about a dozen
persons will be assembled. You will take notes of what each one
will say. Do not be uneasy. It will not be a confused conversation; each one will speak in his turn, though not perhaps con-
nectedly," added the Marquis, resuming his light tone, by far
more natural to him. "While we are speaking you will write
some twenty pages; you will come back here then with me,
and we will just boil it down to four. These four pages you will
recite to me to-morrow morning instead of this number of the
Quotidienne; you will leave soon after, and you must go post

haste, like a young man on pleasure bent. Your destination must not be known to any one. You will come into the presence of a great personage there; you will have to use a great deal of address; you must hoodwink every one around you; for amid all his secretaries and his footmen, some are in the pay of our enemies, and these may lie in wait for our agents.

"You will take with you a letter of recommendation. As soon as his Excellency looks at you, you will draw out of your pocket my watch, which I give you now. Take it, for the arrangement is as good as made, and give me yours in return. The Duke himself will write at your dictation the four pages which you have learned by heart. That done, but not sooner, notice, you can speak of the meeting at which you will be present if his Excellency asks you.

"Something will relieve the tedium of your trip to London, and that is that between Paris and the Minister's residence there will be a great many people who will want nothing better than to make abbé Sorel a target, and then it is all up, and I see a great delay to the whole matter! For, my dear fellow, how can we learn of your death? Your zeal cannot go so far as to make us aware of it.

"Go right away and buy a complete outfit," continued the Marquis in a serious tone; "dress yourself in the fashion of two years ago. You must look badly dressed to-night, but on your journey you will look as you always do.

"Does that surprise you, and are you getting suspicious? Well, young man, one of the venerable personages whom you will hear speak to-night is quite capable of sending instructions to have a dose of opium given you at night at the inn where you will stop to take supper."

"It is better to go thirty leagues out of my way then," said Julien, "than to take the direct route. I suppose it is about Rome?"

The Marquis suddenly gave him that impatient look which Julien saw in him at Bray-le-Haut. "That you will learn, monsieur, when I see fit to tell you. I don't like questions."

"It was not one," replied Julien, effusively. "I swear, monsieur, I was only thinking aloud; I was only trying to find out the most direct route."

"It seems you have lost your balance. Never forget that a diplomat, especially one of your age, should never seek to force confidence."

Julien was greatly mortified, for he felt himself in the wrong. His pride had vainly sought for an excuse.

"Know, then," added M. de la Mole, "that one always has recourse to his heart whenever something foolish is done."

An hour later Julien was in the Marquis's bedroom, looking like some shabby subaltern. A cravat of doubtful whiteness completed his generally seedy appearance. The Marquis burst out laughing when he saw him. Julien's disguise was complete.

"If this young man betrays me," M. de la Mole thought, "in whom can I trust? Yet one must trust somebody in life. My son and his brilliant friends are brave and true. If it is a question of fighting, they will perish on the very threshold of the throne. They are familiar with everything—except with what I need now. The devil if I know if any one of them can learn four pages by heart and travel a hundred leagues without being found out! Norbert is capable of sacrificing his life like his ancestors; but that is the virtue also of a common soldier——"

The Marquis fell into a profound reverie. "And yet, when it comes to sacrificing his life," he said with a sigh, "perhaps this Sorel can do as well as the rest."

"Let us get into the carriage," said the Marquis, as if to banish an unpleasant thought.

"Monsieur," said Julien, "while they were getting this suit for me, I learned the first page of to-day's *Quotidienne*."

The Marquis took the paper, and Julien recited the whole page without making a single mistake.

"Good," said the Marquis, "good for to-night."

All this time the young man took no notice of the streets they were passing. They finally alighted and were ushered into a large drawing-room hung with green velvet. A scowling lackey placed a table in the middle of the room, and soon after converted it into a work table by spreading over it a green baize cloth spotted all over with ink, the mark of some Minister. The host was an enormously large man whose name was not pronounced. Julien saw by his answers that he was a man accustomed to command.

At a signal from the Marquis, Julien sat down at one end of the table. In order to be doing something he commenced cutting the quills. Out of the corner of his eye he could watch the people in the room, but he saw only their backs. Two of them seemed to be speaking to M. de la Mole in a tone of equality, while the rest were more or less respectful in their tone. Then there was a new comer.

"Strange," thought Julien, "no one is announced in the room! Has this precaution been taken in my honor?"

Everybody rose as the man came in. He wore the same decoration which three others in the room had. All talked very low. Julien could only judge the new comer from his features and his general bearing. He was a short, thick, florid-complexioned gentleman, with an eye that had the ferocity of a wild boar.

Julien's attention was diverted by the almost immediate arrival of a very different person. He was a large man, very thin, wearing three or four vests, one over the other. There was a soft look in his eye, and his manners were extremely polished. "It is a face like the Besançon Bishop's," thought Julien. The man apparently belonged to the clergy. He seemed to be only about fifty or fifty-five years of age, yet his manner was very patriarchal.

Then the young Bishop d'Agde came in, who was astonished when, glancing at those in the room, his eye rested on Julien. He had not spoken a word to the latter since the ceremony at Bray-le-Haut. The surprised look embarrassed and irritated Julien.

"Why is it," he said to himself, "that to know a man is always inconvenient to me? All these great lords whom I have never seen do not frighten me in the least, and this young Bishop's look sends shivers through me. Really, I must be very peculiar besides being unfortunate."

A very dark little man entered with a great deal of noise, and began talking even when he was still at the door. There was something bizarre in his every movement. When this unmerciful talker appeared, the company formed themselves into little groups, evidently to spare themselves the annoyance of listening.

As they withdrew from the fireplace they approached the side of the table where Julien sat. He was becoming more and more embarrassed; for, indeed, no matter how hard he tried, he could not understand what was said; and though he was not experienced in such matters, he understood the importance of some things that were said. And how many of those great personages depended on having it all kept secret!

Julien had already cut a score of quills as slowly as possible, but that resource was fast failing him. He looked in vain for some order from M. de la Mole; but the Marquis seemed to have utterly forgotten him.

"What I am doing is ridiculous," Julien said to himself, cutting the quills again. "But men looking as they do and charged either by themselves or by others with large interests must certainly be suspicious. My look must seem disrespectful or inquisitive, and that is why, I suppose, they talk so low; but if I lower my eyes I shall seem to them to be trying to remember every word they say!" His embarrassment was indeed great. There were many things said that were quite astonishing to him.

Chapter 22

The Discussion

> *La république—pour un, aujourd'hui, qui sacri-*
> *fierait tout au bien public, il en est des milliers et*
> *des millions qui ne connaissent que leurs jouis-*
> *sances, leur vanité. On est considéré, à Paris,*
> *à cause de sa voiture et non à cause de sa vertu.*
> —NAPOLEON: *Mémorial*

A FOOTMAN entered hurriedly, announcing the Duke de X.

"Hold your tongue, you fool!" said the Duke as he entered. He spoke with such majesty that in spite of himself Julien thought that the proper way to get angry with a footman was the only mark of distinction in that great personage. Julien raised his eyes, but soon lowered them. He had formed such an idea of the great importance of the new arrival that he was afraid his look might seem indiscreet. The Duke was a man of about fifty, dressed like a dandy. He walked jerkingly. He carried his head straight, his long, curved nose giving to his face unusual prominence. No one could have looked nobler and yet more insignificant. His arrival terminated the preliminaries to the meeting.

Julien was interrupted in his study of the faces by M. de la Mole's voice.

"I beg to introduce to you M. abbé Sorel, who has a wonderful memory. It is only an hour ago that I spoke to him of the mission with which he may be honored, and yet he has learned by heart, in order to give a test of his memory, the first page of the *Quotidienne*."

"Strange news from poor N.," said the host. Taking up the newspaper hurriedly, he gave Julien a look at once pleasant and imposing. "Go ahead, monsieur," he said to him. A great silence ensued, and all eyes were fixed on Julien. He spoke so fluently that at the end of twenty lines the Duke said "Enough!" The little man with the wild boar look took his seat, for he was the Chairman. Hardly had he seated himself when he pointed out a little card table to Julien, making a sign to him to use it. Julien went over there with his writing materials. Twelve persons were sitting around the table with the baize cloth.

"M. Sorel," said the Duke, "please withdraw into the next room; you shall be called." The host looked slightly troubled. "The shutters are not closed," he said, half aloud to his neighbor.

"It is useless to look through the window," he said to Julien, confusedly.

"Here I am," Julien thought, "embroiled in a conspiracy. Fortunately it is not anything that might lead to Place de Grève. If there is any danger, what of it? I owe much more to the Marquis. I should be happy if he gave me an occasion to repay him for all the trouble my follies might cause him some day."

Thus thinking of his own cares, he looked around him as if he intended never to forget the place. He recalled then that he had not heard the name of the street, and that the Marquis had taken a cab, which he had never done before when he was with him. Julien gave himself up for a long time to his own reflections. He was in a room with velvet hangings striped with gold. There was a prie-dieu on which stood a large ivory cross, and on the mantel was a magnificently bound edition of "On the Pope," by M. de Maistre. Julien opened it so as not to seem to listen. From time to time the voices in the other room grew loud. The door suddenly opened and he was called in.

"Now, recollect, gentlemen," said the Chairman, "that from now on we are speaking before the Duke de X. Monsieur," he said, pointing to Julien, "is a young Levite, devoted to our holy cause, who will relate exactly everything we say. The gentleman has the floor," he said, pointing to the paternal looking nobleman with the three or four vests.

Julien thought it would have been more natural to have called him the "vested gentleman." He then set himself to the task of writing. The speeches Julien took down covered some twenty-six pages. What follows is only a bare outline, for it was necessary, as is always the case, to suppress the ridiculous things that were said.

That paternal looking "vested gentleman," apparently a Bishop, smiled quite frequently, and his brilliant eyes, overshadowed by wavy eyelashes, had an expression less indecisive than usual.

This great man who was to speak first before the Duke—"but what Duke," Julien asked himself—and who seemed to be the Attorney-General in expressing the views of the rest, now began to speak in that indecisive way which is frequently charged to magistrates. In the course of his recital the Duke made that identical charge against him.

After expressing his moral and philosophical views, he said: "Noble England, guided by a great man, the great Pitt, has spent forty million francs to suppress the Revolution. If the gentlemen will permit me to speak frankly, I will say that England has not understood yet that if with such a man as Bonaparte they had only good intentions they did nothing decisive, except personally——"

"Ah! again a eulogy on the murder!" interrupted the host, furiously. "You will be kind enough to spare us your sentimental homilies," cried the Chairman, his boar's eye glittering with rage. "Continue," the Chairman said to the previous speaker, his cheeks and brow purple.

"Noble England," resumed the speaker, "is to-day crushed. For every Englishman, before paying for his bread, is obliged to pay interest on the forty million francs which were used against Jacobins. And it has no longer a Pitt."

"But she has the Duke of Wellington," said a military gentleman, looking very important.

"Please, gentlemen, silence!" cried the Chairman, "if we keep on disputing it was useless to call in M. Sorel."

"Every one knows that monsieur has fine ideas," said the Duke, looking fixedly at the interrupter, who was one of Napoleon's generals. Julien saw that there was a reference to something personal that might prove very offensive. Everybody smiled, and the general seemed beside himself with rage.

"There is no longer a Pitt, gentlemen," resumed the speaker, seemingly like a man who despairs of receiving a calm hearing. "Even if there were a new Pitt in England, he could not fool a nation twice the same way."

"That is because a great conqueror, a Bonaparte, is henceforth impossible in France!" cried the military gentleman, interrupting again.

This time neither the President nor the Duke ventured to reply, although Julien could see they meant to do so. They simply lowered their eyes, and the Duke contented himself with a sigh that was heard all over the room. But the speaker was becoming angry.

"I see that you want me to finish," he said, excitedly, laying aside that polite, measured tone which Julien thought was a part of his character; "I see that you want me to stop. You do not seem to realize that I am doing my utmost to offend no one, though what I say might take a long time. Well, gentlemen, I will be brief, I will speak to you candidly. England has not a sou at the service of our great cause. If Pitt himself should come back, he would not with all his genius be able to fool the small proprietors of England again; for they know how much that little campaign at Waterloo has cost them. It cost them a thousand million francs. Well, since brevity is what is required," added the speaker, waxing warmer as he went on, "I tell you, then, *help yourselves.* England has not a guinea for you; and when England does not pay, Austria, Russia, and Prussia, who have only courage, but no money, cannot make against France more than one or two campaigns. It might be hoped that the young soldiers gathered by Jacobinism would be defeated in the first campaign, perhaps in the second, but in the third—may I pass for a rebel!—but in the third you will see again the soldiers of 1794 who were the irregulars of 1792!"

Here he was interrupted by three or four at once.

"Monsieur," said the Chairman to Julien, "please make a transcript in the next room of what you have written." Julien regretfully left.

The speaker had just started on a subject of which he had thought all his life. "They are afraid that I shall think them light," he thought. When they called him back, M. de la Mole was saying, seriously:

"Yes, gentlemen, it is above all the unfortunate people who can ask:

" *'Sera-t-il dieu, table ou cuvette?'*

"A *god* says the fable. It is to you gentlemen that this great and profound word belongs. Act on your own behalf, and France will appear just as our ancestors have made it and as we ourselves have seen it before the death of Louis XVI. England as yet, at least her nobility, despises this Jacobinism as much as we do. Without England's gold, Austria or Prussia could not undertake two or three battles. Would that be enough for our affair if we do not want it to be a fizzle like M. de Richelieu's in 1817? No, indeed!"

Here some one broke in, but the interruption was silenced by hisses from all sides of the room. It still came from that old gentleman who was burning to have the cordon bleu, and to be noticed by those who were preparing the message.

"*I* do not believe it," replied M. de la Mole, with a proud emphasis on the word "I," that seemed charming to Julien.

"That is well said," he thought to himself, as he put down the Marquis's speech. "With that single word M. de la Mole has undone twenty of the general's campaigns."

"It is not to foreign influence," continued the Marquis, in measured tones, "that we can intrust a new military occupation.

The young men who are writing the incendiary articles in the *Globe* will give you three or four thousand captains, among whom will be found a Kleber, a Hoche, a Jourdan, or a Pichegreu.

"There are indeed in France two parties," continued M. de la Mole, "not only in name, but clean cut and well defined; we must crush them. There are the journals, electors, and public opinion; in a word, the youth and all their adherents. While they are confused with the noise of their foolish words, we, we have the advantage of managing the Budget."

Here there was another interruption.

"You, monsieur," said M. de la Mole, haughtily, to the interrupter, "you, you do not furnish the Budget, if the word is disagreeable to you. You put away forty thousand francs furnished by the State and eighty thousand that you receive from the Civil List. Well, monsieur, since you force me to it, I will speak plainly, like your noble ancestors who followed St. Louis to the Crusades. For the one hundred and twenty thousand francs you should furnish us a regiment, a company; what do I say? half a company, if there are only fifty men fit for battle and ready to risk their lives for the good cause! You have only lackeys who, in case of revolt, would make you yourself afraid. The throne, the Church, the nobility may disappear to-morrow, gentlemen, just because you have not placed in each department five hundred who are devoted to our cause. But when I say devoted, I do not mean French bravado, but Spanish constancy. Half that troop is composed of our children, of our nephews, and of fine gentlemen; and each of these has at his side, not a little talkative bourgeois, ready to display the tricolor if 1815 presents itself again, but a good, simple peasant like Cathelineau. Our gentlemen will have taught him he is their brother.

"Let each one of us sacrifice a fifth of his income to form such a group of five hundred men in each department; then you can think of foreign interference. Never will a foreign soldier go as far as Dijon if he is not sure of finding five hundred friends in each department. The foreign Kings will not listen to you unless you tell them beforehand that you have twenty thousand men of the nobility ready to take arms and open the gates of France. Now, that is hard, you say. Well, gentlemen, our heads are at stake. Between the liberty of the press and our existence as the nobility there is war to the death. You must either become manufacturers or peasants, or shoulder your muskets. Be timid if you like, but do not be stupid; keep your eyes open. 'Form your battalions,' I tell you, as the song of the Jacobins goes.

"Perhaps there will be found some Gustave-Adolphe who, moved by the imminent peril to the monarchical principle, will advance three hundred leagues from his country and do for you what Gustave has done for the Protestant princes. Do you want to continue talking without doing anything? In fifty years there will be in Europe only Presidents of Republics and not a single King. And with the letters composing the word 'king' all go, the priests and the nobility. I see only *candidates* fawning at the dirty majorities.

"Yes, you can say all you please that France has not a single general known and beloved by all, and that the army is not organized except in the interest of the King and the Church, and that all the old soldiers have been taken away, while in every Prussian and Austrian regiment can be counted fifty under officers who have seen service. Two hundred thousand young men belonging to the bourgeoisie are burning for war."

"A disagreeable truth," nodded a grave person, apparently representing ecclesiastical dignity, for M. de la Mole smiled in place of becoming angry, and that was always a clue for Julien.

"Yes, it is disagreeable. To resume, monsieur. The man who must have a gangrened leg cut off would be foolish to say to the surgeon, 'This bad leg is all right.' To carry out the simile, monsieur, the noble Duke de X. is our surgeon."

"So now it is out," thought Julien; "it is to X. that I shall ride to-night."

Chapter 23

Clergy, Forests, Freedom

The first law of all creatures is that of self-preservation, of life. You sow hemlock and expect to see ears of corn come up!

—MACHIAVELLI

THE DIGNIFIED MAN followed, apparently very much at home with the matter in hand. He made an eloquent, and, to Julien, a pleasing, exposition of these great truths:

"First, England has not a guinea to spare, economy and Hume being in fashion. The clergy—not even the clergy will give us the money, and M. Brougham will simply laugh at us.

"Second, the impossibility of conducting more than two campaigns with the aid of the Kings of Europe without English gold; and two campaigns will not be enough for the bourgeoisie.

"Third, the necessity of forming an armed force in France, without which the monarchical principle in Europe will not last even through these two campaigns.

"The fourth point which I venture to propose to you is just as evident as the great need of forming an armed force. It is the impossibility of doing it all in France without the aid of the clergy, and I am going to prove it to you. You must yield everything to the clergy. First, because the Church occupies itself with its affairs day and night and is guided by men of the greatest capacity, who are placed away from the storm centre, three hundred leagues from our frontiers."

"Ah, Rome! Rome!" cried the host.

"Yes, monsieur, Rome!" replied the Cardinal with fire. "However ingenious were the pleasantries that were in fashion when you were a young man, I will say it above board, here in 1830 the clergy guided by Rome alone can speak to the people. Fifty thousand priests repeat the same words on the day indicated by their chiefs; and the people, who, after all, furnish the soldiers, will be more touched by the voice of the priest than by all the fine phrases in the world."

There were murmurs heard now.

"The clergy has a spirit superior to yours," continued the Cardinal, raising his voice. "All the steps you have taken to gain your point to have an armed party in France were first outlined by us. Now here are facts. Who has employed eight thousand soldiers in Vendée? Yet the clergy, holding no longer its woods, has nothing. At the first outbreak of hostilities the Minister of Finance writes to his subordinates that there is no money, excepting for the curate. At heart France does not believe, but it loves war. Whoever brings it on becomes doubly popular; for war means the starving of the Jesuits, to use a common phrase, and ridding the French, the monsters of pride, of the threat of foreign intervention."

The Cardinal was listened to with great respect.

"It is necessary," he said, "that M. de Nerval should leave the Ministry; his name is uselessly offensive."

At that everybody arose, and all commenced to speak aloud. "They are going to send me away now," thought Julien; but the prudent Chairman himself had forgotten all about Julien's presence. Everybody looked at the man whom Julien knew. It was M. de Nerval, the Prime Minister, whom he had seen at Duke de Retz's ball. The disorder was "at its highest," as the newspapers say in describing scenes of the Chamber. A quarter of an hour later, when silence was somewhat restored, M. de Nerval rose, saying in a peculiar tone:

"I will not say that I think nothing of the Ministry. But as it has been demonstrated to me, gentlemen, that my name gives additional strength to the Jacobins by having many of the Moderates against us, I will cheerfully retire, for the ways of the Lord are visible to a few of us. However," he added, looking fixedly at the Cardinal, "I have a mission. Heaven has said to me, 'You will mount the scaffold or you will reëstablish the French monarchy and reduce the Chambers to what it was under Louis XV'; and that, gentlemen, *I will do*." He ceased speaking as he sat down, and every one was silent.

"There is a good actor," thought Julien. He was deceiving himself, as usual, by attributing too much cleverness to men. Animated by the debate that had lasted throughout the evening, and above all by the earnestness of the discussion, M. de Nerval at that moment really believed in his mission. But with all his courage the man had no good judgment.

Midnight struck amid the silence that followed the phrase *"I will do."* Julien thought that the sound of the clock had something obsessive and funereal. He was greatly moved. The discussion was then resumed with increased energy and openness.

"These gentlemen will make me poison somebody," thought

Julien at times. "How can they talk about these things before a plebeian?"

At two o'clock the discussion still continued. The host had long ago fallen asleep. M. de la Mole was obliged to ring for a servant to bring in fresh candles. M. de Nerval had left the room at a quarter to two, not without having first observed Julien's face in a mirror that was at the side. His departure put every one at his ease.

While they were lighting the fresh candles, the man with the vests said to his neighbor: "God knows what he is going to tell the King; he can make us out fools and spoil our whole future."

"Yes, he was quite daring to present himself here. He might have come here before being made Minister with impunity, but the portfolio changes everything, undermining all of a man's ideas; he must certainly feel it."

As soon as the Minister had left, the general who had fought under Bonaparte shut his eyes. He began to speak of his health, of his wounds, and, looking at his watch, departed.

"I bet," said the man with the many vests, "that the general is running immediately after the Minister. He is going to excuse himself for being here and to pretend that he has been led away by us."

When the half-asleep servants had finished putting fresh candles in place, the Chairman said: "Let us now deliberate, gentlemen; let us not try to persuade one another. Let us think of the message which will be delivered to all our foreign friends. We have spoken of the Ministers; now, since M. de Nerval has left us, we can see in what way the Ministers can help us. We must see to it that they have the mind to do it."

This the Cardinal approved with a pleased smile.

"Nothing is easier, it seems to me," said the young Bishop d'Agde, with the fiery impulse of the most exalted fanaticism, "nothing is easier than to resume our former position."

Until then he had kept silent. His eye, which, as Julien observed, had first been quiet, had become inflamed at the beginning of the discussion; now his soul welled out like lava from Vesuvius.

"From 1806 to 1814 England was wrong in only one way," he said; "that was in not acting directly and personally against Napoleon. When that man finished making Dukes and Chamberlains, when he had reëstablished the throne, the mission which God had conferred upon him was at an end. There was nothing for him to do than to die. Holy Scripture shows us in more than one place how to put an end to tyrants."

He gave a few citations in Latin.

"To-day, gentlemen, it is not a man that we must sacrifice, it is Paris; all France copies Paris. What is the use of arming your five hundred men in each department? A doubtful enterprise at best, which will accomplish nothing. What is the use of mixing France up in what simply concerns Paris alone? Paris alone, with its newspapers and its drawing-rooms, is the root of all the evil. Let the modern Babylon perish!

"We must decide between the Church and Paris. It concerns even the worldly interests of the throne. Why did not Paris sneer under Bonaparte? Ask the canon of Saint-Roch!"

It was three o'clock in the morning when Julien walked out with Marquis de la Mole. The Marquis was as mortified as weary. For the first time he seemed to have an appealing tone in his voice as he spoke to Julien. He asked him on his word of honor never to reveal anything of the excess of zeal—that was his word—of which chance had made him a witness. "Never speak of this to our friend the foreigner unless he insists seriously upon knowing about our young fools. What difference does it make to them if the State totters? They will become Cardinals and take refuge in Rome, while we should be massacred by the peasants in our own homes."

The secret message which the Marquis wrote from the twenty-six pages which Julien had written was ready at a quarter to five.

"I am tired to death," said the Marquis, and it could be seen that at the end of the note some care was lacking. "I am less pleased with that than with anything I have ever done in my life. Here, my son," he added, "go and rest for a few hours; and for fear of having anyone take this away from you, I myself will lock you in your room."

The next day the Marquis took Julien to a château quite a distance from Paris. They met strange looking men there whom Julien took for priests. A passport was handed to him bearing a fictitious name, but indicating the real aim of his journey. He entered the carriage alone. The Marquis did not have the least doubt about his memory, for Julien had recited the message to him several times; but he feared he would be stopped on the way.

"Above all, look only like some stupid fellow who is travelling just to kill time," he said to him, in a friendly way, as he was leaving the drawing-room. "There was perhaps more than one Judas at last night's meeting."

His journey was rapid but tiresome. Hardly was Julien out

of the Marquis's sight when he forgot both the note and the mission in thinking of Mathilde.

In a little village some few leagues from Metz the post inspector told him that there were no horses for a relay. It was ten o'clock at night. Julien, very much put out, ordered supper. Then he walked about for a little while, passing the stable unintentionally, as it were, and looking inside. He did not see any horses.

"That man looks rather peculiar," Julien said to himself, "he is staring straight at me." He was beginning, as it is seen, not to believe everything he was told. It was his intention to leave the neighborhood immediately after supper, and, in order to learn something about the country, he left the room, pretending he wanted to warm himself by the kitchen fire. To his great joy he found there the singer Geronimo. Seated in an armchair placed near the fire, the Neapolitan was groaning aloud and shouting from time to time at the top of his voice, while twenty German peasants were staring at him with mouths wide open.

"These people are ruining me," he said to Julien, "I promised to sing to-morrow at Mayence; seven sovereign Princes will hear me. Well, let us take a little fresh air," he added, giving Julien a significant look.

After walking a little while, he said to Julien, when he was sure of not being overheard, "Do you know what is the matter? This inspector is a fool. Just as I was walking along a little while ago I gave twenty sous to a little servant, and he told me everything. There are twelve horses in a stable in another part of the village. The intention is to stop some courier."

"Really?" asked Julien, indifferently.

It was not enough to discover the fraud, but they must leave; and that was something Geronimo and his friend could not do.

"Let's wait until morning," said the singer at last; "they look so suspiciously at us. They suspect either you or me. To-morrow morning we will order a good breakfast; while they are preparing it we will take a walk together; we will hire the horses and take the next post."

"And your things?" asked Julien, who was thinking that perhaps Geronimo himself might have been sent to check him. Then they took supper and retired.

Julien was scarcely asleep when he was awakened by the loud voices of two persons talking in his room. He recognized the host in the man who carried the dark lantern. The light was directed to the box which Julien had carried into his room. Beside the host was a man who was quietly searching the box.

Julien could only make out the coat-sleeves; these were black and narrow.

"That is a cassock," he said to himself, softly, taking hold of the pistols he had placed under his pillow.

"Don't be afraid that he will wake," the host was saying; "the wine we served him was the kind that you had prepared yourself."

"I don't find the least trace of a paper," answered the curate. "A good deal of linen, perfume, pomade, and other nonsense; he is a man travelling for pleasure. The courier must be the other one, who affects an Italian accent."

The man then approached Julien in order to go through the pockets of his travelling coat. He had a good mind to kill them for thieves, but nothing could have been more dangerous for himself.

"I should be a fool. I should compromise the whole thing."

When the coat had been overhauled, the priest said: "He is not the diplomat," and he walked away.

"If he touches me or my bed, he had better look out; he might stab me, and that I will not allow."

As the curate turned his head, Julien had half opened his eyes, and to his astonishment he saw it was abbé Castanède. Indeed, although the two men were talking very low, it seemed to him that he recognized one of the voices. Julien was seized with a sudden desire to purge the earth of one of its greatest cowards.

"But my mission!" he thought.

The curate and his satellite walked out.

A quarter of an hour later Julien pretended to have been just awakened. He aroused the whole house, crying, "I have been poisoned. I am suffering tortures." He only wished to go to Geronimo's assistance. He found the latter half poisoned by some laudanum that had been put in the wine. Julien, fearing something of the sort, had had only chocolate served him, which he had brought with him from Paris. With the greatest difficulty Geronimo was aroused from his stupor.

"Oh! I would not take the whole Neapolitan realm," the singer kept on saying, "to deprive myself of a single moment of the delight of sleep."

"But the seven Princes?"

"Oh, let them wait!"

Julien left alone and arrived without further incident at the house of the great lord to whom he had been sent. He lost a whole morning endeavoring to get an interview. Fortunately, toward four o'clock the Duke took a walk. As Julien saw him leave the house, he went up to him and asked an alms. As he approached him, he showily drew out Marquis de la Mole's watch.

"Follow me at a distance," the Duke said, without looking at him. A short distance away the Duke suddenly entered a little coffee-house. There, in the room of a third-rate restaurant, Julien had the honor of reciting the four pages to the Duke. When he had finished the Duke said:

"Begin again, and go slower." The prince took notes. "Now, take the next post; leave your things here in the carriage; go to Strasburg as quickly as you can, and on the twenty-second of the month"—it was then the tenth—"come here to this coffee-house at half-past twelve. Leave in half an hour. Silence!"

That was all Julien heard, but it was enough to evoke his admiration.

"That is the way business should be done," he thought. "How this great statesman would be astonished to hear what went on three days ago."

Julien then left for Strasburg. As he had nothing whatever to do he went in a roundabout way.

"If this devil of a Castanède did recognize me, he is not the man to lose track of me in a hurry, and what a pleasure it would be for him to get ahead of me and thwart my mission." Abbé Castanède, the chief of the Congregation police, happily did not recognize him, and the Strasburg Jesuits, although very zealous, did not think of observing Julien very closely, who, with his Cross and his blue coat, looked like a young military man occupied with his own affairs.

Chapter 24

Strasburg

Infatuation! You have all the energy of love, and all its capacity for misery. Only its enchanting pleasures, its sweet delights, are outside your sphere. I could not say, while watching her sleep: She is all mine, with her angelic beauty and her sweet frailties. There she is, delivered into my hands, just as heaven, in all its mercy, made her to enchant a man's heart.

—SCHILLER

COMPELLED to pass a week at Strasburg, Julien endeavored to divert himself with thoughts about military glory and patriotic devotion. Was he in love? He indeed did not know himself. Only, in his harassed soul he found Mathilde mistress of his happiness as she was mistress of his imagination. He had need of all his energy to keep up his courage. It was not in his power to think of anything that had no connection with Mademoiselle de la Mole. Ambition and little spurts of vanity had often diverted him from his thoughts of Madame de Rênal; Mathilde, on the other hand, absorbed him entirely; he found her everywhere outlining his future. And in this future Julien saw only failure. This young man, so proud and self-confident at Verrières, had become extremely modest. Three days before he would have killed abbé Castanède with pleasure; but now, at Strasburg, if a child had quarrelled with him, he would have admitted he was in the wrong.

Thinking thus of the enemies he had made in his life, he found that he alone, he, Julien, had always been to blame. His greatest enemy now was his imagination. What a treasure would he not have found in a single friend! But Julien said to himself: "Is there yet a heart that beats for me? And even if I should have a friend, honor demands that I should be forever silent."

He was riding leisurely in the neighborhood of Kehl, a little burgh on the banks of the Rhine, immortalized by Desaix and Gouvion Saint-Cyr. A German peasant was showing him the little streams, the roads, and the tributaries of the Rhine, where the courage of these great generals had won such renown.

Julien, guiding his horse with his left hand, held in his right the chart facing the title page of the "Mémoires du Maréchal Saint-Cyr." Just then a joyous exclamation made him raise his head. It was Prince Korasoff, the friend he had made in London, who a few months before had given him the first lessons in love matters. True to his art, Korasoff, who had come to Strasburg, began to explain to Julien all about the siege of 1796, although he had not read a single line about it.

The German peasant gazed at him in astonishment, for he understood enough French to know the egregious blunders that came from the Prince's lips. But Julien had a different opinion. He looked admiringly at the handsome young man, remarking the grace with which he sat on his horse.

"A happy disposition," he was saying to himself. "Ah, his trousers hang so nicely! How elegantly his hair is cut! Oh! if I had been like that, perhaps she would not have despised me after showing me so much love for three days!"

When the Prince finished his description of the siege of Kehl, he said to Julien: "You look like a Trappist; you look even graver than you did in London. A gloomy disposition is not in fashion; rather look blasé. If you are sad it is because there is something the matter, something in which you have not succeeded. That is to show oneself inferior; but if you look annoyed, it is the one who has tried to please you that is your inferior. Just see what a mistake you can make." Julien threw an écus to the peasant, who was listening with mouth wide open.

"Indeed," thought the Prince, "he has a fine manner. What a noble disdain!" and he galloped off. Julien followed with a sort of stupid admiration.

"Oh, if I had been like that, she would not have preferred de Croisenois to me!" The more he ridiculed the Prince's light tone, the more he despised himself for admiring it and thinking himself unhappy for not possessing it.

The Prince found him very gloomy. "Say," he said to him, as they returned to Strasburg, "have you lost all your money, or are you in love with some little actress? The Russians imitate the French, but always fifty years behind the times; they are now in the reign of Louis XV."

All this joking about love brought Julien to tears. "Why don't I ask advice of this clever young man?" he asked himself all at once.

"You see," he said to the Prince, "you see me here in Strasburg head over heels in love, but forsaken. A charming woman, who lives in a neighboring town, left me here after three days of passion; and her change of mind is killing me." Then he painted under fictitious names Mathilde's actions and character.

"Don't stop," said Korasoff. "To make you trust your doctor I will engage to see you through. The young woman's husband must have an enormous fortune, or she must belong to the highest provincial nobility. She must be proud about something."

Julien made a sign with his head, having no longer the courage to speak.

"Well," said the Prince, "here are three kinds of medicine; they are bitter, but you must take them without delay. First, every day you must call on Madame—what is her name?"

"Madame de Dubois."

"What a name!" laughed the Prince. "But pardon me; I suppose you think it is sublime. You must see Madame de Dubois every day. Above all, when you are in her presence, do not look glum. Recollect the great maxim of your age: 'Be the opposite of what you are expected to be.' Show yourself exactly as you were eight days before you came into her graces."

"Ah! I was at peace then," said Julien, in despair. "I thought I would take her——"

"The moth becomes burned by the candle," continued the Prince; "a figure as old as the world. Now, first, you must see her every day. Second, you must court a society woman, but without any appearance of passion, you hear? I do not hide from you the fact that your rôle is a difficult one. You are to enact a comedy; and if it is found out that you are acting, you are lost."

"She is so clever and I—I am lost!" said Julien, sadly.

"No, you are more in love than I thought you capable of being. Madame de Dubois is entirely engrossed with herself, like all women who have received from heaven too much nobility and too much money. She pays attention to herself instead of paying attention to you, yet she does not know you. In those scenes of love she enacted for three days, she thought she saw in you, by sheer force of imagination, the hero of whom she had dreamed; but not you as you really are. But, what the devil! this is but the beginning of it, my dear Sorel; you are still a school boy.

"Pshaw! let us go into this store. This is a charming black collar; I guess they will say it was made by John Anderson of Burlington Street. Now, you will please me by taking it and throwing away that nasty black cord which you are wearing around your neck.

"Now," continued the Prince, as they left the store, "to what sort of society does this Madame de Dubois belong, anyhow? Grand Dieu! what a name! Please don't get angry, my dear Sorel, it is too much for me. But to whom will you pay attention now?"

"To a well known prude, the daughter of an immensely wealthy stocking dealer. She has the finest eyes! No doubt she moves in the very best society, yet with all that grandeur she blushes if any one speaks of stores or of business. And, unfortunately, her father is one of the best known merchants in Strasburg."

"Well, if it is a matter of commerce," said the Prince, laughingly, "you may rest easy that your beauty is thinking of herself and not of you. That sort of foolishness will prove very useful; it will prevent you from losing your head in any way when you are with her. Your success is assured."

Julien was thinking of Madame de Fervaques, who frequently visited the Hôtel de la Mole. She was a beautiful woman, a foreigner, who had married the Maréchal a year before his death. Her whole life seemed to be occupied with an endeavor to forget that she was the daughter of a merchant. To become distinguished in some way in Paris she had taken into her head to make a fad of virtue.

Julien sincerely admired the Prince. What would he not have given to be so clever! For a long time they talked together. Korasoff was charmed with himself, for never before had a Frenchman listened to him so long at a time. "Well," the Prince said to himself, "I have finally made myself heard in giving lessons to my masters. Well, then, it is agreed," he said, aloud, for the tenth time, "not a trace of passion when you speak to your beauty, the daughter of the Strasburg merchant; on the other hand, burning passion in letters. To read a well written love letter is the greatest pleasure for a prude; it is a moment of relaxation; she does not play a comedy, and is only listening to her own heart. And two letters a day!"

"Never, never!" cried Julien, discouraged. "I would rather work in a tread-mill than write as much as three phrases. I am only a corpse, my dear fellow. Don't expect anything of me; let me die by the wayside."

"And who tells you to compose your letters? I have in my grip a volume of love letters in manuscript. There are some for all sorts of characters among women; there are some for those who affect the highest virtue. Didn't Kalisky court Richemond-la-Terrasse, you know, the prettiest Quakeress in England?"

Julien was not quite as unhappy as he had been when at two o'clock he left his friend. Early in the morning the Prince called a copyist, and Julien received fifty-three letters, all numbered, designed for the sublimest virtue.

"I have not the fifty-fourth," said the Prince, "because Kalisky took one away. But what do you care about being snubbed by the stocking dealer's daughter since you are going to act only with reference to Madame de Dubois?"

They went horseback riding every day, the Prince being charmed with Julien. Not having any other way of showing him his great friendship, he had offered him the hand of one of his cousins, a rich Moscow heiress. "Once married, with my influence and that Cross you have, they will make you a Colonel in two years."

"But that Cross was not given to me by Napoleon; far from it."

"Oh! what's the difference?" replied the Prince. "Didn't he start this? That is the first Order in Europe."

Julien was on the point of accepting, but he recollected that his duty recalled him to the great personage. When Korasoff left, he sat down and wrote a letter. He received a reply, and he hastened immediately to Paris; but hardly had two days elapsed when the thought of leaving France and Mathilde seemed to him worse than death.

"I will not marry the millions offered me by Korasoff, but I will follow his advice. After all, the art of seduction is his forte; he has thought only of that for fifteen years, and he is now thirty. He does not lack intelligence; on the contrary, he is clever and cautious. Enthusiasm and poetry are an impossibility in that character. He is a professional, and that is why he cannot be mistaken. Yes, I am going to do it; I will court Madame de Fervaques. Oh, she will weary me a little, but I will look at her eyes, they are so much like those of the loveliest girl in the world. Then, too, she is a foreigner; that is a new character to observe. I shall certainly follow the advice of a friend and not trust to myself alone."

Chapter 25

The Ministry of Virtue

But if I take this pleasure with so much prudence and circumspection, it will no longer be a pleasure for me.

—LOPE DE VEGA

HARDLY had he returned to Paris, when, leaving Marquis de la Mole, who seemed disconcerted by despatches he had received, our hero hastened to the house of Count Altamira. Together with the advantage he had of being sentenced to death, the handsome stranger united a certain amount of gravity and a certain reputation for being true. Those two qualities, and, more than all, the noble birth of the Count, made him an agreeable object to Madame de Fervaques, who saw him very often. Julien avowed to him that he was very much in love with her.

"She is of the purest and loftiest virtue," replied Altamira, "only it is somewhat Jesuitical. There are times when I understand the words she uses, but I do not comprehend her speech as a whole. She sometimes gives me the impression that I do not understand French as well as people give me credit for. Well, such an acquaintance will advance you and will give you some stability in the world. But let's go to Bustos, who is a man to our liking. He has courted Madame de Fervaques."

Don Diego Bustos, lawyer-like, had to have the whole affair explained to him in great detail, himself not uttering a word. He had a long face with a black moustache, and looked extremely severe; but for all that he was a good *carbonaro*.

"I understand," he said, finally, to Julien. "Has not Madame de Fervaques had lovers? Has she not had them? Let us see. And you hope to succeed with her? That is the question. Now, I want to tell you, for my part, I have run aground. Now that I don't feel so badly over it, I reason like this. She has her moods, and, as I will tell you, she does not mean any harm at all. She has not that bilious temperament of genius to spread over her actions a varnish of passion. On the contrary, it is that phlegmatic and calm Dutch fashion to which she owes all her distinction and beauty."

Julien was growing impatient over the measured, phlegmatic

tones of the Spaniard. From time to time, in spite of himself, a few monosyllables would escape him.

"Do you want to listen to me?" Don Diego would ask him.

"Pardon my rudeness, I am all ears," replied Julien.

"Madame de Fervaques has given herself up to hatred, and pitilessly persecutes men she has never seen: lawyers, poor devils of writers who have made songs like Collé. Do you know this?

> *"J'ai la marotte*
> *D'aimer Marote," etc.*

Then Julien had to listen to the entire song. The Spaniard seemed to be well pleased to be able to sing in French; but the divine song was never listened to with greater impatience.

When it was ended, Don Diego continued: "Madame de Fervaques has persecuted the author of this song:

> *"Un jour l'amour au cabaret."*

Julien was afraid he might sing that too; but Don Diego seemed to be content with simply analyzing it. It was indeed quite vulgar and indecent.

"When Madame got angry over this song," continued Don Diego, "I ventured to remark to her that a woman of her rank should not read all the nonsense that is published. However piety and earnestness may flourish, there will always be a carbaret literature in France. When Madame de Fervaques had the author of it, a poor devil of a writer, removed from a position that brought him eighteen hundred francs, I said to her: 'You are attacking this rhymster with your arms; he can pay you back with his rhymes. He might compose a song on virtue. You have gilded drawing-rooms, but there are people who laugh at epigrams.' Now do you know, monsieur, what she said? 'For the sake of our Lord all Paris could see me become a martyr; it would be a new thing in France, and people would then learn how to look upon quality. It would be the happiest day of my life.' Her eyes never looked more beautiful."

"Yes, they are superb," said Julien.

"I see that you are in love. Well," Don Diego Bustos continued, "as I said, she has not that bilious temperament that loves vengeance. If she loves to do a little harm every now and then, it is because she is unhappy; I suspect some secret misery. Might she not be a prude who is tired of her virtue?" The Spaniard looked at him silently for one long minute.

"That is the question," he continued, gravely, "and it is there I can see some hope for you. I thought of it considerably during the two years that I subscribed myself 'Your humble servant.' The whole future of your love depends upon this great problem: is she a prude that is getting a little tired and spiteful because she is discontented?"

"Oh, well!" said Altamira, emerging from a profound silence, "do you know what I have said to you about twenty times? It is all French vanity. It is the thought of her father, that famous cloth merchant, that is making her character shallow and her life unhappy. She would be delighted in only one thing, that is to live in Toledo and to be tormented by a confessor who would show her the terrors of hell all open every day."

As Julien was walking out, Don Diego said to him seriously, "Altamira has been telling me that you belong to us; one day you will help us in regaining our liberty, and so I will help you in your affair now. It is well you should know Madame's style. Here are four letters in her own handwriting."

"I will copy them," said Julien, "and send you these back."

"No one will learn from you what we have said about this?"

"No one, on my honor."

"Well, God help you," added the Spaniard, and in profound silence he conducted Altamira and Julien to the staircase.

Our hero felt somewhat livelier after this scene; he almost smiled.

"There is the pious Altamira," he said to himself, "who is aiding me in an affair of adultery!"

During the entire conversation with Don Diego Bustos, Julien had remarked carefully the hours as they struck in the Hôtel d'Aligre. The dinner hour was approaching, when he must see Mathilde again. He returned to the house quickly and dressed with the greatest care. "That is foolish," he thought, as he was going downstairs. "I must certainly follow the Prince's instructions. He went back to his room and put on a plain travelling suit.

"Now," he thought, "I must look around." It was then only half-past five, and dinner would not be served before six. He had a fleeting desire to go down to the drawing-room, which he saw deserted. At the sight of the blue settee he was moved almost to tears, and he felt his cheeks burn. "I must leave off this foolish sensitiveness," he said to himself, angrily; "it will betray me."

He picked up a newspaper, just to be doing something, and

walked three or four times from the drawing-room to the garden and back again. Tremblingly, and hidden by the great oak, he ventured to lift his eyes to Mademoiselle de la Mole's window. It was closed. He was on the point of sinking to the ground. After remaining a long time leaning against the tree, he went, with a faltering step, to look at the old garden ladder again. The chain he had forced—under what circumstances! —had not yet been fixed. Carried away by his emotion, Julien pressed his lips to it. After all his wanderings from the drawing-room to the garden, Julien felt that he was indeed tired. He saw in it his first success. "I look worn out; then I will not be betrayed."

One by one people arrived, but never did the door open without giving Julien a mortal shock. When they were at table, Mademoiselle de la Mole appeared, faithful to her habit of keeping everyone waiting. She blushed a good deal when she saw Julien, for she had not been told of his arrival. Following Prince Korasoff's instructions, Julien looked at her hands; they were trembling. Troubled himself by the discovery, he was happy to feel that he appeared only tired.

Marquis de la Mole was then praising him very highly. The Marquise then addressed him a few minutes after, referring to his looking so worn out.

Julien was saying to himself all the time, "I must not look too much at Mademoiselle de la Mole. I must look just as I did a week before my misery." He had indeed occasion to be satisfied with his success, and he remained in the drawing-room.

Attentive for the first time to the mistress of the house, he did all he could to engage the men in the drawing-room in conversation. And his politeness was rewarded; for about eight o'clock Madame de Fervaques was announced. Julien, quickly gliding out of the room, came back dressed with the greatest care. Madame de la Mole was infinitely grateful to him for that mark of respect, and, wishing to show her satisfaction, began to speak of his journey to Madame de Fervaques.

Julien sat down near the latter in such a way that his eyes would not be seen by Mathilde. Thus placed, he admired Madame de Fervaques, open-mouthed, according to the rules of the art. It was with such admiration that the first of the fifty-three letters commenced which had been presented to him by Prince Korasoff.

The Maréchale announced that she was going to the Opera Bouffe, and there Julien hastened with the greatest speed. He found there Chevalier de Beauvoises, who led into a box some Gentlemen-in-waiting just opposite Madame de Fervaques's; but Julien did not turn his eyes away from her.

"When I go back to the house," he said to himself, "I must draw up an account of my siege; otherwise I shall forget my plan of attack." He forced himself to write two or three pages on the subject, and succeeded wonderfully well in not thinking of Mademoiselle de la Mole.

Mathilde had almost forgotten him while he was away. "Oh, he is only a common fellow; his name will always recall to me the greatest error of my life. I must return to the ordinary ideas of prudence and honor; indeed, a woman loses everything in forgetting that." She almost consented that the arrangement with the Marquis de Croisenois, which had long been contemplated, should be brought to a conclusion. The latter was wild with joy. He would indeed have been greatly astonished if he had been told that it was only Mathilde's resignation that made him so proud. But all Mademoiselle de la Mole's ideas changed when she saw Julien again.

"Yes, that is my husband," she said to herself. "If I come back to ideas of prudence, it is he whom I should marry."

She was expecting a pleading, constrained manner in Julien, and had even prepared her replies; for no doubt after dinner he would venture to address a few words to her? Far from thinking of that, he had remained in the drawing-room, with never a look toward the garden.

"I must be sure of this right away," thought Mademoiselle de la Mole, going into the garden. But Julien did not appear. Mathilde even walked to and fro opposite the windows. She heard him describing the old ruined castles that picturesquely surmount the steep banks of the Rhine. He succeeded in turning a very pretty phrase that would have been called *esprit* in some salons. Prince Korasoff would have been very proud if he had been in Paris that evening; for everything was exactly as he had foretold. He would have had nothing but praise to give Julien.

A plan among some of the members of the government was hatching to dispose of some cordons bleus. Madame de Fervaques was eager that her great-uncle should become Chevalier of the Order. The Marquis de la Mole had the same intention in behalf of his father-in-law. They combined their efforts, and the Maréchale came almost every day to the Hôtel de la Mole. It was from her Julien learned that the Marquis was going to be named Minister. He was offering the *Camarilla* a very ingenious plan for noiselessly removing the Constitution within less than three years.

Julien could then hope for a bishopric if M. de la Mole became Minister. But in his eyes now all those great interests were hidden as it were by a veil. He looked at them only from a distance, vaguely. His wretchedness, which was almost making him mad, showed him all the interests of life as colored only by Mademoiselle de la Mole. He was thinking that in five or six years, perhaps, he would succeed in making her love him again. This cool, calculating head, as can be seen, had degenerated almost to a state of irrationality. Of all the qualities that had distinguished him formerly, there remained only one, that of firmness.

Following literally the plan of Prince Korasoff, he had placed himself every evening near Madame de Fervaques's chair, without ever finding a word to say. The effort he made at appearing calm in Mathilde's eyes drained him of all his force, and for a long time he would remain almost lifeless beside the Maréchale. Even his eyes lost their former fire.

As Madame de la Mole's manner was only a reflex of the opinions of her husband, who might some day make her a Duchess, she had for some days praised Julien to the very skies.

Chapter 26

Moral Love

> *There also was of course in Adeline*
> *That calm patrician polish in the address,*
> *Which ne'er can pass the equinoctial line*
> *Of anything which Nature could express:*
> *Just as a Mandarin finds nothing fine,*
> *At least his manner suffers not to guess*
> *That anything he views can greatly please.*
> —DON JUAN, XIII. 84

"THERE IS SOMETHING queer about this family," thought Madame de Fervaques; "they are just taken up with this young abbé, who can only listen! He has expressive eyes, though."

Julien found in the Maréchale a vivid example of that patrician calm which exhales a certain polite, colorless emotion. Spontaneity and lack of self-control would have been as scandalous to Madame de Fervaques as lack of majesty toward inferiors. The least sign of sensibility was regarded by her as a sort of moral intoxication, which one must blush at, and which can only injure a person of her rank. Her great delight consisted in speaking of the last chase of the King; of her favorite book, "Mémoires du Duc de Saint-Simon;" and, above all, of genealogy.

Julien knew the place which, after the candles were lighted, would bring the beauty of Madame de Fervaques into greater relief. There he would invariably place himself, but with head turned so as not to see Mathilde. Astonished at the persistence with which he hid himself from her, she left the sofa one day, and took her work to a little table near Madame de Fervaques.

Julien could see her very plainly over Madame de Fervaques's hat. Her eyes frightened him at first; but in the end they only drew him out of his apathy, and he began to speak with great animation. He was speaking to Madame de Fervaques, but his single aim was to work on Mathilde. He was so greatly excited that the Maréchale did not half understand what he was saying. It was his first success with her. If Julien could only have followed up his ideas with some German mysticism and with

358

Jesuitical piety, she would have immediately placed him among the superior men who are called upon to regenerate the age.

"Since he is so ill bred," Mademoiselle de la Mole was saying to herself, "as to talk so long and so excitedly to Madame de Fervaques, I will not pay any attention to him." So throughout the evening she did not open her mouth.

Toward midnight, when she took her mother's candle to accompany her to her room, Madame de la Mole stopped half way up the stairs to say something pleasant about Julien. Mathilde was very angry when she retired. One idea calmed her: "What I disdain may yet be a man of great merit in the eyes of the Maréchale!"

As for Julien, he had done something, and was less unhappy. As his eyes casually fell upon the Russia-leather case in which Prince Korasoff had put the fifty-three love letters, Julien saw a foot-note at the bottom of the first letter: "No. 1 must be sent a week after the first interview."

"I am late," cried Julien, "for it is a long time since I have known Madame de Fervaques!" He immediately set himself to transcribing the first love letter. It was a soul-wearying homily about virtue, full of the shallowest phrases. Julien had the good fortune to fall asleep at the second page.

In a few hours the early sun found him still seated at the table. The most painful incident in Julien's life was that every morning on waking he would learn his misery anew. But that day he finished copying the letter almost smilingly.

"Is it possible," he thought, "that there could be a man who could write a thing like that?" There were phrases nine lines long. At the bottom of the original letter he saw this note in pencil: "The letters must be carried in person, on horseback; a black cravat, and a blue overcoat. The letter must be handed to the porter with a languishing air; look, profound melancholy. If a maid is seen, the eyes must be wiped furtively while speaking to her." All this was followed out to the letter.

"Now I have done something foolish," thought Julien, when he left the house of Madame de Fervaques, "in venturing to write to such a celebrated piece of virtue; but so much the worse for Korasoff! But I may be treated with the utmost contempt, and that will not be at all amusing? This is the only farce I could ever appreciate. Yes, to overwhelm with ridicule this odious creature that I call myself would amuse me! Really, from my present state of mind, I should commit some crime just to take my mind away from myself."

For a month the happiest moment in Julien's life was when

he put the horse back into the stable. Korasoff had expressly forbidden him under any circumstances to look at the woman who had forsaken him. But the clatter of the horse's hoofs that she knew so well, and the way Julien struck the stable door with his whip to call a groom, sometimes drew Mathilde to her window curtain, where the thin muslin permitted him to see her. When he looked from under his hat, he could see Mathilde's figure without seeing her eyes.

"Of course," he said to himself, "she cannot see me, and that is not the same as looking at her."

In the evening Madame de Fervaques looked at him just as if she had never received the philosophical, mystical, and religious dissertation he had handed with so much melancholy to the porter at the door in the morning. The night before, chance had enabled him to be eloquent, when he had placed himself so as to see Mathilde's eyes.

Mathilde, soon after the Maréchale arrived, left the sofa. It was equivalent to deserting the regular group. M. de Croisenois appeared crestfallen over this new caprice; his visible wretchedness removed the sting from Julien's misery. This made him talk as he had never talked before. As pride glides even into the hearts of the most faithful guardians of the temple of virtue, the Maréchale, on returning to her carriage, said to herself:

"Madame de la Mole is right; this young priest has something extraordinary about him. I suppose the first few days my presence intimidated him. Yes, everything is so light and flimsy in this house, I see only virtue that is aided by old age; it requires a reflection in years. That young man can see the difference! He writes well, but I fear that his asking for my advice has been brought about by a sentiment of which he is not even aware. Well, what changes have taken place! What makes me think well of this letter is the difference between his style and that of other young men. It is impossible not to recognize the zeal, the deep earnestness, the strong faith in this young Levite's writing. He may have the sweet virtue of a Massillon!"

Chapter 27

The Best Positions in the Church

Des services! des talents! du mérite! bah! soyez d'une coterie.

—TÉLÉMAQUE

THE IDEA of a bishopric that Julien had, thus occurred also to a woman who, sooner or later, would distribute the best places in the Church of France. But that did not move Julien in the least; he had not yet emerged out of his wretched state. In fact, every moment increased his agony. The sight of his room, for instance, became almost insupportable to him. In the evening, when he came in with his candle, every piece of furniture, every little ornament, seemed to him to proclaim some new feature in his miserable life.

"Now, that time it was a hard piece of work," he said to himself, returning one day with more liveliness than usual. "Let us hope that the second letter will be as wearisome as the first." It was more so. What he was copying seemed so absurd to him that he transcribed line for line without even thinking of the sense.

"That is more emphatic," he said to himself, "than the official notice of the Treaty of Munster, which my professor in diplomacy made me copy in London."

Then he happened to think of Madame de Fervaques's letters, which he had forgotten to return to the Spaniard, Bustos. He looked them over, and he found them just as nonsensical as the young Russian's. There was perfect vagueness in them all. One might gather everything or nothing from them. "It is the Æolian harp of style," thought Julien. "Amid all these lofty thoughts about the illimitable, about death, and about the infinite, I see only an abominable fear of ridicule."

His daily routine for two weeks was to fall asleep in transcribing some sort of a commentary on the Apocalypse, to take the letter with a melancholy air the next morning to the house, to take the horse back to the stable in the hope of seeing Mathilde's dress, to work, and to appear in the evening at the opera if Madame de Fervaques was not at the Hôtel de la Mole.

It was more interesting when Madame de Fervaques was

visiting the Marquise. Then he could see Mathilde's eyes over the feathers of the Maréchale's hat and would grow eloquent. His picturesque, sentimental phrases were becoming striking and elegant. He felt that he appeared absurd in Mathilde's eyes, but he wished to make an impression upon her with the charm of his diction.

"The more absurd I am the more I should please her," thought Julien. And then with abominable hardihood he would exaggerate certain aspects of nature. He quickly perceived that in order not to appear vulgar in the Maréchale's eyes, he would have to eliminate all simplicity and reason from his conversation. He continued, therefore, to make his artificial effusions long or short, according as he saw approval or disapproval in the eyes of the two great ladies whom he tried to please.

On the whole, his life was less unhappy than it was during his days of inaction. But he was saying to himself one evening, "Here I am, copying the fifteenth one of these abominable dissertations. The first fourteen I have already handed to the Maréchale's porter. I will have the great distinction of filling all the pigeon holes in her desk, and yet she treats me as if I had never written to her! Where is going to be the end of all this? Is my constancy wearing on her as much as on me? Really that Russian, Korasoff's friend, who was in love with that pretty Richmond Quakeress, must have been a terrible man in his time, to do any thing so villainous!"

Like all mediocre creatures, whom chance throws in the presence of a great general while executing important manœuvres, Julien did not understand the attack the Russian made on the young English girl's heart. The first forty letters were designed simply to excuse the hardihood of writing.

"I want this fine woman to get out of the habit of receiving letters that are perhaps only a little less insipid than her own life."

One morning a letter was handed to Julien. He recognized the arms of Madame de Fervaques and broke the seal with a haste that would have seemed impossible a few days before. It was only an invitation to dinner. But he remembered Prince Korasoff's instructions. Unfortunately the young Russian wished to be as light as Dorat where he should have used plain common sense; so Julien could not grasp the position he would have to assume at the dinner.

The drawing-room was of the greatest magnificence, gilded like the Gallery of Diana at the Tuileries, and ornamented with fresco paintings. There were some blank places in the pictures, and Julien learned later that the subjects had seemed quite indecent to the mistress of the house, who had put a censorship on the paintings.

"A *moral age!*" he thought.

In the salon he noticed three persons who had been present at the writing of that secret message. One of them, Monseigneur, the Bishop of ____, the Maréchale's uncle, controlled the list of livings, and, it was said, could not refuse anything to his niece.

"What an immense stride I have made," Julien said to himself, with a melancholy smile; "and still I am indifferent to everything! Here I am dining with the famous Bishop of ____!"

The dinner was rather mediocre and the conversation languished. "The table is just like a bad book," thought Julien. "All the great subjects that occupy the human mind are boldly started, and then, after talking for three or four minutes, one asks what it is all about that is inviting the speaker's emphasis or ignorance."

The reader perhaps has forgotten that little literary gentleman, Tanbeau, the nephew of the Academician, and a future professor. By his base calumnies he secretly tried to bring the la Mole drawing-room into bad repute. This little gentleman, Julien hoped, would bring it about so that Madame de Fervaques would look with indulgence on the sentiment revealed in his letters.

M. Tanbeau's dark soul was outraged at the thought of Julien's success. But as, on the other hand, a man of distinction no more than a fool can be in two places at the same time, the future professor was saying to himself: "If Sorel becomes the lover of the sublime Maréchale she would place him in some great position, and I should be rid of him at the Hôtel de la Mole."

Abbé Pirard, also, was addressing long sermons to Julien about his success at Madame de Fervaques's house. There was sectarian jealousy between the austere Jansenist and the Jesuitical drawing-room of the Maréchale, with its hopes for a regenerated monarchy.

Chapter 28

Manon Lescaut

*Or, une fois qu'il fut bien convaincu de la sottise
et ânerie du prieur, il réussissait assez ordinaire-
ment en appelant noir ce qui était blanc, et blanc
ce qui était noir.*

—LICHTEMBERG

THE RUSSIAN'S instructions prescribed never to contradict the lady addressed; that one should not under any circumstances leave off ecstatic admiration. The letters continued in the same strain.

One evening at the opera, while in Madame de Fervaques's stall, Julien admired, with the utmost fervor, the ballet of "Manon Lescaut." His only reason for saying so was that he found it very poor. The Maréchale replied that the ballet was inferior to abbé Prévost's novel.

"What!" thought Julien, astonished as well as amused, "a person of that calibre to praise a novel!"

Madame de Fervaques affected, two or three times a week, the greatest disdain for the scribblers who, with their insipid writing, tried to corrupt the youth, who, alas! were only too much disposed to the errors of the flesh.

"In that immoral and dangerous class," continued the Maréchale, " 'Manon Lescaut' is in the first rank. The weaknesses and anguish of a wicked soul are pictured with a truth that is indeed profound; yet that did not prevent your Bonaparte from saying, at Saint Helena, that the novel was written only for servants."

That word restored all the energy to Julien's soul.

"They want to discredit me with the Maréchale," he said to himself. "Some one has told her of my admiration for Napoleon." That discovery amused him; it made him cheerful throughout the evening.

"Now, remember, monsieur," she said, "that no one must love Bonaparte who pretends to love me. We must accept him as a necessary evil imposed by Providence. Besides, that man had not the temperament to appreciate masterpieces."

" 'When one loves me,' " Julien repeated to himself. "That

means nothing, and it might mean anything. That is the secret of speech which is lacking in us poor provincials."

He was thinking of Madame de Rênal while he was copying an enormously long letter destined for the Maréchale.

"How does it happen," she said to him the next day, with an indifference that was only half concealed, "that you are always speaking of London and Richmond in a letter which it seems you wrote yesterday evening when you came back from the opera?"

Julien was greatly embarrassed. He had copied the letter word for word and had apparently forgotten to substitute the words Paris and Saint-Cloud for the words London and Richmond in the original. He began a few phrases, but he could not finish; he felt as if he would laugh like a fool. Finally, in groping about for something to say, he caught on the idea of saying:

"Exalted by the discussion of those sublime things that are of the greatest interests to human life, my soul, when I wrote to you, became oblivious of its environment."

"I am producing an impression," he thought. "Still, I might be bored the whole evening." And he ran out of the de Fervaques mansion.

In the evening, when he looked at the original letter from which he had copied the night before, he came to the place where the young Russian was speaking of London and Richmond. Julien was really astonished to find the letter had something tender in it. It was the contrast between the apparent lightness and the sublime depth of Apocalyptic phraseology that distinguished it. The long sentences were particularly pleasing to the Maréchale. "There was not that light, airy style that was made fashionable by Voltaire, that immoral man," she said.

Although our hero did everything in the world to banish all appearance of common sense in his conversation, there was still an anti-monarchical and sceptical strain which did not quite escape Madame de Fervaques. Surrounded as this great lady was by persons who were eminently moral, but who could not express a single idea throughout an evening, she was profoundly impressed by anything that resembled originality. Yet she felt that she was being outraged. She called that weakness the impress of the frivolity of the century.

All the time that Julien spent in connection with Madame de Fervaques, Mademoiselle de la Mole had great need of self-control not to think of him. Her soul was a prey to a great conflict. Sometimes she would say to herself that she despised this gloomy young man; but in spite of herself his conversation captivated her. What astonished her more than anything else was his falsity, which was as clear as day. He did not say a word to the Maréchale that was not a lie, or at least an abominable disguise of what he really thought; that Mathilde knew perfectly. This Machiavellianism seemed most striking to her.

"What finesse!" she said to herself; "how different he is from those sentimental noodles or common souls, such as Tanbeau, who all talk the same way!"

Yet Julien experienced some horrible days. It was a frightful punishment for him that he had to appear every day at the Maréchale's house. His effort in playing a part deprived him of all energy. Frequently at night, when he crossed the immense courtyard, it was only through the sheer force of a tenacious resolve that he did not lose all heart.

"I conquered despair at the seminary," he said to himself, "and yet how terrible it seemed there! I am making or losing a fortune in my career in the one case as in the other; I am obliged to pass my whole life in a class of society which is the most damnable and disgusting on the face of the earth. The following spring I was, perhaps, the happiest young man in the world."

Nevertheless, all his fine reasoning was not proof against the horrible reality.

He saw Mathilde at breakfast and dinner every day. According to the letters which Marquis de la Mole dictated to him now, she was going to marry M. de Croisenois. Already that happy young man appeared twice a day at the house. The jealous eye of an abandoned lover did not lose a single circumstance of the entire arrangement. When he thought that Mademoiselle de la Mole was pleasant to her admirer, Julien, on returning to his own room, could hardly refrain from looking longingly at his pistols.

"Ah! I should indeed be wise," he said to himself, "to take the marks off my linen and go to some solitary wood about twenty miles away from here, and put an end to my terrible life. As I am unknown in the country, my death would not be learned for two weeks; and who would think of me after two weeks?"

It was very good reasoning; but the next day Mathilde's arm, seen from the shoulder to the top of her glove, sufficed to plunge that young philosopher into the most cruel recollection and to attach him more than ever to life.

"Oh, well!" he said to himself, "I am going to follow this Russian diplomacy to the very end. How will it end, anyhow?

As regards the Maréchale, certainly after finishing the fifty-three letters I shall not add another line! As to Mathilde, the six weeks of this horrible comedy have not removed the least bit of her anger or obtained for me the least recognition. Good God! I should die of joy——" he did not dare even to finish his thought.

When, after a long reverie, he succeeded in resuming his reasoning, he said to himself: "Well, one day I shall obtain that happiness; and it may all be again as it is now, just because I have not been able to please her! Then there would not be a single resource left to me; I should be ruined, lost forever! What guarantee could she give of her constancy? Pshaw! My manners are rude; my way of speaking is clumsy and monotonous. Why am I as I am?"

Chapter 29

Ennui

Se sacrifier à ses passions, passe; mais à des passions qu'on n'a pas! O triste dix-neuvième siècle!

——GIRODET

AFTER reading Julien's long letters indifferently, Madame de Fervaques in the end became interested in them. Only one thing disconcerted her. "What a pity it is that M. Sorel is not really a priest! One could then enter into some intimacy with him. With his Cross and his bourgeois dress, one is exposed to cruel questions. What can one say in reply?" She did not finish her thought, which was that some malign soul might suppose that he was a little cousin, one of her father's relatives, some little trader decorated by the National Guard.

Up to the moment when she saw Julien, Madame de Fervaques's greatest pleasure had been in writing the title of Maréchale beside her name. "It would be so easy," she thought, "for me to make him a grand vicar in some diocese around Paris; but M. Sorel is so insignificant, and then he is only a little secretary of M. de la Mole."

For the first time she, who had her doubts about everybody, began to question her pretensions to rank and social prestige. Her old servant remarked that when he brought her a letter from this handsome, gloomy young man, he was sure that the distraught and discontented air which the Maréchale always assumed in the presence of one of her servants disappeared. The weariness of a life that depends altogether upon the effect on the public had become so intolerable since she began to think of Julien, that if she did not treat her maids outrageously for an entire day it was because the night before she had spent an hour with that singular young man.

His influence, that was now making itself felt, was proof against all anonymous letters, even when they were well composed. In vain Tanbeau furnished de Luz, de Croisenois, de Caylus, and the others with two or three plausibly arranged calumnies which these gentlemen took pleasure in spreading, without troubling themselves as to the truth of the accusations.

The Maréchale, whose spirit was not strong enough to resist such vulgar tricks, related her troubles to Mathilde, and was always consoled.

One day, after asking three times if there were any letters for her, Madame de Fervaques suddenly resolved to answer Julien. That was a victory over her wearisome life. At the second letter the Maréchale was almost constrained to stop, from the inconvenience of writing in her own hand, an address as vulgar as "M. Sorel, care of Marquis de la Mole."

In the evening she said to Julien, drily: "You must bring me some envelopes with your address on them."

"Here I am installed as a footman playing the lover," thought Julien, and he inclined his head, smiling like Arsène, the Marquis's valet. The same evening he brought the envelopes to her, and early next day there was a third letter awaiting him. There were five or six verses at the beginning and two or three at the end, all covering pages of close writing. Gradually she adopted the good habit of writing every day. Julien replied with faithful copies of the Russian manuscript.

Such was the advantage of a forceful style, that Madame de Fervaques was not at all astonished at the incongruity between his answers and her letters. Her pride would have suffered a great deal if little Tanbeau, who constituted himself a voluntary spy on Julien's movements, had informed her that her letters were sometimes thrown unopened into a drawer.

One day, as the servant was bringing him a letter from the Maréchale into the library, Mathilde met the servant and saw the letter with the address in Julien's handwriting. Entering the library just as the valet left, she found that the letter was still on the table, and that Julien, who was busy writing, had not put it away.

"That I will not allow," Mathilde cried, taking possession of the letter; "you have forgotten me altogether, I who am your wife. Your conduct is abominable, monsieur!"

At these words, her pride, disturbed by her unconventional proceeding, almost killed her. She burst into tears, scarcely able to breathe for her sobs.

Surprised, dumbfounded, Julien did not at first comprehend the happiness the scene had in store for him. As he assisted her to a seat, she threw herself with abandon into his arms. At first his joy was boundless, but on second thought he recalled Korasoff.

"I may lose everything now by a single word." His arms became rigid, though indeed the effort was painful.

"I must not permit myself to press this supple and charming figure to my heart; otherwise she would despise me. What a queer character!" While thus berating Mathilde's character, he in fact loved her a hundred times more than ever; he seemed to hold a queen in his arms. Julien's impassive coldness redoubled the wretchedness that was tearing Mademoiselle de la Mole's heart. She was not self-collected enough to try to read in his eyes what he really felt for her at that moment. She could not bring herself to look at him; she was trembling lest she might encounter an expression of contempt.

As she sat on the library sofa silent, and with her head turned away from Julien, she was a prey to the most cruel pain that mingled pride and love can bring to the human heart. Into what a terrible plight had she come!

"It has remained to me, wretched as I am, to see my advances repulsed, and repulsed by whom?" she added, almost mad with proud disdain; "repulsed by my father's servant!

"I will not stand it," she said in a loud voice; and, rising furiously, she opened the table drawer before her. She froze with horror when she saw eight or ten unopened letters like the one the valet had just brought. In all the addresses she recognized Julien's handwriting more or less disguised.

"So," she cried, beside herself, "not only have you come into her good graces, but you despise her; you, a nobody, despise the Maréchale de Fervaques! Ah! pardon!" she adde, throwing herself on her knees. "Slight me if you will, but love me! I cannot live deprived of your love!" Then she fell completely exhausted.

"There she is, that proud woman, at my feet!" thought Julien.

Chapter 30

A Box at the Opera

As the blackest sky
Foretells the heaviest tempest.
—DON JUAN, I. 73

IN ALL THIS Julien was more astonished than happy. Mathilde's
upbraidings showed him how wise the Russian maxim is: "To
say little is to do little." "That is my only means of safety," he
said to himself.

Raising Mathilde, he seated her on the sofa without saying a
word. Then she began to cry again. She took Madame de
Fervaques's letters in her hand, slowly opening them. She moved
nervously when she recognized the Maréchale's handwriting.
She turned over the pages of the letters without reading them.

"Answer me, at least," Mathilde said, beseechingly, without
daring yet to look at Julien. "You know I am proud; it is the
misfortune of my position and character, I admit it. Has
Madame de Fervaques taken your heart away from me? Has
she made for you that sacrifice to which this fatal love has
drawn me?"

A frightful silence was Julien's only answer. "What right has
she," he thought, "to ask me about an indiscretion unworthy of
a man of honor?"

Mathilde then tried to read those letters, but, with her eyes
filled with tears, that was impossible. For a month she had been
unhappy, but her proud heart would not avow the fact to itself;
pure chance alone had led to the sudden outburst. For a single
instant jealousy and love had carried the day over pride.

She was seated on the sofa very close to Julien, and he saw
her beautiful hair and neck. In a moment he forgot his entire
plan. Passing his arm around her waist, he pressed her against
his breast. Slowly she turned her head toward him; he was
astonished at the misery he read in her eyes. He could hardly
recognize her.

Julien felt his strength disappear, so frightful was the act of
courage which he had outlined for himself. "Those eyes," he
said to himself, "will soon express only disdain if I allow
myself to be drawn into the allurements of love."

Then, faintly, in words that she could hardly utter, she repeated to him her humblest apologies for what her pride had suggested to her.

"I, too, am proud," Julien said to her, in an unsteady voice, and his features showed the great physical strain. Mathilde suddenly turned to him; to hear his voice was a happiness of which she had almost lost all hope. At that moment she recalled her pride only to curse it. She wished to do something extraordinary, something incredible, to show him how much she adored him and detested herself.

"It was probably because of your pride that you treated me so well for a while; it is certainly because of my courage and firmness that you esteem me at this moment. Yes, I may have some feeling for the Maréchale."

Mathilde trembled. There was a strange look in her eyes, as if she had heard at that moment her death sentence pronounced. That movement did not escape Julien, and he felt his courage fast leaving him.

"Ah," he thought, as he listened to the sound of his empty words, "if I could only cover those pale cheeks with kisses, and if she would not feel them! Yes, I may love the Maréchale," he continued, his voice gradually weakening, "but certainly I have no decisive proof of any feeling for me on her part."

Mathilde looked at him. He bore up under the look, hoping that his face was not betraying him. He felt love penetrating to the innermost depths of his heart. Never had he adored her so much; he was almost mad over Mathilde. If she had had self-possession and courage he would have fallen at her feet, abjuring forever his foolish comedy. He had just enough strength to continue.

"Ah! Korasoff!" he was saying, inwardly. "Oh, that you were here! How badly I need a word to guide me!" But he was saying aloud: "In default of all sentiment, mere friendliness has sufficed to attach me to the Maréchale; she has been indulgent to me; she has consoled me when I was despised. I, of course, cannot have illimitable faith in appearances that are flattering, no doubt, but not liable to last very long."

"Oh, God!" cried Mathilde.

"Well, what guarantee will you give me?" replied Julien, finally seeking for a chance to abandon the prudent forms of diplomacy.

"What pledge can I give?"

"What god will tell me that the position which you are disposed to give me now will last for two days?"

"My great love and misery, if you do not love me any more," she replied, taking his hands.

The movement removed the shawl for an instant, and Julien saw her charming shoulders, her disordered hair recalling to him a certain pleasing scene; and he was about to yield.

"One imprudent word," he said to himself, "and I begin again that long series of days of despair. Madame de Rênal was right in doing what her heart dictated; this fine girl does not give way to her heart except when good sense tells her to." He saw the truth of this in the twinkling of an eye, and in that instant he regained all his firmness. He withdrew his hands from Mathilde and moved away a little. He began putting in order Madame de Fervaques's letters which were scattered on the sofa; and it was with the greatest politeness, which was indeed cruel at that moment, that he added:

"Mademoiselle de la Mole will kindly permit me to reflect over all this?"

He withdrew quickly from the library, and she heard all the doors close in succession.

"The wretch was not affected even! But what am I saying— wretch? He is wise, he is prudent, he is good; it is I who have done more wrong than one can imagine!"

Her way of looking at it continued all that day. Mathilde was almost happy, for she gave herself up to love; one might have said that her heart had never been moved by pride—and what pride! She trembled with horror when, in the evening, a servant announced Madame de Fervaques. The man's voice seemed to have a foreboding. She could not look at the Maréchale and stopped short in her greeting.

Julien, who was not over-proud over his painful victory, was himself fearing her looks, and had not dined at the house that night. His love and happiness increased rapidly the moment he was removed from the scene of battle. Then again he began to blame himself. "How could I have resisted her? Suppose she does not love me any more? In a moment she can change, and I must admit I treated her shamefully."

In the evening he felt that it was absolutely necessary for him to appear at the Bouffes with Madame de Fervaques, who had given him a special invitation. Mathilde would not fail to know of his presence or his absence in the house. In spite of his courage he had not the strength in the beginning of the evening to appear in public. While talking he lost half of his happiness. Ten o'clock struck. He must absolutely show himself. Happily he found the Maréchale's box filled with women, and he found himself relegated to the door, almost hidden by their hats. That position saved him from making himself ridiculous. The scenes of *Caroline's* divine despair in *Matrimonio Segreto*, made him shed tears. Madame de Fervaques saw him cry. It was such a contrast to the masculine firmness in his face that the soul of the great lady, long saturated as it was with the unfeeling pride of a parvenu, was indeed touched. She began to speak to him. She wished to enjoy the pleasure of hearing his voice at that moment.

"Have you seen the de la Mole ladies?" she asked him; "they are in the third box."

And just as Julien leaned over, supporting himself on the edge of the box, he saw Mathilde. Her eyes were glistening with tears. "And this is not their day for the opera," thought Julien. "What insistence!"

Mathilde had induced her mother to come to the Bouffes in spite of the inconvenience of the kind of box which a friend of the house had offered. She wanted to see if Julien would spend the evening with the Maréchale.

Chapter 31

Make Her Afraid

Voilà donc le beau miracle de votre civilisation!
De l'amour vous avez fait une affaire ordinaire.
———BARNAVE

JULIEN hurried into Madame de la Mole's box and found Mathilde in tears. She wept without restraint, for there were only persons indifferent to her in the stall—the man who had kindly offered it to them, and other acquaintances. Laying her hand on Julien's, she almost forgot her mother's presence. Choking with sobs, she could only utter the words, "A guarantee!"

"Anyhow, I must not talk to her," thought Julien, himself greatly moved, shading his eyes with his hand, as if to protect them from the brilliant light. "If I talk she might suspect my emotion; the sound of my voice would betray me, and all would be lost again." Self-command was even more painful for him now than in the morning, for he had had time to think over what had happened. He feared that Mathilde would be piqued from vanity. Though he was intoxicated with love, he still determined not to talk.

Mademoiselle de la Mole insisted upon taking Julien with them to the house. Happily it was raining. The Marquise made him sit opposite, talking to him all the way, and thereby preventing him from talking to her daughter. One might have thought that the Marquise herself was caring for Julien's welfare.

Fearing no longer that he would lose all by showing his emotion, he gave himself up to it altogether when alone. It need hardly be said that Julien, on returning to his room, fell on his knees before Prince Korasoff's letters. "Oh, great man! what do I not owe to you?" he said, madly. Yet he did not entirely lose his self-control; he compared himself to a great general who had just won a battle. The advantage is certain, but what will happen to-morrow?

He opened the "Mémoires" dictated by Napoleon at Saint Helena, and for two long hours he read, but only with his eyes.

Throughout, his mind and heart were soaring to the greatest heights of grandeur and beauty.

"Her heart is different from Madame de Rênal's," he was saying to himself; but he went no farther in the comparison. "I will make her afraid," he cried out, all at once, throwing the book aside; "the enemy will not obey me until she fears, and then she will not dare to despise me." He walked about his room wild with joy, but more of pride than love. "Yes, I will make her afraid," he repeated. Had he not a right to be proud?

"Even in her happiest moments Madame de Rênal feared that my love was not equal to hers; here it is a demon that I am to subjugate, for I must subjugate her." He knew very well that the next morning Mathilde would be in the library at eight o'clock; but he did not appear until nine, burning with love, yet master of himself. Not a single moment passed without a repetition on her part, distracted by the doubt of, "Does he love me?" Her brilliant position, the flatteries she received on all sides, were not enough to reassure her.

He found her pale, calm, seated on the sofa, but unable to make a single movement. Holding out her arms to him, she said:

"Dear, I have offended you, it is true. Can you be angry with me?"

Julien did not expect such a simple remark; he almost weakened.

"You speak of a guarantee, my dear," she added, after a silence which she hoped would be broken by him. "That is so. Take me; let us go to London. I should then be lost forever—dishonored!" She had the courage to withdraw her hand from Julien's to cover her eyes. All the sentiments, all the feelings of maidenly modesty returned to her. "Well, dishonor me," she said, with a sigh; "that is a guarantee!"

"Yesterday I was happy because I had the courage of being severe with myself," thought Julien. After a moment of silence he was sufficiently master of himself to say, in a chill tone:

"Once on our way, and once, as you say, ruined, as a pledge of what you say, who would tell me that you still love me, that my presence in the coach would not be disagreeable to you? I am not a monster! To see you pilloried by public opinion would be wretchedness for me. It is not your position with the world that is the obstacle, it is yourself. Can you answer for yourself that you would love me in a week?"

"Oh, if she would only love me a week," Julien was saying to himself, "then I should die of sheer happiness! What do

I care about the future, about this life? And this divine pleasure may begin at once if I so desire; it depends upon me alone!"

Mathilde saw him pensive. "Well, then, so I am indeed unworthy of you," she repeated, taking his hand. Julien kissed her, but immediately the iron hand of duty was laid on his heart.

"If she sees how much I adore her, I shall lose her," and before disengaging himself he had resumed again the firmness proper to a man.

That day, and for some days following, he was able to hide his great happiness. There were times when he refused himself even the pleasure of pressing her in his arms. At other times his great happiness carried him beyond the control of his prudent course. It was near a honeysuckle vine in the garden, where he had stood to look at Mathilde's shutters and to mourn her inconsistency, a large oak hiding him from view. Now, passing with Mathilde in the same place where he had experienced so much misery, the contrast between past despair and present happiness was almost too much for his nature. His eyes would well with tears, and he would say, kissing her lips: "Here, here, I have passed my time thinking of you; here I waited for hours for the moment when your hands would appear."

His weakness was complete. In colors too vivid to be false he painted his great despair at that time. A word, a monosyllable, would bear witness to the actual happiness which had now taken its place. "But what am I doing? Good God!" Julien said to himself, "I am lost." In his alarm he thought he saw less love in Mathilde's eyes. Julien's face changed immediately; he became mortally pale; his eyes lost their brilliancy. An expression of pride, not unmixed with malice, succeeded his look of love, of the greatest abandon.

"What is the matter, my dear?" asked Mathilde, tenderly.

"I am lying to you," said Julien. "I am reproaching myself; and God knows that I love you well enough not to lie to you. You love me and you are devoted to me, and I have no need to talk to please you."

"My dear, were those mere words you have been saying for the last ten minutes?"

"Yes; and I am sorry for it, my darling. I said the same thing before in the presence of a woman who loved me and of whom I tired. That is my weakness, I confess. Pardon me!"

Mathilde's cheeks were bathed with bitter tears.

"Something has had a stifling effect on me," continued Julien, "and I had a moment of reverie; and then my execrable memory, which I curse at this moment, prompted me, and I am abusing it."

"Have I done anything that has displeased you?" asked Mathilde, with charming simplicity.

"Well, one day, I remember, when you were near the honeysuckle, you picked a flower, and M. de Luz took it from you, and you let him have it, and I was only two feet away from you."

"M. de Luz?" replied Mathilde, "that is impossible; indeed, it is not so!"

"Well, I am sure of it," replied Julien, testily.

"Oh, well, it is so then, my dear," replied Mathilde, lowering her eyes. But she knew positively that for months she had not given M. de Luz such a privilege. Julien looked at her with inexpressible tenderness.

"No," he thought, "she does not love me any less."

In the evening she reproached him, laughingly, for his flame for Madame de Fervaques. "A bourgeois loving a parvenu! Such creatures are perhaps the only ones that Julien cannot make adore him! She has really made of you a veritable dandy!" she said to him, playing with his hair.

While he was embroiled with Mathilde, Julien had become one of the best dressed men in Paris, and he had this advantage over the men of fashion: once dressed, he no more thought about it.

Only one thing piqued Mathilde. Julien continued copying the Russian letters and sending them to Madame de Fervaques.

Chapter 32

The Tiger

Hélas! pourquoi ces choses et non pas d'autres?
——BEAUMARCHAIS

AN ENGLISH TRAVELLER tells of the intimacy with which he had lived with a tiger. He had raised it and was always caressing it, but he always kept a loaded revolver on his table.

Julien did not give himself up to the happiness he found, except when Mathilde could not read it in his eyes. He acquitted himself of his duty faithfully by speaking to her harshly from time to time. When Mathilde's tenderness and devotion, which quite astonished him, were on the point of making him lose his self-control, he had the courage to leave her abruptly.

For the first time Mathilde was really in love.

Time, which was for her unending torment, now passed quickly for him. Yet, as her pride had to have some expression, she wished to expose herself rashly to all the dangers which her love might bring. Julien alone was prudent; and it was only when there was a question of danger that she did not yield to his wishes. But subdued, almost humble toward him, she showed more hauteur than ever to every one in the house, to her parents as well as to the servants.

In the drawing-room, in the evening, in the presence of nearly sixty people, she once called Julien aside to speak to him a long time alone. Little Tanbeau happened to be near, and she asked him to go to the library for the volume of Smollett that described the Revolution of 1688. When he hesitated, she said: "You need not be in a hurry," with an expression of disdain that was balm for Julien's soul.

"Did you notice how the little fellow looked?" he asked her.

"His uncle has seen ten or twelve years' service in this drawing-room, otherwise I should drive him out immediately."

Her conduct toward MM. de Croisenois and de Luz was formal and polished, but, indeed, no less provoking. Mathilde reproached herself for all the confidences which she had made to Julien, and, more than all, for the fact that she did not dare to declare to him that she had exaggerated all the innocent marks of affection she had shown those gentlemen. In spite of her fine resolutions, her womanly pride prevented her from saying to Julien:

"It is because I was speaking to you that I found such pleasure in describing my weakness in not withdrawing my hand when M. de Croisenois touched it on the marble table."

Now, hardly would one of those gentlemen speak to her, when she would have some question to ask Julien and find a pretext for keeping him by her side.

She was becoming large. With joy she told the news to Julien.

"And now, do you doubt me? Is not that sufficient guarantee? I am your wife forever!"

Her announcement astonished Julien profoundly. He was on the point of forgetting his principle of conduct. "How, how can I deliberately be cold and cruel to this poor young girl who has actually ruined herself for me?"

When she seemed to suffer, he had no longer the courage, even when prudence raised her voice, to say anything rude to her about her inconstancy.

"I wish to write to my father," Mathilde said to him one day. "He is more than a father to me—he is a friend. It is so unworthy of me and of you to hide it from him, if only for an instant."

"My God! what are you going to do?" Julien asked, frightened.

"My duty," she replied, her eyes blazing with joy. She seemed nobler than her lover.

"But he will drive me away in disgrace. That is his right, and we must expect it."

"I will take your arm and we will go out together in broad daylight."

The astonished Julien begged her to defer, to wait a week.

"I cannot," she replied; "my honor speaks. I have seen my duty and I must obey it instantly."

"Well, then, I command you to wait," Julien replied, firmly. "Your honor is not tarnished. I am your husband. Our mutual relations are now changed. I, too, have rights. To-day is Tuesday; next Tuesday is Duke de Retz's day; in the evening, when M. de la Mole returns, the servant will hand him the fatal letter. He is thinking of making you a Duchess, I am certain of it. Just see my misfortune! Judge of his vengeance! I might have had pity for my benefactor, but I do not fear, and I will fear, no one!"

Mathilde obeyed. Since she had told Julien of her condition it was the first time he had spoken to her with authority, for never had he seen himself so loved. It was with a great deal of happiness that the tenderness in his nature found a pretext for dispensing with the necessity of saying anything harsh. He was greatly moved by the thought of her confession to M. de la Mole. Is he to be separated from Mathilde? And however sadly she might look upon his departure, would she think of him a month after he left? He had a horror, too, of the just condemnation of the Marquis.

In the evening he confessed to Mathilde the second cause of his emotion, and then, led away by his love, he also confessed the first. She changed color.

"Really," she said to him, "would six months away from me be an actual misfortune for you?"

"Terrible! the only thing in the world I look upon with terror."

Mathilde was indeed happy. Julien had followed his plan so assiduously that he began to think it was the only one that gave him all this love.

The fatal Tuesday came. At midnight, when the Marquis returned to the house, he found a letter with the superscription telling him that it should be opened by his own hand and when no one else was present. It read:

"My Father:—All social ties are broken between us and only those of nature remain. After my husband you are, and always will be, the only being that is most dear to me. My eyes are filled with tears when I think of the grief I cause you, but I do it only in order that my downfall may not become public and that you may have time to deliberate and to act. I have not been able to put off any longer the confession I owe you. If your generosity, which has always been so great to me, will grant me a little pension, I will retire wherever you like, to Switzerland, perhaps, with my husband. His name is so obscure that no one will recognize your daughter in Madame Sorel, the daughter-in-law of a Verrières carpenter. To write that name has caused me indeed great pain.

"I fear your anger for Julien, and it would only be just. I shall not be a Duchess, my father, but I knew that while I loved him; for it was I who loved him first, and it was I who have led him into this. I know your good heart only too well to have me do anything that may be or seem common. In vain I tried to think of M. de Croisenois, with the view only of pleasing you. Why did you place real worth under my eyes? You told me yourself, on my return from Hyères, 'This young Sorel is the only person who is interesting to me.' The poor boy is as grieved as myself, if that is possible, over the pain which this letter will give you. I cannot prevent your being angry as a father, but yet love me as a friend.

"Julien respected me. If he spoke to me sometimes it was only through his great gratitude to you; for his natural pride caused him to say nothing, except formally, to any one above him. He has a lively and innate sense of the difference between social classes. It is I—and I confess it blushingly to my dearest friend, and that confession will never be made to anyone else— it is I who one day pressed his arm in the garden.

"After a day has passed would you still be angry with him? My conduct is irreparable. If you like, it will be only through me that the assurance of his profound respect and of his despair at displeasing you will pass. You will not see him, but I will rejoin him wherever he goes. It is his right; it is my duty; he is the father of my child. If you will be good enough to give us six thousand francs for living expenses, I will accept it with the greatest gratitude. Julien may establish himself at Besançon, where he will begin again his profession as teacher of Latin and literature. In whatever low estate he may find himself, I am certain he will rise. With him I care nothing for obscurity. If a revolution takes place I am sure he would act a great part. Could you say as much of any of those who have asked for my hand? They have fine lands: is that enough cause for my admiration? My Julien would reach a high station, even in the actual state of affairs; if he had a million and the influence of my father——"

Mathilde, who knew the Marquis to be a man of impulse, had written eight pages.

"What shall I do?" Julien was saying to himself, while M. de la Mole was reading the letter. "What is my duty? What are my interests? What I owe to him is indeed great; without him I should have been a mere fool of a subordinate and not enough of a fool even not to be hated and persecuted by others. He made me a man of the world. My foolishness now will be, first, more rare, and second, less ignoble. That is more than if he had given me a million. I owe this Cross to him and the appearance of diplomatic services which drew me into the company of peers. If he should prescribe my conduct for me, what could he write?"

Julien was rudely interrupted by M. de la Mole's valet.

"The Marquis wishes you to come to him immediately, dressed or not." The valet whispered, as he walked by Julien's side: "He is beside himself with anger; take care!"

Chapter 33

The Hell of the Weak

En taillant ce diamant, un lapidaire malhabile lui a ôté quelques-unes de ses plus vives étincelles. Au Moyen Âge, que dis-je? encore sous Richelieu, le Français avait la force de vouloir.

—MIRABEAU

JULIEN found the Marquis furious. For the first time in his life, perhaps, the great peer was rude. He called Julien all the vile names he could think of.

Our hero was overwhelmed, yet his gratitude was not extinguished. How many beautiful plans, cherished for so many years by the poor man, disappeared in a moment! "But I must answer him, or else my silence will increase his anger." He began with the rôle of Tartuffe.

"I am not an angel, I have served you well and you have paid me generously. I was grateful, but I am twenty-two years of age. In this house I was never understood by anyone but yourself and that adorable person."

"You scoundrel!" cried the Marquis. "Adorable! adorable! The moment you found her adorable you should have left— fled!"

"I tried to when I asked you for leave to go to Languedoc."

Weary of walking madly about the room, the Marquis, overcome by his exasperation, threw himself into an arm-chair. Julien heard him say half aloud:

"He is not such a bad fellow!"

"No, I am not to you," cried Julien, throwing himself on his knees. But he was ashamed of that action, and he quickly rose. The Marquis was really beside himself with anger. When he saw him fall on his knees, he began again to curse him in trooper fashion. It was the novelty of hearing himself curse that diverted him somewhat from his anger.

"What! my daughter will be called Madame Sorel! my daughter not a Duchess!" When those two thoughts presented themselves definitely to him, M. de la Mole was tortured. Julien was afraid of being struck. In the intervals of calm, while the

383

Marquis was becoming accustomed to his grief, he spoke to Julien a little more reasonably.

"You must leave, monsieur," he said to him; "your duty is to go. You are the last man in the world——"

Julien, approaching the table, wrote:

"For a long time life has been insupportable to me; I will put an end to it. I beg the Marquis to accept the assurances of my great gratitude, and my great regret for the embarrassment which my death will cause in his house."

"Will the Marquis be kind enough to read this paper? Kill me!" said Julien, "or let your valet kill me! It is one o'clock in the morning; I am going to walk in the garden, toward the lower wall."

"Go to a thousand devils!" cried the Marquis, walking away.

"I see," thought Julien; "he would not regret having his valet take the burden of my death on his shoulders. Let him kill me! Indeed, that is the only satisfaction I can give him. But, God! I love life! I owe it to my son!"

This thought, appearing for the first time clearly to his imagination, absorbed him entirely during the first few moments of his walk. "This new interest makes one prudent; I must be careful with this furious man; he is bereft of reason; he is capable of anything. Fouqué is too far away. Besides, he will not understand the feelings of such a man as the Marquis.

"Count Altamira—am I sure of silence on his part? But my asking advice of him would complicate my position. There remains only the glum abbé Pirard, and his heart is shrivelled up with Jansenism. A fool of a Jesuit would know the world and my condition far better. M. Pirard is capable of beating me the very first time I tell him of my trouble."

Tartuffe's genius again came to Julien's aid. "Well, I will go to confession to him!" It was the last resolution he made in the garden after walking for two hours. He no longer thought of becoming the mark for a bullet.

He retired to his room to rest; but early in the morning Julien was at some distance from Paris, before the door of the severe Jansenist. To his astonishment he found that the abbé was not too much taken by surprise by what he told him.

"Indeed, I can reproach myself for a great deal," said the abbé, more anxious than irritated. "I thought I suspected that love. My friendship for you, oh my unfortunate friend, has prevented me from warning the father!"

"What is he going to do?" asked Julien. He loved the abbé that moment, and anything like a scene would have been very painful to him. "I see three things," continued Julien. "First, M. de la Mole can kill me"; and he repeated the suicidal letter which he had given to the Marquis. "Second, I can be shot point blank by Norbert, who will ask for a duel."

"Would you accept it?" asked the abbé furiously, rising.

"You don't let me finish. I will certainly not take aim at my benefactor's son. Third, he can have me put away somewhere. If he tells me to go to Edinburgh or to New York, I shall obey; then it is quite possible that Mademoiselle de la Mole's condition can be hidden. But I will not allow them to make away with my child."

"I do not for a moment doubt that is the first idea of that man."

Mathilde, at Paris, was in the greatest despair. She had seen her father at seven o'clock, and he had shown her Julien's letter. She trembled lest he might think it proper to put an end to his life, and without telling her anything about it.

"If he is dead, I will die," she said to her father. "You are the cause of his death; perhaps you will find pleasure in it; but I swear by his shade that I will first put on mourning, and I shall be known publicly as Madame Sorel the widow. I will send out my cards. You will find me neither hesitating nor cowardly." Her love was indeed driving her mad.

On his part, M. de la Mole was nonplussed; but he began to see things with a ray of reason.

At breakfast Mathilde did not appear, and the Marquis was relieved of a great weight and felt considerably flattered when he found that she had not said a word to her mother. Then Julien came back.

Mathilde called him and threw herself into his arms almost before the eyes of her maid. Julien, not over grateful for this transport, seemed more diplomatic and prudent since his conference with abbé Pirard and his calculation of possibilities.

Mathilde, with tears in her eyes, told him that she had read his letter announcing his suicide. "My father may think better of it; but leave at once for Villechières. Mount your horse again, and leave before they get up from the table."

As Julien's hesitating manner did not change, she burst into tears anew. "Let me manage our affairs here," she cried, pressing him in her arms. "You know I do not separate myself from you voluntarily. Write in care of my maid, and let the address be in someone else's handwriting. I will write you volumes. Good-by—go!"

Though wounded in his pride by the command, Julien nevertheless obeyed. "It is terrible," he thought, "that even in their pleasant moments these people have a way of giving me pain."

Mathilde firmly resisted all her father's prudent plans. She wished the matter to be settled under no other conditions than these: that she should be Madame Sorel, and that she should retire to Switzerland, or remain in her father's house in Paris. "And if people should talk," she urged, "two months after our marriage I will go travelling with my husband, and then the birth of my child would cause no comment."

Her firm position, though at first assailed by bursts of anger, finally turned the Marquis. In a moment of tenderness he said to his child:

"Here is a note for ten thousand livres; send it to your Julien, and let him make it impossible for me right away to take it back."

In order to obey Mathilde, whose love for him expressed itself in a command, Julien had covered forty useless miles. He was at Villechières managing the affairs of the farmers. The Marquis's generosity gave him occasion to return. He went to ask an asylum of abbé Pirard, who, during his absence, had become Mathilde's most useful adviser. As often as the Marquis questioned him, he proved that anything else than a public marriage would be a crime in the eyes of God. "And, happily," the abbé would add, "worldly wisdom is here in accord with religion. Could you for a moment count on a secret, with Mademoiselle de la Mole's temperament, unless she chose to keep it? If you do not have a public marriage, society would busy itself a long time over this strange *mésalliance*. Everything must be told at once without the least mystery."

"That is so," added the Marquis, pensively; "in this life of ours to talk of a wedding three days after belongs only to a man who has no ideas. I must profit by some anti-Jacobin measures on the part of the government to pass unobserved in this matter." Two or three of M. de la Mole's friends thought like abbé Pirard. The greatest obstacle in their eyes was Mathilde's firmness. Yet, after so many good reasons, the Marquis could not accustom himself to renouncing the hope of a *tabouret* for his daughter. His memory was crowded with the scenes of force and falsity that were enacted in his youth. To yield to necessity, to fear the law, was something absurd and dishonoring to a man of his rank. He paid very dearly for such enchanting illusions ten years before the arrival of his dear daughter.

"Who could have foreseen it?" he would say to himself. "A

girl of such a determined character, of such a lofty disposition, prouder even than myself! Her hand has been asked by every one that has been most illustrious in France! Well, I must renounce all prudence; all is confusion worse confounded. We are marching straight to chaos!"

Chapter 34

A Man of Intellect

Le préfet cheminant sur son cheval se disait:
Pourquoi ne serais-je pas ministre, président du
conseil, duc? Voici comment je ferais la guerre.
. . . Par ce moyen, je jetterais les novateurs dans
les fers . . .

—LE GLOBE

NO ARGUMENT could destroy a resolution that had been fixed
by ten years of thought. The Marquis could not at heart find
any reason for being angry, yet he could not make up his mind
to forgive. "If only Julien would suddenly die!" he said to himself now and then. He found some consolation in following up
many chimerical projects; they nearly withstood the reasonable
arguments of abbé Pirard.

A whole month passed unmarked by any decisive step. In
this family affair, as in matters of state, the Marquis had certain
brilliant ideas about which he would be very enthusiastic for
three days. Then any line of conduct would seem inadequate
because supported only by good reasoning; and yet he would
reason only as was suitable to his favorite plan. For three days
he had worked with the ardor and enthusiasm of a poet to
bring the matter to a certain head. Then the next day he did
not think of it again.

Julien felt troubled by the Marquis's slowness. After some
weeks he began to think that M. de la Mole had really adopted
no plan of action. Madame de la Mole and the entire house
thought that Julien was in the provinces to take care of the
lands. He had only hidden himself with abbé Pirard, and saw
Mathilde almost every day. She would spend an hour with her
father every morning; but for weeks, sometimes, not a word
would be uttered about their great trouble.

"I do not want to know where that man is," her father said
to her one day. "Send him this letter." Mathilde read:

"My lands in Languedoc yield twenty thousand six hundred
francs. I will give ten thousand six hundred to my daughter and
ten thousand to M. Julien Sorel. Of course I give the lands, too.

Notify the notary to prepare two separate deeds and to give them to me to-morrow. After this all is over. Monsieur, can I expect an answer to this?

"MARQUIS DE LA MOLE."

"I thank you so much!" Mathilde cried gayly. "We are going to live at Château Aiguillon, between Agen and Marmande; they say the country there is as beautiful as in Italy."

The gift came as a great surprise to Julien. He was no longer that harsh and cruel man that we have known. The future of his child absorbed his every thought. Such a fortune, coming unexpectedly to a man as poor as he, gave rise to great plans. He saw already an income of thirty-six thousand livres for his wife as well as for himself.

As for Mathilde, all her thoughts were absorbed in adoration of her husband, for so she proudly called him. Her sole ambition was to have the marriage recognized. She spent her time exaggerating the great prudence she had shown in uniting herself to such a superior man. His personal worth alone occupied her mind. His absence, the complexity of the affair, the little time they could pass in speaking of their love, combined to bring out the good results which his prudence before had begun.

Mathilde gradually became impatient at the thought that she saw so little of the man she adored. In a moment of anger she wrote her father, beginning like Othello:

"That I have preferred Julien to all the advantages that society could offer to a daughter of Marquis de la Mole, my choice has proved. The pleasures of a society life are nothing to me. As weeks have now passed since I have been separated from my husband, it is long enough to show my respect for you. Before next Thursday I shall leave home. Your kindness has made us rich. No one knows my secret except abbé Pirard. I will go to him, and he will marry us. An hour after the ceremony we will be on our way to Languedoc, never to appear again in Paris except at your request. But what is like a stab to my heart is the fact that it will all be a good tale at your expense and mine. Will not the epigrams of a foolish public oblige my excellent Norbert to quarrel with Julien? Under such circumstances I know I have no influence with him; we should then find in his heart only a discontented plebeian. I beg you on my knees, my father, to be present at our marriage in M. Pirard's church next Thursday. Then the public talk will not be so poignant; and the life of my child, as well as that of my husband, will be spared."

The Marquis was greatly embarrassed by that letter; he must then come to some decision! All his habits, all his ordinary friends, had lost their influence over him. At this juncture, the traits of his character, impressed by the great events in his youth, became again manifest. The misfortunes of the Emigration had made him a man of reflection; for after enjoying for two years an immense fortune, and all the distinctions of the Court, he had been thrown, in the year 1760, into the greatest wretchedness. That hard school had changed the heart of a young man of twenty-two. Indeed, he was not enslaved by his great fortune. Yet his heart, preserved from the corrosion of gold, was mastered by one ambition: to see his daughter the possessor of a great title.

During the six weeks that had passed, the Marquis had been thinking of making Julien rich; for poverty seemed ignoble, almost dishonoring to M. de la Mole, and impossible for his daughter's husband. He himself was always throwing money away. The next day it seemed to him that Julien might learn the mute eloquence of his great gift, change his name, and go to America, and write to Mathilde that he was dead to her. The Marquis was already thinking that the letter had been written, and was wondering what effect it would have on his daughter.

On the day when he was drawn out of his dreams by Mathilde's real letter, after he had been thinking a long time of making away with Julien in some way, the idea came to him of building up an immense fortune for him. He would give him the name of one of his estates; and why could he not have the peerage passed to him? Duke de Chaulnes, his father-in-law, had frequently spoken to him, after his only son had been killed in Spain, of his desire to transmit his title to Norbert. It could not be denied that Julien had a singular aptitude for affairs. "He is daring, even brilliant at times," the Marquis was saying to himself; "but at the very bottom of his character I see something terrifying. That is the impression he invariably makes; there is something in that!

"My daughter was telling me the other day that Julien is not connected with any salon or any clique. He has not a single support against me, not a single resource if I abandon him. But is that from ignorance of the actual state of affairs? Two or three times I have already told him there is no real or profitable candidacy except from the salon. No! he has not that adroit and cautious spirit of a procureur who never loses a minute or an opportunity. There is nothing of the Louis XI. in him. On the other hand, I see something antagonistic to nobility in him. Would he use it as a dam against his passions?

"Well, one thing remains, he cannot stand a slight, and I will hold him by that. There is no religion in noble birth, that is true; he does not respect us instinctively. Of course, it is wrong; and a seminarist's soul should not be touched except by want. He, on the other hand, will not brook a single slight."

Pressed as he was by his daughter's letter, M. de la Mole saw the necessity of immediate action. "Now, here is the great question: has Julien's audacity gone so far as to court my daughter because he knows that I love her more than anyone else and I have an income of one hundred thousand livres? Mathilde says no. No, Monsieur Julien, I will not be deceived on that score. Was there real, sudden love, or simply the common desire of raising himself to a fine position? Mathilde has a clear head; she knew that that suspicion would lose him forever in my eyes, and hence the confession she made that she loved him first! To think that a girl of such a lofty character would forget herself so far as to make advances, to press his arm in the garden of a night! Preposterous! As if she could not have found a hundred other occasions, less indecent, to let him know that she thought something of him! 'He who excuses himself, accuses himself.' I have reason to suspect Mathilde." And the Marquis was more decided that day than he had ever been before. Yet he thought he would wait and write to his daughter. M. de la Mole did not dare to have an argument with Mathilde; he was afraid he would make a complete and sudden concession. And he wrote:

"Do not do anything more stupid. Here is a commission of a Lieutenancy of Hussars for M. Chevalier Julien Sorel de la Vernaye. See what I have done for him! Do not oppose me; do not ask any questions. Let him leave for Strasburg, where his regiment is stationed, in twenty-four hours. Enclosed find an order on my banker. Obey!"

Mathilde's love and joy were infinite. Wishing to profit by her victory, she replied immediately:

"M. de la Vernaye would be at your feet, proffering you thanks, if he knew all that you have been kind enough to do for him; but with all this generosity, my father has forgotten me. Your daughter's reputation is in danger; one indiscretion is enough to give her everlasting shame, which an income of twenty thousand écus could not repair. I will not send the commission to M. de la Vernaye unless you give me your word that in the course of the next month my marriage shall be celebrated in public at Villechières. Soon after that your daughter will not be able to appear in public except under the name of Madame de la Vernaye. I thank you, dear papa, for having delivered me from the name of Sorel."

The answer was unexpected, and so the Marquis wrote again:

"Obey, or I take everything back. Take care, imprudent one! I do not know who your Julien is, and you know him less than I do. Let him leave for Strasburg immediately. I will inform you of my wishes in a fortnight."

The firm reply astonished Mathilde. "I do not know Julien!" The fact threw her into a reverie which ended with most enchanting ideas. "My Julien's genius has not been clothed in the little salon uniform, and my father cannot believe in his superiority just because he proves it. However, if I do not obey, I see a possibility of a public scandal; my position in the world will become wretched, and I may make myself perhaps less lovable in Julien's eyes. Poverty for ten years and the choice of a husband for his own sake must in the end be crowned by wealth to escape ridicule. My father, at his age, might at a distance forget me. Norbert will marry some amiable, clever woman. Old Louis XIV. was led astray by the Duchess de Bourgogne——"

She resolved to obey him, but did not communicate her father's letter to Julien. That strange character might be led to do something rash! In the evening, when she told Julien that he had been made a Lieutenant of Hussars, his joy was beyond all control. A life-long ambition and his love for the coming child—all was seen in his wild delight. The change of name astonished him most.

"Now, at last, my dream is fulfilled, and I have only myself to thank! I know how to make myself esteemed by this proud creature!" he added, looking at Mathilde. "Her father cannot live without her, nor she without me."

Chapter 35

A Storm

Mon Dieu, donnez-moi la médiocrité!
——MIRABEAU

JULIEN seemed to be in a dream. He scarcely replied to the tenderness she showed him, but remained silent and pensive. Never had he appeared so grand, so adorable in her eyes. She had a vague fear of the pride which was about to change their entire position. She saw abbé Pirard arrive almost every morning at the house. Could not Julien find out from him some of her father's intentions? Has not the Marquis, in a capricious moment perhaps, written to him? After all this happiness, how could she explain Julien's cold looks? She did not dare ask.

She did not dare—she, Mathilde! Then at that moment in her love for Julien appeared something vague, something unforeseen, something that resembled terror. Her heart had all the passion of which a person raised in the effete civilization which Paris admires was capable.

Early next morning Julien was at abbé Pirard's. The post horses had come into the courtyard, dragging a dilapidated coach that had been hired at the neighboring village.

"Such an outfit is not proper," said the severe abbé to him. "Here are twenty thousand francs which M. de la Mole has presented to you. He wishes you to spend them in a year, but try to do it with as little foolishness as possible." Such a great sum thrown at a young man could only breed sin in the eyes of the priest.

"The Marquis adds that M. Julien de la Vernaye will receive this money from his father, whom it is unnecessary to call by any other name now. M. de la Vernaye might think it proper, perhaps, to make a present to M. Sorel, a Verrières carpenter, who took care of him as a child. I can take care of that part of the arrangement," added the abbé. "I have induced M. de la Mole to make some arrangement with abbé de Frilaire, that Jesuit, whose influence is decidedly stronger than ours. The recognition of your high birth by the man that governs Besançon is one of the tacit conditions of the arrangement."

Julien was beside himself with joy, and ran up to kiss the abbé.

"Here, here!" said the abbé, pushing him away, "what do you mean by this worldly nonsense?" And he kept on reading the letter.

"As to Sorel and his sons, I will give them, in my name, an additional pension of five hundred francs, to be paid to each one as long as I am satisfied with them."

Julien instantly became cold and haughty. He thanked him, but in measured and not very effusive terms. "Is it possible," he said to himself, "that I am the natural son of some great lord who was exiled by the terrible Napoleon to the mountains?" That idea seemed less improbable to him every moment. "My hatred for my father would be a proof! I am no longer an outcast."

A few days later the Fifteenth Hussars, one of the crack regiments of the army, had a battle-drill at Strasburg. Chevalier de la Vernaye was on the most beautiful charger in Alsace. It had cost him six thousand francs. He had received the Lieutenancy without being a sub-lieutenant except on the muster-roll of which not a word was to be said.

His impassive air, his severe and masterful eyes, his pallor, his unalterable sang-froid, gave him a reputation from the very first. Soon his perfectly polished manners, his skill with pistols and other arms, which he showed without too much affectation, removed all occasion for making unpleasant remarks on his account. After five or six days of hesitation the opinion of the regiment declared itself in his favor.

"That young man," said the old officers, "has everything except—youth."

Julien wrote from Strasburg to M. Chélan, the old curate of Verrières, who was now in the ripest old age.

"You have no doubt learned with pleasure of the events which have given me my new rank. I enclose five hundred francs, which I wish you to distribute without any form, without even mentioning my name, to those who are unfortunate and poor as I was, and whom no doubt you are helping as you formerly helped me."

Julien was intoxicated with ambition, but not with vanity. Nevertheless, he gave a great deal of attention to his outward appearance. His horses, his uniform, the livery of his men were correct enough to have done honor to an English nobleman. Hardly was he a Lieutenant, which he had become only through influence, than he calculated already that he would become

Commander-in-Chief at thirty at the utmost, like all the great generals. He should have been more than a Lieutenant at twenty-three.

He was thinking only of his glory and of that of his son, when he was surprised by the arrival of a servant from the Hôtel de la Mole with a letter.

"All is lost," wrote Mathilde. "Come as quickly as you can; desert if necessary! When you arrive, wait for me in a carriage near the little garden door at No. – X street. I must talk to you! Perhaps I could let you in by the garden gate. It is all over, I fear. You can count on me, though! You will find me always devoted and firm, even in adversity. I love you."

In a few minutes Julien obtained permission from the Colonel and left Strasburg at full gallop. But the uncertainty that devoured him did not permit him to continue his mad ride beyond Metz. There he jumped into the mail coach, arriving soon at the place indicated, near the little door of the de la Mole garden. The door opened, and Mathilde, forgetting everything, threw herself into his arms. Fortunately, it was only five o'clock in the morning, and the street was still deserted.

"All is lost! My father, fearing that he would weaken at the sight of my tears, left Thursday night."

"But where?"

"No one knows. Here is his letter; read it!" and she came into the cab with Julien.

"I could pardon him everything except his idea of seducing you because you are rich. This, my poor child, is the terrible truth. I give you my word of honor that I will never consent to a marriage with that man. I can assure him of an income of ten thousand if he moves away from here, away from France, or, better still, if he goes to America. Read the letter which I have received in reply to my request for information. Why, he had even asked me himself to write to Madame de Rênal. I will never read anything from you relative to that man; I have a horror of Paris and you. I beg you to keep everything that may happen secret. Leave that vile man, and you will find a father again."

"Where is Madame de Rênal's letter?" Julien asked, coldly.

"Here it is. I did not want to show it to you until you were prepared."

"My duty to the sacred cause of religion and morality, monsieur, impels me to discharge this obligation to you. A rule that cannot fail orders me to speak ill of a fellow man in order to avoid a greater scandal. The grief that I feel should be conquered by my sentiment of duty. It is only too true, monsieur, that the conduct of that man, relative to whom you have asked for information, would seem inexplicable. It might be proper to hide or disguise a part of the truth; prudence would require it more than religion; but his conduct, concerning which you inquire, has been indeed damnable and worse than I can tell. Poor and wretched, it was through consummate hypocrisy, after leading astray a weak and unfortunate woman, that this man has tried to get on in the world and become somebody. It is also my painful duty to add that I am forced to think that M. J. has not a particle of religion; in truth I am constrained to believe that one of his means of success in a house is to try to lead astray the woman that is loved the most. Under the cover of disinterestedness and fine phrases he aims only to be able to control in some way the master of the house as well as his fortune. He leaves behind him grief and eternal regret."

This long letter, half effaced by tears, was in Madame de Rênal's own handwriting. She had written it with more care than usual.

"I cannot blame M. de la Mole," cried Julien, after finishing. "He is prudent; he is right. What father wants to give a cherished daughter to such a man? Good-by!"

Julien leapt from the cab and ran to the coach that had remained at the end of the street. Mathilde, whom he seemed to have forgotten, attempted to follow him; but the looks of the tradesmen who appeared at their doors, and by whom she was known, compelled her to retreat into the garden.

Julien left for Verrières.

During the journey he tried to write to Mathilde, but his hand traced only illegible lines.

He arrived at Verrières on a Sunday morning. He went straightway to an arms dealer, who congratulated him on his recent good fortune. It was the talk of the neighborhood, he said. With great difficulty Julien gave him to understand that he wanted a pair of pistols. These, at his request, the merchant loaded for him.

The "three bells" were heard—the well-known signal in French villages, announcing the beginning of Mass—as Julien entered the new church at Verrières. The lofty windows of the sacred edifice were draped with crimson curtains. He took a seat a little in the rear of Madame de Rênal's bench; it seemed to him she was praying with ther greatest devotion. The sight of the woman he had adored made his arm tremble, and he could not at first execute his design.

"I cannot do it," he said to himself; "I cannot do it! It is a physical impossibility!"

At that moment the young clergyman who was celebrating Mass sounded the Host. Madame de Rênal lowered her head, which at that moment was almost entirely hidden by the folds of her shawl. Julien could not take very good aim; he fired one shot and missed, but at the second she fell.

Chapter 36

Painful Details

> *Don't look for weakness on my part. I have*
> *avenged myself. I have deserved death and here*
> *I am. Pray for my soul.*

—SCHILLER

JULIEN remained motionless; there seemed to be a mist before his eyes. When he came to himself somewhat, he noticed that the worshippers were fleeing from the church, and the priest had left the altar. Julien unthinkingly followed a few women who were leaving the church shrieking. A woman who wished to go out more quickly than the rest pushed him rudely aside so that he fell. His foot caught in a chair that had been over-turned by the crowd; as he arose he felt himself seized by a gendarme. Mechanically he felt for his pistols, but another gendarme caught his arm. He was led to jail. After taking him into a cell they handcuffed him and then left, locking the door with both locks. It all happened so quickly that he did not know what had taken place.

"Great God! all is at an end now!" he said aloud. "Yes, in two weeks the guillotine, or suicide here!" His reasoning carried him no further. His head felt as if it were pressed by a vise, and he looked around to see if he was between any one's hands. After a few moments he fell into a profound slumber.

Madame de Rênal was not mortally wounded. The first ball had passed through her hat; as she was turning around the second one had lodged. The ball had hit her shoulder, and, glancing off after breaking the bone, had struck the Gothic pillar where it removed a large piece of stone.

When, after a long and painful examination, the physician said to Madame de Rênal: "I am as sure of your life as I am of mine," she seemed to be greatly afflicted.

For a long time she had sincerely prayed for death. The letter which her confessor had dictated to her, and which she had written to M. de la Mole, had given the finishing stroke to a spirit enfeebled by continuous misery. It was because of Julien's absence. Her confessor, a young and fervent ecclesiastic who had recently arrived from Dijon, was not deceived in his suspicions.

"To die like this, and not by my own hand, is not a sin," thought Madame de Rênal; "God will pardon me, perhaps, if I say that I am glad death is at hand." She dared not add, "And death at Julien's hands is my greatest happiness!"

Hardly had the surgeon and her friends left when she called Elisa to her.

"The warden," she said, blushing, "is a cruel man. Of course he will maltreat him, believing that I should like it. It is horrible to think of it! Won't you go, as of your own accord, and give this to the warden? There are some louis in it. You can tell him that our holy faith does not permit cruelty. Above all, he must not speak of this little gift of money."

From this came the constant kindness with which Julien was treated by the warden. It was the same M. Noiroud, a model of an official, whom we have seen frightened by the appearance of M. Appert.

A magistrate appeared in the prison. "I killed her. I intentionally killed her," said Julien to him; "I bought the pistols and had them loaded. Article 1342 of the Penal Code is explicit; I deserve death, and I expect it."

The judge, astonished by such a reply, wished to multiply the questions so as to bring out possibly a *se coupât*.

"But, don't you see," said Julien to him, smilingly, "that I make myself as culpable as you desire? See, monsieur, you shall not miss the prey you are pursuing; you shall have the pleasure of sentencing me to death. Please leave me! There remains only one sad duty to perform," thought Julien, "I must write to Mademoiselle de la Mole."

"I am avenged," he wrote to her. "Unfortunately my name will appear in the papers, and I cannot withdraw unknown from this life. I shall die in two months. My vengeance was terrible; just like my grief at being separated from you! From this moment I forbid myself to write or to pronounce your name. Never speak of me, not even to my child. Silence alone can honor me. Among men generally I shall always be thought of as an assassin.

"Permit me to tell the truth at this last moment. You will forget me; this great catastrophe, about which I beg you never to open your mouth to a living soul, will in a few years remove all that is romantic and beautiful in your character. You were made to live with the heroes of the Middle Ages. Show their firm character! All that has happened is secret, and you will not be compromised. You can go under an assumed name, and you need have no confidante. If it is absolutely necessary for you to have the aid of a friend, I advise you to take abbé Pirard. Do not speak to anyone, especially the people of your class, like de Luz and de Caylus. A year after my death marry M. de Croisenois; I command you, as your husband, to do it. Do not write to me, for I will not answer. Less wicked by far than Iago, to whom I may be compared, I am going to say like him:

" *'From this time forth I never will speak word.'*

I will not be seen nor will I talk. You have from me my last words as my last homage. "J.S."

It was after sending that letter away that Julien, fully conscious of what he had done, first felt his wretched state. Every hope his ambition had given him was now successively torn from his heart by the thought: "I shall die!" Death itself did not seem terrible: all his life had been only a long preparation to endure the evils of life, and he had not forgotten all that had passed, to be afraid of the greatest evil of all.

"What!" he said to himself, "if within sixty days I were to fight a duel with a great fencer, should I have the weakness to think of it all the time, and should I be frightened?" For more than an hour he reasoned with himself in that strain. When he had looked clearly into his soul again, and the naked truth appeared distinctly before his eyes, there crept in the form of regret.

"Why should I have remorse? I have committed a horrible crime; I have murdered; I deserve death; and there it is. I die after settling my account with humanity; I leave no duty unfulfilled; I owe no one. My death will not be disgraceful except in the means that will be employed. That alone, it is true, is enough for my shame in the eyes of the Verrières public. There remains one thing, though, to stand well with them, and that is to throw money to them when I begin my death march; my memory linked with gold will shine resplendent with them."

After such reasoning, he concluded: "I have nothing more to do on earth!" and he fell asleep again. At nine o'clock in the evening the warden awakened him to hand him his supper.

"What do they say in Verrières?"

"Monsieur Julien, the oath that I took before the crucifix in the royal chamber on the day I was installed in office obliges me to be silent." He was silent, but remained in the room. The evident hypocrisy amused Julien.

"I must let him wait a long time for the five francs he wants to sell his conscience for."

When the jailer saw the meal finished without being tempted in any way, he said, in a soft, hypocritical tone:

"The friendship I have for you, monsieur Julien, forces me to speak, say what they might that it is against the interests of justice, because that might help you in your defence. Monsieur Julien, who is a good person, I know, will be pleased if I inform him that Madame de Rênal is doing well."

"What! she is not dead?" cried Julien, beside himself.

"Why, don't you know?" replied the jailer, stupidly, more than ever anxious for a tip. "It would be wise if monsieur Julien would give something to the surgeon who in pursuance of law and justice should not open his mouth; but in order to please monsieur, I went to his house and he told me everything."

"So, then, the wound is not a fatal one, after all!" muttered Julien. "Would you answer for it with your life?"

The warden, a giant six feet tall, fearful of bodily harm, shuffled away toward the door. Julien, seeing that he had taken the wrong means for getting at the truth, sat down again and threw a napoleon to M. Noiroud.

The more he heard of what the man had to say about the slightness of Madame de Rênal's wound, the more he felt tears coming into his eyes.

"Go!" he said all at once. The warden obeyed. Hardly was the door closed when Julien cried out: "Great God! she is not dead!" and he fell on his knees, his tears streaming over his cheeks. At that crisis he felt himself becoming religious again.

"What do I care for the hypocrisy of the priests? Can they remove anything from the truth and the sublimity of the idea of God?" Only then did Julien begin to repent of his crime.

The information he received relieved him of his despair, as well as of the intense physical strain under which he labored since leaving Verrières. His tears flowed freely; he awaited death with resignation.

"She will live, then"; he said to himself, "she will live to pardon me and to love me again!"

Late the following morning the jailer, on awaking him, said: "You have a brave heart, monsieur Julien. I have been here twice, but I did not want to wake you. Here are two fine bottles of wine which M. Maslon, our curate, has sent you."

"What! Is that fool here yet?" asked Julien.

"Yes, monsieur," replied the guard in a whisper. "But don't talk so loud; it might injure you." Julien laughed outright.

"Where I am now, my friend, you are the only one that can do me any harm if you are not humane. You shall be well paid," continued Julien, resuming his imperious air and justifying his manner with another tip.

M. Noiroud, disgustingly obsequious, recounted again with great detail all he had learned about Madame de Rênal; but he did not say anything about the visit of mademoiselle Elisa.

A new idea came to Julien. "This man may make perhaps three or four hundred francs, for the jail is not filled; I can assure him of ten thousand francs if he wants to go to Switzerland with me. The difficulty would be only to persuade him of my good faith." But the idea of a long discussion with such a creature was disgusting to Julien, and he began to think of something else.

The evening was made short, for at midnight he was taken away in a coach. The gendarme who accompanied him was very kind. In the morning, when he arrived at the Besançon prison, a cell on an upper tier of a Gothic dungeon was assigned to him. He thought the architecture was of the fourteenth century, and he admired the graceful, cheering effect. A narrow space between two walls, across a deep courtyard, permitted of a beautiful view.

He was examined that morning, and then he was left alone for several days. He was calm and resigned. The matter seemed very simple to him: "I wanted to murder; I should be put to death." Beyond that he did not go. The trial, the annoyance of appearing in public, his defence—all that he considered simply embarrassing details, annoying formalities, of which there was time enough to think during the trial. He did not even think of death. "I will think of that after I am sentenced." Life, indeed, was not annoying to him now; he looked at everything in a new light; he no longer had any ambition.

He thought only rarely of Mademoiselle de la Mole. Remorse overwhelmed him, nevertheless, and he thought very often of Madame de Rênal, especially during the silence of the night, when he would be disturbed in his high cell only by the cry of ospreys. He thanked heaven for not having wounded her fatally.

"It is remarkable," he said to himself. "I thought by her letter to M. de la Mole that she had forever destroyed my happiness, and less than two weeks after that I think no more of what occupied me then. An income of two or three thousand livres to live quietly in a mountain country like Vergy—I was happy there; I did not know how happy I was!"

At other times he would rise abruptly from his chair, saying:

"If I had killed Madame de Rênal I should have killed myself—
I must be certain of that if I don't want to commit suicide. Kill
myself? That is the great question," he thought. "These formal
judges, who are so wrought up against the poor defendant, and
who would hang the best citizen for touching a Cross—why, I
should deprive them of their power, of their abuse, and that in
vile French, which the department newspapers will call eloquence! I shall live five or six weeks yet, at most. Kill myself?
No!" he said after a while. "Napoleon lived—besides life is
agreeable now; it is calm and peaceful here. I am not bored,"
and he began writing an order for some books which he wished
to have sent from Paris.

Chapter 37

A Dungeon

The tomb of a friend.
—STERNE

SUDDENLY he heard a noise in the corridor, though it was not the time when visitors were admitted in the prison. An osprey flew away shrieking. The door opened, and the venerable curate Chélan, tremblingly leaning on his cane, entered and threw himself into his arms.

"O good Lord! is it possible, my child? Wretch, I should say," and the good man could not add another word.

Julien, fearing he would fall, led him to a chair. The hand of time had rested heavily on the good old man, who was formerly so energetic. He appeared to Julien to be only a shadow of himself. When he regained his breath, the old man said:

"Day before yesterday, only, I received the letter from Strasburg with your five hundred francs for the poor of Verrières. It was brought to me in the mountain at Liveru, where I have retired at my nephew Jean's. Yesterday I learned the terrible news. O heaven! is it possible?" The old man no longer wept, he seemed dumbfounded. He added, mechanically: "You will need your five hundred francs here now; take them."

"I have need of you, my father," Julien cried, tenderly. "I have other money"; but he could not obtain a satisfactory answer. From time to time a tear trickled down M. Chélan's cheeks; then he would look at Julien, almost overcome on seeing his hands kissed. That face formerly so expressive of energy and noble sentiment now showed only the deepest apathy. Soon a peasant came to fetch the good old man home.

"He must not be tired out," he said to Julien, who recognized him as the nephew.

This visit plunged Julien into the most cruel despair. He could not even shed tears. Everything appeared to him hopelessly gloomy. He felt the blood freeze in his veins.

It was the most cruel moment he had yet experienced since committing the crime; it revealed death to him in all its horrors. All his thoughts of firmness and fortitude disappeared like a mist. And in this cruel state he continued for several days.

With such dejection he had need of a physical stimulant. Julien thought himself a coward for having recourse to it.

At the end of a horrible day, spent walking to and fro in his narrow cell, he cried out:

"What a fool I am! I have got to die like everybody else. It is the thought that I might die looking as the poor old man did that has made me so downcast. But a quick death, in the flower of my youth, puts me above such sad decrepitude."

Yet with all his reasoning, Julien remained low-spirited and wretched after that visit. There was no longer any rude, rugged courage in him; no more of the Roman stoicism; death had seemed at a greater height and less easy of reach.

"Now, this will be my thermometer," he said to himself. "This evening I am ten degrees below the courage line with which I should go to the guillotine; this morning I was up to the line. Oh, well! what's the difference if it comes back to me at the last moment?" The idea of a thermometer diverted his mind somewhat from his wretched condition.

On awaking the next morning, he was ashamed of his feelings of the preceding day. "My happiness and peace are at stake!" He resolved to write to the Attorney-General to ask that no one be admitted to see him. "And Fouqué," he thought; "suppose he took it into his head to come to Besançon, what would not be his disappointment!" For two months, perhaps, he had not thought of Fouqué.

"I was such a fool in Strasburg, my thoughts did not go farther than my coat collar."

The thought of Fouqué engrossed him now, and his heart became tender. He walked about in great agitation. "Here I am now, decidedly twenty degrees below the mark; if this weakness continues it would be better if I killed myself. What joy for Maslon and Valenod if I die a coward!"

Fouqué really came. That plain, good man was beside himself with grief. His sole idea, if he had one, would have been to sell all he had in order to bribe the warden and save Julien. He spoke for a long time about the escape of de Lavalette.

"You make me feel bad," Julien said to him. "M. de Lavalette was innocent; I am guilty. Without being aware of it, you made me think of the difference. But is it really so? Really, you want to sell everything you have?" asked Julien, becoming suddenly the critical observer again.

Fouqué, overjoyed at the thought of a consent on Julien's part, began with the details, even to a hundred francs of what he would receive from his various holdings.

"What a sublime effort on the part of a bourgeois! What economy! What little scrapings and savings! It makes me blush now when I see him sacrifice everything for me! Would one of those handsome young men whom I have seen at de la Mole's and who read René think of such a ridiculous thing? Except those who are very young and had their money left to them, who of those fine Parisians would make such a sacrifice?" All of Fouqué's shortcomings and coarseness disappeared and Julien threw himself into his arms. Never had the provinces received such homage from Paris. Fouqué, wild over the enthusiasm which he saw in his friend's eyes, took it for a consent to escape.

This view of the sublime in human character restored to Julien all the force which M. Chélan's visit had removed. Yes, he was still young; if, instead of inviting him to cool judgment, old age had only brought him emotion, he would have been cured of one misgiving.

The examinations now came more frequently. "I have killed, or at least wished to kill, with malice aforethought," he repeated every day. But the judge was for the niceties of form above everything else. Julien's declarations did not make the examinations any shorter and only piqued the judge's pride. Julien did not know that an effort was made to have him transferred to a horrible dungeon, and it was due to Fouqué's efforts that they left him in his little cell a hundred and forty-eight steps above the ground.

Abbé de Frilaire was among the important men who gave Fouqué orders for wood. The good merchant even went so far as to call on the grand vicar. To his great delight M. de Frilaire told him that, touched by Julien's good qualities and by the services he had before rendered at the seminary, he was thinking of speaking a good word for him to the judges. Fouqué saw a ray of hope for his friend, and upon leaving bowed almost to the ground, begging the grand vicar to distribute in Masses for Julien's acquittal the sum of ten louis.

Fouqué was greatly mistaken; M. de Frilaire was not a Valenod. The abbé refused and tried to convince the good peasant that he would do better to keep his money. Seeing that, short of imprudence, it was impossible to make him clear on that point, he advised him to spend that sum in gifts to the poor prisoners, who indeed were in need of everything.

"That Julien is a singular creature! His conduct is inexplicable," thought M. de Frilaire; "yet nothing should be so to me. Perhaps it will be possible for him to become a martyr

in this. At all events, I will know the end of the whole affair
and find perhaps the means of holding Madame de Rênal in
my power. She does not care much for me; indeed, at bottom,
she detests me. Perhaps I can find some way of becoming recon-
ciled with M. de la Mole, who has a weakness for this little
seminarian."

The trial had been placed on the calendar some weeks before.
Julien saw only one disagreeable thing: a possible visit from
his father. He consulted Fouqué about writing to the Attorney-
General to be spared that visit. The horror which the prospec-
tive sight of his father gave him just at this time was like a stab
to the good honest heart of the wood merchant. He could see
then why so many people hated his friend. Out of respect for
his great trouble, he disguised his thought as best he could.

"Anyhow," he replied, coldly, "this order cannot be applied
to your father."

Chapter 38

A Powerful Man

But there is such mystery in her movements and elegance in her form! Who can she be?

—SCHILLER

THE DOOR of his cell opened early the next morning, and Julien woke up with a start. "Good God!" he thought, "that is my father! What a terrible scene is coming!"

At the same instant a woman dressed peasant fashion threw herself into his arms. It was Mademoiselle de la Mole. He could hardly recognize her.

"Cruel one! I knew only by your letter where you were. What you call your crime, which is only a noble revenge, shows me more than ever the courage that is in your heart. I did not know that in Verrières——"

Though he had tried to prevent Mademoiselle de la Mole from visiting him, he found her now very attractive. Could anyone fail to see in her manner, in her speech, this noble, disinterested love? Was she not far above most women? He believed he was indeed loving a queen. After a few moments he said, with rare eloquence:

"The future is outlined very clearly before me. After my death, you are Madame de Croisenois, my widow. The noble, romantic soul of that widow, converted again to ideas of prudence by a singularly tragic circumstance, will perhaps appreciate the real worth of the young Marquis. You must yield to the happiness that is awaiting you from the side of riches and high rank. But, dear Mathilde, your arrival in Besançon, if it is at all suspected, will be a mortal blow to M. de la Mole, and that is something I shall never forgive myself. I have caused him enough grief. The Academician will say he has warmed a snake on his hearth."

"I must confess I did not expect such unfeeling reasoning from you," replied Mademoiselle de la Mole, half angry. "My maid is almost as prudent as you are. I received a card of admission in her name and have come here under the name of Madame Michelet."

"And Madame Michelet could arrive so quickly here?"

"Oh, you are always the superior man—the man that I have

loved! First, I have given a hundred francs to the judge's secretary, who first said that admission was out of the question; but after receiving the money the good man made me wait a while, then raised more objections, until I thought I should be robbed here——" She stopped.

"Well?" asked Julien.

"Don't get angry, dear Julien," she pleaded, embracing him. "I was obliged to tell my name to the secretary. He first took me for a young shop woman in love with the handsome Julien. Indeed, he would not let me in under any other condition. I swore to him that I am your wife, and now I shall have permission to come and see you every day."

"She is stark mad," thought Julien. "I could not have possibly prevented her. After all, M. de la Mole is a great peer, and public opinion will find a good excuse for a young Colonel who will marry this charming widow. My death will hide everything, and he will give himself up with delight to Mathilde's charms. It is the daring of a great soul. Most singular!"

She earnestly pleaded that they should commit suicide together. After she had become somewhat calm and had her fill of looking at Julien, she became all at once possessed by curiosity. She looked her lover all over as if she were trying to find something that she had imagined in him. Yes, Boniface de la Mole seemed to be resurrected in him, but of more heroic mould!

Mathilde engaged the best lawyers in the district. These, indeed, were at first offended by her extravagant offers, but they eventually yielded. She discovered this fact: that all doubtful affairs in Besançon were in M. de Frilaire's balance. Under her obscure name of Michelet she had at first found insurmountable difficulties to gain an audience of this all-powerful Congregationist, but the rumor of the beauty and of the charm of the "modiste" who had come all the way from Paris to console the young abbé, Julien Sorel, spread rapidly throughout the town.

Mathilde walked alone through the streets of Besançon, hoping that she would not thus be recognized. At all events, she did not think it would be damaging to his cause to produce a great impression upon the people. Mademoiselle de la Mole believed that she was plainly dressed, as becomes a sorrowing woman, but not plainly enough to avoid attracting great attention. She had gained considerable notice when, after a week's trial, she obtained an audience of M. de Frilaire.

With all her courage, her ideas of the influential Congregationist were so linked with prudent knavery that she trembled when she rang the door-bell. She could hardly walk when she was told to go up the stairway to the grand vicar's apartments.

The solitude in the Episcopal palace chilled her. "I might be sitting here in the chair and all at once I might be seized and made away with! For whom could my maid ask? The gendarme captain would be very slow. Indeed, I am lost in this great city."

After looking round the apartment Mademoiselle de la Mole became more reassured. A valet in fine livery had opened the door for her. The waiting-room was furnished with much delicate luxury, quite different from the coarse magnificence of some of the best houses in Paris. When she saw M. de Frilaire with his paternal look coming toward her, all ideas of the crime disappeared. She did not even find in his handsome face the imprint of that energetic, rugged virtue which is so antagonistic to Parisian society. The covert smile that played on the features of the man who was all powerful in Besançon, announced a man of the world—the learned prelate and prudent administrator. Mathilde thought she was in Paris. It required only a few minutes for Mathilde to declare to him that she was the daughter of his powerful opponent, the Marquis de la Mole.

"Indeed, I am not Madame Michelet," she declared, assuming her proud tone, "and I don't care if I make this confession. I have come to consult you, monsieur, about the possibility of having an acquittal secured for M. de la Vernaye. In the first place, he is guilty only of a blunder. The woman at whom he shot is doing well. In the second place, I can immediately dispose of fifty thousand francs and promise twice as much again. Finally, my own gratitude and that of my entire family will find nothing impossible for any one who saves M. de la Vernaye."

M. de Frilaire appeared astonished at hearing the name. Mathilde showed him several letters from the Minister of War addressed to M. Julien Sorel de la Vernaye.

"You see, monsieur, my father has charged himself with his welfare. We have had a clandestine marriage. My father desires that he shall become a superior officer before announcing a marriage which might be deemed rather singular for a de la Mole."

Mathilde noticed that the kind and benevolent expression in the abbé disappeared as he became more and more interested. Shrewd hypocrisy was plainly visible on his face now.

The abbé had his doubts, and so he read again the official documents. "What advantage can I gain from such a strange confidence?" he asked himself. "Here I am all at once in close relation with a friend of the celebrated Maréchale de Fervaques, the niece of the all-powerful Bishop of ____, who may appoint anyone Bishop of France. What I was looking for in the distant future presents itself immediately under my eyes. This may bring me to the realization of my fondest hopes!"

At first Mathilde was frightened to see the change of expression in the face of the influential man. "But, indeed," she said to herself, "the worst thing would have been if I had not made an impression on this egotistical priest, puffed up as he is with power and wealth."

M. de Frilaire, dazzled by the view of the rapid road to the Episcopacy, and, moreover, astonished by Mathilde's intelligence, was for a moment off his guard. Mademoiselle de la Mole almost had him at her feet, trembling with ambition.

"It is all clear now," she thought. "Nothing is impossible here for a friend of Madame de Fervaques." In spite of her jealousy she had the courage to explain that Julien was an intimate friend of the Maréchale and had met at her house Bishop of ____ almost every day.

"When they draw four or five panels for a list of thirty-six jurors among the titled citizens of the department," said the grand vicar, slowly measuring his words, "I should consider myself a bad guesser if in each list I could not count on eight or ten friends who are the most intelligent of the lot. Almost always I shall have a majority over those voting for a death penalty. You see, mademoiselle, with what ease I can relieve you of all your trouble——"

The abbé stopped all at once, surprised at his own words. He was telling things that should never be told to the laity. But in his turn he stupefied Mathilde when he informed her that what astonished and interested the Besançon public most of all in this strange affair was that Julien had inspired such a passion in Madame de Rênal. M. de Frilaire saw quickly how much pain he gave her by his account.

"I have the advantage now!" he thought. "At least I have a means of turning this headstrong person to my purpose. I was fearful that I might not succeed." The distinguished, decisive air increased in his eyes the charm of the rare beauty which he saw almost suppliant before him. Regaining his sang-froid, he did not hesitate to turn the knife in her heart. "I should not be surprised, after all," he said, lightly, "if you learn that M. Sorel had shot this woman, whom he formerly loved so much through sheer jealousy. Indeed, there may be some truth in that; for a long time she was visiting a certain abbé Marquinot from Dijon, a sort of an immoral Jansenist, like all the rest."

M. de Frilaire delighted in this torture of the pretty girl, in whom he had found the weak spot. "Why," he said, looking at Mathilde's brilliant eyes, "why should M. Sorel have chosen the Church, if it was not because at that very moment his rival was celebrating Mass? Everybody gives the man whom you think of so much great credit for intelligence and prudence. Would it not have been much simpler for him to hide himself in M. de Rênal's garden, with which he is so familiar, with the greatest certainty of being neither seen nor seized, nor even suspected? He could there have given the mortal blow to the woman of whom he was jealous."

Such reasoning, apparently irrefutable, made Mathilde almost beside herself. That strong spirit, passing in high society as the reflex of the true human heart, could not appreciate the pleasure of such sneering at prudence. In the society in which Mathilde moved in Paris passion very seldom went beyond the range of prudence, and it was only from the fifth story that people ever threw themselves out of the window.

Abbé de Frilaire was now sure of having her in his power. He gave Mathilde to understand that he could influence the magistrates who were charged with sustaining the prosecution. After the panel was drawn he could approach directly and personally thirty out of the thirty-six jurors. If Mathilde had not appeared so pretty to M. de Frilaire he would not have talked to her so plainly before the fifth or sixth interview.

Chapter 39

Intrigue

> *March 31, 1676. He that endeavoured to kill his sister in our house, had before killed a man, and it had cost his father five hundred écus to get him off; by their secret distribution, gaining the favour of the counsellors.*
>
> —LOCKE

WHEN SHE LEFT the Bishop's house, Mathilde did not hesitate to send a courier to Madame de Fervaques. The fear of compromising herself did not stop her for an instant; she begged her rival to get a letter for M. de Frilaire, written in the Bishop's own handwriting. She even begged her to go herself to Besançon. That was indeed heroic on the part of a jealous and proud girl.

Following Fouqué's advice, she was prudent enough not to tell Julien of what she was doing. Her presence alone was sufficiently distracting to him. More sincere at the approach of death than he had ever been in his life, he felt remorse not only with respect to M. de la Mole, but also as regards Mathilde.

"How is it," he asked himself, "that I feel so happy and yet wearied in her presence? She loses everything for me, and this is the way I pay her back! Am I indeed a wretch?" The question would have disconcerted him when he was ambitious; then his only shame would have been not to succeed.

His position with respect to Mathilde was the more painful to him since he inspired in her every moment the most extraordinary love imaginable. She could only speak of the strange sacrifices which she proposed to make in order to save him.

Carried away by the feeling that extinguished all her pride, she did not wish to pass a single moment without doing something unheard of for him. The strangest and most perilous projects filled her conversations with him. The wardens, who were well paid, gave her the freedom of the jail. Mathilde was not content with the sacrifice of her reputation; it was nothing to her to have her affair made known to society. To ask pardon for Julien on her knees before the King's carriage, to invite the Prince's attention at the risk of being overwhelmed with contempt, was the least of the chimeras that crowded her imagination. With friends of hers near the King, she was sure of being admitted in the private grounds of Saint Cloud!

Julien was aware that he was not worthy of such devotion. Indeed, he was becoming distraught by such heroism. He was sensible only of a simple and obscure tenderness; while, on the other hand, in Mathilde's proud soul, the idea of a public entered as an essential element. For, in the midst of all her anguish, in the midst of all her fears for Julien's life, which she did not wish to survive, she had a secret satisfaction in astonishing the public by her great love and extraordinary devotion. Julien was growing angry with himself at not being touched by such heroism. He would have been more touched than ever if he had known with what madness Mathilde was assailing the devoted but eminently reasonable Fouqué. This one saw a good deal that he could blame in Mathilde's devotion; as for himself, he would have sacrificed everything he had in the world and risked his life a hundred times for Julien's sake. He was overwhelmed by the quantity of gold that Mathilde threw away right and left. During the first few days the sum thus spent was stupefying to Fouqué, who had all the provincial veneration for gold; but he discovered that Mademoiselle de la Mole's projects changed frequently; and to his own relief he found a word that characterized such foolish actions—she was *fickle*. That epithet is only one remove from *blockhead*—the severest censure in the province.

"Strange," said Julien to himself, as she left the jail one day, "that such a passion, of which I am the object, leaves me so cold, and two months ago I worshipped her! I have frequently read that with the approach of death a man loses interest in everything; but it is horrible to think that one is ungrateful, without the ability of changing! Am I, then, such an egoist?" He experienced the most humiliating self-reproach.

Ambition was dead in his heart, but another passion arose from its ashes. It was remorse, he thought, for having attempted to murder Madame de Rênal. Indeed, he had the greatest love for that woman. He was singularly happy when, left alone and fearing no interruption, he could give himself up entirely to thoughts of the happy days he had passed in Verrières and in Vergy. The slightest incident connected with those days—alas, only too swiftly passed!—had irresistible charm for him. He never gave a thought to his brilliant career in Paris; that, indeed, bored him. This trait, becoming accentuated from day to day, was partly guessed at by Mathilde. She clearly saw that she had to struggle with an inordinate love of solitude. Sometimes she would pronounce with evident terror Madame de Rênal's name, and then she would see Julien tremble. Then her passion would become immeasurable.

"When he dies, I will not survive him a moment," she would say to herself. "What will they say in the Paris drawing-rooms when they see a girl of my rank worshipping a man on the brink of execution? To appreciate such a feeling we must go back to heroic times. It is like the loves that inflamed hearts in the days of Charles IX. and Henry III." In the midst of these reflections the horrible thought would come, as she pressed Julien's head to her breast: "Oh, this charming head must soon drop! Well," she would add, spurred on by generous heroism, "my lips, which are now kissing his pretty hair, will be cold twenty-four hours later." These moments of abandon and passion attached her to Julien as she had never been before. The idea of suicide, which now took possession of her—formerly so far removed from her heart—now urged her on, ruling her with irrepressible force. "No, the blood of my ancestors has not become thinned in me," Mathilde would say to herself with pride.

"I have a favor to ask of you," said her lover to her one day. "Let your child be nursed in Verrières. Madame de Rênal will see to its nursing."

"What you ask is indeed hard," replied Mathilde, turning pale.

"Yes, and I ask your pardon a thousand times!" cried Julien, emerging out of his reverie and pressing her in his arms.

After drying his tears, he came back to his first thought, but a little more circumspectly. He had given a tone of melancholy philosophy to his conversation. He spoke of that future which would soon be closed to him. "Indeed, my darling, passion is an accident in life; but that accident cannot occur except to superior hearts. My child's death would no doubt be the greatest piece of good fortune for your family. Neglect alone would be the fate of that child of misery and shame. I trust some day—which I do not want to fix, but which I clearly see—you will follow my instructions to the letter: that you will marry the Marquis de Croisenois."

"What, disgraced as I am?"

"Dishonor cannot overtake a name like yours. You will be a widow, and the widow of a madman. That is all. I'll go farther. My crime, since it was not instigated by love of money, cannot be a disgrace. Perhaps at that time some philosophical legislator will effect the abolition of capital punishment. Then some friendly voice will say, for example: 'See, Mademoiselle de la Mole's first husband was mad, but not a criminal! It was shameful to cut off his head.' Then my memory will not be infamous, at least not after a little time has elapsed. Your position in the world, your fortune, and, permit me to add, your character, will enable M. de Croisenois, after he becomes a husband, to play a part in the world which he could not obtain himself. He has only birth and courage; and these qualities, which would have made a man in 1729, become an anachronism a century later and are fruitful only of pretensions. There is something else necessary to place oneself at the head of young France. You will bring as an aid to him a firm and initiative character to the political party to which your husband will belong. You might succeed the Chevreuses and the Longuevilles of the Fronde. But then, darling, the divine spark which animates you now may be extinguished! Let me also say," he added, "in fifteen years you will look back upon your love for me as an excusable folly, but nevertheless a folly." He stopped all at once, lost in reverie. He again had those ideas that were so distasteful to Mathilde. "In fifteen years Madame de Rênal will adore my boy, and you will have forgotten him!"

Chapter 40

Peace of Mind

> *It is because I was mad then that I am sane now.
> O philosopher who sees nothing but that of the
> moment, how short your vision is! Your eye is
> not made to follow the underground workings of
> the passions.*
>
> ——GOETHE

THE CONVERSATION was cut short by an official examination,
which was followed by a conference with the attorney charged
with his defence. Those were the only disagreeable moments
in a life that was full of tender reveries. "There was a murder
and premeditated murder," said Julien to the judge as well as
to his attorney. "I am sorry, gentlemen," he added, smiling; "but
it makes the matter a little less complicated."

"Indeed," Julien said to himself, when the two men left him,
"I must be brave, and apparently braver than these two men.
They look upon the matter as the greatest evil, the very prince
of horrors; and yet I will not concern myself about it until the
time comes. That is because I have known a greater misfortune,"
continued Julien, philosophizing; "I suffered much more on
my first trip to Strasburg, when I thought that Mathilde had
abandoned me; and yet to think I desired the intimacy with so
much passion which leaves me so cold to-day! Indeed, I am
much happier alone than when that pretty girl is with me."

The attorney, a man of great formality, really believed him
mad, thinking, like the public, that it was jealousy that put a
pistol in his hand. One day he ventured to tell Julien that this
idea, whether true or false, would make an excellent plea. But
the prisoner could show only contempt and anger. "Not on
your life, monsieur," cried Julien, beside himself, "must you
think of such an abominable lie!" The prudent advocate was
for a moment afraid of personal injury.

He prepared his case. The fateful day was fast approaching.
Besançon and the entire department could speak only of that
cause célèbre. Julien was indifferent to this detail and begged
to be spared all reference to it.

That day, as Fouqué and Mathilde came to inform him of

417

what the public was saying, being, as it seemed to them, very favorable, he stopped them abruptly by saying:

"Leave me my ideal. The petty chicaneries, the little details you bring here from real life, draw me away from my heaven; they run counter to my heart. One should die the best way he can. As for myself, I want to think of death only in my own way. What do I care for others? My relations with others are to be abruptly cut short. Please don't talk to me about them; it is enough to have to see the judge and the attorney."

"Really," he then began to muse, "it appears that it is my destiny to die dreaming. An obscure person like myself, sure of being forgotten in a fortnight, would indeed be a fool to enact a comedy now. Strange, I haven't known how to enjoy life until I see my end so close!"

He passed his last days walking to and fro in the narrow corridor on the top floor of the prison, smoking excellent cigars, which Mathilde had ordered from Holland by a courier. He was not aware that all the field-glasses in town were daily ranged to see him appear. His mind was far away in Vergy. He never spoke of Madame de Rênal to Fouqué, but two or three times his friend told him that she was rapidly recovering. The news fairly mastered his soul.

While Julien dwelt almost entirely in the realms of ideas, Mathilde, occupied with real things, as is proper for an aristocratic person, advanced so well the relations between Madame de Fervaques and M. de Frilaire through direct correspondence, that there was already a suggestion of the Episcopate.

The venerable prelate, who controlled the list of livings, added in a postscript to a letter to his niece: "This poor Sorel has only been foolish; I hope we shall get him back."

On receiving these lines M. de Frilaire was beside himself with joy. He no longer had any doubts as to saving Julien.

"If it weren't for this Jacobin law, which provides for a long panel, and which has for its only aim to remove all influence from people of quality," he said to Mathilde, before the list of the thirty-six jurors was drawn up for the session, "I could answer for the *verdict*. It was I who saw to it that the curate N. was acquitted."

Next day M. de Frilaire found with pleasure that among the names drawn from the panel there were five Congregationists from Besançon, and among the others the names of Valenod, de Moirod, and de Cholin. "I can answer for these eight jurors," he said to Mathilde. "The first five are *machine* men. Valenod is my agent; Moirod owes everything to me; de Cholin is an imbecile, afraid of everybody."

A list of the jurors was published in the newspapers, and Madame de Rênal, to her husband's great horror, wished to go to Besançon. All that he could obtain from her was that she would not leave her bed, so as not to have the disagreeable duty of being summoned as a witness. "You don't understand my position," said the ex-Mayor of Verrières. "I am now a Liberal from *defection,* as they call it. No doubt, that rascal of a Valenod or M. de Frilaire would see to it with the prosecuting attorney about making the affair as disagreeable to me as possible."

Madame de Rênal soon submitted to her husband's wishes. "For if I appeared at the assizes," she said to herself, "I should appear as if I came for revenge." In spite of all her promises to be prudent, which she made to her confessor and to her husband, she wrote with her own hand, when scarcely arrived at Besançon, the following letter to each of the thirty-six jurors:

"I will not appear at the trial, because my presence might be prejudicial to M. Sorel. I only wish one thing, and that ardently: that he might be saved. You must know that the horrible idea of an innocent man being sentenced to death on my account would no doubt poison and shorten the rest of my life. How can you sentence him to death since I am alive? No, society has not the right to take away a life and, such as Julien Sorel's! Everybody at Verrières has known him to have had moments of aberration. True, the poor young man has a great many enemies. But even among his enemies is there one who does not appreciate his admirable talents and his profound learning? It is not an ordinary person on whom you are going to pass sentence, monsieur. For eighteen months we have all known him as a pious, good, industrious young man; but two or three times a year he would be seized with a fit of melancholy that would drive him almost to insanity. All Verrières; all our neighbors in Vergy, where we spend the summer season; my whole family, and the sub-prefect himself, will bear testimony to his exemplary piety. He knows the whole Bible by heart. Would a wicked man spend years in studying the Holy Book? My sons will have the honor of presenting this letter to you. They are children. Please question them, monsieur; they will give you details about this young man that will convince you of the barbarity of sentencing him to death. Far from avenging me, it would kill me.

"What can his enemies say? The wound inflicted in a fit of temporary insanity, which even my children remarked in their tutor, is so slight, that in less than two months I have been enabled to travel from Verrières to Besançon. If I learn, monsieur, that you hesitate to apply such a barbarous law to an innocent man, I will leave my bed, where I remain only in obedience to my husband's wishes, and come to embrace your knees. Declare, monsieur, please, that premeditation has not been proved, and you will not have occasion to reproach yourself for having shed innocent blood!"

Chapter 41

The Trial

*Le pays se souviendra longtemps de ce procès
célèbre. L'intérêt pour l'accusé était porté jusqu'à
l'agitation: c'est que son crime était étonnant et
pourtant pas atroce. L'eût-il été, ce jeune homme
était si beau! Sa haute fortune, sitôt finie,
augmentait l'attendrissement. Le condamneront-
ils? demandaient les femmes aux hommes de leur
connaissance, et on les voyait pâlissantes at-
tendre la réponse.*

—SAINTE-BEUVE

THE DAY of trial came that was dreaded alike by Madame de
Rênal and Mathilde. The strange appearance of the town redoubled their terror. Even the phlegmatic soul of Fouqué was
touched. The whole province had flocked to Besançon to witness the trial amid such romantic circumstances. For several
days, already, there was no room to be had at any of the inns.
The judge of the assizes had been assailed by requests for tickets
of admission; for all the women in town wished to be present
at the trial. In the street, pictures of Julien were in great demand.
Mathilde held in reserve, as a last resort, a letter written entirely
by the Bishop of ____. That prelate, who directed the affairs of
the Church in France, and controlled the appointment of the
Bishops, had agreed to ask for Julien's acquittal. The day before
the trial Mathilde brought the letter to the all-powerful grand
vicar.

At the conclusion of the interview, M. de Frilaire, half-moved
himself, laid aside his diplomatic reserve, and said to Mathilde,
just as she had burst into tears: "I can answer for the verdict.
Among the twelve persons charged with ascertaining if your
protégé's crime is habitual, and, above all, if there was any
premeditation, I can count on six who are devoted to me. And
I have given them to understand that it depends upon them
whether I shall one day mount to the Episcopacy. Baron
Valenod, whom I have made Mayor of Verrières, controls two
of his officials—de Moirod and de Cholin. True, chance has
given us in this affair two jurors whose views are rather queer.

But although ultra-Liberal, they are true to me in all matters of weight, and I have asked them to vote like Valenod. I have learned that the sixth juror, an immensely wealthy manufacturer and Liberal, aspires to an office under the Ministry of War, and no doubt he is not desirous of acting contrary to my wishes. I have given him to understand that M. de Valenod is my representative."

"And who is this M. Valenod?" asked Mathilde, uneasily.

"If you knew him, you would not have the least doubt about our success. He is a bold, impudent, coarse fool, a born leader of fools. In 1814 he was poor, and now I am going to make him a prefect; he is capable of striking the other jurors if they do not vote to suit him."

Mathilde was not altogether reassured. Another conference took place in the evening. Julien had resolved not to say a word in defence, in order not to prolong a disagreeable scene of which the result seemed to him only too certain. "My lawyer will speak," he said to Mathilde. "As it is, I shall be exposed only too long to the sight of my enemies. These rich provincials are sour over the rapid progress I owe to you, and, believe me, there is not one of them but desires my death, even though he may shed tears like a fool when I am executed."

"They want to see you humiliated; that is only too true," replied Mathilde; "but they are not cruel. My presence in Besançon and my distress have interested all the women. Your face will do the rest. If you only say a word before the judges, everybody will be with you."

Next day at nine o'clock, when Julien walked down from the jail to go to the courthouse, the guard succeeded only with difficulty in making way for him through the crowd that were massed in the hall. Julien, after a good night's rest, was self-composed. He only had a feeling of pity for that vast crowd, who, without intending the least cruelty, would, he thought, applaud a verdict for death. He was greatly surprised when, after a quarter of an hour in the midst of the crowd, he was obliged to recognize the fact that the public had only pity for him. Not one unfavorable word reached his ears. "These provincials are less bloodthirsty than I thought," he said to himself. He was impressed by the appearance of the court-room, which was in real Gothic style; all around there were pretty little stone columns, gracefully carved. He thought he was in England.

Soon his attention was attracted to a dozen handsome women who filled the balcony over the places reserved for judges and jury, opposite the prisoner's dock. Running his eyes over the crowd, he saw that the space behind the railing to the rear was entirely filled with women. Most of them seemed young and handsome; and their eyes, he thought, were alive with interest. An immense crowd filled the rest of the hall. At the doors they were fighting for admission, and the guards could hardly maintain silence. When all eyes were turned to the accused, as he stood in the dock on a slight elevation, he was received with looks of astonishment and tender interest.

One might have thought he was not twenty years of age. He was dressed simply but neatly. His hair and brow were indeed charming. Mathilde, herself, wished to superintend his dress for the occasion. He was indeed extremely pale. Hardly seated, he heard on all sides: "Lord, how young he is!" "My, he is only a boy!" "He looks even better than his picture!"

"Defendant," said the gendarme to him, on his right, in a friendly tone; "you see the ten ladies who are in the balcony?" pointing to a little place alongside the part occupied by the jurors, "that's the prefect's wife, and right near her is the Marquise de M. She takes a great deal of interest in you. I heard her speak to the judge. Then right beside her is Madame Derville."

"Madame Derville!" cried Julien, blushing. "When she leaves here," he thought, "she will write to Madame de Rênal." He did not know of Madame de Rênal's arrival in Besançon.

The witnesses quickly gave their testimony. As soon as the prosecuting attorney commenced, two women in the gallery opposite Julien burst into tears. "Madame Derville is not moved like that!" thought Julien. He noticed, however, that her face was flushed.

The prosecutor spoke pathetically, in bad French, of the barbarity of the crime, and Julien observed that Madame Derville's neighbors seemed to disapprove of it. Several jurors, who were evidently acquainted with these ladies, spoke to them, seeming to reassure them. "That isn't a bad sign," thought Julien.

Up to this point, Julien seemed to have only contempt for the men who were in the courtroom. The vapid eloquence of the prosecuting attorney served only to increase it. However, Julien's apathy disappeared when he noticed the interest that was taken in him. He was well pleased with the firm look of his attorney. "No wind now!" he said to the latter, as he arose to speak.

"All the eloquence that was taken from Bossuet will only help you," replied his lawyer. In truth, he had not spoken five min-

utes when all the women were nervously fingering their handkerchiefs. Encouraged by this, the lawyer continued with even
greater emphasis. Julien was greatly moved, feeling as if he
were about to burst into tears. "Good Lord, what will my
enemies say!" He was about to give way to his emotion, when
he surprised a scowling look on Baron Valenod. "That fool's
eyes are glittering!" he said to himself. "What a triumph for
that despicable soul! If my crime would have led only to this,
I should have cursed him! God knows what he will tell Madame
de Rênal about me!"

That thought made him insensible to everything else; but he
was recalled to himself by the evident marks of public sympathy.
The attorney had just finished. Julien thought that it was proper
he should shake hands with him.

Time had passed quickly, and the attorney and the defendant received some refreshment. Julien was struck by one circumstance: not a woman had left her place to go to dinner.

"Lord, I am just dying of hunger," said the lawyer; "aren't
you?"

"Yes," replied Julien.

"Look, there is the prefect's wife, who has had her dinner
brought to her," said the lawyer, pointing to the little balcony.
"Now, cheer up; everything is going all right," he said, as the
case was resumed.

It was midnight when the judge of the assizes summed up
the case. He was obliged to stop; the sound of the clock sounded
ominously in the midst of the silence and anxiety.

"There is the beginning of my last day," thought Julien. He
was soon seized by his idea of duty. Up to this point, he had
mastered his emotion and kept to his resolution not to speak;
but when the judge of the assizes asked him if he had anything
to say, he arose. He saw before him Madame Derville's eyes,
shining brilliantly in the light. "Is she crying on my account?"
he asked himself.

"Gentlemen of the jury," he said, "I can brave contempt now,
and I will speak. Gentlemen, I have not the honor of belonging
to your class; you see in me only a peasant who rebelled against
the lowliness of his station.

"I ask no favor of you," continued Julien, firmly; "I am not
deceiving myself. Death is awaiting me, and that will be just.
I have made an attempt on the life of a woman who was worthy
of the highest respect and consideration. Madame de Rênal was
like a mother to me. My crime is atrocious, for it was premeditated; I therefore deserve death, gentlemen of the jury.

But if I should appear less culpable, I see men here who, without stopping to think of any allowance to be made for youth, would like to punish and discourage forever, through me, a class of young men who, born in a lowly station in life and borne down by poverty have the good fortune of becoming well educated, and have dared to mix up with what the pride of the rich calls 'society.'

"That is my crime, gentlemen, and I shall be punished with a greater severity, since I am not judged by my peers. I do not see on the juror's bench any rich peasant, but only bourgeois who are feeling they have been outraged."

In that strain Julien spoke for twenty minutes. He said everything that weighed on his heart. The prosecuting attorney, who was eager for aristocratic favor, bounded from his seat. In spite of the abstractness of Julien's speech, all the women were in tears. Madame Derville herself was holding her handkerchief to her eyes. Before concluding, Julien came back to his criminal intention, to his repentance of the act, and to his respect and almost filial adoration which in the happy days he had for Madame de Rênal. Madame Derville gave a cry and fainted away.

One o'clock struck when the jurors retired. Not a single woman had left the place. Even men had tears in their eyes. The conversation was first animated, but gradually, as the verdict of the jury was long in coming, the strain of the people present produced an ominous quiet. It was a solemn moment. The very light seemed dimmer than usual. Julien, worn out with trouble, was hearing the question discussed by his side whether the delay was a good or a bad sign. It gave him pleasure to find that he had the good wishes of everyone. The jury did not come back, and yet not a single woman had left the hall.

When two o'clock struck there was a general movement in the courtroom. The door of the jurors' room was opened, and Baron Valenod advanced theatrically, followed by the rest of the jurors. He coughed a little, then declared that on their soul and conscience the jury found it as their unanimous verdict that Julien Sorel was guilty of murder, and of murder with criminal intent. That verdict meant a death sentence, and, soon after, that was pronounced. Julien looked at his watch, thinking of M. de Lavalette. It was a quarter-past two. "To-day is Friday," he thought. "Yes, but this is a happy day for this Valenod who has condemned me. I am too closely watched to be saved by Mathilde, as Madame de Lavalette had done. So in three days, at this very hour, I will know what is in store for me in the great hereafter."

Just then he heard a cry that recalled him to his mundane existence. The women all around him were sobbing. He saw that all faces were turned to a little balcony built around the capital of one of the Gothic pillars. He found out later that Mathilde had hidden herself there. As the cry was not renewed, everybody turned to Julien again, for whom the guards were trying to make a way through the crowd.

"I must try not to give this rascally Valenod an occasion for triumph," said Julien to himself. "With what a contrite and humble air he delivered that verdict that has sent death to me! And yet this poor judge, on the bench for so many years, had tears in his eyes, even while he was sentencing me. What a joy for Valenod to revenge himself for our former rivalry about Madame de Rênal! I shall not see her again, that is certain. A last farewell is impossible for us; I feel it. How happy I should be to tell her what horror my crime has caused me."

He kept on repeating the words: "I have been justly condemned."

Chapter 42*

WHEN he was led back to the jail, he was brought into the condemned cell. Though ordinarily attentive to every little circumstance, he was not aware that he was not led back to his usual cell. He was thinking what he would say to Madame de Rênal if he were fortunate enough to see her before the end came. He thought that she might interrupt him, as he would strive at the very first word to describe his repentance of his act. After such a deed, how could I persuade her that I love her *alone?* For really, did I not want to kill her from ambition and my love for Mathilde? When he retired, he saw that the curtains were of a rough texture. Then his eyes told him the truth. "Ah, I am in the condemned cell. That is right. Count Altamira has told me that before his execution Danton said in his loud voice: 'It is singular how the verb guillotine cannot be conjugated in all the tenses.' You can say, 'I shall be guillotined,' 'Thou wilt be guillotined,' but not, 'I have been guillotined.'

"Why not," Julien mused, "if there is another life? My God, if I meet the Christian God, I am damned forever; for he is a tyrant, and as such, he is moved only by thoughts of revenge. His Bible tells only of fearful punishment. I have never loved him; I have never even wished that he should be loved sincerely. He is pitiless!" and he recalled several passages from the Bible. "He will punish me cruelly!

"But suppose I find the God of Fénelon? He will tell me, perhaps: 'Much wilt thou be forgiven, because thou hast much loved.' Have I loved much? Yes, I have loved Madame de Rênal, but I have been so cruel to her! See, there as elsewhere, simple, modest worth was abandoned for tinsel!

"But what a perspective! A Colonel of Hussars if there had been war; Secretary of Legation in peace; then Ambassador; for I should have known how to get on. And even if I were only a fool, could Marquis de la Mole's son-in-law fear any rival? All my stupidity would have been pardoned, or, rather, thought clever. I should have been a man of importance, enjoying the greatest life in Vienna and London.

"Not so fast; softly, monsieur! The guillotine in three days!" Julien laughed outright at his own thoughts. "In truth," he

* The last four chapters are untitled.

thought, "a man has two personalities in him. Who the devil would think of this malign reflection? Well, my friend, the guillotine in three days!" he said to his "other self." "M. de Cholin will hire a window together with abbé Maslon. Of course, one of these worthy personages will steal the price of that window from the other."

Then this passage of Rotrou's *Venceslas* occurred to him all at once:

Ladislas.—My soul is prepared.
The King (father of Ladislas)—The scaffold is also ready. Take your head there.

"Not a bad answer!" he thought, as he fell asleep.

Someone awoke him in the morning with a pressure of the hand.

"What, already!" Julien said, opening his sunken eyes. He thought he was in the hands of the executioner.

It was Mathilde. "Happily," he thought, "she has never understood me;" and that thought made him self-collected again. Mathilde looked as if she had been sick for six months; he could hardly recognize her.

"That infamous Frilaire was a traitor," she said, wringing her hands; and she could not continue.

"Didn't I do well yesterday, when I spoke?" asked Julien; "it was extempore, and the first time in my life, too! True, I had a fear that it was the last." At that moment, Julien played on Mathilde's feelings with as much self-possession as a pianist on the keys. "The advantage of noble birth illustrates my weakness. True," he added, "but Mathilde's soul has raised her lover to her level. Do you believe that Boniface de la Mole appeared better before his judges?"

That day Mathilde was pathetically tender, like a poor girl in an attic; but she could not get the simplest word out of him. He tormented her in the same way he often did before.

"Nothing is known of the sources of the Nile," Julien was saying to himself. "It has not been given to the eye of man to see the king of rivers in its state as a simple stream. So no human eye will ever see Julien weak; it is because he *is* not weak. But I am easily touched; the simplest word, uttered without affectation, can make my voice falter and bring tears to my eyes. How often those dry and apathetic souls have despised me for this weakness! They thought that I would ask for clemency; that's what they could not bear!

"It is said that Danton at the foot of the scaffold was moved by thoughts of his wife; but Danton had given strength to a nation of coxcombs and prevented the enemy from reaching Paris. I alone know what I could have done; all the rest—they know me only at best as a *possibility*.

"If Madame de Rênal were here in my cell, in place of Mathilde, could I answer for myself? My great despair and my repentance would appear in Valenod's eyes and the rest of the patricians as a cowardly fear of death; their weak little hearts are so proud that their pecuniary position puts them above temptation. 'See what it is,' de Moirod and de Cholin may have said, who have condemned me to death, 'to be a carpenter's son!' One may become prudent, educated; but the heart never learns. Even with poor Mathilde, who is crying now, or, rather, who cannot cry any more," he said, looking at her red eyes. He pressed her in his arms. The sight of real grief made him forget his cool reasoning. "She has cried, perhaps, all night; but one day how ashamed she will be to think of it all! She will look back upon herself as a young, misguided girl who had ignoble thoughts about a plebeian. De Croisenois is weak enough to marry her, and, really, he would do well; she would give him a rôle to play,

> " *'Du droit qu'un esprit ferme et vaste en ses desseins*
> *A sur l'esprit grossier des vulgaires humains.'*

"Oh, yes, that's pleasant. Since I am going to die, all the verses I ever learned in my life come back to me. It may be a symptom of the end."

Mathilde said, in a choking voice: "He is there in the next room." He really listened to her then. "Her voice is so weak," he thought, "yet her whole imperious character is heard in it." She lowered her voice so as not to aggravate him.

"And who is it?" he asked, softly.

"Your lawyer, to have you sign your appeal."

"I will not appeal!"

"What, you will not make an appeal?" she cried, as she rose, her eyes aflame with anger. "And why not, pray?"

"Because, just now, I feel I have the courage to die, without causing too much laughter at my expense. And who tells me I should feel the same way after two months in this damp cell? I see already interviews with priests, with my father—nothing in the world would be so disagreeable to me; I'd rather die!"

This unforeseen stubbornness aroused again Mathilde's proud nature. She had not been able to see abbé de Frilaire before the prison doors were opened in Besançon, and her anger spent itself on Julien. She adored him, and yet for a quarter of an hour he found again, in her condemnation of his character and in her regrets at ever having loved him, all that fiery temperament which had formerly overwhelmed him in the de la Mole library.

"Heaven owes it to the glory of your race to have you give birth to a son," he said to her. "As for myself," he thought, "I should be a fool to live two months longer in this hole, a prey to all the infamy and humiliation to which the patrician party will subject me, with only such a conversation as this to console me. Well, day after to-morrow I shall fight a duel with a man known to be self-possessed and remarkably adroit; so remarkable," continued this Mephistopheles, "he never misses!"

"Well, then, you will come round?" Mathilde continued, eloquently.

"No, indeed, I will not appeal," he said to himself.

Firmly fixed in this resolution, he fell into a profound reverie. "The carrier will bring the newspaper at six o'clock as usual. At eight o'clock, after M. de Rênal has read it, Elisa, walking on tiptoes, will put it on her bed; later she will wake up, and then, all at once, while reading, she will feel moved. Her pretty hand will tremble; she will even read the words: 'At five minutes after ten he ceased to breathe.' She will cry; I know her. In vain did I try to murder her; all that will be forgotten; and the person whom I wished to deprive of life will be the only one who will sincerely mourn my death.

"Oh, that is an antithesis!" he thought; and throughout the scene with Mathilde, lasting for over a quarter of an hour, he only thought of Madame de Rênal. In spite of himself, even while replying to what Mathilde was saying, he could not tear himself away from his memories of her bedroom. He saw the Besançon newspaper on the counterpane of yellow taffeta; he saw that white hand which had pressed him so frequently; he saw Madame de Rênal weep; he followed each tear as it flowed down her cheek.

Mademoiselle Mathilde, despairing of Julien's consent, called the lawyer. He was an old captain of the Army of Italy of 1796, when he was a companion of Manuel.

As a matter of form he combated the prisoner's resolution. Julien, wishing to treat him with consideration, then explained to him all his reasons. "Indeed, you are almost right," he said to him; "but you have three full days for an appeal, and it is my duty to come back to see you every day. If a volcano should open under the prison within the next two months, you would be saved; and you might die of a disease," he added, looking at Julien.

Julien shook him by the hand. "I thank you; you are a man. I will think of that."

As Mathilde walked out with the lawyer, he had more friendship for the lawyer than for her.

Chapter 43

AN HOUR LATER, after a deep sleep, he was awakened by the flow of tears on his hand. "Oh, it's Mathilde yet!" he said, only half awake. "Faithful to her resolution, she comes now to attack mine with her love." He did not open his eyes at first, gloomy over the prospect of another scene. The verse about Belphégor's flight from his wife came to him; but he heard a deep sigh. Opening his eyes, he saw Madame de Rênal.

"Oh, I see you then again before I die!" he cried, throwing himself at her feet; "or am I dreaming? But pardon, Madame, I am only a murderer in your eyes," he said, quickly, coming back to himself.

"Monsieur, I have come to beg you to appeal; I know you do not want to do that——" but her sobs would not allow her to continue.

"Please forgive me!"

"If you want me to forgive you," she said, throwing herself into his arms, "make the appeal right away."

Julien covered her with kisses.

"Will you come to see me every day during these two months?"

"I swear I will, every day; unless my husband forbids me."

"I will sign it," cried Julien. "Really, you forgive me? Is it possible?" He pressed her in his arms, wild with joy. She gave a little cry. "Oh, it's nothing," she said, "but you hurt me a little."

"Oh, it is your shoulder!" cried Julien, bursting into tears. Disengaging himself, he took her hand and kissed it. "Who would have told me that the last time I saw you in your room at Verrières?"

"Who would have told me then that I would write an infamous letter to M. de la Mole?"

"You know that I have always loved you, and only you!"

"Is it possible?" cried Madame de Rênal, herself wild with delight. Leaning over Julien, who was on his knees, she mingled her tears with his.

Never in his life had Julien experienced such happiness.

Some time afterward, when they could speak, Madame de Rênal said: "And this young Madame Michelet, or, rather, this

Mademoiselle de la Mole? For I am beginning to believe in the strange romance."

"It is all appearance," replied Julien. "She is my wife, but not my mistress."

Interrupting each other for a hundred times, they finally told each other as to what they had done. The letter that had been written to M. de la Mole had been dictated by a young priest who directed Madame de Rênal's conscience, and she had copied it. "What horror hasn't my religion caused me! And yet I have softened some of the horrible things in that letter!" Julien's happiness proved to her that he forgave her. Never was she as wild with love.

"I think I am religious," Madame de Rênal said to him. "I certainly believe in God. I equally believe, and I have seen it to be a fact, that the wrong I am doing is great; but since I see you, even after you shot me——" Here Julien could only kiss her.

"Please, I want to talk reason to you, for fear of forgetting it. When I see you, all duty disappears. I feel only love for you; indeed, the word 'love' is too feeble! I feel for you what I should feel for God alone—respect, love, obedience. I don't know what you inspire in me! If you should tell me to stab the guard, I would do it without further thought. Explain this to me, please, before I leave you. I want to look clearly into my heart, for in two months we shall part. Really, shall we part?" she asked, smiling.

"I take back what I said," replied Julien. "I will appeal from the sentence if you quit thinking of harming your life in any way."

Madame de Rênal's face changed all at once. The greatest tenderness followed her deep reverie.

"Supposing we died together right now?" she said, at last.

"Oh, who knows what is going to be in the next world?" replied Julien. "Perhaps frightful punishment, or perhaps nothing. Can we not pass two months together in delight? Two months!—that is a great many days. I shall never be as happy again!"

"You will never be so happy?"

"Never!" replied Julien, ravished. "I talk to you as if I were talking to myself. God knows I am telling the truth."

"It is to command me when you talk like that," she said, with a timid, melancholy smile.

"Well, then, you swear on the love you bear me that you will never make an attempt on your life—neither directly nor indirectly? Remember, now," he added, "that you must live for my child, whom Mathilde will abandon to some servants when she becomes the Marquise de Croisenois."

"I swear," she replied, coldly; "but I am going to take your appeal myself, written in your own hand. I will go myself to the Attorney-General."

"Take care; you will compromise yourself."

"After having come to see you in jail, I am forever a by-word for Besançon and for all Franche-Comté," she said, visibly affected. "The limits of modesty have been overstepped long ago. I am a woman lost to honor. It is true that it was all for you!"

Her tone was sad in the extreme, and Julien embraced her again with renewed fervor. It was not the intoxication of love, but rather great gratitude. He had just appreciated for the first time all the sacrifices she had made for him.

Some charitable soul, no doubt, informed M. de Rênal that his wife was making long visits to Julien in jail; for in three days he sent his carriage to her, with command to return to Verrières immediately. The cruel separation made a bad day of it for Julien. He was informed, two or three hours later, that a certain priest, who was not able to push himself forward among the Jesuits in Besançon, had stationed himself, early in the morning, in the street just outside the prison gate. It rained, and there in the rain the man was trying to play the martyr. Julien felt wretched as it was, and this foolishness caused him even greater dejection.

He had already refused a visit from this priest in the morning, but the man took it into his head to become Julien's confessor, so as to stand well with the young women of Besançon by pretending to have received great confidences. He loudly declared that he would pass day and night at the prison gate. "God has sent me to touch the heart of this backslider;" and the common people, always anxious for a scene, began to flock around him.

"Yes, my brethren," he said to them, "I will pass day and night here, and as many other days and nights as necessary. The Holy Ghost has spoken to me. I have a mission from on high. It is I who will save the soul of young Sorel. Let us pray."

Julien had a horror of notoriety and of everything that might attract attention to him. He was thinking of seizing a moment when he could pass out of the world by his own hands; but he had some hope of seeing Madame de Rênal, being still intoxicated with love.

The prison gate was in one of the most frequented streets. The thought of that squalid priest gathering a crowd around him tortured his soul. "And no doubt every moment he is mentioning my name." This was more painful to him than death. Two or three times an hour he sent the warden, who was friendly to him, to go out and see if the priest was still at the door.

"Monsieur, he is on both his knees in the mud," always brought back the warden. "He is praying at the top of his voice, and reciting Litanies for your soul."

"The rogue!" thought Julien. That moment, in fact, he heard a murmur. It was the people responding to the Litanies. To add to his impatience, he saw the warden himself move his lips, repeating the Latin words. "They are beginning to say," added the warden, "that your heart has been indeed made hard, to refuse the aid of that holy man."

"Oh, my country! How barbarous you are yet!" he cried out, angrily; and he uttered his thought aloud, without thinking of the warden's presence.

"That man wants an article in the newspaper, and he is sure of getting it now. Cursed provincials! At Paris I should not have been subjected to these vexations. There they use more finesse with their roguery.

"Let the holy priest enter," he said at last to the warden, the perspiration rolling off his brow. The warden crossed himself and left with great joy. The holy priest was horribly ugly, and was literally covered with mud. The cold rain made the cell gloomier and damper than ever. The priest made a pass as if to embrace Julien, and began talking to him very affectionately. The barest hypocrisy was evident in all this. Never in his life was Julien so disgusted.

A quarter of an hour after the priest's entrance he found himself a coward for the first time. Death appeared horrible to him. He thought of the state of putrefaction in which his body would be two days after his execution.

He either had to betray himself by some mark of weakness, or throw himself upon the priest and strangle him with his chain. But the sudden idea came to him to beg the saintly man to go and offer a Mass for him for forty francs that day. It was noon then, and the priest immediately left.

Chapter 44

WHEN HE LEFT, Julien wept as if his heart would break. Every now and then he said to himself that if Madame de Rênal had been in Besançon he would have confessed his weakness to her. Just when he was regretting most the absence of the woman he adored he heard Mathilde's footsteps. "The worst thing about being in jail," he thought, "is that you can't keep your door shut." All that Mathilde could say only served to irritate him.

She told him how, on the day of the trial, M. de Valenod, with the nomination of prefect in his pocket, wished to spite M. de Frilaire and to enjoy the pleasure of giving a verdict for death. "What a strange idea your friend had," M. de Frilaire just said to me, "to attack the petty vanity of the bourgeois aristocracy! Why did he speak of caste? He only indicated to them what they had to do for their own interests. Those fools were not thinking of it at all and were almost ready to cry. That caste interest just shielded their eyes from the horror of a death sentence. Indeed, we must confess M. Sorel is inexperienced in the affairs of life. If we do not succeed in saving him by an appeal to clemency, his death will be a sort of suicide."

Mathilde did not care to tell Julien what she suspected, namely that abbé de Frilaire, seeing Julien doomed, thought it would serve his ambition to aspire to become his successor. Almost beside himself with impotent anger, he said: "Go and hear a Mass for me and give me a moment's peace!" Mathilde, already very jealous of Madame de Rênal's visits, understood the cause of Julien's anger. She burst into tears. Her grief was indeed real. Julien, however, became only the more impatient. He had need of solitude, and he did not know how to get it. Finally, Mathilde, after trying everything to win him over, left him, and almost at the same moment Fouqué appeared.

"I want to be alone," he said to his faithful friend; and, when he saw the latter hesitate, "I am composing a memoir as a mark of my return to grace. Well, give me the pleasure never to talk of death. If I need anything particularly to-day let me speak first."

When at last Julien was alone he found himself in a more cowardly state than ever. The little strength that he had left was spent in trying to hide himself from Mademoiselle de la Mole and Fouqué. Toward evening one idea consoled him.

"If in the morning, at the time when death appears worst to me, I should be informed that my execution is at hand, my fear would cause some comment; like a gawk entering a drawing-room. Some of the clear-sighted among the provincials might look for my weakness, but no one shall ever see it." And he felt a little less cowardly. "I am a coward now," he repeated to himself, "but no one will know it."

Even a more disagreeable scene awaited him the next day. For a long time his father had said that he would visit him. That day, before Julien was awake, the old, white-haired carpenter entered the cell.

Julien was weak, and resigned himself to the reproaches he expected. To cap his disagreeable sensations, he had that morning a lively sense of remorse for never having loved his father.

"Chance has placed us on the earth together," the latter said, while the warden was putting the cell in order, "and we have done each other as much evil as possible; but this execution is the last straw——" Then when they were left alone the old man began to overwhelm him with the vilest abuse. Julien could not restrain his tears. "What an unworthy weakness," he said to himself with rage. "He is going to tell everybody of my want of courage. What a triumph for Valenod and for all the other hypocrites that rule Verrières! In France they indeed seem great. They have all social advantages. Up to this moment I could say to myself they all have money, it is true; they have honors heaped upon them. But I—I have nobility of heart, and here is a witness whom all will believe, and who will certify to all Verrières that I was nothing but a coward before my death!"

Julien was on the brink of despair. He did not know what to do to send his father away, and to attempt to hoodwink that sharp old man was at this moment beyond his power.

As his mind ran over all possible means, he finally hit on this idea: "I have saved up money." This stroke of genius immediately changed the old man's face.

"How should I dispose of it?" continued Julien, more calmly. The effect he produced now removed all sense of inferiority from him.

The old carpenter was burning to have not a penny of the money escape him; Julien had said that he would divide it among his brothers. He talked long and vivaciously.

"Ah, well, the Lord has directed me in this. I will give a thousand francs each to my brothers and the rest to you."

"Very good," replied the old man, "the rest is due me; but since God has been so gracious as to soften your heart, if you want to die like a good Christian you must pay your debts. There was the expense for your rearing and your education of which you are not thinking now."

"There is a father's love!" Julien repeated to himself, when he found himself alone at last.

The warden then appeared. "Monsieur," he said, "after parents' visits I always bring a good bottle of champagne. It is a little dear, six francs a bottle, but it gladdens the heart."

"Bring three glasses!" cried Julien, with the impatience of a child, "and invite the two prisoners whom I hear walking in the corridor."

The warden led in two convicts who had been sentenced for the second time to the galleys. These fellows were remarkable for their cleverness and courage.

"If you give me a twenty-franc piece," said one of them to Julien, "I will tell you everything about my life."

"But you will lie to me?"

"No, indeed," he replied; "my friend here, who is jealous about the twenty francs, will say when I am not telling the truth."

His record was an abominable one. It revealed a daring heart in which the ruling passion was money. When they left, Julien was no longer the same man. All his despair vanished. The misery his pusillanimity engendered from the time Madame de Rênal had left made way only for melancholy now.

"Whenever I was not fooled by appearances," he said to himself, "I saw that Paris drawing-rooms were peopled by men like my father, or by such clever rascals as these galley convicts. Oh, yes, they are good! A fashionable man never arises in the morning with the poignant thought: 'How will I get my dinner?' And still they vaunt their probity, and when called as jurors they sentence a man to death because he has stolen silver plate with which to buy bread! But if there is an intrigue at Court, or if there is a question of gaining or losing a portfolio, my virtuous drawing-room gentlemen commit exactly the same crime as those do whose hunger transports them to the galleys.

"There is no *natural* right. That is only an old piece of nonsense, worthy of the attorney who summed up my case the other day, and whose ancestors became rich from the confiscations under Louis XIV. There is no *right* except when there is a law to prohibit such and such a thing under penalty. Previous to the law there is nothing *natural*, except the strength of the lion or the crying necessities of a human being suffering from hunger and thirst. The men that are honored are only rascals who have the good fortune not to be found out. The prosecutor whom society has hurled at me got rich through infamy. I have committed a crime and I am justly condemned; but as far as that is concerned, Valenod has been a hundred times more harmful to society.

"Oh, well," Julien added, gloomily, with no longer a trace of anger, "in spite of his avarice my father is worth more than all of them. He has never loved me. I have dealt him a mortal blow by dishonoring him with my disgrace. This fear of want of money, this exaggerated view of the sin in men that is called *avarice*, gave him the only means for consolation in the sum of three or four hundred louis I am going to leave him. On a Sunday, after dinner, he will show his gold to all the simple people in Verrières. 'At this price,' his look will say, 'who of you would not be charmed at having a son guillotined?'"

This philosophy might not be true, but it was of a nature to make death lose its sting. Five long days dragged out. He was kind and gentle to Mathilde, whom he saw writhing under the most cruel jealousy. One evening Julien thought seriously of committing suicide. His heart was crushed by the deep despair into which Madame de Rênal's departure had thrown him. There was nothing more in life to charm him. Lack of exercise, too, began to tell on his health, giving him the spiritual, feeble look of a German student. He lost that manly force which can resist the attack of the most painful thoughts.

"I have loved the truth—where is it? There is everywhere hypocrisy, or, at least, charlatanism, even among the most virtuous and the greatest." His lips expressed disgust. "No, man cannot be proud of man!

"Madame de X——, making a donation to some orphan children, tells me that such a prince has just given ten louis. Lies! but what am I saying? Napoleon at Saint Helena—charlatan!—a proclamation in favor of the King of Rome!

"Good God! if such a man, after all the misfortune that should have recalled him to duty, lowers himself to deception, what can you expect of the rest of the race?

"Where is truth? In religion? Yes," he added, with a bitter smile. "In the mouth of Maslon, or Frilaire, or Castanède? Perhaps in the true Christianity, whose priests are not paid more than the Apostles have been? But St. Paul was paid by the pleasure of speaking; of hearing himself talked about! Oh, if there were a true religion! Fool that I am! I see a Gothic cathedral with venerable windows. My feeble heart imagines itself to be the priest in these windows. My heart would understand it all; my soul is yearning for it. But what do I see? Only a sleek rascal. But the real priest; a Massilon, a Fénelon. Massilon has cursed Dubois. The "Mémoires de Saint-Simon" has spoilt Fénelon for me—but anyhow a real priest! The real tender souls will be together. We shall not be alone. This good priest will tell us about God. But what God? Not the God of the Bible—a little, cruel tyrant thirsting for revenge? No, the God of Voltaire—good, just, infinite!"

The recollections he had of the Bible, which he knew by heart, moved him deeply. "But how, when there are *Three* together, we believe in the name of God, after all the horrible abuse on the part of the priests?

"But to live alone, what torture! But I am getting foolish and impatient," said Julien to himself, passing his hand over his brow. "I am alone in this cell, but I have not lived alone on earth. I have had a strong idea of duty, right or wrong, and I see it has been to me a mighty tree on which I leaned through storm and stress. I hesitated, yet I have never failed to act. After all, I was only a man, but I was never swept off my feet!

"It is the damp air of the cell that is making me think as I do. And why should I be a hypocrite yet, even while condemning hypocrisy? It is neither death nor the cell nor the damp air; it is only Madame de Rênal's absence that is working on me. If I should be compelled now, at Verrières, to live for six weeks in the cellar in order to see her, should I complain? I am still influenced by the times," he said aloud, with a bitter smile. "Even when I talk to myself, a step away from death, I am still a hypocrite. Oh, nineteenth century! A huntsman discharges his fowling piece in the forest, his prey falls, and he rushes forward to get it. His boots destroy an ant hill and crush the ants, and not only the ants but also the eggs. The most philosophical among the ants would only know of a black body, immense, frightful—the huge boot that crushed their dwelling amid much noise and the flash of red flame.

"And so death, life, eternity, is a mystery. It is simple only when one can comprehend it. The ephemeral insect is born at nine o'clock in the morning of a summer's day, to die at five o'clock in the afternoon. Does it know what night is? Give it five hours more of existence and it will know all that is meant by 'night.' And so I—I shall die at twenty-three! Give me five years yet to live with Madame de Rênal." Then Mephistopheles-like, he began to laugh.

"What foolishness to talk of these great problems! First, I am only a hypocrite, for I talk as if there were someone here to listen to me. Second, I forget both life and love when I have only such a few days left. Oh, Madame de Rênal is gone! Perhaps her husband will not let her come any more to Besançon and persist in her imprudence. That is what makes me so desolate, and not the absence of a just, all-powerful God, who is all good and not revengeful. Ah! if He existed, indeed, I should fall at his feet. I have deserved death. I would tell him—but great God! good God! gracious God! give back to me the one I love!"

The night was then far advanced. After an hour or two of peaceful slumber, Fouqué arrived. Julien was strong and resolute like a man who was master of himself.

Chapter 45

"I DON'T want to play such a trick on abbé Chas-Bernard as to send for him," he said to Fouqué. "He would not dine for three days. But try to find me a Jansenist, a friend of M. Pirard, and who is likely to be above intrigue."

Impatiently Fouqué had been awaiting such a proposition. Julien acquitted himself with all the decency required by public opinion. Thanks to abbé de Frilaire, Julien, in spite of his bad choice as to a confessor, became in his cell a protégé of the Congregation. With just a little more cleverness he could have made his escape. But the atmosphere of the cell had produced its enervating effect. He had no heart for any undertaking.

He was happier than ever when Madame de Rênal visited him again.

"My first duty is to you," she said, embracing him. "I just stole away from Verrières."

Julien was no longer held by pride in her presence, and he told her all of his fears and doubts. She was sweet and tender to him. In the evening, as soon as she left, she had the priest, whom Julien could not shake off, call at the house of her aunt. As he only wished to stand well with the society women of Besançon, Madame de Rênal quickly induced him to have a *neuvaines* sounded at the abbey Bray-le-Haut. No word could express Julien's great love.

By throwing away a great deal of money, and by abusing even the credit of her aunt—a celebrated, rich woman—Madame de Rênal obtained permission to see him twice a day. At this Mathilde's jealousy became almost frantic. M. de Frilaire had told her that his influence could go no farther than to permit her to see her friend once a day only. She dogged Madame de Rênal's footsteps in order to find out everything she was doing. M. de Frilaire exhausted all the resources of a clever mind to prove to her that Julien was unworthy of her. Yet, in the midst of all her torment, she only loved him the more, and almost every day she created a scene with him.

Julien wished to act the upright man even to the end with this poor girl whom he had so strangely compromised; but his wild love for Madame de Rênal carried him completely away.

When he could not persuade Mathilde of the innocence of her rival's visits, he would say to himself:

"Well, the end of this drama is near; it is an excuse for me if I do not know how to dissimulate any better."

Then Mademoiselle de la Mole heard of the death of the Marquis de Croisenois. The rich M. de Thaler had permitted himself indiscreet remarks as to Mathilde's sudden disappearance, and M. de Croisenois had demanded that he should deny them. But M. de Thaler showed him anonymous letters describing the whole matter with such detail as to make it impossible for the poor Marquis not to realize the truth. Then M. de Thaler said many things that were quite coarse. Beside himself with misery and anger, M. de Croisenois immediately demanded such an apology that the millionaire preferred a duel. Folly triumphed, and the one of the two—a most lovable young man—fell mortally wounded. That death made a strange impression on Julien's heart.

"Poor de Croisenois," he said to Mathilde, "was really kind to us! He might have hated me after your imprudent acts in the drawing-room. He might have quarrelled with me, for hatred that comes from a slight is ordinarily uncontrollable."

M. de Croisenois's death changed Julien's ideas completely as to Mathilde's future. For several days he tried to prove to her that she should accept M. de Luz's hand.

"He is not a daring man, not too much of a Jesuit," he said to her, "and will without doubt reach a high mark. With a lower but steadier ambition than poor de Croisenois, and without a Duchy in his family, he would not make the least difficulty about marrying Julien Sorel's widow."

"And a widow," Mathilde replied, coldly, "who despises all passion; for she has lived long enough to know that her lover after six months prefers another woman, the source of all our misery!"

"You are unjust. Madame de Rênal's visits will give the most telling points to the Paris lawyer who is charged with my appeal for clemency. He will paint the murderer as cared for tenderly by his victim, and that will produce its effect; and perhaps——"

A mad jealousy that could not avenge itself, the continuation of a hopeless despair—for supposing even that Julien were pardoned, how was she to win back his heart?—the shame and anguish of loving her unfaithful lover brought Mademoiselle de la Mole to a silence from which neither the officious attentions of M. de Frilaire, nor even the rude brotherliness of Fouqué could draw her out.

As for Julien, he lived, except when Mathilde was present, a life of love. Not a thought did he give to the immediate future. By the strange effect of a pure passion Madame de Rênal shared the same indifference, the same absence of care.

"Formerly," Julien would tell her, "when I should have been so happy during our walks in the woods of Vergy, a terrible ambition dragged my soul into unknown lands. In place of pressing my breast against the charming arm which was so near my lips, the future took me away from you. Even after much struggling I should have succeeded in playing a great part in life; I should have died without knowing the real happiness that has come to me from your visits here."

Two events began to trouble his heart. Julien's confessor, Jansenist though he was, was not a novice in Jesuitical intrigues. He indeed gave himself up to them entirely. He told him one day that in order not to commit the terrible sin of suicide he should do all that was possible to obtain grace. Now, since the clergy had the greatest influence with the Minister of Justice in Paris, an easy means presented itself to him—to become converted with *éclat*.

"Ah! with *éclat*," repeated Julien. "That is your word. You, too, my father, are enacting a comedy like the missionaries."

"Your age," replied the Jansenist, gravely; "that interesting face of yours, which Providence has given you; even the very motive of your crime, which remains inexplicable; the heroic acts of Mademoiselle de la Mole in your behalf; even to the marvellous friendship your victim shows you—all have contributed to make you the hero of the young women of Besançon; they have forgotten everything for you, even discretion.

"Your conversion will take deep root in their souls. It will make a profound impression. You can be of great service to the cause of religion, and I—I should hesitate at the frivolous reason which the Jesuits would give on such an occasion. Even in a case which has no concern with their rapacity, they still have a means of doing injury.

"The tears which your conversion will bring will wipe away the corrosive effect of ten editions of Voltaire."

"And what will I have then if I despise myself?" Julien replied, coldly. "I have been ambitious; but I don't want to tarnish myself. I have acted with the world in view; now I live only from day to day. With a reward before me, I should indeed consider myself unfortunate in the extreme if I gave myself up to such cowardice."

The other incident to which Julien was even more sensible

came through Madame de Rênal. Some intriguing friend had succeeded in persuading her naïve, timid soul that it was her duty to go to Saint-Cloud and there throw herself at the feet of King Charles X.

She had made sufficient sacrifices in separating herself from Julien; yet, after such efforts, the disagreeable incidents connected with such a spectacle, which at other times would have appeared worse than death to her, were nothing in her eyes now.

"I will go to the King; I will confess freely that you are my lover. A man's life, and such a man as Julien, should be above everything. I will say that it was through jealousy that you tried to kill me. There are numerous instances of poor young men who have been acquitted in such a case by the humaneness of a jury or of the King."

"I will not see you again; I will have the jail closed to you!" cried Julien. "To-morrow I will kill myself in despair if you do not swear to me at once that you will do nothing to make a public spectacle of both of us. That idea of going to Paris is not yours; tell me the name of the designing woman who suggested it to you! Let us be happy during the few days of this short life of mine; let us hide our existence from the world. Mademoiselle de la Mole has all the influence necessary in Paris; you may surely believe that she has done everything that is humanly possible. Here in the province I have against me all the rich, substantial men. Your action would more than ever incense these rich people for whom life is such an easy thing. Let us not make ourselves a laughing stock to Maslon, Valenod, or their betters."

The bad air in the jail was becoming insupportable to Julien.

Fortunately, the day set for his execution, all nature was bathed in bright sunlight, and Julien was strong with courage. To walk in the open air was as delicious a sensation for him as walking on land is for the sailor who has been a long time at sea.

"Well, it is all right," he said to himself; "I am not wanting in courage!" Never had he felt as exalted as at the moment when his head was about to fall, and the tender moments he had experienced formerly in the woods of Vergy won him again.

Everything passed off simply, unaffectedly, on his part.

The day before he had said to Fouqué, "I cannot answer for my emotion; this cell is so horribly ugly! so damp! I get feverish at times, and I am not myself; but never fear! You will not see me flinch."

He had made all the arrangements for the following morning.

Fouqué was to take away Mathilde and Madame de Rênal together.

"Get them in the same carriage," he said to him. "See that that postilion's horses are kept at a trot. They will either fall into each other's arms or they will vow eternal hatred. In either case the poor women will have their minds taken off their terrible grief."

Julien had received Madame de Rênal's oath that she would live to care for Mathilde's child.

"Who knows? Perhaps we have sensations after death," he said one day to Fouqué. "I should like very much to rest—yes, rest is the word—in that little cave on the high mountain overlooking Verrières. Several times I have told you how ambition inflamed my heart when I lay in the hollow that night and gazed far away over the rich provinces of France. It was my passion then. Yes, that grotto is dear to me—though it cannot be denied that it is not situated to suit a philosopher's soul.

"Well, those good Congregationists in Besançon make money out of everything; if you know how to go about it they will sell you my mortal remains."

In that Fouqué succeeded.

He was spending the night alone in his room beside his friend's corpse, when, to his great surprise, he saw Mathilde enter. A few hours before he had left her ten leagues from Besançon. She looked haggard.

"I want to see him!" she cried.

Fouqué had not the courage either to speak or to rise. He pointed with his finger to a pall over a board. Thus covered rested all that remained of Julien.

She threw herself on her knees. The thought of Boniface de la Mole and of Marguerite of Navarre gave her superhuman courage. Her trembling hands lifted the mantle. Fouqué turned his eyes away.

He heard Mathilde walk quickly across the room. She had lit several candles. When Fouqué had courage enough to look round, he saw that she had placed Julien's head on a little marble table before her and was kissing the brow.

Mathilde followed her lover even to the tomb which he had selected. A large number of priests escorted the coffin. Unknown to all, she carried on her knees, as she sat in the mourning carriage, the head of the man she had adored.

Arrived at the most elevated spot on one of the high mountains of the Jura, twenty priests, in the middle of the night, celebrated Mass for the dead in that little cave, which was made resplendent with numerous tapers. All the inhabitants of the little mountain villages, who had met the procession, followed it, attracted by the strange ceremony.

Mathilde appeared in the middle in heavy widow's weeds, and at the end of the service had several thousand five-franc pieces scattered.

When she remained alone with Fouqué, she buried her lover's head with her own hands. Fouqué was nearly mad with grief.

Mathilde had the rough grotto adorned with sculptured Italian marble.

Madame de Rênal was true to her promise. She made no attempt to take her own life; but three days after Julien's death she died as she was kissing her children.

Further Reading

Works by Stendhal

Rome, Naples and Florence, 1817
On Love, 1822
Racine and Shakespeare, 1823
Armance, 1827
Walks in Rome, 1829
The Red and the Black, 1830
The Charterhouse of Parma, 1839

Posthumous Works

Lamiel, 1889
The Life of Henri Brulard, 1890
Memoirs of an Egotist, 1892
Lucien Leuwen, 1894
A Roman Journal, 1911 (Collier Book BS 7)

Critical and Biographical Studies

For its clarity and genuineness, Joseph Wood Krutch's chapter on Stendhal in *Five Masters: A Study in the Mutations of the Novel* (Bloomington: Indiana University Press, 1959) is a useful first reading. Robert M. Adams' *Stendhal: Notes on a Novelist* New York: Noonday Press, 1959) yields many hints for further exploration. Jean Dutourd's *The Man of Sensibility* (New York: Simon and Schuster, 1961) is a recent comprehensive study. A classic of Stendhal criticism, textual and yet encompassing, is Erich Auerbach's chapter in *Mimesis: The Representation of Reality in Western Literature* (New York: Doubleday, 1957).

For readers interested in French views of the novelist, Léon Blum's *Stendhal et le Beylisme* (Paris: Albin Michel, 1930) is of historic importance. Jean Starobinski's L'Oeil vivant (Paris: Gallimard, 1961) is already considered one of the best studies. Francine Marill Albérès' *Le Naturel chez Stendhal* (Paris: Nizet, 1956) is a brilliant, difficult and advanced attempt to demonstrate Stendhal's pursuit of naturalness.